Soulbound

Arlyn wanted to meet her elven father...
not spark the plot to kill him.

BETHANY ADAMS

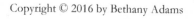
Book Layout ©2013 BookDesignTemplates.com
Book Format Design by Machovi Creative facebook.com/machoviprods
Cover designed by Eve Milady, http://www.venetian-cat.com

Soulbound/ Bethany Adams. -- 1st ed.
ISBN 978-0-9975320-0-5

To my family:
My parents, who always encouraged me
My husband, for his patience and unswerving enthusiasm
My children, simply for being.

Acknowledgements

I hope you're sitting down, because this is going to be a long one. So many people have touched my life on this journey, and I have so much to be grateful for.

First, I'd like to thank my parents. They bought me countless books and encouraged my love of reading. Especially my mom, who patiently defined countless words instead of telling me a book was too hard. They got me notebooks to scrawl stories in and never laughed at my early attempts. My dad didn't live to see my first book published, but I'm sure he'd be just as proud as my mom. I love you, Mom and Dad! Thank you.

Next, my long-suffering husband, who'd rather read the next chapter of my latest project than come home to a home-cooked meal. He's my first reader for everything, and I never would have made it this far without his support. Thank you for believing in me when I forgot to believe in myself. I love you!

Thanks also to my extended family: my siblings, nieces and nephews, and in-laws. I've received nothing but encouragement from you, and that means the world.

To Dr. Allison Smith and the MTSU McNair Scholars program. My path didn't take me to a doctorate, but the lessons I learned with you were invaluable. Dr. Smith, no words can express how grateful I am to have worked with you. You taught me how to complete a big project and how professional collaboration should be.

Thank you to my awesome critique partners, Catherine, Shiloh, Natasha, and Jessica. Not just for helping me hone my words but for listening to my woes. And thank you Shantele (aka S.E. Summa) and Jody for being great friends and talking me off the ledge of writerly panic more than once.

And Eve Milady! Your cover rocks my socks. Check out her awesome art at http://www.venetian-cat.com

Last but not least, my wonderful writing groups. Prose Pirates, AMG, SASS, and Music City Romance Writers—you guys rock. I've learned so much from all of you. I hope we all have great success and much happiness in the years to come.

A rlyn shoved trembling hands into her pockets as the elf approached, his long hair shifting in the breeze. Though he moved with relaxed ease, his sharp gaze scanned her from head to toe. Thank goodness she'd left her weapons at camp. The elf carried only a dagger, but Arlyn's mother had warned her he was a formidable warrior, more than capable of taking her on. She did *not* want to be mistaken for a threat.

Her fingers brushed the smooth, useless glass of the cell phone in her pocket. It slid against her sweaty palm as she gripped it, though she doubted they'd have service on this world anyway. Her mother had said these Moranaians were different than the elves of legend, but the myths surely weren't *that* wrong. Arlyn grinned, despite her nerves, drawing a frown from the approaching elf. Strangers must not often smile at him in the middle of the forest path.

The dappled light shadowed the elf's young-looking face and made blotches in his dark brown hair. As he stopped a couple of feet away, Arlyn's breath caught. He looked exactly like the man in the picture her mother had given her, except then he'd been sitting in the forest near her family home. But this was a different world. Though the shadows might look the same, the leaves that cast them were another shape and the trees another species.

Say something, she ordered herself, but only a strangled gasp slipped from her lips.

"You appear to be lost," he said, his voice smooth and calm. "May I help you?"

Arlyn took a deep breath. *He's not going to hurt me. Probably. I'll deliver the message and leave.* "Are you Lord Lyrnis Dianore?"

With a small, polite smile, he inclined his head. "I am. Forgive me if we have met, for I do not know your name."

"We haven't," she said, "met, that is. My name is Arlyn."

"A pleasure to make your acquaintance." He stared at her, his brows pinching with another frown. "If you have come with a request, you may make an appointment for a formal meeting."

She opened her mouth, but no sound worked loose.

Lord Dianore's expression tightened, a hint of irritation shifting into his gaze. "Very well. If you have no further need of me, I'll bid you good day."

He bowed, then continued forward, moving around her. Arlyn's eyes went wide, and the words she needed to say tangled in her throat. Forgetting the phone she held, she pulled her hands from her pockets to grab him as he passed. Her left hand wrapped around his forearm, and he twisted, crouching into battle stance as he jerked free. His hand settled on the hilt of the knife he wore, his eyes narrowing on the phone in her right hand.

"You have moments to explain," he snapped.

Arlyn shivered at the coldness of his tone, so different from the polite warmth of his initial greeting. She tried to slip the thin phone back into her pocket but missed. The device thudded into the dirt as she lifted her hands. "I'm sorry. I'm just nervous."

"What is that thing?" He drew his dagger. "That is not from Moranaia."

Her brows lifted. "It's a phone. You're speaking my language. Shouldn't you know?"

Eyes as green as emeralds focused on her face. "You're from Earth."

"Yes." Arlyn stiffened her spine at his flat statement and hoped she appeared confident instead of scared. "My mother sent me to find you."

He tensed. "Your mother?"

"Her name was Aimee." Arlyn took a deep breath. "Aimee Moore."

Only centuries of training kept the knife from slipping out of Lyr's hand. A shudder rippled through him as he examined her. Gods, the girl *did* resemble Aimee with her dark red hair and slender form, though Arlyn was more muscular, closer to the female scouts who guarded his estate. *Wait, what had she said?*

"Was?" His hand convulsed around the hilt of the blade as he straightened. "Her name *was?*"

Arlyn twisted her fingers together. "Her final wish was for me to find you."

Pain forced the air from Lyr's lungs, and his hands trembled. After two tries, he finally returned the dagger to its sheath. "How long ago?"

"A few months, I guess. But it's impossible to tell time in the mists, so I'm not really sure."

Lyr stumbled over to one of the benches that lined the path and plopped down. His soulbonded. The only woman he had ever loved. *Dead.* His stomach heaved, and he closed his eyes against the agony. Could he believe this girl? He had no doubt she was Aimee's daughter. The resemblance was too uncanny.

He rubbed his face, struggling to regain a modicum of composure, before meeting the girl's eyes once more. "Why would she send you? She knows…knew how dangerous the Veil would be for a human."

"Haven't you guessed?" Arlyn tucked a strand of hair behind her ear and ran a finger along the pointed tip. "She wanted you to meet your daughter."

"Impossible." The blood drained from his face, leaving him pale beneath his tan. "In all my years, I have never—"

"Oh, I assure you, you did once." Her teeth ground together. Why had she dared hope he would believe her? "Maybe you should have checked on her instead of abandoning her. And me."

He shot to his feet, hands clenched at his sides. "I did not abandon her. An emergency required my immediate return. Surely, she told you."

"She did. But she loved you."

The implications floated between them, as unbearable as the heat beating down from the sun. Arlyn had grown up hearing tales of her father. Of him and all Aimee had known of his land. But love had colored her mother's stories, and Arlyn had always wondered how much that emotion altered the truth. Had love made her mother believe he possessed a kindness that wasn't really there?

"Perhaps she was mistaken." He took a few steps closer, then paused. The frown deepened between his brows. "I'd hoped she would find another. Half-bloods are rare, and I was only there for a single moon."

His denial pierced the doubt within and splattered it wide. Arlyn flushed. "Are you saying my mother slept around? That's low."

"What?" His eyes widened at the fury in her tone, and he lifted his hands, palms out. "At peace, Arlyn. I meant no offense. Our customs are different here. Whether she took other lovers or not would make no difference among my people."

The pain burned like the arrow that had sliced her thigh during practice last spring. "Fine. I get it. I've delivered the news, and now I'll head back home. Is there a place I can barter for supplies? I have a few things from Earth that might be of interest."

His expression twisted, but Arlyn couldn't decipher the emotion behind it. "No."

Arlyn threw her hands up in frustration and spun to head back to her camp. There'd been fountains of water scattered through the otherwise formless mists of the Veil but no food. Would she get in trouble for hunting in these woods? Maybe she could add *being arrested by her own father* to her failures on this trip.

Warm fingers curled around her arm.

"Hey!" Arlyn yelped and twisted, struggling to tug herself free, but his grip held firm. "Let go."

"I didn't mean you couldn't have supplies. I meant you couldn't leave."

Arlyn's brows rose. "What, you have other insults to add?"

"Forgive me." He stared into her eyes. "I was shocked. A claim like this…"

Her shoulders slumped as her anger deflated. What had she expected? That he would sweep her into his arms as she'd dreamed when she was a child? He had a right to his doubt. "Mom seemed to think you'd believe me without question."

Boom! A rumble of thunder split the air, and Arlyn jumped. Her gaze darted to the canopy above, but she found no sign of clouds between the leaves of the ancient trees. Still, the scent of rain floated on the wind, and the already-stifling heat clung to her clothes and skin as the humidity increased. Just one more bit of discomfort.

A soft squeeze on her arm drew her attention back down. "What was that?"

"A storm, as on Earth." He smiled, although it didn't wash the hint of grief from his eyes. "It's on the north end of the valley, still some distance away. But it's moving faster than I expected. Come with me to Braelyn, my home. We'll work this out."

Should she? Her chest still ached from the pain of his denial, but she *had* crossed worlds to meet him. Only he could answer her questions about her heritage. "Okay. If you promise to let me leave when I wish."

He nodded. "I will provide you a guide through the mists."

A gust of wind rattled the canopy above. Lord Lyrnis released her to rush back up the path, and Arlyn followed quickly on his heels. Her attention alternated between him and the trees, resembling oaks or maples but as large as redwoods, as their branches tossed back and forth. Could those Earth varieties even grow this big if left undisturbed? She just hoped *these* trees were sturdy. If one of those branches fell, they'd be dead for sure.

The trail split at the edge of a long valley. To the right, the path descended to the floor below. The route on the left followed the line of the ridge to a large estate woven around the base of the ancient trees. Arlyn had only glimpsed his house from a distance, and then from another section of the trail that led to a large garden. But he didn't take her in the back way. A matter of trust? She couldn't withhold the hurt that speculation caused.

Lightning flashed from the windows and across the tan stone walls of the estate, making the carvings on its surface seem to dance. Arlyn squinted at the designs. Stylized trees, leaves, and flowers were clear enough, but the animals... Not-squirrels and almost-deer shifted eerily with each lightning strike. *Yeah, so not Earth.*

Lyrnis dodged down a side path, avoiding the double doors at the front, and moved to a small door tucked next to a gently curved wall full of windows. Arlyn drew up short at the sight of the soldier, a tall, dark-skinned woman dressed in leather, who guarded the entrance. On Earth, Arlyn had usually seen elves depicted as one of two things: pale and fair or dark and deceitful. Was the whole light elf versus dark elf thing a myth? A reflection of human racism? Did Moranaians not make the same distinction? Something in Arlyn relaxed. Maybe these elves weren't as cold and unaccepting as she'd feared.

With a nod to the guard, Lord Lyrnis opened the door and gestured for Arlyn to precede him. She paused a few inches over the threshold as her eyes adjusted to the decreased light. The cool interior drew a shiver as her clothes, damp with sweat and raindrops, chilled around her. A heartbeat later, she could make out the small hallway that linked the oval room at the right to the main building on her left, separated by a door.

"If you'll move into my study?" Lyrnis asked, his voice calm. Unlike the thunder that cracked outside, putting Arlyn even more on edge.

"Sorry," she muttered.

Arlyn took a few steps into the room and stopped. Book-shelves alternated with windows around the two wider walls of the oval, and a massive desk sat on a small dais at the end. She caught her reflection in the tall mirror placed behind it and winced. Damn. She'd worn some of the clothes she'd made for her Ren Faire booth, but as the only short-sleeved set she had brought, they were well-worn. She wouldn't want to claim her dirty, sweat-stained self, either.

The sight of Lord Lyrnis, impeccable in a thin, silken tunic and loose pants, brought a blush to her cheeks. Arlyn turned her face away and focused on the chairs arranged in the center of the room, all four placed in precise order beneath their own skylights. Though wood-framed, the seats were covered in cushioned fabric that was probably worth more than the car she'd left on Earth. The two tables positioned between them were exquisite, solid wood carved with leaves and inlaid with tiny, gemstone flowers. Not particle board.

"Please, have a seat."

Distracted, Arlyn jumped at the sound of his voice. She turned to find him staring at her, his hand held out toward one of the chairs in the center. "No way. I am entirely too dirty."

"They've seen worse." His lips curved up. "I used to sit in here with my father after a day spent chasing frogs in the gardens. They are spelled to resist stains."

Though he clearly meant to reassure her, Arlyn paled. These chairs had to be over five hundred years old. "Still, it doesn't seem like a good idea."

"Watch." Before she realized what he intended, Lyrnis wiped a smudge of dirt from her arm and walked to the closest seat. He knelt, smearing the trail of grime along the bottom cushion. Almost instantly, it evaporated. At her gasp, he smiled again. "Our artisans are quite clever. Come. Our discussion will be more pleasant if you are comfortable."

Arlyn stared at the seat for a long moment before taking a few hesitant steps. As though to reassure her it really was clean, Lord Lyrnis chose the chair he'd used as an example. Biting her lip, she relented, though she perched on the edge and tried not to touch the polished wooden armrest.

"There."

From above, light gilded him, softening the serious lines of his face. Pain burned through her. Her mother had been a shadow, all bones and wrinkles, by the time the cancer took her. This man could have been mistaken for Arlyn's brother. Then he caught her gaze, and the sorrow darkening his eyes dispelled the image. All the long centuries he'd lived glinted there.

His fingers tapped the armrests. "How did you find the way here?"

"Mom showed me where you emerged." Arlyn shrugged. "Unlike most humans, I grew up knowing that magic is real. I studied all I could find, though most of the knowledge out there is guesswork or pure fantasy. Mostly, I had to experiment."

"Experiment." His hands gripped the wood. "You experimented with the portal to the Veil?"

Arlyn winced at his dry tone. "No. Well, not exactly. I meant things like creating shields against attacks and lighting fires. I can make a mean campfire."

"And the portal?"

"Honestly, I'm not sure what I did," she answered. "It's like something came to life when I stepped within the stones."

A frown pinched his forehead. "Would you be offended if I test you?"

"Test me how?"

"Energy doesn't lie, Arlyn." He leaned forward, his eyes focused on her face. "For elves, our magic is a part of us. Unique, like our souls. I can sense where my own energy merged to create yours."

"A magical paternity test?" She shook her head at the questioning lift of his brow. "Never mind. I guess you aren't going to take my word for it."

"I am sorry." His mouth turned down. "I am eighteenth in line to the throne of Moranaia, Arlyn, and a leader of many. I want to believe you, but I can't."

She stared at her hands gathered in her lap. "It's too much of a risk."

"More than you understand. It is no small thing to acknowledge an heir."

Lyr studied Arlyn as she froze, her eyes going wide. Was she afraid of being proved a liar, or did the idea of being his heir cause such unease? Which would he prefer? His gut twisted with a mix of fear and hope. A daughter with Aimee. A miracle he'd never expected. Yet if it were true, then so was Aimee's death. He'd pretended she would stay as he had left her, young and full of life. That illusion would be shattered.

"Will you allow the test?" he asked again.

Arlyn's lips flattened. "I guess I don't have much choice."

"There is always a choice." A grim smile crossed his face. "I gave my word to see you back to Earth. That promise will be kept either way."

Lyr didn't blame her for her doubt-filled frown. She peered into his eyes for a long moment before nodding. "Fine. What do I need to do?"

He pulled his chair forward until he could reach her. "Just give me your hands and relax."

Arlyn paused for so long he wondered if she was about to change her mind, but she finally placed her trembling hands onto his own. He sucked in a breath at the connection—the sense of family—that flowed through him. But he'd still have to test her. Lyr let his eyes drift closed and opened his mental shields to touch upon her energy. Brushing the energy of another was a simple thing, especially as unskilled as she was in controlling it. He needed only a few heartbeats to search for remnants of his own signature. Then several more before the truth slammed into him.

Lyr dropped her hands as though they were aflame and leapt to his feet, the chair toppling behind him. Arlyn winced at the clatter, alarm filling her gaze as it darted between him and the seat. He barely registered it. Pain clawed through him so hard he almost doubled over. Running a hand through his hair, tugging strands haphazardly from the band that constrained it, Lyr paced the room. A daughter. He had a daughter.

Clechtan, he cursed to himself. *How had he not known?*

He should have checked. He'd only been with Aimee for a moon, but he still should have checked for signs of a child before he'd left. Lyr leaned a hand against a windowsill where rain pounded the glass, a fitting match for his mood. Thunder shook the panes as if in sympathy. He wanted to pound his fist through the glass and had to dig his fingers into the wood of the sill to stay the impulse.

"What did you find?"

Lyr turned to focus on Arlyn. *His daughter.* The shake in her voice caught him. She'd taken a few steps forward but seemed hesitant to get close. He supposed he couldn't blame her. "You are mine. It's all true."

Her shoulders sagged. "I'm sorry."

"What?" Lyr's chest tightened. "What reason do you have to be sorry?"

"You don't seem pleased." Her gaze lowered to the floor. "I guess it's some dishonor to have a half-human bastard."

Pain and anger mingled until the air around him throbbed with it. Lyr strode forward, taking her hands once more. "Never say such. None of this is directed at you. I'm the one who should apologize, though no words can ever make up for this."

Gods. The eyes she lifted were the same shade of green as his own. He should have noticed that, too. She shook her head. "Mom didn't tell you."

His brows rose. "She knew?"

"I'm not sure. Maybe."

Lyr cursed under his breath the entire time he turned to right his chair. He and Aimee had both agreed that crossing through the Veil at the speed he'd needed was too dangerous for a human. Had she worried for their unborn child and not told him? Betrayal mingled with grief. It would explain why Aimee had not fought for a way to go to Moranaia, even knowing they would be forever parted.

He sank into the chair, giving in and doubling over from the pain of it. Aimee, his soulmate, gone. Arlyn, their daughter, unintentionally abandoned. And he'd treated her like a fraud. How could the girl not hate him? At that moment, he hated himself with an intensity that stole his breath. Lyr damned himself for not checking in on Aimee. He could have sent Kai or could have even gone himself. Coward, coward, coward.

A hand settled on his back, and he startled. Shame streamed through to dampen the violence of his emotions, if only a little. Control was prized among their kind, but he had shown none of it. Lyr needed to focus on Arlyn, a child who had been too long without a father. Body heavy, he pushed up to a sitting position, feeling older than his 549 years. Right then, he could have been an ancient.

"Forgive me."

Stunned by the violence of his reaction, Arlyn's mouth worked, but no sound came out. Her mother had called him steady, calm, and lighthearted. None of that was in evidence now. For years, doubt about him had picked at the confidence her mother had tried to instill. Had he known and left anyway? Well, that was one worry she could let die.

"I understand if that is too much to ask," he said in a voice hoarse with emotion.

"Lord Lyrnis—"

"Call me Lyr." He grimaced. "*Laial*, father, is a title I must earn."

"I didn't come here to ask for anything from you." Arlyn huffed out a breath and threw up her hands. "Honestly, I'm not sure why I came. For acknowledgment, I guess. Maybe closure. I've seen you, met you, and now we both know the truth."

Lyr shot to his feet. "You aren't still considering leaving?"

"Shouldn't I?"

"All this time." He took a step closer, lifting his hand to cup her cheek. "I've mourned since the day I left, never knowing the half of it. You can't tell me such a thing and then go."

Arlyn bit her lip. "I don't know what you want. A few minutes ago, you didn't even believe me."

Wincing, he jerked his hand back and looked away. "I—"

"No, you had the right." She shook her head. "I shouldn't have said that."

He brushed past her to pace around the room. Feelings flew from him, thudding against her meager shields like foam-covered practice swords. Arlyn had studied the concept of empathy, even sensed others' emotions from time to time, but this? The impact reverberated through her own energy with a decided sting. Arlyn rubbed her chest as the ache compounded.

At the sound of the knock, both of them turned to stare at the door that led to the rest of the estate. Out of the corner of her eye, Arlyn saw Lyr run a hand through his hair. The tie that had held it back was gone, leaving it spilling around his shoulders in a tangled mass. She almost smiled watching him try to smooth it.

"You may enter," he said though the door had already opened.

A slight woman gowned in flowing blue silk swept in, her white braid whipping behind her as she rushed up to Lyr. "What happened?"

"*Laiala,*" he murmured, grasping the woman's shoulders. "Be calm. I'm fine."

The woman's lips thinned. "You are *not* fine."

Arlyn shuffled her feet, her eyes moving to the window. The rain had stopped. She could slip out and spare Lyr further embarrassment. But the slight movement had caught the other woman's attention, and the elder turned, the intensity of her gaze capturing Arlyn's. There was a fierceness in her blue eyes. The look of a mother.

"Are you responsible for this?"

"I..." Arlyn took a step back. "I suppose."

"She is not," Lyr said, voice firm. "She brought important news, but the blame for my distress is my own."

"Perhaps you might introduce our guest so this discussion can continue."

Arlyn's brow pinched, but Lyr nodded. Did she really need to know the woman's name to be yelled at? Apparently so. Lyr released the elder's shoulders and gestured to the chairs in the center. "You might want to sit down."

The woman flicked an incredulous look at him. "I am not so old that an introduction is going to fell me, Lyrnis."

"You might change your mind about that." He moved next to Arlyn, and she jumped when his hand wrapped around her own. "Honored daughter, I present to you Callian Myernere i Lynia Dianore nai Braelyn. Lady Lynia, I present to you Callian Ayala i Arlyn Dianore nai Braelyn."

The elder paled, her hand darting out to grasp the back of one of the chairs she'd just declined. "If you are jesting..."

"Do I often joke about having children?" he countered, lips twisting.

"Excuse me." Arlyn squeezed his hand, then regretted the impulse when his surprised gaze found hers. With a blush, she pulled free. "I have no clue what you just said. Was my name somewhere in that mess?"

Lyr stared at her a moment, then stifled a cough. Had she imagined the smile that had briefly flickered in his eyes? "I'm sorry. It is custom to introduce guests according to title."

Arlyn shook her head. "I don't have a title."

"On the contrary—"

"Lyrnis Dianore," the other woman snapped. "If you do not explain this at once..." The elder paused to take a deep breath, and some of the tension eased from her shoulders. "I do believe we are all confused. Perhaps we *should* sit."

Though a brief dream of darting out the side door and hauling ass for the portal tempted her, Arlyn took the seat next to Lyr. "Could you at least introduce us in English?"

"Of course," he answered. "Arlyn, this is my mother, Lady Lynia. Mother, this is Arlyn. My daughter."

"So I gathered." The lady's brows rose. "I would love to know why I am just now meeting her."

His face reddened. "I didn't know."

The lady canted her head. "What do you mean, 'didn't know'?"

"When I left Aimee, I never thought to check."

"Lyrnis!" Lady Lynia's eyes widened. "If we taught you anything, it was to always check for such things. Children are important. I cannot believe you were so irresponsible."

If Lyr's blush could ignite, they would all be on fire. "I was in a hurry, and we'd been together for such a short time. Half-bloods are even rarer than full-blooded children. But I should have checked regardless."

Arlyn crossed her arms at her waist. She should tell him what her mother had said, but the words caught in her chest, squeezed tight by the pain in her heart. Lady Lynia examined her, her expression softening. "Aimee's, you say? Did Kai bring her?"

"Kai is on a mission." Lyr cleared this throat and shifted in his seat. "She found the way on her own."

The elder scowled. "And you haven't taken her to the healer? That's no small task for one of full blood if they do not have the talent for it. Honestly, I cannot believe you let her—"

"Hey!" Arlyn interrupted. "I'm not five. There's no need to talk around me. I'm sure he could tell that I'm fine."

Both turned tense faces her way. Arlyn tapped her fingers on her arm and glared. After a moment, Lyr chuckled, and her grandmother let out a long breath. The elder grimaced. "Forgive my rudeness. I suppose it has been long enough for you to reach adulthood."

"Twenty-two years," Lyr whispered.

Arlyn frowned. "I was twenty-three when I left Earth."

"Hmm." Lyr ran a hand along his jaw, his eyes narrowed. "Time flows differently here. By my count, you should be nearly twenty-six there."

"No way."

"You must have wandered through the mists longer than you believed."

Arlyn's forearm burned with pain, and she realized she was gripping it. She uncurled her fingers one by one. "I couldn't have been there for almost three years. I only had supplies for a month. Maybe two."

"It's possible you were there for a month yet lost a few years of Earth time," Lyr said. "The Veil is a strange place. A transition zone. Guides among us can pass through quickly, but it takes great effort. Some have wandered there for decades. Even centuries."

"Like the myths of people getting lost in fairy hills."

"There's more truth in those tales than most humans realize. We are cousins to the Sidhe though our people left Earth long before them." His mouth pinched. "The Ljósálfar as well. Not that they would admit to it. They all use the Veil to travel between worlds."

Heedless of the dirt on her clothes, Arlyn sank back against the seat. There were humans on Earth who would give anything to know the myths were real. "Well, then."

"Lyr," Lady Lynia interrupted. "You can give her history lessons later. Surely, she would like to rest."

"Of course." He stood, solemn eyes staring into hers. "Will you stay?"

K ai walked through the portal and paused to shake off the last whispers of power whirling through his mind, disoriented by the final shift back into his own world. He wavered on his feet for a moment, then started down the path, anxious to make his report and get some rest. The lack of sleep had grown dangerous, his energy levels so low he could barely shield himself. How long had it been? A week? Two? Slowing, he scanned the small clearing for Lyr but found it empty.

Kai leaned against a nearby tree and gathered as much energy as his strained personal resources would allow. His reserves were so meager his head throbbed with the effort of converting natural magic into something he could use. Where was Lyr? Kai had notified his friend that he would return this afternoon, and Lyr had never failed to meet him before. Unease thrummed in Kai's blood like a pulse.

He scanned as far as he was able but could sense no sign of his friend. Too bad telepathy was one of Kai's weakest skills. After a moment, he pushed away from the tree and closed his eyes against the sudden spinning. Gods curse the Sidhe and their idiocy. More than a week spent in fruitless discussions, and Kai had nothing to show for it but exhaustion. He was about ready to tell them to find their *own* solution to the poisoned energy creeping into their realm.

Mud sucked at his shoes as he strode along the trail. Though it was traditional to keep the path as natural as possible to avoid drawing attention to the portal, days like today made Kai want to call in artisans to pave. He huffed out a breath. It wasn't as if the portal's existence was much of a secret. If only he could convince Lyr.

By the time Kai reached the main path, he was soaked through from the raindrops falling from the branches above. The bulk of the storm was gone with the thunder rumbling away to the south, and the moisture had begun to gather into mist around the bases of the trees. Humid air would have cloaked him in water even if the droplets had not. Had the storm delayed his friend?

The crunch of glass beneath his boot brought Kai to a halt. Glass, out here? He took a step back and crouched down to investigate. A rectangle a few inches smaller than his hand was mashed into the mud, fractured reflections of the canopy above shining from the cracked top. Was that *a phone?* He'd admired them on his last scouting mission to Earth, but there was no reason for one to be here.

No *good* reason.

His body tensed for action as he glanced around the small clearing. Wind gusted the leaves above and a few birds sang in the distance, easing from their shelter after the storm. Animals skittered through the underbrush. Insects called. But he detected no signs of the person who'd dropped the phone. Kai examined the device before stretching out a finger to poke it. Cool to the touch. Possibly ruined by the rain.

He had to find the owner of the phone even if he had to drain his energy dry to do it.

Trying not to gawk, Arlyn followed her grandmother down the hallway that led away from the study. In human houses, everything was so square, the construction based on right angles, but here hallways and rooms curved gently, probably in part to accommodate trees. Carved or painted walls resembled the forest, and gentle globes of light hung from branches so real they seemed alive. Twice, she'd noticed interesting devices that dripped water from a carved flower into a glass container with strange markings. Before she could ask about the object, the beautiful room at the end of the hall claimed her attention.

Directly before her, a wide set of steps curved around a large tree trunk. Beyond that, huge wooden doors stood, their carvings a match for the large outside doors she'd noticed earlier. The main entry, then? The room was certainly large enough. An elaborate stone arch took up part of the center wall, and at the far end of the room, another, more massive tree trunk stretched across the entire side. If this were the main entrance, what was the importance of the arch and the tree? Another thing to learn about her new, probably temporary, home.

Arlyn followed her grandmother up the stairs, focusing on her feet to keep from being distracted by the room below. She'd rather not trip on a step because she couldn't stop staring. After a short walk down another beautiful hallway, the other woman stopped at the second door on the right.

"This will be yours. I am across from you and one door down, and your father is at the end of the hall. I thought you might want some extra privacy."

Arlyn opened the door and strode inside, admiring the unique beauty of the room. Unlike the study, the chamber was square. Each corner was gently rounded instead of sharply angled, and the bottom half of the walls was paneled in a dark wood engraved with intricate, forest-themed carvings while the top half was painted a soft cream. Directly across from the entrance, windows overlooked a garden, and on the right-hand side, an enormous, wooden four-poster bed took up much of the space. Matching chairs, a desk, and another door filled the wall on the left. A smaller version of the strange water device in the hall hung above the desk.

"That door leads to a bathing and dressing chamber," Lynia said, gesturing to the left. "Someone will come in to clean if they sense your desire. We do not precisely have servants in the way humans think of them, but we can speak more about that after you have rested."

"Thank you."

Lynia stepped near the water device, piquing Arlyn's curiosity. Her fascination grew as her grandmother pointed at the lines carved into the delicate glass. "This is the water clock. I assume you do not know how to read our numbers, so if you would like to count the hours, just start from the bottom."

Arlyn nodded her understanding. "I have hated not knowing the time."

Lady Lynia moved back, wringing her hands. "Please forgive my rude greeting earlier. He has hurt for so long, and when I sensed a surge, I worried."

"I understand." Arlyn gave a gentle smile. "Thank you for showing me to my room. I guess I need to go collect the rest of my things."

"The rest?"

"I had a small camp off the trail."

The elder frowned. "I am amazed the *sonal* did not find you."

"The what?"

"They scout the grounds for danger." Lady Lynia gestured to the window. "The *sonal* are all around, there in the trees. Though I suppose they might have mistaken you for a guide from another House. We guard the portal to Earth, so we do get travelers."

Arlyn wanted to ask for more information, but a sudden shyness caught at her tongue. With a nod, her grandmother started back toward the door, her braid swinging behind her. As the elder's hand gripped the handle, she glanced over her shoulder. "Welcome to the family, Arlyn. I am pleased you found us. You give me hope."

Lady Lynia slipped out before Arlyn could come up with a reply. For a long moment, she stared at the door, uncertain if she wanted to stay or run away. Why had she agreed to remain here? Arlyn walked to the window and ran a finger along the smooth sill as she gazed out at the garden. Such beauty. Such an idyllic world. But nothing was ever perfect.

Arlyn's thoughts scattered like the drops of water clinging to the glass in front of her. Suspended, stuck. Not sure which way to go. Her experiences on Earth had been no different, because she had never quite fit there either. Now she had the chance to discover if this world would be better for her. If darkness lurked beneath the seeming perfection, she would soon find out. Because every culture had *some* darkness.

How long had it been since she'd left Lyr's study? Arlyn stepped over to the clock and examined the markings. Maybe ten minutes. Lyr had received an important message through the mirror behind his desk not long after she had agreed to stay. From his grim expression and profuse apologies, she gathered the conversation would be lengthy. Plenty of time to collect her things from her camp. Her lips turned up into a smile as she strode from the room and down the stairs that curled around the tree. The mirror had been a surprise. Elves might not have cell phones, but they'd found spells that let them communicate just as easily. Elven Skype.

The more things changed, the more they stayed the same.

The broken branches were small, but Kai had scouted these woods with Lyr since boyhood and knew they signaled strangers in the area. Travelers weren't allowed in this section, and larger animals ranged far from the portal. Slipping between the trees, Kai followed the subtle trail left by their intruder. Scuffed grass here. A shoe print there. He frowned. The print was smooth like the flexible soles the sonal favored, but a scout would have passed without a trace.

Kai almost tripped into the camp as he slammed through a thin barrier and snagged a foot on a large lump of cloth. He righted himself, hand reaching for his dagger, and checked around the small clearing. A moment before, it had been empty. Now, a small, banked campfire appeared in the middle, surrounded by a bedroll and the bag he'd almost fallen over.

No sign of their owner.

Pain pierced his head as he used a precious bit of magic to examine the spell surrounding the clearing. Thin, subtle, and an awkward imitation of Lyr's own energy. Similar to an apprentice who hadn't mastered their art. The edges of the spell were ragged, and the whole thing wavered like a leaf in the wind. *Cell phone. Inexperienced mage.* The signs weren't good.

Then a ray of sunlight escaped the thinning clouds above and glinted silver near the bedroll. Frowning, Kai knelt, brushing away the blanket that had been tossed aside. And the breath left his body. A steel sword. Great Goddess Bera protect them. Kai's allergy to iron, and thus steel, was fairly mild, but Lyr was not so fortunate. If the intruder wielded either, his friend would be at a serious disadvantage.

Kai spun, darting around the pack and through the field of energy. He pulled his shields tight, though the draw on his energy had him swaying on his feet for a few strides, and rushed back the way he'd come. In moments, he'd made it to the main trail. He slowed to a fast walk and forced his expression to neutral. If their uninvited guest didn't know they'd been discovered, Kai would rather not give them a hint.

Could a human have made it through the Veil to Moranaia? It was a long, treacherous crossing for those without the talent of the guide. Humans were much more likely to stumble into Sidhe hills than a world as far removed as this one. But the cell phone was a human invention, something only found on Earth, and couldn't be here otherwise. Unless a Moranaian exile had found their way through the magic that kept them from returning through the portal? They'd certainly have cause to hate Lyr. Their gatekeeper.

At the sight of the woman approaching along the path, Kai slowed. Nothing about her screamed threat, and yet something about her bothered him. His eyes narrowed on the clothes she wore, the cut different from any in this area of Moranaia. Really *any* area he knew of, but he hadn't traveled to every holding on the vast continent. Perhaps she was a visitor from a distant branch.

Then again, the camp had also been different.

The red of her hair blurred into the brown of her tunic as he pulled energy into his hands. Kai shook his head against the dizziness and tried to focus. By the time his vision cleared, the woman's brow had pinched into a concerned frown. Had he wavered on his feet? She'd certainly picked up her pace. When she drew to a halt in front of him, her hand lifted as though to touch him. Then her green eyes met his gray, and she froze.

With a shuddering breath, Kai opened his energy to scan the woman for any sign of a threat. As his energy found hers, his mind went blank. "Gods," he gasped.

"Are you okay?"

All the power he'd gathered seemed to drain out at once, leaving him hollow. Kai pulled his essence back and scrambled for something resembling reality. It couldn't be this. Finding one whose soul could join with one's own was rare, and after five hundred years, Kai had long ago given up hope of meeting his soulbonded. But he knew—*knew*—it was her. This stranger.

"Seriously, do you need a doctor?" She shifted on her feet and glanced behind her before returning her attention to him. "You've gone pretty pale."

Why did she seem so familiar? The cast of her eyes and her high cheekbones reminded him of someone, but he couldn't have met her before and not recognized her as his bonded. "Where are you from?"

Her brows rose. "Are you just going to ignore my questions?"

"I'm sorry." He ran a shaky hand across his face. "I'm in a rush, and you startled me. I'll be fine."

He hoped. The woman's lips twisted as she studied him, but she let him get away with the evasion. "I'll let you be on your way, then." She stared at his still form. "If you'll let me by?"

The mental image of Lyr impaled on a steel blade, as Lyr's father had been, warred with Kai's fear of losing the woman. His bonded. "You didn't tell me where you're from."

She shrugged. "Far away. Really far. I'm visiting relatives."

The dull throb of energy depletion twisted in his head to mingle with the rising panic. What if she left before he could find her again? Kai lifted a hand to his burning chest and wrapped it around the pendant that had slipped free as he ran. *The pendant.* How different were her customs? Even the distant branches should understand bonding. If she took it, he could find her again. Always.

"There is danger near, my lady, and you are unarmed." Kai pulled the chain over his head and held it high, the round medallion glimmering in the sun. "I would prefer to see you protected."

Uneasiness filling her eyes, she stepped back. "I'll be okay."

"I can't take that risk. This will shield you." And it would, for if he sensed her in danger, he would kill any who caused it. Didn't she understand that? "I have to find Lord Lyr at once, but I hate to leave you."

Her mouth pinched into a thin line, and she shook her head. "That looks important. I couldn't accept it."

Kai tried to send a mental call to Lyr but was still too far away. He swayed, pain sparking behind his eyes. He had to go while he still could. Surely, she would recognize the bonding magic once he activated it. *"i'Tayah ay nac-mor kehy ler ehy anan taen."*

The flash of light from the pendant reflected for a moment in her widened eyes. "What?"

"Please, take it." Pain crashed through his skull as the forming bond pulled at his energy. "It's yours now."

She reached out a hand, her fingers almost brushing his. "Are you sure?"

"Very sure." More light flared as she accepted the necklace. Kai almost dropped to his knees from the surge of power. He tried to smile around rising nausea. "Be careful. At the first hint of danger, call for me."

His bonded frowned up at him as the chain settled around her neck. "Thank you. I think."

Before she could say another word, he was gone.

Arlyn stood for a moment, her gaze following the strange, black-haired elf as he rushed away. What the hell had just happened? On weakened legs, she sank onto a bench, the same one Lyr had used earlier. She tried to lift the medallion, still warm from the stranger's body, but it slipped from her trembling fingers the first couple of attempts. Finally, she raised the shiny metal to eye level and examined the symbols tracing each side. The writing was incomprehensible.

She let the pendant drop between her breasts as she huffed. Like she needed something *else* unusual to happen today. *Ah, but his eyes!* Arlyn shivered, a bolt of desire catching her off guard. Really, the man had looked ill, his face gaunt and skin unnaturally pale. So what if he'd been built and gorgeous? She should have insisted on taking him to a doctor instead of ogling him. Anything besides standing there like an idiot.

Though she was far from an expert, Arlyn doubted the magic the stranger had used was for protection. A sort of connection sang through her, almost as though she could sense where he was located even after he had moved out of sight. Her stomach lurched as she leapt to her feet. She would ask Lyr. If the man had done something to her, maybe her father would know how to fix it.

Arlyn tucked the chain between her tunic and her undershirt, then headed for camp. No matter how hard she tried to shuffle the encounter to the back of her mind, it lingered. Those words had sounded familiar, but she was certain she'd never heard them before. Had it been Moranaian? Something niggled at her on the edge of conscious thought, something important, but she couldn't bring it forth. With a growl, she kicked a rock out of her way and swore.

As she crammed her belongings into the pack, his eyes still haunted her. Pulled at her. So gray, just like the mists swirling endlessly in the Veil.

As soon as Kai was within range, he sent a mental call to Lyr. Kai's pace increased as he waited for his friend to respond, every terrible scenario possible flitting through his mind. What could be taking so long? If someone held Lyr captive, Kai feared the result. Lyr had never been the same since leaving Aimee behind on Earth and might take unnecessary risks. He wouldn't hesitate to sacrifice himself to save others.

"Kai?" Lyr finally answered. A wave of emotion slipped through as their energy connected enough for mental communication, the intensity causing Kai to stumble and slow. *"I forgot you were returning."*

"I just talked to you this morning." Kai's brows rose even though Lyr couldn't see. *"How in Emora's name could you have forgotten?"*

"Meet me in my study, and we'll talk."

"But I found—"

"In my study."

Without warning, Lyr cut off their communication. Kai broke into a jog despite the calm tone of Lyr's voice. His friend had not leaked emotion through a link that way in over twenty years. Not since the murder of Lyr's father, an event that had forced him to leave his soulbonded on Earth to search Moranaia for the person responsible. The entire ordeal had left Lyr more reserved and habit-bound than he'd once been.

Kai slipped around to the front of the house, not wanting to run into anyone he knew in the gardens. Politeness would require a longer discussion than he wanted to risk. Ignoring the main entrance, he took the side path to Lyr's study. His friend Kera stood guard at the outer door. Her face lit with pleasure, and maybe relief, at his appearance.

"Welcome back, Lord Kaienan."

"You haven't called me that since our training days." He shook his head, frowning. "Is all well?"

"You know I cannot betray what passes at my post without the Myern's command." She shrugged. "Unless there's an emergency. Which there isn't."

"But?"

A grin split Kera's face. "You'll be interested in speaking with Lord Lyr. Trust me."

"Thanks," Kai answered, his tone wry.

Kera winked at him as he stepped past her to open the door. No doubt she'd corner him later for more details about whatever she'd seen. His eyes adjusted quickly to the gloom of the little hall, and Kai strode into the study, blinking against the brightness that greeted him once more. Half-turned behind his desk, Lyr sat staring out the nearby glass. Kai studied his profile for some clue of what had happened but found nothing.

Restless, Kai shifted on his feet before deciding to damn protocol. "What is going on?"

As he turned to face Kai, Lyr smirked. "Is that any way to greet me after returning from a diplomatic mission?"

"Today it is." Kai strode forward to stand in front of Lyr's desk. "First, you fail to meet me at the portal. Then, I find a camp hidden in the woods. And you're leaking emotion like a cloth waterskin."

All amusement dropped from Lyr's face. "I have good reason. Do you remember the day I left Aimee?"

Kai jerked back in surprise. "Yes, but—"

"It's important," Lyr interrupted. "Did you notice anything different about her?"

"No, but I was hardly in the best state of mind." Kai gritted his teeth against the echo of remembered pain. Telien had been like a father to him. "I was more concerned with finding your father's murderer."

"As was I." Lyr closed his eyes. "Much to my own misfortune."

Kai frowned. "How so?"

"I'm fairly sure I know who the camp belongs to." With a sigh, Lyr glanced up. "I had a visitor today. My daughter.

Aimee was pregnant with our child, and I never even suspected."

For a full five drips of the clock, Kai stared at him. Lyr had
a child? "How?"

Lyr's brow rose. "Didn't your father have that discussion
with you centuries ago?"

"You know what I meant." Kai huffed. "You didn't
check?"

"Obviously not." Lyr rose, scowling. "I wouldn't abandon
a child. I was too busy trying to think of a way to get Aimee
through the portal at the speed we'd need."

Kai swayed on his feet and leaned forward to grip the desk.
"*Clechtan.* What a mess. Where is she now?"

Lyr's eyes narrowed, finally taking in Kai's appearance.
"Are you unwell?"

"Nothing sleep won't fix." Kai forced himself to straighten.
"The girl?"

Lyr stared at him for a moment but let the topic of Kai's
weakness drop. "She went to collect her things."

Kai recalled the camp he'd found. The clumsy shield with
energy resembling Lyr's. And the sword. "*Your* daughter carries steel?"

Lyr grimaced. "Perhaps. She came from Earth. What other
metal would she be likely to find?"

"I've been to Earth more recently, but even when you last
traveled there, humans didn't often use swords. Why would
she have one?" Kai paced from the window and back, brow
furrowed. He dug the phone out of the pouch at his waist and
set it on the desk with a click. "Yet she carries their technolo-

gy. Something isn't right here. Are you certain she's telling the truth?"

Lyr picked up the device to examine it more closely. "What *is* this?"

"A phone. Humans use it to communicate much as we do with the mirrors. Except I can't play games on my mirror."

"Games?"

"Never mind." Kai's mouth tightened. "Did the girl bring proof?"

Lyr sank back into his chair and rubbed a hand across his brow. "She let me test her. It's true."

"What about Aimee?"

Kai regretted the question as soon as it slipped free. Lyr paled, lines of grief etching his face. "Gone."

"I'm sorry." Another wash of leaked emotion made Kai turn his head away. "I should have guessed."

"I always knew—" Lyr's voice choked off.

"That doesn't make it easy."

Kai went back to the window, giving Lyr a moment to collect himself. Late afternoon sun glimmered across the flowers planted next to the study where it bordered the garden. In the distance, a couple wandered one of the paths that meandered through the trees. Such a bright day after the storm, a contrast to the pain humming through the air of Lyr's sanctum. Only when it eased did Kai turn.

"Would you like to give your report so you can go rest?" Lyr asked wearily. "I sense Arlyn returning."

Unease trickled into Kai's body. "She's on the path? What does she look like?"

"Tall and leanly muscled like a scout, with long, red hair like her mother's." Lyr's expression softened. "And my green eyes."

Kai coughed out a breath. *Miaran!* His soulbonded. She *had* seemed familiar. He rubbed a hand through his hair, sending up a prayer to the Nine Gods. All of them. Any of them. Could he have started the bonding process with his best friend's daughter? He searched for the connection between them and sensed her getting closer. *Iron in the heart,* Kai cursed to himself. How was he going to explain this? He hadn't even asked the woman her name.

"Was the mission that bad, then?"

He met Lyr's concerned gaze. "No. Well, yes, but that isn't—"

"Come. Let's get the formal part over." Lyr flipped open a leather-bound book resting on his desk and murmured a few words until the pages glowed. "*Taysonal,* what news do you bring to the stewards of Moranaia?"

Kai suppressed a groan, bound by the formal question and by duty. He could not talk to Lyr about the bond now, not until the report was finished. Kai clenched his hands behind his back and straightened his body. "Lord Meren seems conflicted about ending the treaty with the humans. If it were up to him, I think he'd send mages to the surface. But many among the Sidhe have no desire to leave their underhill cities after all this time."

"Did you receive an audience with the queen?"

"Once again, I was denied. My access to the Seelie court was severely restricted." Kai scowled. "I'm not even sure why they've asked for our help just to delay any discussions."

Lyr leaned forward, his brow furrowed. "What about the energy poisoning?"

"Worse. I dared not draw in energy to replenish my stores lest I risk contagion. I didn't even chance sleeping. I don't know how any of the Sidhe function."

"So we're no further than before your mission."

Kai let out a long breath. "I fended off two assassins if that makes it clearer."

"I see." Lyr tapped his fingers on the desk. "Something isn't right here. The Sidhe are still blaming the humans?"

Kai nodded. "They believe aboveground pollution is trickling down and perverting the energies of the underhill realms at an increasing rate. They have had to abandon entire cities because the tainted energy makes those areas uninhabitable unless the people are willing to put themselves at serious risk. But humans have been polluting the environment heavily for a couple of centuries. In fact, there may be less pollution now than even fifty years ago. I see no reason why it's just now affecting the underrealms. And physical pollution shouldn't cross dimensions."

Lyr's sigh echoed Kai's thoughts. "We're going to have to act soon, no matter what they say."

"Very soon. I'd rather not have maddened Sidhe overrunning everything." Kai grimaced. "It may not have infected the energy here, but the Veil has grown increasingly turbulent with each crossing. Even as far removed as we are from Earth, we're not without risk."

"Anything else?"

"Nothing that can't wait for my written report."

"It appears I have a great deal to consider before bringing this matter to the king. I thank you, *Taysonal*, for the news you have brought." As the traditional words ended the spell that had recorded their words in the book, Lyr relaxed. Pale and drawn, he returned the tome to its drawer and faced Kai. "I must admit I am thankful there is not more. This much is unwelcome but hardly unexpected. I am not certain I could handle another surprise this day."

Fuck it all, Kai muttered to himself, his favorite human curse. How could he tell Lyr now? *Oh, speaking of surprises, I'm fairly certain I started the bonding process with your daughter without courting her first.* Lyr was going to kill him. But Kai had believed she was from a distant branch. That she'd recognized the bonding magic. He attempted to examine the memory, but it was shrouded in a haze of pain.

Only one thing rang clear: if she was from Earth, then *she hadn't known.*

Kai stumbled over to the chairs, sinking into the first one he reached. He dropped his head into his hands and struggled not to throw up. Unforgiveable. Making the decision in haste had been bad enough, but without her knowledge? The sound of Lyr's chair scraping back thundered through Kai's pounding head, but he didn't look up. Even when his friend's footsteps drew near.

"Kai?"

Before he could form an answer, the door to the outside opened. Kai glanced up and found the woman from the path now standing inside the study. She bit her lip as she looked with uncertainty between him and Lyr. Kai straightened and forced down the bile rising with the action. Only now did the resemblance between the two become clear. How could he have missed it?

She slung a large pack off her shoulder and propped it against the wall. The hilt of the sword and a couple of bows peeked over the top. When she turned back, her brow had risen. "Still haven't found a doctor?"

Lyr's startled gaze flew to Kai. "You've met?"

"I was going to tell you about it before you asked for my report."

The woman approached, her fingers tangling in front of her. "Looks like you found Lord Lyrni—Lyr. Have you taken care of whatever danger had you worried earlier?"

"Danger?"

Kai grimaced at Lyr's startled expression. "I found the cell phone, then the camp with the steel blade. I thought there was trouble."

"My phone!" The woman patted her pockets. "I can't believe I lost it."

"It will hardly do you any good here."

"Still, I'd like it back."

Lyr grabbed the device from his desk and held it up. "This is yours, correct?"

She strode over and took it from his hand, examining it closely before scowling over at Kai. "The screen is cracked. This thing was expensive, you know."

"It was in the middle of the trail, and I didn't see it." Kai shrugged. "Don't worry about it. I'll replace it. Surely, it can't cost more than a couple of diamonds."

"A couple of…" She paled. "Just like that, you're going to give me *diamonds?*" Shaking her head, her hand went to the small lump just visible beneath her shirt. The pendant. "You certainly do give things away easily."

Panic shot Kai to his feet. If Lyr saw that necklace before Kai could explain, Lyr might kill him before he had the chance. "Diamonds are a common trade item here, but I think they're worth enough on Earth. Wealth is counted differently on Moranaia." He took a gasping breath while his mind scrambled for a topic to distract her. "We even have an alternative to steel."

"It isn't like you to ramble." Lyr gave him a puzzled frown. "You really don't seem well. Your favorite tower is free if you'd like to rest."

"Sounds like a great plan to me," the woman muttered.

Kai flushed even as he wavered on his feet. His own bonded considered him a fool, and she certainly had every right. His mind was so muddled by energy loss he hardly recognized himself. But how could he rest with so many issues unresolved? The woman deserved his confession, as did Lyr. Kai had to find a way to pull her aside.

"My lady," Kai began, then paused, frowning. "Forgive me. I don't believe I know your name."

Lyr appeared stunned for one moment, then shook his head. "I have lost all sense of politeness this day. I forgot to introduce you."

The woman shrugged. "You mentioned his name earlier, I believe."

"It is not the same. Indeed, it would be an unforgivable breach to some. Pray gods you do not tell my mother. She has despaired of my manners ever since I returned from my last visit to the human world." An unexpected twinkle of humor in his eyes, Lyr bowed politely to Kai. "Honored friend, I present to you Callian Ayala i Arlyn Dianore nai Braelyn. Lady Arlyn, I present to you Callian ay'iyn Tayern pel Taysonal i Kaienan Treinesse nai Oria."

Kai couldn't stop himself from bowing over her hand, though he shouldn't have touched her, even innocently. Not after what he'd done. "It is a pleasure to meet you, my lady. Please call me Kai."

"If you will call me Arlyn." She smiled for a moment before pulling her hand free. "Especially since I still don't understand the rest of what he called me."

"Our long names show our place in society," Lyr explained. "The first word tells which of the three great branches of government the person belongs to. Next usually comes a title or description of their trade. Then the given name and place where they live."

Arlyn grimaced. "Why so complicated?"

"Most Moranaians are more order-minded than humans." Lyr's lips twisted. "And when you have thousands of years to deal with offending someone, you tend to set up ways to avoid it. Knowing a person's position in society from the beginning often helps with that."

"So Callian is the branch, which means Kai and I belong to the same one. I'm lost after that." She examined Kai as though his presence could somehow make it clear. "I think you had a lot of titles."

Kai grinned. "It mostly translates to 'second son of an earl and assistant to Lyr.'"

"Sounds kind of feudal."

"There's more flexibility than it might seem," Lyr said. "Titles can and do change. If Kai here were to bond with someone on a higher branch or even a different branch, much of what you just heard would change."

The breath rushed out of Kai in one long gasp, and he sank back into the chair. Pain, a match to the constant thrum in his head, filled his chest. He couldn't talk to Arlyn first, as she deserved. He had to correct Lyr now. For lying about one's name or title was considered a grave misdeed, and Lyr had just incorrectly introduced him. *Kai didn't even have the same damn name.*

"Go rest, Kai."

He met Lyr's puzzled gaze. "We need to talk."

"You look like you're about to collapse. It can wait."

"No." Kai stiffened his spine, trying to appear stronger than he felt. "It can't. We have to talk *now*. Alone."

Arlyn glanced between them, her brow furrowed, and Kai caught a hint of concern from her along their growing bond. Could she sense his turmoil? Gods, he hoped not. "Why don't I go get settled in?"

Lyr nodded. "I will find you when we are finished."

Kai tensed as his bonded gathered her pack and left, but there was no avoiding what had to be done. What Lyr would do about it was less clear. Kai hadn't done anything illegal, so he was unlikely to be exiled, but his actions had been dishonorable no matter how unintentional. Even centuries of friendship might not survive this breach.

The pain in his chest wound ever tighter.

5

Lyr turned to Kai with an irritated scowl. "What is wrong with you? I have not seen you like this since your first journey through the Veil. Even then you were not so ill. Did something else happen while you were away?"

"No, it was after my return." Kai ran a hand through his hair. "Remember that I haven't slept for a week. It was stupid, unpardonably stupid."

"*Miaran,*" Lyr cursed. "By Arneen, just say it."

"You see, I have a new name." Kai paused, winced. "Calli-an Myal pel Taysonal i Kaienan Dianore nai Braelyn."

It only took Lyr a moment to process. Myal—mate to the female heir—matched with his family name. His face went white with the anger that swept through him. "Did you do what I think you did?"

"I encountered her on the path, and my soul resonated with hers. I'd just drawn energy, so my head was pounding, and I couldn't focus." Kai gripped the arm of the chair. "She said she was just visiting, and I was in a rush to get to you after seeing that steel sword. But when I spoke the words, I assumed she knew about bonding. I thought she was from a distant branch."

"*You thought.*" Lyr's hands fisted, and he took a few deep breaths. Anything to keep from pummeling the man standing before him. "I don't suppose you bothered to ask."

"All I could see was you, impaled like your father. But I couldn't stand to lose her after I'd just found her."

Sick pain twisted through Lyr, propelling him forward. He paced the room, his mind in disarray and emotions tangling until he wasn't certain of anything. *His best friend. His daughter.* "When did you realize who she was?"

Kai leaned forward. "Not until I spoke to you."

Lyr turned on him, fury winning out. "And you didn't tell me then?"

"I was about to when you asked for my report." Kai stared him in the eye, unflinching as Lyr approached. "Then she came in. I wanted to tell her first, but I realized I couldn't after your introduction."

Lyr stared at Kai, his friend of more than five hundred years. "I believed you to be a better man than this."

Kai dropped his gaze. His hands clenched the arms of the chair. "As did I."

Lyr spun around to pace once more, trying to work out some of his anger so he could think. Should he call for a priest of Arneen to sever the bond? No. No, that would steal Arlyn's choice as surely as Kai had. Lyr could call her in to explain the soulbond, but that would ease the burden for Kai. Gods, what a mess. Kai was rash, but Lyr never would have expected this of him. Never.

Lyr's chest ached as if it were splitting. Though he'd just met his daughter, she was *his*. His child. He hadn't even had a chance to get to know her. He wasn't entirely certain he even trusted her. And still, he gripped his hands behind his back to keep from hurting his closest friend.

A friend whose pain thundered through the air like the earlier storm.

Kai stood, his head held high. "Whatever you decide I will not dispute."

"It is hardly for me to decide." Lyr's lips twisted in a satisfied smirk. "I'll leave that to Arlyn as is her right. You'll have to tell her yourself."

"Will you give me enough time to rest so I can do so coherently?"

Lyr watched Kai sway on his feet but found he could no longer summon sympathy. "Only so you don't muddle things worse. I will give you a day before I tell her myself. Go collect your things from your father's house, then get some sleep."

"You want me to gather my things?"

"You are part of this House now, like it or not." Lyr sank into the chair behind his desk and rubbed his face, his anger deflating. "Chances are good she'll decide to sever the bond, but it might take some time to find the proper priest. Until then, your place is here."

Kai paled, knowing full well what Lyr hadn't said. A severed bond would be a disgrace, a shame so deep that Kai's father might refuse to let him back into his home. Soulbonds were treasured, broken only for the worst offenses. If Arlyn decided to sever it, Kai might end up leaving Moranaia altogether.

"Go." Lyr motioned to the door. "The sooner you leave, the sooner you can face Arlyn. Take the portal."

Expression tense, Kai nodded and turned, heading for the door that led into the house. Oria, his father's estate, was not far, but the portal would be faster. Lyr dropped his head onto his hand when he heard the door open, then looked up when it didn't close. Kai stood, half-turned, glancing at Lyr over his shoulder.

"How long will it take you to forgive me for this?"

"I do not know, Kai. I do not know."

The door clicked closed, leaving sudden silence.

Though the rock was rough beneath her thin pants and sweat dampened her skin, Arlyn couldn't bring herself to leave her spot on the edge of the small bluff. She wasn't sure how long she'd been out here since dropping her things off in her room, but the green of the trees in the valley below was almost black with shadow as the last rays of sunlight trickled through the forest behind her. If not for the lights she could see flicking to life, she'd think the entire area was uninhabited.

Her breath caught at the reality of it all. This wasn't myth or legend. This was her life. And though the valley reminded Arlyn of her home in the Blue Ridge Mountains, the huge trees that swayed around her indicated otherwise. As far as she knew, no other human had ever seen these mountains or the sky that darkened overhead. Her heart pounded in equal parts terror and exhilaration.

As her arms tightened around her knees, she heard the footsteps behind her and knew it was Lyr. Arlyn could just *sense* him. She'd always had a feel for people, but the talent seemed heightened by this world. Most things seemed heightened. She had arrived on this world almost a week before confronting her father and had struggled to sleep each night since she'd stepped through. Energy throbbed beneath her skin. Her body was jittery with it, like she'd had too many espressos.

Lyr settled cross-legged beside her, and they sat together for a long moment, both staring into the darkening valley. Finally, he turned. "Why are you sitting out here?"

She shot a glance over her shoulder at the front of the estate, then shrugged. "It's one of the few places I know how to find. I got restless, but I didn't want to disturb your discussion." She looked back at the lights teasing from below. "Besides, the view is amazing. So long as the rock doesn't crumble under us."

"It won't." Lyr patted the ground. "The scouts regularly check for any sign of weakness or instability, and we call in mages yearly to reinforce. It's also not as steep as it looks."

"Good to know."

"I hope you realize you may explore wherever you like. I offered you a home here." Pebbles skittered beneath his restless fingers as he drew them over the rock. "You may not wish to stay, but the invitation is for life. You are my family."

Arlyn lifted a brow. "Just like that?"

"As I said earlier, energy doesn't lie." He met her eyes. "Blood matters. Family matters. Maybe there will never be affection between us, and maybe we can never overcome the past. But I'd like to try."

Her throat tightened, and she looked away, blinking rapidly to clear the sudden tears. "I'd like that, too. I'm not sure I can fit in here, but if nothing else, we can get to know each other. I'll probably embarrass you."

She heard him shift beside her. "I doubt it. But if anyone should cause you trouble, tell me at once. I'll take care of it."

"You know, you're nothing like I expected" She looked over to see his lips twist in a half-smile. "I didn't expect much of what has happened, really."

Lyr lifted his knee and rested his arm on it as he turned to stare into the growing darkness. "So tell me. How do I differ? Did your mother not speak of me?"

"She did," Arlyn hastened to reassure him as what little smile he'd had slipped from his face. Something about him seemed so bleak. An eternity in his eyes. She didn't want to care so much about his pain with the hurt of his absence still echoing in her heart. Arlyn hugged her knees close to her chest to keep from offering…what? A hug? A pat of reassurance? She doubted either would be welcome. "She said you were different than she would've expected an elf to be. Humans have plenty of legends about elves, you know. And she's right. You don't quite match them."

"Indeed?" A touch of humor lifted his fallen expression once more. "How so?"

"Elves are supposed to be formal. Stuffy. Self-important. You aren't." Arlyn glanced back at the house again. "Although I have to say your home is about right."

"Most Moranaians *are* formal." Despite the steady loss of light, she could still make out his grin. "I trained with the guard for about two hundred years, for combat magic is my greatest strength. Then I traveled on estate business for my father. In the last three centuries, I've been to Earth often. At least once every year or two, until I took his place as Myern. I suppose it has rubbed off on me."

Arlyn wanted to ask why he'd spent so much time on Earth, but Lyr continued before she could. "The same could be said for Kai. He acted as my guide through the Veil then and continues to travel for me as I did for my father."

That distracted her. "What's the deal with him?"

"The deal?"

She ground her teeth together, frustrated at his inconsistent grasp of her language. Why did he know some slang and not others? "What's wrong with him? Is he sick?"

"Energy depletion." Lyr's face tightened, and he opened his mouth as if to continue before snapping it closed. Was he annoyed at her for asking? Then the faint smile returned, and she wondered if it had been a trick of the dim light. "Elves live on energy as much as food. Maybe more. He'd been a week or so without sleep, and sleep is how we restore our natural energy stores."

"A week? Damn." Could a human even survive a week without sleep? The guy's strange behavior suddenly made a lot more sense. "I hope you sent him to get some rest."

When Lyr's expression hardened this time, there was no mistaking it. He averted his eyes and straightened, the casual ease of moments before gone. "After an errand," he ground out.

Interesting. Whatever they'd discussed, it must not have gone well. *None of my business*, she reminded herself. No matter how drawn she was to Kai. No matter the odd connection between them. One she had to be imagining. "Okay, then."

In one fluid motion, Lyr rose to his feet, so suddenly that Arlyn flinched back. At her movement, he froze, and some of the tension eased from his body. "Forgive my ill temper. Are you hungry? The evening meal is held around sundown this time of year."

Bile rose into her throat. There was no way Arlyn could face whatever strange dinner customs this world held, not after all that had happened this day. "Would it offend you if I eat in my room? Today has been…"

"Overwhelming." He winced. "I should have considered that. I'll walk you there, then see that food is sent."

Arlyn took his offered hand and let him help her to her feet. Lyr turned toward the house, and she followed, trying to dust off the back of her pants without being obvious. She should have known better than to sit outside in her only summer outfit since *she* didn't have spell-enchanted fabric. *Dammit.* It had been chilly when she'd left Earth, so she'd packed her warmest Ren fair clothes. Of the three sets of pants, shirts, and tunics, only one was short-sleeved—the clothes she was wearing. Anything clean she had left in her pack would be hell in this heat.

Outside her door, Lyr's hand closed around Arlyn's forearm as she started to enter. With a puzzled frown, she released the door handle and turned to face him. His expression was neutral once more, no hint of emotion left to indicate what he wanted. Though he released her, his head dipped in a bow, the gesture more formal than any she'd seen from him before.

"Before we part, I need to give you the key to the estate."

Arlyn's brow quirked. "I don't think I'll go out in the middle of the night. I doubt I'll need a key to the door."

"Not that kind of key." The corners of his mouth twitched. "This is a formal offer, made to few. The estate is shielded by many layers of magic and many forms of defense. With the key to that, you'll grow accustomed to this place more readily. It will also give you a mental map of all of the buildings."

She bit her lip. "Are you sure you want to give me that information?"

"I am certain," Lyr answered, voice firm. He lifted a hand, sketching symbols that glittered with his next words. "*Laeial abh-i nai'Braelyn dae ghere nach-mor.*"

Without warning, the symbols flared with light, and the energy poured through her, stealing her breath. Arlyn reached blindly for the wall as information slammed into her brain. The mental map. Impressions of protection spells, a magic beyond anything she'd ever seen. Even flickers that might be people, but she recoiled at that. Did he spy on everyone?

She slumped against the wall as the spell settled in, her eyes squeezed tight. Lyr's hand gripped her shoulder, and his voice, when he finally spoke, sounded worried. "Arlyn?"

"That was crazy." Arlyn swallowed against the tightness in her throat. "I don't even know how to process all of that."

"I will help you decode it later."

"Were those people I could sense?" Her eyes shot open. "That doesn't seem right."

He nodded. "If you focus, you will know the general location of all who work on or protect the estate. But nothing more than that. Only use it for true need, for this key is a trust granted the guardians of Braelyn."

"Why did you give me this?" Though he released her, Lyr met her eyes without hesitation. "Surely, you don't trust me so much in less than a day."

"Not entirely, no." His brows pinched together. "Forgive me for that truth. But I do believe you are my child, and I offered you a place here. I've accepted you as family. All of our blood who reside at Braelyn receive this key by right. If you have hidden ill-intent, then I suppose I will soon know."

Hurt stole her breath, though what he said was more than reasonable. They *were* strangers. "I see."

"Please understand—"

"Stop." Arlyn darted around him to her door. "Really, I do see. I get it. I have no reason to be upset."

But she was, and the frown that creased his brow told her he knew it. As he opened his mouth to say more, Arlyn shook her head and opened the door to her room. "Arlyn…"

"Leave it," she snapped. Then found herself softening a little at the hurt and confusion in his eyes. "We can talk about this tomorrow. I think we both need to sleep on it."

His shoulders slumped, but he nodded. "I will make sure a tray is sent. We'll talk in the morning."

Arlyn bit her lower lip as he strode away. *That could have gone better.* Sighing, she entered her new room. The door clicked closed behind her, and she slumped against it. *So much to take in.* She slid down the smooth wood, her head dropping to her knees. What did she really want out of all this? She wasn't even sure who she was anymore. Energy curled through her, still shimmering from the spell Lyr had cast. Magic greater than anything she'd guessed existed.

And still a thin thread of power that led to the elf named Kai.

The manor was quiet, like a cursed ruin out of myth. As
usual. Not even Kai's boots dared to echo on the
stone floor as he walked toward his father's study. Kai
searched along his inner map and found none of the household workers near. Only his father was in this section of the
house, a poor sign for the coming confrontation.

Everyone avoided Allafon when he was in a mood.

Kai would, too, if he had the time or energy. But what was
one more argument with his father? Kai could not fathom how
his older brother, Moren, could tolerate being here so often,
much less live in relative peace with Allafon. Then again, Allafon didn't blame Moren for their mother's death. It was Kai's
birth that had weakened Elerie so much that she'd been unable
to survive the fall down the stairs. Their father never let him
forget it.

Gods, how Kai hated this place and all its coldness. Not even the heat of Belen, month of the summer solstice, could warm the stone his ancestors had chosen for their keep. It could have been a world away from Lyr's home, though there was only an hour's walk between them. Just being here had the muscles of Kai's shoulders knotting before he even opened the door to the study.

He entered without knocking. His father would have already sensed his approach. "Good evening, father."

Allafon glanced up from his work, his customary scowl in place. "So you have finally returned from whatever fool mission Lyrnis sent you on."

Kai let the insult pass. "You know I cannot discuss the task with you."

"You could if you were *sonal* to me." His father's scowl deepened. "Though I doubt you are here because you wish to act as a scout for our House. What brings you to seek me out? You usually do not bother."

"I have news." Kai smiled and hoped his father could be happy for him for once. "I have found my soulbonded."

Allafon's face *almost* managed to arrange itself into something pleasant. "Is that so? When will she be arriving? Your brother will surely wish to celebrate this rare event."

Kai held back a frown. At least his father had attempted to seem happy. Too bad Kai was about to ruin the effort. "She will not be coming here. Her branch is higher than mine so I will live with her."

"You are leaving?" Allafon paused for a moment, then his eyes narrowed. "Who is this lady, then?"

Kai tensed, bracing himself for the outburst. "Lyr's daughter."

His father's chair screeched along the floor as Allafon leapt to his feet. Energy sparked to life, unheeded, around his frame. "What mockery is this? I am no fool. I know as well as anyone that Lyrnis has no daughter. You dare to lie to me?"

Kai winced at the venom in his father's voice. "Perhaps my first bit of news should have been the arrival of Lyr's daughter. No one knew of her until this day, not even Lyr."

"I do not believe you," his father snapped. The sparks around him danced, an unusual display of Allafon's agitation.

"You already know that Lyr found his mate in the human world but was forced to leave her. Unfortunately, he did not realize he also left a child."

Allafon stared at him a moment more, no doubt searching for a hint of deception, before he sank back down in his chair. His face went curiously blank as the energy around him winked out. "Gods, you are telling the truth. Well, you always did want to be part of that family. Now you have your wish."

Kai tried to school his expression to indifference, but he failed to cover his surprise. "What are you talking about?"

"Come now, Kaienan. You and Lyrnis have been inseparable almost from birth. You practically live at Braelyn, always have. In truth, you have spent more time with Lyrnis and his family than me and your own brother."

"Moren is three hundred and twenty years older than me," Kai said, throwing up his hands in frustration. "He already had responsibilities well beyond entertaining one young child."

"Even so, you still show him, or us, no favor. You spend all your time working for Lyrnis. Honor though your position as *Taysonal* may be, I have always wished you worked here with us instead. I have little else of your mother but you and Morenial."

Kai's mouth opened, but he had no idea how to respond. His father had never talked to him like this, never given him any indication he wanted him near for any reason except pride. Finally, he shook his head. "I have never seen the point of wishing to be in another family. But I have always envied Lyr this—he always knew his father loved him. Sometimes, I think you detest me."

"You *think?*" Sudden anger flashed in Allafon's eyes. "Then you know nothing of me."

"So I was wrong?"

"I would have thought my feelings for you were always obvious, but it seems you have had doubt."

"Obvious? But—"

"Go, Kaienan. I can bear this no longer." Allafon turned away. "I'll expect you gone before the dawn."

Arlyn stared at the water clock, but the number of lines didn't change. She'd been in a rush earlier and hadn't paid attention. But after tossing and turning for what seemed like forever, she had gotten up to see how much time had passed. Water dripped steadily into the vial as she counted yet again. Full to the twenty-fifth line. Twenty-five out of *thirty* lines.

Were their days really longer, or did they just count differently? Arlyn pulled the phone from her pocket and tried to turn it on, but either the battery was dead or Kai had broken it beyond repair. *Too bad I stopped wearing a wristwatch years ago.* She paced the room, her stomach rumbling from nerves and the new food she'd eaten for dinner. Even foods as simple as cheese, meat, and bread were different here. She had no idea what animal she'd even eaten.

Consumed by the restless energy that had plagued her since her arrival, Arlyn slipped from her room and down the curved stairs. The lights placed along the halls were dim, the quiet surprising. It hadn't seemed loud during the day, not until the peace of midnight, or whatever they called it, eased around her. Maybe she could absorb enough of that peace to finally sleep.

At first, she wandered with no specific destination in mind, her mental map directing her away from any private rooms. Lyr's study was empty—had she hoped to find him?—as were a couple of other chambers that appeared to be sitting rooms. She circled down another winding hall and opened the door to the dining room. Like the study, it was oval, the walls full of windows looking out on the moonlit garden. An oval table took up much of the space, and a pleasant, spicy-sweet scent lingered in the air.

How many meals had this room seen over millennia? Certainly beyond her counting.

With a small shudder, Arlyn closed the door and made her way to the largest room she'd found on her inner map. The hall was wider and less twisting, finally ending at a set of carved double doors. She ran her fingers across the intricate forest scene, her stomach taking another roll at the mix of odd and familiar. The unique leaves of the trees were hard to make out, but not the animals. She squinted at a small creature with a fuzzy squirrel tail but long ears like a rabbit. That was just wrong.

Arlyn shoved the door open before she could make out anything else odd and stepped inside. Then froze. Nothing about the manor had hinted that such an impossibly large room could exist within its walls. But here it was. Between tall windows, intricately carved and painted trees stretched in magnificent detail to the ceiling. Delicate light globes dangled from false branches entwined above, a dark, star-studded sky beyond them.

Her eyes narrowed as her gaze darted between the ceiling and the windows. The colors didn't match, and the hint of moon—*moons?*—didn't seem quite real. Enchanted, then? Maybe the ceiling changed to match the outside, becoming day when the light rose. She would have to come back tomorrow to see.

The floor was smooth beneath her feet as she walked over to the windows. Her eyes caught on the pattern inlaid into the wooden floor, the colors and designs so seamless that she paused before stepping on a rock. A rock that turned out to be another color of wood. With a shake of her head, Arlyn continued forward, though her toes curled to step barefoot where her mind said she shouldn't.

At first, all she could see in the window was her own reflection, and she let out a short laugh. She was wandering the house in her nightgown, a luxury she'd argued with herself about packing. Maybe somewhere deep inside, Arlyn had hoped all along that she could stay here, if only for a short while. She'd certainly stuffed the nightgown in her pack despite thinking it foolish. Too bad she hadn't thrown in a robe.

A few steps closer and she could make out the world beyond the window. Arlyn's hand gripped the window frame as she stared into the sky. *At the two moons.* The image on the ceiling hadn't been a fantasy. She spun away, her feet thumping against wood as she hurried to the door. To her room. She'd known, looking into the valley, that this place was different. Now she *felt* it.

Lyr had said something about the years being off from Earth's. For the first time, she considered the implications. How long did it take this planet to circle its sun? Or to spin an entire day? Maybe they *didn't* count the length of an hour in a different way. The days here might actually be longer.

Out of breath, Arlyn paused at the base of the stairs leading to her room. She pressed her hand against her chest and forced herself to relax. To take in air. Yes, this world was strange. But how many humans had ever stepped onto another planet? Zero, as far as she knew. She could let fear take her, or she could embrace the adventure.

Her hand dropped to her side, and she straightened. Chances were good she wouldn't be here long. Her ignorance of elven ways would surely prove to be an embarrassment to her new family, and they'd be happy to see her leave. Why not enjoy being in a place none on Earth even knew existed? Her gaze landed on the massive tree trunk on the far side of the room, so different from anything she'd seen before. If she fled, she would never know its significance.

Arlyn found herself approaching with slow steps. The map in her head said this tree was important, but it didn't say *why*. It didn't tell her about the history or culture of this world. Even without it, the way the room was built around the trunk with obvious care, coupled with the intricate carvings on the columns that framed it, told her of the tree's significance. That and the energy that seemed to waft from it like a spring breeze.

She stopped an arm's reach from the smooth trunk, but she couldn't bring herself to touch it. What if it was taboo? Her mom hadn't mentioned anything about Moranaian religion, if she'd even been told about it. For all Arlyn knew, she'd be hauled off by a bunch of priests for defiling the sacred tree. Or something. Who even knew?

Her eyes drifted closed as the tree's gentle energy flowed through her. Arlyn's stomach muscles unclenched as some of her tension eased, and the restlessness that had driven her began to fade. She drooped where she stood, the exhaustion long-masked by the energy of this world overtaking her. Rubbing a hand over her face, she forced her gritty eyelids to rise. If she didn't go to bed now, they'd find her sleeping at the base of the sacred tree come morning.

Arlyn forced her leaden limbs to carry her to the stairs. As she climbed, the peace of the tree followed her. Was there some magic at work? Did the tree contain a soothing spell to help the home's inhabitants rest? Still pondering, Arlyn settled into bed and snuggled into the soft blanket. After a week of fractured sleep, she just didn't care.

Only one of the moons was visible, its half-full face partly hidden by clouds. Two marks until dawn. It had taken Kai longer than expected to pack his things and arrange for all of them, except for the one bag he carried, to be sent to Braelyn in the next couple of days. How had it been possible that his room contained so many possessions? He was rarely there. But he had boxed up several crates worth during the last few hours.

As he sent his senses out in a sweep, Kai examined the trees around him. There were few problems on this path, but anything was possible. Except for sleep, which seemed destined never to be his. Though he barely had the energy left to shield himself and monitor his surroundings, his father had demanded he leave at once. Kai hadn't even had the energy to use the transportation portal between the two estates. Over a week now since he had properly rested. He reminded himself again that sleeping on the side of the path would be a bad thing.

He used a great deal of energy to cross the Veil in a matter of minutes, sometimes nearly half of his reserves if the path was difficult. In his early days of being a *sonal*, it had not taken as much to go to the human world, and if he'd been traveling to the underhill, he would have simply rested before returning. But now that the energies there had become polluted, the risk was too great. Kai did not want to take such unhealthy stuff into his body or, worse, contaminate his own world. Not to mention the newer threat of assassins. So instead, he wore himself down to this exhaustion every trip.

Something would have to be done about the Sidhe and their thrice-cursed poisoned energy. And soon.

Kai slowed as the hairs on his arms stood on end. Had something flickered on the edge of his senses? He dropped his hand to his knife and sent his power sweeping farther ahead, pain shattering in his skull from the effort. As best he could tell through the haze of agony, no sign of life existed beyond the normal assortment of forest creatures, yet he was not reassured. If he possessed more energy, he could cast something stronger. Doing so now would collapse his already-meager shields.

With the perimeter of Braelyn only a few minutes away, Kai sped up, hoping to make it to the safety of the estate shields before the threat he sensed could show itself. The land guards could search the area to see if they could find anything. Besides, the energy depletion might be messing with him, jumbling up his perceptions.

A rustle of fabric and quick jolt of power were his only warnings. Out of reflex, Kai drew his knife, but it was too late. The slide of the blade under his ribs brought a new kind of agony, and energy slipped from his body as steadily as blood. He fell hard, each gasp of breath twisting the knife ever deeper into his flesh.

Hands closed around his shoulders, and his world tilted. Rough bark bit into Kai's back. He could see little this deep in the shadows, but a form hovered above him. Tall. He tried to pull energy from his surroundings, but what was left of his reserves was gone, dispersed by the blade in his side.

Must be steel.

"You'll make a nice warning," a deep voice murmured. "If you manage to live, tell your lord this: leave Sidhe business to the Sidhe. If not, well, let's hope he figures it out, hmm?"

Kai attempted to rise, to fight, but he couldn't get his limbs to move. The stranger chuckled, then disappeared in another swirl of fabric. Kai blinked, trying to clear the sweat from his eyes, but he could make out nothing but the forest. Gone. He struggled to breathe as the trees swirled around him.

So near Braelyn, but not close enough. He'd never be able to send out a mental call to Lyr from this distance. *Miaran.* He couldn't even pull up enough energy to call the closest land guard. Kai's eyes drifted closed, and he let his head fall back against the tree. Agony screamed through him, a match for the fear pounding his heart.

Not just for himself, but for Arlyn.

rlyn woke screaming. Her hands darted to the source of pain along her left side, but her skin was smooth with no sign of injury. She struggled to draw breath, to make sense of the sudden agony. Frantic, she searched the room, still lit by the mage light she hadn't known how to extinguish. No one there. No tormentor to account for the pain gripping her. She lifted a shaking hand, certain there must be blood even if she couldn't find a wound. Nothing.

The door slammed open, and Lyr rushed in, Lynia just behind. They scanned the area as she had before taking in the sight of her writhing form. Lyr ran over to the bed. "Arlyn, what is it?"

"I...don't..." she said, trying to pant through the unrelenting pain, "know. No blood. No wound. But my side..."

Lyr pushed her hands away and pressed down where the wound should have been. "Does that hurt?"

"No different."

"It is not her pain."

Her grandmother stepped closer. "What do you mean?"

"She is soulbound. We have to get to Kai."

"Kai?" The elder frowned when she noticed the necklace Arlyn wore. "Gods. When did he have time? Well, never mind that. Teach her to control it."

"I'm not sure she can with the bond incomplete." He brushed Arlyn's hair from her face with trembling fingers. "The healer can put her to sleep while I go find Kai."

Arlyn grabbed his wrist. "Take me with you."

"Do not be ridiculous. I doubt you could walk."

Her grip tightened. "You will find him faster with me. I can sense where he is."

"Arlyn—"

"I think they used steel."

"How could you know such a thing?"

"I…" She panted around a surge of pain. "I'm not sure. An impression."

With a curse, Lyr gathered her in the blanket and lifted her in his arms. At least moving her physical body did not increase the pain. Though it made no logical sense, she would allow nothing to stop her from getting to Kai. The link she'd believed imaginary clearly *wasn't*.

When they reached the outside, Lyr's men surrounded them. He paused, looking at her expectantly. It took her but a moment to trace the link and gesture toward the forest to the west. "That way."

Arlyn closed her eyes against the swirling of the stars above. Apparently, Lyr was not an idle lord. When she dared to look again, he was running full out, though his expression showed no sign of strain. Only a worried frown. His gait as he sped through the trees was so smooth she was barely jostled. Stories of elven strength and grace given life.

A faint voice broke into her thoughts. *"Arlyn?"*

Another wash of agony came with it, taking her breath. When some of the pain cleared, she looked for the mental path. *"Kai?"*

It took him so long to answer that she assumed she had gotten the connection wrong, but when his voice returned, the pain flowing through their bond seemed muted. *"Yes. I sense you nearing. Do not come alone."*

"Lyr is with me, along with some guards. What's going on?"

"Surprise attack. Tell him to contact me. I am too weak to contact anyone but you."

"Lyr." He looked down at her when she spoke but did not slow. "I just spoke to Kai. He said he does not have the energy to contact you himself."

"That weak? *Miaran.*" He fell silent, then, likely seeking out Kai himself.

A few moments later, a new flash of pain seared her side, and her body jerked as she stifled the scream. Blind with it, Arlyn motioned to the right, following the invisible line that linked her to Kai. "Hurry."

After cutting off the link to Lyr, Kai braced himself to pull out the blade. He would have left it in until he reached a healer, but the steel was more of an issue than the wound itself. Already, the poison of the metal seeped into his body in a slow burn. At least his allergy was relatively mild. His body would heal almost as fast as with any other injury, but not if he left the metal in the wound. The longer the contact, the harder it would be to heal by magic.

With one hand, he ripped the sleeve off his tunic and wrapped it around the blade where it met flesh. Then he grabbed the hilt with the other and pulled. As his body exploded in fresh agony, he pressed the fabric down tight, knowing it would do little good. The cloth was already growing slippery with the blood soaking through. He tried to block the pain from Arlyn again, but his strength had ebbed too much. For the first time, feeling his life pooling on the ground and knowing he was too weak to stop it, he accepted that he might die.

But the worst part? He'd been stupid enough to start the bond. Incomplete and tenuous as it was, Arlyn might be pulled with him when he died. Kai's throat convulsed around a moan. He had to try to contact Lyr again, tell him to take her far away. Maybe distance could save her. He'd gladly give up his own slim chance of survival to keep from taking her with him.

"Don't you think highly of yourself?" Arlyn's voice interrupted, making him jump. How could she read his thoughts so soon?

"You heard that?"

"You were practically shouting. I'm sure everyone heard."

"No, Lyr would have said something. Probably would have shielded me, too." He struggled to keep his shaking hand pressed against the wound. *"Are you near?"*

They appeared out of the darkness before she could answer, mage light illuminating Arlyn bundled in Lyr's arms. Five others ringed him and began to cast in an arc around them in an attempt to break the attacker's invisibility, but the assassin was probably long gone. His warning had been well delivered. With a groan, Kai glanced up to see that Lyr had set Arlyn on her feet. She sank down beside him, heedless of the pool of blood. Her energy flowed around him, soothing, though it could barely bolster what he'd lost.

"Go, Arlyn. The farther away you are, the less likely you will be pulled with me."

Lyr stooped down beside him and examined the wound, then blanched. "Great gods, Kai, why haven't you stopped the bleeding? Your allergy is certainly mild enough."

"No energy left." He lost focus, using the power he'd gained from Arlyn to search inside himself. "Think it nicked my stomach, maybe a kidney. Missed heart. Can't just seal outer layer."

Lyr's jaw clenched. "I'll give you energy. Your healing gift is mild, but surely—"

"Won't be enough." Kai's eyes slipped closed. He tried to open them again, but it was too much effort. "Not enough personal reserves to convert it. If Arlyn knew…"

"Knew what?"

"Energy that passes along a *taenac*, a soulbond, is more useable. Something in the link," Lyr answered for him. "But it takes a great deal of training to learn how to transfer power that way."

Her gaze filled with resolve. "I can try."

"Just go," Kai whispered. "Please. All of this is my fault. I'll not…" His voice trailed off as he struggled for air. Each pant seared his side like a brand, and he heard Arlyn gasp with the echo of it. "Please."

"No." He forced his eyes open and focused on her face. Frowning, she shook her head. "If anyone or anything is going to kill you, it'll be me."

He smiled at her words. A blessed bit of numbness spread through him, and his hand dropped to his side. The cloth went lax against his wound. "I fear not."

Lyr placed a hand on her shoulder. "Arlyn—"

"No!" Arlyn grabbed Kai's arm.

Then the world exploded.

Lyr's groan reverberated against the cold floor as consciousness slammed into him. Had there been an earthquake? It took a few heartbeats to realize that a hand, and not the earth, shook his body. He twisted, trying to see over his shoulder, and caught sight of his mother, eyes wide and face drawn. What had happened? The last he'd seen her—

Arlyn. Kai. The injury. Lyr shoved himself up to sitting and looked around. How had he gotten to his daughter's bedroom? An arm span away, Arlyn slumped over Kai, both of them unconscious. With Lyr awake, his mother rushed over to them and reached out, then pulled her hand back with a hesitant frown. "What happened?"

"Kai was stabbed." Lyr slid himself closer, every muscle in his body screaming against the action. He placed a hand on Kai's chest and shuddered in relief to find it still moving, however slowly. When he glanced to Arlyn, he found her pale but breathing, too. "Did you call Lial?"

His mother nodded. "Just before you came to. Should we move the girl? I am not even certain you should be touching Kai."

"I—"

The door flew open, slamming against the wall, as Lial rushed in. With deft hands, the healer bundled his long, auburn hair at his nape, tying it as he walked, his gaze taking in the scene. Lynia scrambled back, making room, and Lial dropped to his knees beside the unconscious pair. He rested a hand on Arlyn's brow, then pinned Lyr with his gaze.

"Her channels are blasted wide and raw, but she's otherwise unharmed." Lial nodded toward the bed. "Take her there for now so I can see to Kai."

Stifling a groan from the ache moving brought, Lyr stood and gathered up his daughter's still form, cradling her against him as he carried her to the bed. Despite the healer's words, her lack of movement caused Lyr's chest to tighten with worry. What if she didn't wake? What if he lost her? One of the last things he'd told her was that he didn't trust her. His own daughter.

Lyr tucked the blankets around her and smoothed the hair away from her face. What had he ever done for her? The reasons he'd clung to for staying away from Aimee crumbled around him. He might have had to search for his father's murderer, and he might have had to take his place as Myern. But, *clechtan,* he still could have visited. Lyr had let himself be ruled by fear. Fear that Aimee hadn't fought to come with him because she didn't love him.

And their daughter had paid the greatest price.

His mother's hand settled on his shoulder, and he lifted his to cover it. For a long moment, she said nothing, though some of his tension eased all the same. "She will be fine. You know Lial would not give you false hope."

Lyr snorted, glancing over at the man in question. Lial's assistant had joined him, and they worked in silence over Kai. The assistant stitched with needle and thread while Lial sat in a trance, energy streaming from his outstretched hands. Lyr's stomach pitched at the sight of the open wound, and he averted his gaze. He'd been friends with the terse healer for several centuries. If there was one thing Lial didn't do, it was placate. "True."

"How did you get here?" She gestured toward the window. "I was waiting over there when all three of you just *appeared.*"

Lyr let out a quick breath, remembering the surge of energy that had blanked his mind. A transportation spell? But none of them had that ability. His gaze darted to Arlyn, and Lial's words finally registered. Her channels had been blasted open. Could she have done the spell without knowing how? Surely not. Such magic took decades of study to master.

Yet here they were.

"I think it was Arlyn."

A frown pinched his mother's brow. "None in our family possess that talent."

The glow faded from Lial's hands, its absence drawing Lyr's attention. He let out a long breath, bracing himself, and left his mother with Arlyn while he spoke with the healer. Steps slow, Lyr approached, throat tightening to see the healer's pallor. Was the news so dire, or had the healing needed that much effort? Lyr ran a hand through his hair, dislodging the tie that held it. It could be both.

After a long, shuddering breath, Lial's eyes opened, focusing on Lyr. "I'll not lie to you. He is still at great risk. The wound is barely knit."

Lyr's hand tightened, pulling at his hair. "Barely?"

"The knife was steel. It leaves less iron in the wound, and I have no allergy." Lial motioned to the stitches binding Kai's side. "But his weakness to the metal makes it difficult to heal him with magic. Even with all I expended, the wound is grave."

"Will he…" Lyr swallowed around the lump in his throat. "Will he live?"

"Likely. But nothing is certain."

Lyr sent up a quick prayer to Bera. "What about Arlyn?"

"The girl?" Lial pushed to his feet, then swayed for a moment before he could stop himself. "I'll see to her." The healer glanced over his shoulder. "Elan, monitor Lord Kaienan for any signs of weakening."

"No," Lyr answered, then shook his head at Lial's raised brow. "I mean, yes, watch him. But I was going to say that Arlyn is bound. She and Kai. If he dies, she's at risk."

Lial's other eyebrow lifted to match the first. "Soulbound? That was fast. Did he find her during his mission?"

"Not exactly." Lyr let out a breath. "He found her after he returned. She's my daughter."

Lial choked on a surprised cough as his gaze shifted to the bed. "Well."

"Heal her. Then we'll talk."

Lial's mouth tightened, closing off the questions that lingered in his eyes, and strode past Lyr to the bed. The healer paused to pull in more energy, and some of the color returned to his face. A few more breaths and he stretched his hands out over Arlyn. Blue light flowed from his palms as he hovered them along the length of her body, finally returning to settle his hands across her head.

Lyr had to look away from the flare of light, but Arlyn's soft moan drew his eyes back just as the glow faded. She blinked up at Lial for a moment, her expression blank, before shoving herself upright. The healer stumbled back as she pushed at him, her other hand going to her chest. Her frantic gaze darted around the room until it landed on Lyr.

"What? Who?" Arlyn's hands gripped her head, and she let out another moan. "God, make it stop."

With a furious look at Lial, Lyr took the healer's place at her side. "You are still in pain?"

"I think my skull is trying to strangle my brain."

"Move," Lial snapped, nudging Lyr out of the way. "I couldn't heal the pain until she was awake. The mind is a tricky thing to work with."

Arlyn's mouth fell open as light flowed from Lial's hands to surround her head. But she didn't argue. From her expression, the tension eased, and her body relaxed. As the healer pulled back, she rubbed a hand across her face, then stared at it as though some of the blue might remain. "Wow."

"Might I recommend learning *how* to use a transportation spell before you try it again?"

"Enough, Lial." Lyr's hands clenched. "Ayala Arlyn does not deserve your ill-humor. She knows nothing of this world."

The healer's eyes widened at the title. "Ayala, is it? I believe you promised me an explanation."

"She is my child with Aimee," Lyr bit out. "I did not know of her until this day." He glanced to the window, the sky beyond lightening with the dawn. "Yesterday now."

Lial snorted. "That's your explanation?"

"Later. Have you forgotten Kai?"

Arlyn's eyes widened, and she swung her legs over the side of the bed. "Kai!"

Lial grabbed her shoulders. "Steady, Ayala. You should rest. I have seen to him."

"Let go of me." She pushed at his hands, but the healer held firm. "I am not a child to be told to rest."

"I just healed—"

"Release. Me." Arlyn bit out. "Or I will gut you while you sleep. With my *steel* knife."

Lial let go and stepped back, hands lifted. "Gods save me from the Dianore line," he muttered. Lyr almost grinned at that. He, too, was an ofttimes-difficult patient.

Arlyn slipped past them, not even sparing a glance for the healer. Lyr frowned as he followed her to Kai. What had happened in her past to cause such a strong reaction to Lial's hold? Lyr would have to make it his business to find out. Later. His heart twisted to see Arlyn sink down beside Kai, much as she had in the clearing, and lift a hand to his cheek. Her face was pinched with an odd mixture of worry and confusion.

Lial joined them. "I believe he will live. If we can keep him still between my workings, he should heal well."

"I'm not even sure why I care this much," Arlyn whispered. Her eyes met Lyr's. "Whatever he did to me must be powerful."

Lial ran a hand across his drawn face. "She doesn't know?"

"She came from Earth," Lyr answered. "Kai was going to tell her of his foolishness upon his return."

"What?" Arlyn's eyes narrowed. "You obviously know what's going on. You should have told me earlier."

Lyr's jaw clenched as frustration poured through him. "It was his to tell. I did not want to ease his burden by taking some of it from his shoulders."

"Still—"

"Enough," Lial interrupted. "We need to get him settled, or he won't survive to face your wrath. Where should I put him? The guest tower he usually stays in is too far."

"Next door is fine."

"No!" Arlyn tensed, her fingers tightening around Kai's arm. "Leave him in here. I'll watch over him."

"Are you certain, Ayala?"

"I know it's stupid, but I don't care." A frown creased her forehead. "For whatever reason, I need to know he is safe. I *have* to know."

Lial's brow lifted in question, and he looked to Lyr, who nodded. "Very well."

R alan stared absently out the window of his estate as the sky shifted toward day, highlighting his land in a dull, blue-gray tone. He winced at the encroaching light. Although he had seen hundreds of thousands of dawns, both on his home world and here on Earth, now each one reminded him of his failure. Another dawn closer to losing his beloved Eri.

He spun away from the window and began to pace the length of his spacious bedroom. Ralan had tried everything he could think of to save her. He spent months at a time here, away from the pollution of the cities, feeding Eri the regenerative energy her own body seemed unable to gather. For a while, infusing her weekly had seemed to work. But now, at nearly seven years old, she was so ill she spent most of her time in bed. He sustained her fragile life with nightly infusions of the natural energy he gathered and purified.

Finally, Ralan had given in, had used his gift of Sight to see what needed to be done. And there was only one thing left, one choice that would ensure she lived.

He would have to return to Moranaia.

He'd sworn never to go back, but he had no choice. The magic was wrong here. Ralan had lived on Earth for more than three hundred years without difficulty, but lately even he had to filter the energy with care. The humans argued over pollution and global warming, but while that was certainly a problem, this gave the impression of something else. Perverted magic. If his child were to live, they could not stay. He no longer merely suspected as much. He *knew*.

Soon, he'd have to move on from this lifetime, anyway, or glamour himself to appear older. Hardly worth the effort, no matter how much he enjoyed being a fashion designer. And not just the process of creating but also the reactions of the humans. Ralan had heard it whispered that he preferred the company of men, as though designing clothes should have an effect on his sexual orientation. Why did humans treat sexuality like a fragile thing that would change at the least provocation?

The joke was on the men who avoided such jobs. Ralan worked with some of Earth's most beautiful women, and few of them would hesitate to strip at his command. Though he never dated the models who worked directly for him, it was no hardship to find companionship. What male could complain about that?

His pocket vibrated, causing Ralan to jump as the phone buzzed against his leg. Frowning, he reached for it. He'd made it clear during the last several months that he was not open to social engagements due to his daughter's illness. Thankfully, few bothered to contact him even during normal hours. When he pulled the phone out, Mandy's face lit up the screen. His assistant must be working early.

Ralan smiled at the almost frantic tone of her text questioning one of the designs for the Paris show in a couple of months. She'd worked on this one mostly by herself, and it would be her first look to go down an haute couture runway. Ralan's thumbs tapped quickly across the glass in a short, hopefully reassuring, reply. Mandy would be able to take over for him when he left if he could only build her confidence.

A whimper sounded from his daughter's room as his phone vibrated a reply. He tossed it on his bed, knowing from experience how poorly electronics fared during energy work, and rushed from the room. As Ralan opened Eri's door and ran to her side, she sat up in her little, canopied bed, golden eyes wide and chest heaving. "*Laial,*" she whispered.

"Hush, *tieln.*" He sat beside her and gathered her trembling form into his arms. "I am here, precious one."

For hours, he rocked her, smoothing his hand down her long, black hair. He whispered words of comfort in Moranaian and in English and fed her as much rejuvenating energy as he could gather and purify. Even when his own body grew tired and strained, he continued. Until finally, as morning shifted toward noon, she slipped into a normal sleep. He tucked her back beneath the covers and sat in the chair he kept by the bed.

As he closed his eyes and prepared to gather more energy into himself, Ralan knew he could no longer deny it. He would have to contact Lyr, and soon. Ralan squeezed his hands against his skull, the ache of purifying the natural magic burning his channels after such extended use. Lyr would have to send Kai to guide them home.

Though Kai's face was in shadow, Arlyn's eyes had long adjusted to the dim light well enough to make out his features. Carved cheekbones, a strong jaw a male model would kill for, tanned skin, gorgeous black hair—God, he was hot! A lock of hair tangled across his forehead, and Arlyn finally gave into temptation and brushed it aside. Her fingers tingled and burned where they made contact with flesh. She jerked her hand back with a gasp.

Soulbound. That's what she'd heard over and over since waking in pain. His pain. Arlyn clenched her hands in her lap and worried her bottom lip with her teeth. The word sounded serious. Like a wedding. Like *more* than a wedding. She glanced down at the pendant resting on the nightgown her grandmother had offered to replace Arlyn's blood-soaked one. The metal seemed to glimmer against the thin fabric in the dim, morning light. Whatever Kai had started by giving the necklace was serious business.

Arlyn had to know more. Had to know why she'd threatened to gut a man for keeping her from Kai. She'd hated being restrained ever since elementary school, when bullies had almost beaten her up because of her ears, but she had never had such a strong reaction before. She was just that drawn to Kai. Even now, she had to grip her fingers together to keep from caressing the lines of pain and tension from Kai's mouth. Her toes curled against the desire to lie down beside him, rest against him. She was sure she could give him energy if only she understood how.

Blaming him for the bond would be too easy. The anger that had been in Lyr's eyes and the shock that had registered on the others' faces told her well enough that Kai's actions hadn't been proper. If she were less honest, she could let it go at that. But the connection between them had coursed through her well before he'd offered the necklace. He might have been tricky about its purpose, but she'd known, somewhere deep, that it had been more than a talisman of protection. She had taken the pendant anyway.

Her initial denial of the bond seemed silly after last night, and not just because she had experienced Kai's pain. Arlyn would have been concerned for others hurt like that, too. Anyone would. But that all-consuming drive to save him had taken her like fire. Lyr claimed she had transported them here. He wasn't around to argue with, but she still shook her head. *No way.*

Yet something had happened, and Arlyn had no idea how else they could have returned to her room in time. And the pain in her head when she woke had been more intense than a normal headache. Could she have been that desperate? On Earth, she'd managed to spark a fire with her meager power. That was it. Besides making her way through the mists, she had shown no other signs of the kind of ability she would need to transport three people. Maybe her link with Kai held more answers. If she only understood more.

"Stop worrying, mialn,*"* Kai whispered into her mind, so softly she almost didn't hear.

"Kai? I thought you were sleeping."

"Your concern reaches into my dreams. Talk to Lyr if this bothers you so. I cannot stand you so upset."

"He would tell me?"

"He would do anything for you."

Kai slipped back into a tenuous sleep. As much as Arlyn wanted to stay, as much as she wanted to wait for him to explain, he would not rest with her there, not until she calmed her mind. Though she doubted Kai's last assertion, she had to ask Lyr. Would he give her an answer? She wanted to believe her father cared for her that much, but it was too soon. He had given her little in her life so far, and all of it, except for her life itself, had been given within a day.

Arlyn found Lyr in his study, slumped in a chair nearly hidden by a bookcase, his face turned to the last moments of sunrise visible through the opposing window. He stared unseeing, not seeming to notice the glorious colors, but her breath caught as she paused. The trees in this spot were thin enough to reveal the valley that dropped away to the east of the estate, and the light skimmed in a beautiful display across the floor of the vale. *Magnificent.*

"Do you see such beauty so often that it no longer holds meaning?" she murmured.

Shaking free of his thoughts, Lyr turned to look at her. "No, I am rarely here this early. Usually, I am either resting or enjoying one of my own pursuits, not working on estate business. But when Kai stays here, he always sits in this spot to view the sun rise over the valley. His father's house has no such view."

"Then maybe you should enjoy it." She stepped closer, stopping by his chair to watch the sun creep higher.

As the colors of dawn began to fade, he smiled. "Thank you for that. I sat here because Kai does, but I was so lost in worry I forgot to notice *why* it is his favorite spot. You are more elven than you realize. Literally, perhaps."

"What do you mean by that?"

"My original intent was that it's a very elven thing to admire beauty even in the middle of a crisis. But it reminded me of a speculation I'd had." He paused and took a deep breath. "I have to wonder if there is more to your bloodline. Either your mother wasn't entirely honest, or she didn't know."

With a gasp, Arlyn spun away, pain cleaving her chest. "I knew you would not accept me. I should have expected no less."

"Arlyn, wait." He grabbed her hand and squeezed gently until she turned. "I know you are my daughter. That is not in question. But you see, the Dianore line does not have the power of teleportation, at least not until now. It's mostly found on the Taian branch, and they guard it jealously."

Her brows pinched. "If I'm your daughter, then where do I get it? *If* I was the one who did the spell in the first place. I'm still not sure I believe it."

"Oh, it was you." Lyr released her hand to rub his fingers against his temples. "I still ache from it. The spell was wild. Untrained."

"So it's some kind of human magic?"

"It felt elven. Moranaian." His gaze captured hers. "We need to find out why."

Arlyn's teeth ground together. "Mom never lied to me."

"If she had our blood, she might not have known."

"Wouldn't you have noticed?"

"Not necessarily. I do not have the skill to test another's bloodline, only to detect my own, and she did not have any particularly obvious elven traits." His face twisted with pain. "Which is unfortunate. If it's true and I had known, I would have been more likely to risk bringing her here. The healers could have cured her."

"Maybe not," she murmured.

"You saw how easily Lial helped Kai. Could a human doctor repair a wound so quickly?"

"No," she answered. "But her grandmother loved to cook on cast iron. It wasn't until after she met you that she avoided it. If she was part elf, she might have inherited the allergy and never known."

"Oh gods, I remember that now. She offered me some kind of bread out of one of those pans before she knew better. I half feared she was trying to kill me." Laughter filled his eyes at the memory before pain stifled it. "All those years, she could have been eating poison."

"I'm not sure anyone could have helped."

"I suppose it does little good to consider it." He averted his gaze and rubbed a hand across his brow. For a moment, he sat in silence, a range of emotions flickering over his face, before his expression closed and he drew himself up. The pain lingered in his eyes, but he said nothing more about her mother. "Will you permit Lial to do a deeper test of your bloodlines? If you have more hidden talents, we need to know."

"What does it matter?"

"Uncontrolled magic is a danger to all." The corner of his mouth quirked up. "You said you'd stay to learn more about this part of your blood. Looks like you're going to get more than you bargained for."

"Great," she muttered. "So you were as surprised as I was to appear in my room."

He laughed. "You cannot imagine. I have never been teleported before."

"Really?" she asked, her voice full of doubt. "Surely, you know someone who can do it."

"Well, yes, I know you," he teased. At her frustrated groan, a true smile lit his face. "I wasn't joking when I said the Taians guard the talent. It's one of that branch's greatest prizes."

"And what does our branch prize?"

Lyr paused, tapping a finger on the arm of the chair. "Our guides, as we have the bulk of them, followed by our scouts, diplomats, and warriors. The Rieren branch holds our greatest craftspeople, our inventors. Not that all of these talents do not and cannot exist in other branches; as more time goes on, these traditional distinctions become more and more blended. But the Taians can be difficult."

"What about you? This family?"

"We keep order. I am a general of one of three segments of our military. Scouts, called *sonal*, are usually part of that. Diplomatically, I am in charge of dealing with Earth and the fae who are closely connected to that world. A fairly boring job until just recently. Events have been escalating, and poor Kai has been having to work hard as my *Taysonal*. My right hand, you might say. Of late, he's away on diplomacy as often as he's here."

"Kai? A diplomat?" Arlyn snorted, remembering how careless he'd seemed. "Right."

Lyr chuckled. "You would be surprised. As a rule, most elves are not as formal with family and close friends, but Kai goes beyond most. I think he spends so much time being diplomatic with others that he has none left for us."

"Speaking of Kai—"

A knock interrupted her before she could finish the question she had come to ask. Arlyn wanted to scream in frustration, but the delay was her own fault. She should have asked about the soulbond as soon as she entered. While she berated herself, Lyr rose, bidding the person to enter. Arlyn stepped back, almost falling into a bookcase, as her father moved in front of his desk. Should she leave? Lyr's neutral expression gave her no hint.

Before she could decide, a slightly familiar elf with long, blond hair and full leather armor, except for the helm, strode in. Judging from the armor and the small arsenal of knives and swords he wore, Arlyn guessed he must be one of the warriors Lyr had mentioned. She frowned. What *did* they make all of those weapons out of, if not steel? Before she could think to ask Lyr, the elf stopped several feet from the desk, tapped his chest twice with his right fist, and bowed to her father.

He stood that way, head bent down, until Lyr spoke. "Good morn to you, Belore Norin. How do you fare this day?"

"I am well, Myern. I trust you and your family are the same."

"Indeed, all but one." Lyr inclined his head. "You may relax, Norin."

As the warrior shifted to a more casual stance, Arlyn noticed the small bundle he held in his left hand. It was a bloody bit of cloth wrapped around a small knife. Was that the blade that had injured Kai? It had to be. She recognized the man, then, as one of those who had gone with them into the forest the night before. Had her father not noticed the knife? He seemed so relaxed.

Fingers twisting wrinkles in her gown, Arlyn stepped forward. "Lyr."

The surprised glance of the soldier warned her she had probably just interrupted something she should not have. But damn, they were exchanging pleasantries while the warrior held Kai's blood in his hands. Unsure what to do, she turned to her father. His eyes held either exasperation, amusement, or both, but it was difficult to tell. Lyr's expression was more guarded than she had seen it since their first meeting on the forest path the day before.

With barely a pause, Lyr gestured for her to approach. "I must beg your forgiveness, Belore Norin. The lady Arlyn is not accustomed to our ways and meant no offense. I would offer introduction so you might be made comfortable."

Arlyn blinked, stunned. She had never heard Lyr speak like *that*.

"Certainly." The other elf nodded.

"Honored Captain, I present to you Callian Ayala i Arlyn Dianore se Kaienan nai Braelyn. Lady Arlyn, I present to you Callian iy'dianore Belore i Norin Tialt nai Braelyn."

Had Kai's name entered her title? She wanted to ask, but first, she needed to respond to the warrior, a daunting task since she had no idea what most of his title even meant. There was the branch name, Callian, but then she was lost. Arlyn bit back a groan. How had her father addressed the other elf when greeting him? As she tried frantically to recall, the warrior turned to her and repeated the chest tap and bow he had done earlier.

If the elf was surprised by her presence, Arlyn couldn't tell it from his neutral expression. "It is a pleasure to make your acquaintance, Ayala Arlyn, honored daughter of the Dianore line. May good health be yours for many happy centuries."

"It is a pleasure to meet you, too, Belore Norin." Thank all the gods everywhere she had actually remembered what Lyr had called the warrior. "May you remain safe in the hands of the gods through many victories." Out of the corner of her eye, Arlyn caught her father's slight smile. "Please excuse me for my interruption. I'm just concerned about Kai."

"Of course, Ayala." The warrior nodded politely, though she was certain he did not understand the situation. It had to seem strange to him that Lyr suddenly had a grown daughter, a complete stranger, who was so worried about Kai. Someone the warrior had likely known for several centuries.

Arlyn jumped at Lyr's laugh. "Come, Norin, let us abandon such formality now that basic politeness has been met. It is difficult to maintain with you, considering you taught me to hold a sword. And I'm sure you are bursting with curiosity."

With a grin, Norin relaxed. "That I am. I saw her earlier, of course, but I had no time to consider who she might be. Where have you been hiding a daughter all this time? And when did she become mated to Kai?"

Mated? So the necklace exchange *had* been some form of wedding. Shouldn't she have to agree to be someone's mate? Just as she stiffened in anger, a sound somewhere between a laugh and a snort caught her attention. She turned to see Lyr lean back against the edge of his desk as his mouth twisted in a grimace.

Frowning, Norin looked between them. "Did I say something wrong?"

"She doesn't know about soulbonds yet. She just met me and Kai yesterday." Her father released a long, drawn-out breath. "Arlyn grew up in the human realm. I had a daughter with Aimee, and I never knew."

"Which of the nine gods have you offended, Lyr?" Norin's chuckle held little real amusement. "I do not even need the full story to see that you have had an amazing tangle of events— and in less than a day. Unfortunately, it is only going to get worse."

"Surely not."

Norin strode forward and held out the blood-stained bundle. "I would take a look at this dagger before you get your hopes up."

K ai drifted to semi-wakefulness but was uncertain
why. It was not pain; Lial had blocked that during
healing. Arlyn was not near enough to pull him
from such a deep sleep with her worry. Perhaps it was a
dream, if one could dream of being awake. His mind wandered, unfocused. His soulbonded was beautiful. One of the
last things he remembered was the gleam of her red hair when
she bent over him. Maybe she would not hate him. Maybe it
would work.

"I always said you were too hasty. But congratulations anyway."

Was that Moren? It couldn't be. If it had been a few days
since the attack, Lyr would have already notified his brother.
But why hadn't Arlyn come back? Surely...

"Leave here, Kai, and go far away. I would not see you harmed."

"What are you talking about, Moren? I already am."

Silence. Was he hallucinating? Lial would have killed any infection, but maybe the steel had affected Kai's mind. It took him several moments to force his eyes open. No one hovered in view. He tried to turn his head, but his body refused to obey.

"I fear the next attempt on your life will not end this well, so heed me now. Take your mate and leave. I can give you no other warning."

Before Kai could ask another question, he heard a door open, then footsteps. He still detected his brother's presence, watching, but as soon as the hand touched his shoulder, Moren disappeared completely from his mind. Or had he ever even been there? Everything was muddled.

"Rest, Kai." Lial's face appeared above him. "Or you will delay your recovery. I do not want to block you from mental communication, but I will if I must. Who was agitating you so much?"

"Moren," Kai whispered though he was surprised he could manage even that.

Lial's brows rose. "Your brother is not here." Kai could hear the frown in the healer's voice. Or maybe he could feel it. He wasn't sure anymore. "No one in your family has been notified of the attack, and the few here who *do* know what happened have been ordered to silence. Now let me help you rest while I check for infection. Perhaps I missed something."

Between one thought and the next, Kai fell back into the darkness.

Moren jerked the hood of the cloak over his head and disappeared once more. His eyes slid closed as he slumped against the tree. *Too close.* He shouldn't have stayed until the healer touched Kai, but Moren had wanted a glimpse of Lial's intentions. And had almost been caught in the process.

Pulling the fabric tight around his frame, Moren straightened. Even with his head uncovered, the cloak let him slip through the estate shields, but allowing himself the freedom to use telepathy also left him vulnerable to mental scans. He had to go, and fast, in case he'd been found out. Lial might have noticed something amiss.

Though no one could see Moren beneath the cloak, he took a reflexive glance around before turning to dart back down the path. He'd done all he could. If his brother wouldn't take his advice, then so be it. Though he *had* sworn to their mother he would protect Kai. Moren bit back a curse. How could his brother have gotten caught up in this?

He needed to make himself scarce. If his father found out what Moren had been up to, Kai would be the least of his problems.

The explosiveness, not to mention the creativity, of Lyr's curse surprised Arlyn. As she gaped at him, her father straightened from where he leaned against the desk and grabbed the knife, the *steel* knife, only the bloody cloth between his hand and the hilt. Before she could blink, he had turned the blade to examine the pommel. He made a sound almost like a choke, every ounce of blood seeming to drain from his face.

"Father?" He glanced up sharply at her voice, not missing what she had called him, but she did not give him time to dwell on it. "What is it?"

Lyr clutched the hilt in his hand so hard his knuckles were white. "I have seen this seal before. Once before."

"Then you know who it belongs to?"

"No." He spun, slamming the knife down on his desk. The metallic clank rang loud in the quiet room. "The last time I saw it, it was attached to the sword sticking out of my father's back."

"What?" The sudden wail drowned out Arlyn's gasp. All three turned at the sound to see Lynia standing in the doorway, her mouth open in horror.

"*Laiala*," Lyr whispered, aghast.

"It was an accident. They told me it was an accident. He had been experimenting with those damn steel swords, trying to find a way to overcome the allergy." Lynia shook her head. "You were not even here. You were with Aimee."

"Norin had Kai come get me right after he found father. Lial had sedated you by the time I arrived," Lyr said in a soft, pained voice.

"You!" Lynia advanced on Norin, her hands fisted as though she would hit the warrior. "Why did you tell me it was an accident? You said he slipped in his workshop while testing spells on the blade. You lied to me." She turned on Lyr. "And you continued the lie. Why?"

Lyr rushed over to his mother. "You were already insensible with grief at the severing of your bond. For a while, I believed you'd be lost, too. Would you have had us add to that?"

"It has been more than twenty years, but you have never told me the truth."

"What would have been the point?" Lyr touched her face gently, lovingly. "I have worried about you every day since it happened. For years, it seemed you would never recover, but you have finally begun to return to yourself. I did not want to upset that."

Lynia's fingers wrapped around his wrist. "That was not your decision to make."

Tension swirled through the room like mist, clinging. Arlyn lifted a fist to press against the ache in her own heart at the sight of her father and grandmother, their faces pinched with grief. After a moment, Lyr hung his head. "Forgive me. I should have. Everything was in so much upheaval."

"Ah, *tieln*." Lynia released Lyr's wrist, then pulled him into her arms.

Eyes closed, they clung together, mother and child bound by love and shared pain. Arlyn lifted her other hand to her mouth to stifle a sudden sob. Her own mother had once held her just like that when she needed comfort.

When Lynia pulled back, tears glimmered on her cheeks. "I will always forgive you."

"I know." Lyr let out a shuddering breath. "Even when I don't deserve it."

"Did you stay here for me?"

"*Laiala*, please."

"No, I know it. If not for me, you might have gone back." Lynia brushed the tears from her face, but more fell to replace them. "You ruined your life, and your daughter's, by upholding this lie. I am certain you spent much time shielding me from what truly happened."

Arlyn gasped as understanding hit. Her father had been with Aimee when Kai had come to get him. He must have rushed home at once. And who wouldn't have? Short of breath, Arlyn clutched at her throat. All the years of bitterness over her father's perceived irresponsibly, all the hurt she had held close—a waste laid bare by the truth. Rather than carelessly slipping through her mother's life, he must have left in a panic. Arlyn had always been told there was some kind of emergency, but she'd assumed her mother had only been trying to make her feel better. Why hadn't Lyr told her about the tragedy when she'd confronted him?

Lyr's hands balled into fists. "There was more to it than that."

"I suppose you looked for Telien's murderer."

"Yes," Lyr answered. "For years."

Lynia's brow furrowed. "If it wasn't those things, then what?"

"She told me not to return," he snapped, the pain in his voice stabbing like a blade. "We both agreed it would be too risky to take her through the Veil in a rush, but I tried to convince her." Lyr's jaw clenched. "I told her I would come back when I could though it might be a few years. She said it would be too late."

"Oh, my love," Lynia whispered.

"I might have tried anyway, but the search for the assassin took so long. For over ten years, I looked, following every lead. And I found nothing." Lyr's shoulders slumped. "I let fear rule. Fear that she hadn't loved me. I stayed away. And now it will forever be too late."

In the charged wake of his words, he pushed past Lynia and strode from the room.

Arlyn found him in a tower rising near the edge of the garden. Her fingers tightened on the small silk pouch in her hand as she looked up the staircase that spiraled up the center. From her mental map, she knew it was an observation tower. A lofty one. Blowing out a breath, she began the long climb, her steps growing ever heavier with the pain that emanated down from her father.

Either she was getting better at connecting with his energy, or her talent for empathy was growing in this place. Maybe both. From her limited experience, what Lyr had said—that energy didn't lie—was true. Arlyn found in him a certain similarity to herself. To the power she'd struggled to grasp for years. And a certain resonance, like a song perfectly in tune, with Kai.

The staircase opened into a single room at the top of the tower, the walls almost entirely glass. Arlyn drew to a halt, her eyes going wide. She'd marveled at the view from her father's study, but this? With a shake of her head, Arlyn tore her gaze from the window and searched for Lyr. He had to know she was there, either by her energy or the sound of her gasp, but he didn't turn from where he stood, one hand braced against a column framing a window. Unsure of her reception, she took a few steps into the room, then paused.

"I should have told you earlier," Lyr murmured.

Arlyn shifted a little closer. "About your father?"

"Yes. And that your mother denied me." He turned enough for her to see his face in profile. "My cowardice. All of it."

Her stomach pitched. And not because of the height. "I had no idea she told you not to come back. It makes no sense. She always spoke of you with longing. She loved you."

His fingers whitened where he gripped the column. "So I'd believed."

"No, I mean it. She did." Arlyn lifted a hand to offer comfort, then pulled it back. "She never even dated anyone else to my knowledge. Mom told me over and over not to blame you for leaving. I grew up hearing stories of you and all you'd told her of this world."

Lyr spun, his face pinched with frustration and hurt. "Then *why?*"

"I don't know." Arlyn lifted the bag between them. "Maybe this will tell you. Mom would not rest until I swore to bring it to you."

With a frown, he took the smooth silk from her hands and unwrapped the ties. For a moment, he hesitated, then plunged a hand in. First came a chain with a pendant attached, much like the one Arlyn wore around her own neck. Lyr held it, a trembling thumb caressing the inscription carved into the metal. "My medallion. I never started the bonding, but I—"

His mouth pinched closed, cutting off the rest of his words, and his hand tightened around the chain. Lyr closed his eyes, then let out a long breath. A few heartbeats and he opened them again to loop the chain around his wrist and reach into the bag once more. This time, he pulled out a letter.

Sealed. Arlyn had almost opened it several times but had never quite found the courage.

At first, she worried that her father would have the same problem. Lyr stared down at the envelope, one finger running along it with reverence, until Arlyn wanted to scream. Didn't he want to know? But finally, he tore it open and pulled out the letter within. He paced the room as he read, his brow furrowed. Arlyn tapped her foot and forced herself not to snatch the paper from his hand.

Just as her patience was nearing its end, Lyr stopped, then folded the letter and slipped it back into the envelope. The eyes he lifted to hers were so full of loss that tears gathered at the back of Arlyn's throat and teased at her eyelids. "What did it say?"

"She knew." His voice was rough. Raw. "She knew she would meet me. That I would leave. That we could never be together beyond a month."

"What?"

"She said she had visions."

Arlyn let out a long breath as flashes of memory sprang forth. The times her mom had warned Arlyn away from danger. The things she'd just *known*. "She used to joke about being psychic. But psychics aren't real. Are they?"

"I have no idea about humans, but seers are quite real on Moranaia." Lyr unwound the chain from his wrist and held it up, his gaze drawn to the swinging pendant. "Aimee wrote that she'd seen more pain for all of us if I'd returned. Her body was too weak even then to make the crossing, and I'd be forever torn by my duties here."

"She never said a word to me."

"That she *didn't* explain." Some of the tension seemed to ease from her father as he slipped the chain around his neck. "But if I were to guess, I'd say she wanted you here now and thought telling you might change the timing. Then again, guessing the plans of a seer is almost always impossible."

Arlyn's eyes narrowed on the necklace. "She wore that for as long as I can remember but never said it was yours. Now that you have it back, does it mean you can bond again?"

"We never bonded in the first place. I didn't want to speak the words until she was here." Lyr shook his head as his hand closed around the metal. "But no. I've never heard of anyone finding a second *aenac*—soulbonded. There are a few rare bondings with more than two partners, but that isn't quite the same. I've never been drawn to multiple partners, in any case."

"Ugh." Arlyn coughed. "I didn't need to know that."

A slow smile split his face, although his eyes barely lightened with it. "Sorry. I wasn't thinking."

"Yeah. So." Arlyn gestured at the pendant he still held. "It's something you wear anyway, even with no intention of bonding?"

"Each necklace is unique to the owner. It is engraved with indicators of our House and family and imbued with our own energy." He let the pendant drop against his chest. "Many wear it their whole lives and never find a bonded. Your mother asked me to put it back on. In her letter."

"Why?"

Lyr shrugged. "In her memory. That's all she said. And I will do so." His face twisted with the pain that seemed to hum through the air. "Even unto my grave."

A rlyn stared down at her food, uncertain what she was about to eat or if she even wanted to eat it. After they had checked on Kai and found him resting peacefully, her father had insisted she come with him to the dining room she'd found on her rambles the night before. The room was even more beautiful in daylight, the broad windows giving the impression of eating in the garden. Well, attempting to eat.

Their bread was easy enough to understand. It was dark and seemed to consist of several types of unfamiliar grains, but she could still tell exactly what it was. Beside the plate of bread, there sat a bowl of some kind of large, nut-looking objects, a saucer filled with a dark, syrupy liquid, and a small, steaming cup of tea. No utensils in sight. Frowning, she picked up the napkin that lay on the table next to her food and placed it in her lap.

"Arlyn," Lyr said with amusement. "This is not a formal meal. Just follow what I do and stop worrying."

"It isn't just that." She held up one of the nut-things. "I have no idea what most of this is. Last night, I was sent a tray with bread, cheese, and meat. Different, but nothing this unusual."

"Ah, yes." His lips curled up into a smile. "I wasn't thinking. Your mother was quite confused when I asked for nuts and fruit in the mornings. Watch."

Lyr took one of the nuts and dipped it in the syrupy substance, twisting it over the saucer until nothing dripped off, then ate it. After a brief hesitation, Arlyn did the same. The taste of honey burst upon her tongue, blending with the warm tones of the nut. Her eyes slipped closed as she savored each nuance. Like macadamia dipped in chocolate-infused honey.

When she opened her eyes, her father had sliced off a piece of the bread and was dipping it, too, in the honey. Instead of copying him this time, she decided to try the tea. The odd, light mix of minty, sweet, and spicy was more pleasant than it should have been. So far, the breakfast was strange but delicious.

Her father offered her some fruit, and Arlyn took a wedge, lifting it closer to examine it. It had a pale center like an apple or pear but with a thick, light orange skin. With a frown, she sniffed. It smelled for all the world like a grape. "What is this?"

"*Kehren* fruit."

"Is this world different?" Arlyn watched him settle a few pieces of fruit around the rim of his syrup bowl. "Am I on another planet?"

"Yes." Lyr shrugged. "And no. There is much debate on the subject. Our best theory is that this is a dimension far, far removed. So far away the planet that takes up this space is not the same at all. But it is impossible for us to prove."

With a wince, Arlyn set her own fruit in the syrup. "I don't think I understand. You mean this planet takes up the same space in the universe? But it has two moons."

Lyr took a bite, frowning as he chewed. "You've heard of alternate realities? Parallel dimensions?"

"Sure," Arlyn answered. "There are tons of theories on that. Different timelines, even."

"Though we cannot cross time, the fae are quite deft at traveling between dimensions. When the humans began to grow in numbers and power, many of our kind did just that. But they stayed fairly close to Earth."

"Like the Sidhe and their hills."

"Yes." He nodded. "Our queen searched the Veil for a place much farther removed. And found this place. Much of it is a mystery even after millennia."

Arlyn stared at the bowl of syrup as she processed his words. Too bad she couldn't take in what Lyr had said as easily as the fruit absorbed the syrup. Another planet that *wasn't?* She groaned. "Never mind. I'm going to have to think about this."

He grinned. "You and a few hundred Moranaian philosophers."

With an answering smile, she braved the slice of *kehren*. Then her eyes slid closed on a moan. What magic was this? *Like eating a grape-flavored candy apple.*

At her father's chuckle, she shrugged. "Sorry."

"Don't be. *Laiala* has much the same reaction."

"What does that mean?"

"*Laiala?* It means *mother.*"

Arlyn enjoyed a couple more slices of fruit, then pushed the dish of syrup away. She took a deep breath, bracing herself, and met Lyr's eyes. "So are you going to tell me about the soulbond?"

He pushed aside his own dish. "Now is as good a time as any, I suppose."

She lifted a brow. "That dire?"

"No." Lyr let out a huff. "I'm still upset at Kai."

"Okay. So spill it." Arlyn grimaced at her father's blank look. "Sorry. Tell me about it."

Lyr leaned back in his chair. "Elven relationships are both extremely complicated and quite easy. We have many levels of courtship, from satisfying physical needs to alliances for the purpose of producing children to long-term commitments. And then we have the soulbond."

"But what *is* it?"

His lips twisted wryly at her interruption, but he didn't comment on it. "Each of us has one, or rarely more, whose soul matches ours perfectly, called our soulbonded. It's similar to the human concept of a soul mate, except we do not see ourselves as being *completed* by our mate. We are not each one half of the same soul. It is simply that one is able to bond with the other. Literally."

"Are you saying—" Her mouth worked a few times before she could force the words from her throat. "Kai connected our *souls?* Oh my god, I *am* going to kill him. How dare he!"

"Arlyn, let me finish." His smile slipped away. "Few elves ever find their soulbonded, yet that is the most sought-after relationship for our kind. It is something to be treasured above all things."

"So you think it's okay for him to bond to me without making sure I understand what it means?"

"Absolutely not." Lyr shifted forward to grip her hand. "It was not okay. Even he knows that."

Arlyn pulled away, then regretted the move at her father's stricken expression. She took a deep breath to steady herself before putting her hand back in his. "I'm sorry. It's not your fault. You just seem so calm about it all."

His grip tightened. "I almost throttled my best friend of five hundred years."

"Oh."

Lyr looked down at their hands, and his expression tightened. "Kai only started the bond. To be complete, you would have to give him a token in return. Then there is consummation."

"Consummation?" Her brow wrinkled. "So this is a male/female kind of thing?"

His lips quirked. "No. It's not about how sex is done. It's about intimacy."

This time, when she pulled at her hand, he released her with no sign of upset. Really, though, this was not a discussion she wanted to have with her father. "That's—" Arlyn almost choked on her nervous laugh. "Anyway. So can I undo what he started?"

Lyr seemed to pale some as he leaned back. "A priest can break the bond. But it can't be reforged."

Her mouth fell open on a gasp. If soulbonds were so rare, then severing this one would end her only chance. Why had she taken that necklace? She should never have been so hasty. "What would happen then?"

"Little would change for you." Lyr looked down at the table, where his fingers tapped a restless tune. Then his eyes met hers again. "But for Kai? Severing a bond is only done when one of the partners has done something unspeakable. Everyone would assume he had committed an unforgivable act. Something horrible, anathema. He would no longer be part of our family, and I doubt his father's house would take him back."

Arlyn pressed a hand against the ache in her chest. "Harsh."

"None would blame you if you decided to go before a priest." Lyr sighed. "But give it time. Consider what you really want. I'd not see you be as hasty as Kai in this."

"I will think about it."

"Good." Lyr stood, offering her a hand. "Now, go get some rest. Then we'll go see Lial and have him test you."

Arlyn winced but let him help her to her feet. "If we have to."

Kai's head was thrashing back and forth across the pillow when Arlyn returned to her room. She checked herself at the last moment, closing the door gently instead of slamming it, before she rushed to his side. The healer had said the wounds were barely knit together, and Kai's movements could reopen them. With soft, meaningless murmurs, she stroked a hand through his hair, over and over, until he stilled.

Kai broke into her thoughts. *"Arlyn?"*

"Why aren't you sleeping?"

"Nightmares, hallucinations. I don't know anymore."

She pulled a chair up to his bed, sat, and took his hand. *"You have to lie still, Kai. I will stay if it helps."*

"Yes. Please." He fell silent for a moment. *"Have you seen Moren? I thought he spoke to me earlier, but Lial said he wasn't here. Then I dreamed he was trying to kill me. He wouldn't do that. We've never been close, but he's my brother."*

"Kai, hush. Your brother has not been here. As a visitor, he would have spoken to Lyr before coming to your room, right?"

"Of course."

"I have been with Lyr since I left you, and no one named Moren spoke to him. It was just a dream." At her words, he relaxed. He drifted back to sleep as she continued stroking his hair.

The door clicked open, and the healer strode in. Glaring at Arlyn, he halted on the other side of the bed. "Please stop upsetting him. I have already had to calm him once."

"It's not my fault." Arlyn scowled back. "He was thrashing around when I came in. After I got him settled down, he told me he was having nightmares and that his brother had been here."

"That again. I do not understand it. He is not feverish, nor does he have an infection. No reason for hallucinations. But after such a trauma, and as sleep-deprived as he was, nothing should have been able to wake him. I am surprised he is even capable of dreaming."

Lial stopped speaking long enough to sketch some kind of symbol over Kai. It glowed for only a moment before disappearing. "*Clechtan.* Kai has not regained any of his energy since being here. In fact, he has lost some. He is low enough to be delirious."

"But why?"

"I am not certain." Frowning, Lial ran a hand through his hair. "I made sure the foreign iron from the blade was flushed from his system, but I can think of little else that would drain energy in such a steady stream."

A sudden suspicion sank into Arlyn's chest, tightening it. She tossed a look over her shoulder, then groaned. The sword she'd brought from Earth was propped in the corner next to her pack. "Damn," she breathed.

She heard the healer mutter something in Moranaian. Probably a curse. Arlyn stood and retrieved the sword, then took it to the far end of the room. When she looked back, Lial's glare had intensified so much she began to worry what he might do. Healers didn't usually hurt people. Did they?

"Are you *trying* to kill him?"

"*Excuse* me?" She stiffened. "That was uncalled for."

Letting out a long sigh, Lial rubbed his forehead, some of the tension seeming to drain from his body. "Forgive me for my ill temper. In the last thirty hours, I have attended a difficult birth, set and healed two broken bones, and stitched up Kai, a long-time friend. Every time I go to rest, he stirs. But I should not have taken out my frustration on you."

Arlyn stared at him, noticing then the white lines of exhaustion around his mouth and the dark circles under his eyes. Meeting his gaze, she hefted the sword. "Fine. I get that. If you're done harassing me, do you happen to have any ideas about this?"

His lips twisted up. Considering his own attitude, maybe he appreciated her snark. "Put it in the closet for now. I'll see if I can find some silk to wrap it in later."

"Okay." Arlyn opened the door leading to the changing area and waved back toward Kai. "You go do...whatever you do."

When she returned, Lial was sitting in the chair she'd pulled up to the bed, his fingers massaging his temples. He looked even more pale and drawn than he had moments before, and Arlyn wondered what cost he paid for healing. From the looks of him, a high one. Her stomach muscles unclenched as the anger she'd been nursing released.

He glanced up. "I placed Kai into a deep sleep. You should take the opportunity to rest."

"You're one to talk." She smiled, softening her words. "But yeah, I should. Lyr wanted me to. He wants you to test my bloodlines later."

"I can do that now." Lial stood. "Come, sit. I'll take care of that before I go."

Arlyn hoped he didn't notice how her hands trembled as she approached. "Now? Surely, it can wait. I'm sure Lyr will want to be here. And you're tired."

Lial moved aside and gestured to the chair. "Sit. It's a simple spell, and I'd like a few solid hours of sleep without interruption. I'll have to check on Kai soon enough as it is."

Her fingers twisted together as she took the seat, her stomach tightening once more. Arlyn had no reason to be nervous. None. But she was. As his magic swirled around her, she squeezed her eyes shut. Whatever the healer found, she would just have to face.

Despite all that had happened in the last day, Lyr could not afford to ignore his work. He had countless tasks to attend to for his estate and the nearby village, and many of them had been forgotten in the wake of Arlyn's arrival. Since the season had just turned to Toren, which began the day after the solstice, everyone wanted to finish outdoor projects before the harvest. He had to review requests for home repairs and additions and even a few for new houses to be built, though that was usually done in the spring when the weather was cooler.

Lyr signed yet another paper and shuffled it into a stack. As he slid the pile aside, the back of his hand brushed something hard, and he shifted a few more papers to find the source. His palm hovered for a moment over the leather cover of the book before he settled his hand on the top. His record book. The one he always returned to the drawer of his desk. He opened it to the latest page and found it wrinkled as though someone had tried to rip it out. Lyr had spelled it against being torn or copied, either physically or magically, but someone with a good memory could have gained quite a bit of information.

He read the last words recorded: *Nothing that can't wait for my written report.* It seemed too coincidental that someone had tried to remove the record of Kai's latest mission about the same time he was attacked. But why? Lyr was not accustomed to this kind of intrigue. For at least a millennium, diplomatic relations with Earth and its related fae had been quiet. The underhill elves had rarely spoken to them, and the Moranaian ones cared little for the humans. Everything had changed.

Lyr traced an additional glyph over the book, ensuring only someone keyed to the estate could read it. He should have done so sooner, but it had seemed unnecessary. Now he had to discover how word of the negotiations with the Seelie had gotten out and to figure out the apparent connection between Kai's attack and his father's murder.

When he'd reached out to Kai after the attack, Kai had said something about the Sidhe, but his words had been jumbled by pain. A warning about interfering in their affairs? But if a Sidhe assassin had made it undetected onto Moranaia, Lyr had greater problems. The portal was spelled to alert the land guards of any such access. Someone powerful enough to interfere with that could cause a great deal of harm.

Lyr tucked the book back in its drawer and added another locking spell. The warning had probably been a false one. No, it was more likely that a Moranaian was to blame. But finding who would dislike his work with the Sidhe to this extent? Next to impossible. It would be easier to find someone who *did* want to travel to Earth on behalf of the Sidhe.

Forty or so millennia of relative peace—well, except for the early wars with the dragons—tended to make a people complacent.

As Lyr lifted a report on potential crop yield from yet another stack, he sensed Lial's presence, seeking communication. *"Yes?"*

"I have completed my analysis of your daughter's bloodlines."

Lyr sat the paper down before he wrinkled it. *"And?"*

"Her mother was a quarter Moranaian. Aimee's grandfather was from the Baran family on the Taian branch."

"You are certain?" He let out a long breath, ruffling the stacks on the desk. *"You have no doubt?"*

A bit of Lial's impatience slipped through their link. *"I trained for ten years alone on identifying every bloodline on Moranaia. I am sure."*

"Of course." Blood was vital to the elves. Lyr should have considered how stringently the healer would have trained. *"Thank you."*

"Disturb me for anything less than a birth or a mortal wound within the next three hours, and I'll slip something unfortunate in your drink."

Lyr grinned and sent his assent along the link. His sharp-tempered friend was always at his worst when tired. But as their connection ended, Lyr's smile slipped. *Baran family.* Like all elves, he'd had to remember the placement of each House along all three branches during his schooling, but after five hundred years, the more distant ones had grown hazy.

He pushed away from his desk and walked to the nearest bookshelf. Stooping, he ran his hand along the books on the bottom shelf. He knew the Barans didn't descend from one of the first three dukes along the Taian branch because he'd memorized those the most stringently. *Could it have been...?* He pulled out a large tome detailing the branchings of the fourth and fifth dukes and carried it back to his desk.

Lyr didn't bother to sit as he flipped through the index. *Baran. Yes.* The current head of that family was on a sub-branch four down from the fourth duke. A minor lord with no other Houses under his command. How had he or one of his people made their way to Earth to father a child? Lyr tapped a finger on the page. He could search through the records the guides had left of the people they transported through the Veil, but he'd rather not go through that chore if it could be avoided.

Lord Loren Baran would surely know.

After drifting in and out of sleep for over an hour, Arlyn gave up on getting any real rest. She rubbed a hand across the back of her neck, sore from the way she'd been curled up in the chair. No wonder she hadn't been able to sleep. Tired though she was, Kai was a virtual stranger, and even though he was unconscious, it hadn't seemed right to lie down beside him. Arlyn couldn't trust him that much.

She grabbed some of her clothes from beside the bed and went into the changing room. It was only when she clutched the edge of her nightgown that she realized she'd been wearing it all evening. Arlyn closed her eyes as her face flamed. *Great!* She'd been introduced to the captain of her father's guard while wearing her nightgown. Some impression she was making. At this rate, she would probably become the laughingstock of her father's house within a couple of days. What little there seemed to be of that household. She had seen few outside of family since she'd arrived.

The odd emptiness continued as Arlyn made her way into the garden. The people she *had* seen in the distance always managed to be gone before she could reach them. She bit her lip, her gaze darting along the path. What the hell? Was it because she was a stranger? Part human? Maybe elves weren't particularly social. Yet another question for her father.

Well, at least she didn't have to worry about stopping to exchange pleasantries.

Like the house, the garden was entwined with the trees. Flowers seemed to be planted without any pattern in mind and paths seemed to wander without design, but she was certain a plan existed behind the apparent disorder. Hearing a trickle of water, she turned to the right to look for the stream, confident that if she could hear water she would be able to find it. Of course, she could have consulted her inner map, but what would be the fun in that?

Though everything was foreign in this world, somehow Moranaia was more like home than Earth. She'd *never* fit in there. After a few disastrous years of elementary school, her mother had taught her at home. Arlyn had loved to run through the forests near her house, learning how to survive in the woods. As a teenager, she'd joined a medieval society and taken lessons on how to wield a sword and use a bow. And instead of getting a traditional job once she reached adulthood, she had made and sold longbows at medieval and renaissance festivals.

No wonder her mother had understood. She'd been part elf, too.

Arlyn stopped by the small stream where it trickled between two willow-like trees, enjoying the soothing sound of water. At least now she knew why her mother had encouraged her strange hobbies. Most parents would have tried to direct her toward sports or cheerleading, but not Aimee. Her mother had taken pride in her daughter's odd accomplishments. Pictures of sword fighting tournaments and archery awards had lined their mantle.

How was Arlyn supposed to feel about what she'd learned? With a grimace, she sat down on a small log beside the stream and watched the water burble along the rocks. For the briefest moment after Lial's test, she'd wondered if her mother had known. But no. Aimee's father had been an iron worker, of all things, and had died before he was thirty. Surely, he would have chosen another profession if his heritage had been common knowledge.

Damn, it's hot. Arlyn pinched the front of her long-sleeved shirt and waved it against her body, but the slight breeze did little good. She eyed the stream. Did she dare put her feet in? Was there some rule against it? This world might sing to something in her soul, but she was still clueless about elven etiquette.

Before she could decide, the sound of footsteps caught her attention, and she glanced up to find Lyr approaching. Lines of frustration and exhaustion crossed his grim face. Concerned, she drew in a breath. "Is everything okay?"

"Mostly." He sighed, then took in her appearance with a quick look. "Gods, Arlyn, how can you stand being out here in that? You must be sweltering."

She rolled her eyes at him. "I don't think I *can* stand it much longer. It was early spring when I left, so I packed for chilly weather. My other clothes are all dirty."

"I will see about getting you something more appropriate to wear. Lial will not be pleased if I let you faint from the heat." He held out his hand. "Walk with me back to the house, if you would not mind. Inside, at least, is magic-cooled. I need to speak with you."

She let him help her up. "That sounds ominous."

"It is not, truly, but the news is not necessarily pleasant either."

"Great." She followed him along a different path that followed the course of the water. "I'm afraid to ask."

He turned abruptly to the right and the estate returned to view. "I just spent the last half hour talking to the head of the Baran family."

"And?"

"He wants to send a teacher for you right away."

Her heart skipped a beat. "What? Why?"

Lyr stopped by one of the doors to the manor. "Your magic is growing, Arlyn. I can detect it swirling around you, but my talents do not work in the same way. You need a magic teacher before you lose control."

"Aren't I a bit old for this?" She pinched the bridge of her nose against a building headache. "I could barely spark a fire before."

"On Earth," he answered. "Magical energy is lower there. It's one of the many reasons the fae left. Something shifted, lessening the flow. A skilled magic user can work around it, but it's possible many of your talents were latent due to lack of energy. You didn't have the knowledge to augment it."

"I'm not ready for this."

"For magic?"

"No. Yes." Arlyn wrapped her arms around her waist. "Everything is moving so fast. I'm sure to offend this teacher as soon as he arrives. Or she. Whatever. I don't understand your rules."

"Calm down, Arlyn." He lifted a hand to her cheek. "I have an idea about that."

"Do you have a spell to teach me etiquette?"

He smiled. "No. There is no spell that can give you the lived experience of a culture. But I believe reading a few books about it will help. Your new teacher will know you aren't from our world. They will not expect you to know anything."

"How long do I have?"

Arlyn caught his wince as he turned to open the door. He gestured for her to precede him. "Lord Loren wanted to send someone today, but I put him off. Your new teacher will arrive tomorrow evening."

She stopped so abruptly that he almost ran into her. She spun, then took a couple of steps back. "Tomorrow?"

"I know this is a great deal to take in, Arlyn. I do." He lifted his hands, palms outward. "But we really do need a full mage here. If there were another attack, you might lose control."

Seeing the worry in his eyes, Arlyn slumped. "Fine."

"I'm sorry." Lyr's mouth turned down as he lowered his hands. "The library is right over here. I'll do my best to help you prepare. We all will."

After a few more steps down the hall, he opened yet another door for her. Arlyn paused on the threshold, her breath drawing in on a gasp. Her mental map had told her the library was in a tower. But the reality went beyond expectation. She peered up, then up some more, at the countless levels of bookshelves practically piercing the sky. A staircase spiraled up the center, stopping at the landing of each level before continuing on. *Beautiful.*

Arlyn finally pulled her eyes down to the base. The floor of the tower was lower than the ground outside to allow yet another level. Large tables took up the center, a few books left here and there. At the far table, her grandmother sat, holding something over a huge, ancient-looking tome. Arlyn and Lyr followed the short flight of steps down to the bottom, and Lynia looked up, her eyes glazed in thought.

"*Laiala?*"

Arlyn heard the question in her father's voice and suspected it was about more than her grandmother's presence in the library. Lynia focused on Lyr's face, and the smile she gave was knowing. "I'm fine, love."

"After earlier…"

"I had my cry." Lynia tapped the book. "Now I'll help bring justice."

Lyr's expression blanked with surprise. "You think you'll find father's murderer in a book?"

"You can find almost anything in a book if you're patient enough." Lynia's grin could only be described as wicked. "Never anger a researcher."

"But how—"

"You connected Telien's murder with Kai's attack through the design on the blade. But why now, after all this time? You told me only yesterday about Kai's mission. The energy poisoning. So I'm searching the records for any mention of this type of problem happening before. It will help to know if it is natural or intentional. And if you'll give me the blade, I'll see if I can find out more about the design on the pommel."

Lyr stared at her, his mouth open, before shaking his head. "I should have asked you sooner."

Arlyn had to admire her grandmother's serene smile. "Yes. You should have."

Though his expression turned sheepish, Lyr chuckled. "Point taken. I'll let you get back to what you were doing."

"Thank you." Lynia lifted the small, round piece of glass she held in her hand. "It is difficult enough working through this tiny print. Remind me to spell-copy these to larger tomes when I have more time."

Obviously not expecting an answer, Lynia bent over the book once more. As Arlyn followed her father to the base of the spiral staircase, she kept looking over at her grandmother. A scholar. Arlyn would have to remember that. She had so many questions about this world, and maybe Lynia could help answer some of them.

They climbed to the second walkway before walking along the shelves. Lyr stopped a few bookcases away, then searched through the titles for a moment before pulling several down. With a smile, he handed her one of them. "This is likely the best source."

A quick glance had a line forming between her brows. "You do realize that I can't read this, right?"

He frowned. "What?"

"Haven't you noticed that we have been speaking English since I arrived?" Arlyn asked as she handed the book back to him. "As a matter of fact, everyone I've met has. This is not in any language I've ever seen."

"Oh!" He chuckled, giving a sheepish wince. "I had forgotten completely, to be honest. Eight years ago, I ordered everyone on the estate to speak English, unless we had a visitor who did not know it. In two more years, we will switch to French."

"But why?"

"Remember that our people once came from Earth. House Dianore is responsible for keeping up with our original planet. We stand as the guardian between the two realms." Some of the levity dropped from his face. "Every year, I grow more certain we will have to reestablish contact with the human world, a difficult task if we cannot speak to anyone."

Arlyn followed him to the stairs. "That doesn't mean you have to speak it here."

He looked back over his shoulder. "I have a spell that can transfer the vocabulary, and to some extent the grammar, of a language, but it takes practice to truly be able to communicate with it. Not to mention that some people have been spelled with earlier forms of English over the years, which is not easy to overwrite."

"You're really so certain that you feel the need to practice?" Arlyn nibbled the tip of her finger, the pinch a distraction from the unease creeping into her chest. "Must not be an effective spell."

Smiling, Lyr paused at the bottom of the stairs and waited for her to join him. Across the room, Lynia still bent over her book, not bothering to even look up. "Language is a social construction," her father said, "Constantly evolving as it is used, and it is not made by one person alone. You may technically know what a word means, but you won't truly understand it until you try it with others."

She laughed. "You would if you had a good dictionary."

"Really?" His smile twisted into a smirk as he crossed to the door, still open from their entry. "Tell me, then, expert. What does *hello* mean?"

"That's easy. It means…" Arlyn grimaced. "Well, it means *hello*. It's just a greeting."

"And what use is the word unless spoken to another?"

"I see your point. But I doubt you guys will use the words the same way people on Earth do."

He nodded. "That is true. But we should at least have an understandable dialect. Your presence will help, actually."

"Me?" She followed him from the library and down the hall to the study. "I'm not an English teacher."

"No, but as a native speaker, you truly *are* an expert. Kai and I have spent time in the human world in recent years and are the best here at English, but even we sometimes sound old-fashioned."

"Well, don't expect much from me when you switch to French. I learned a little bit of Spanish when I was younger, but I don't remember it well." She paused, grabbing his arm in panic. "Oh no! I won't be able to talk to anyone, then, will I?"

"Arlyn." He looked at her with raised eyebrows. "I'll spell the language to you just as I do everyone else on the estate."

Relaxing, she let go of him so they could continue along the hall. "How many languages do you know, anyway?"

"Let me think." His gaze grew distant. "I know English, French, Spanish, Mandarin, Japanese, Arabic, Gaelic, German, Russian, and more dialects of fae than I want to count. Though I still haven't found anyone to teach me the Ljósálfar tongue."

"The what?"

"Norse elves," Lyr answered. "They are reclusive, if not hostile. They are related to us just as the Sidhe are, but you'll not likely hear a Ljósálfar admit it."

"They sound lovely." Arlyn shared a smirk with her father at her sarcasm. When they reached the door to his study, she held the door open for him so he wouldn't have to juggle the books. "So you're a scholar, too?"

"I'm not. Before I met your mother, I traveled the human world for my father ensuring nothing major was happening that might warrant our attention. Many of those languages I learned with magic many years ago and would likely not speak well with modern people. But it probably would not take me too long to adapt if necessary."

As Lyr set the books on a side table, Arlyn shuddered. What could possibly warrant a return of the elves to Earth? Echoes of overheard conversations flickered through her mind. *Other dimensions. Sidhe. Energy poisoning.* Could humans be involved? And if so, where would her loyalty lie?

Arlyn had only been here for a day, and already, she didn't know.

Lyr turned, a smile crossing his face despite the seriousness of their discussion. "I hope *Laiala* finds something with her research. I really should have asked her sooner."

His daughter's distant gaze returned to his face. "Sorry. I was lost in thought." She bit her lip. "Though now that I think of it, why isn't your mother in charge? Are only men allowed to lead here?"

He shook his head. "Why would you think such a thing? Your own title, Ayala, names you as my heir. But the position is usually hereditary, passing to the firstborn child regardless of gender."

"Wait, what?" Arlyn paled, and her chest tightened. "I'm your heir? I assumed that was some kind of courtesy word. I can't take over for you. I don't even know how to start a conversation here. You said you didn't even trust me."

"Breathe, Arlyn." His smile faltered, and he took a few steps closer. "And I'm sorry for that. You didn't deserve it."

"The title?"

He ran a hand through his hair. "My doubt in you. After I had left your mother, after *you* had to find *me*. It was not well-done of me to treat you so."

"It made sense." He opened his mouth to argue, but she lifted a hand. "No, it did. Still does. But being your heir? That does not."

How could he calm the panic lighting her eyes? Lyr crossed the gap between them and rested his hands on her shoulders. "You are my firstborn child. It would be a dishonor not to name you as such. Anyway, you are still thinking like a human."

A spark of anger eased some of the panic in her eyes. "Is that an insult?"

His mouth quirked up. "No. It's an observation. Even with your human blood, you'll likely live a couple of millennia at the least, probably a few more. I am only five hundred and forty-nine. If you decide to stay, to accept your place as Ayala, you will have more than enough time to learn our ways. If elves have anything, it's time."

"God." Arlyn sagged a little beneath his hands. "I didn't even think about that."

Lyr winced. So much for comforting her. "Just let it be. How about I give you our language? That should provide plenty of distraction."

"Now?"

After a glance at the water clock, he nodded. "The sooner, the better."

She sighed. "Might as well."

Lyr guided her to one of chairs in the center of the room, then pulled his own seat to face her. At her nod, he began.

Her father stilled, all but his right hand, which he used to sketch a series of symbols in the air faster than she could process. Arlyn sensed the power building, could almost follow the near-invisible strands that wrapped together to form a glowing ball of light in the center of his left palm. Before she realized what he was about to do, he turned his hand over and pressed the ball against the center of her forehead. Arlyn gasped at the impact as the energy took off, racing its way down pathways inside her skull she'd never even imagined. She shuddered against the tingling almost-pain of it. The spell seemed to struggle for a moment before she forced herself to relax and let it through. Instantly, the tingling eased as the spell settled in her brain.

"*Lae'ial hy maliar na Moranaia dae gher,*" he whispered, pressing his forefinger to the middle of her forehead. "I imbue the Moranaian language into you."

The energy flared, distracting her for a moment from the burning pain building in the left side of her head. Then words started flowing through her mind faster than she could grasp them, and every single one seemed to heighten the agony. Like someone was poking sticks into her brain. For a moment, Arlyn stopped trying to understand each word, hoping the pain would ease if she relaxed, but nothing helped. Clutching her head, she bent over and gasped for air. It was too much. *Too much.*

The world faded to black.

"Arlyn."

As sound trickled in, Arlyn winced. Her hands lifted to her head, and she squeezed against her aching skull. When she dared to open her eyes, light speared through her in a fresh rush of agony. "Damn."

Laughter eased some of the concern from his face, and she noticed then that he was kneeling beside her chair. "Of all the words you just learned, *clechtan* is your favorite?"

"Don't the elven children in the dictionary look the bad words up first?" Arlyn fumbled out, mangling what she wanted to ask.

"That was an interesting way of saying it." He chuckled again and returned to his own seat. "And no, not in general. Curse words are not as strong of a taboo for us. We are more likely to look up certain courtship traditions. How do you think I knew where to find the etiquette books?"

She groaned, eyeing the books he had brought. "Do you mean those tomes have some sex rules?"

"Ah." His face twisted into an odd expression as he choked off a laugh. "The books I brought do not have anything like that, but the ones that do are near them in the library. Please tell me we do not need to have *that* talk."

"Nope." She grinned and shook her head, an action she quickly regretted. "I think maybe I should try more of speaking when I *can* think."

"Perhaps so." Lyr looked toward the door. "Lial will be here in a moment to heal the pain."

As if he'd been cued, the healer entered, customary scowl in place. "A quarter-mark past three hours, Lyr? I should slip something into your drink anyway."

Arlyn caught her father's eye roll. "I've no doubt you were already awake."

When Lial bent next to her chair, Arlyn caught the hint of humor in his gaze, and she wondered how much of his temper was bluster. "Sorry to again bother you."

The healer shrugged. "It's my job. Just relax."

She let her eyes slipped closed and forced some of the tension from her limbs. Arlyn wasn't sure how, but she'd almost stopped her father's spell only moments before. The last thing she wanted was to keep Lial from fixing her pain. She tried to blank her mind as the healer's energy flowed around her. Within a few heartbeats, her headache eased, then faded completely.

Arlyn smiled up at the healer. "Thanks."

"I can hardly say 'my pleasure,' since the injury required the healing, but I appreciate the sentiment." Lial stood and wasted no time in striding across the room. When he reached the door, he turned back. "I'm about to go check on Kai. If you could both abstain from grave injury for a while?"

Lyr's low laugh sounded as the door clicked closed. Arlyn found her own lips curling into a smile. "Is he always like this?"

"Most of the time," Lyr answered. "But we keep him around anyway."

There was a wealth of affection in his tone, built from a lifetime of memories Arlyn didn't have. She sensed some inside joke and wondered if she'd ever be close enough to any of them to understand it. "What now?"

He lifted one of the books from the table and started flipping through it. "Now you read."

Arlyn tried to focus on the book in her lap, but her gaze kept straying to Kai. After her father had marked several passages for her to review, she'd returned to her room, settling into the chair next to the bed. Despite her confusion about her relationship with Kai, she couldn't help glancing up from her book to check on him. She would rather study him than etiquette, as though she could divine the nature of their connection and his intentions in establishing it simply by analyzing his every feature.

God, what a sappy idea. If she weren't careful, this bond would turn her into a starry-eyed romantic, and then where would she be? Instead of learning anything useful about her elven heritage, she would start writing sonnets about his finely chiseled face, long black hair, and—

With a snort of derision, Arlyn turned her eyes resolutely back to her book. It would be harder to yell at him when he finally woke up if she spent all of her time beforehand ogling him. Protocol. She had to focus on protocol.

When greeting a guest, it is imperative to make said personage feel both comfortable and important. Their ease must be sought before one's own. This is doubly so if the guest has come to provide aid for one's House or is recognized as a Sage, Teacher, or Priest. Such important personages must be greeted with the highest respect owed their station.

Arlyn's brow furrowed as she paused to reread the passage. What made someone a recognized teacher? Was there some nuance to the phrasing that she didn't understand?

She would need to ask her father, but it would be impractical to go looking for him every time she had a question. Could she reach him telepathically as she had Kai? It was possible she could only speak to Kai that way because of their bond, but maybe not. With a frown of concentration, she searched for the energy that felt like her father, and once she found it, she pushed against it with her own essence. She caught his surprise as she established the connection.

"Lyr?"

"Arlyn!" She winced as an outpouring of jumbled emotions hit her with the words. Her breath left her in a rush and her vision swam with the power of it. *"Calm the connection! Pull back!"*

"What?" she managed to gasp. Blindly, she retreated until their energies barely touched. As soon as she managed it, his emotions faded from her awareness. *"What did I do?"*

"You created quite a strong link, tieln.*"* His amusement came through with the words. *"For future reference, it is considered rude to do so without invitation."*

She flushed with embarrassment. Thank goodness he wasn't there to see. *"Sorry. I didn't know what I was doing."*

"I am aware. Next time, brush your energy against mine and wait for a response. If I do not establish a connection, then you should assume I do

not wish to be disturbed and will reply when possible. Only reach through and create the connection yourself if it is a true emergency."

Arlyn grew redder. *"Okay."*

"Do not distress yourself." He sent reassurance along their link. *"Now, what led you to come seeking me?"*

"I am trying to prepare a greeting in the way this book suggests, but I do not have enough information about my mentor. For instance, is this person a recognized teacher?"

"Her formal title is Taian ia'Kelore ai'Flerin ay'mornia Tayerna pel Rorian i Selia Baran nai Fiorn. You should be able to get all the information you need out of that if you look it up in those books."

"If I can remember it."

"The way I sent it, you should remember long enough to write it down." He paused for a moment, and she sensed a bit of his uncertainty. *"I do not wish to upset you, Arlyn, but I must return to work. Do not hesitate to contact me, but please do not be offended if I cannot answer immediately."*

"Of course. I'm sorry I disturbed your work."

She sensed his relief as he bid her a good afternoon and ended their connection, and it made her smile. At least he was as uncertain of her as she was of him. How long would it take for them to be at ease with one another? Considering their life spans, they had plenty of time to find out. With a grimace, she stepped over to her desk to write down the name her father had given her, then stared down at the neat, elven text that appeared by her own hand.

It was one thing to read the lettering in the books; she had spent more time making sure she had the meaning correct than paying attention to the script. But after writing it herself, she was forced to admit the language *had* been put in her head just a couple of hours earlier. That morning, she would have seen nothing but random lines.

Arlyn took the paper back to her chair and reopened the book. It would probably take her hours to decipher such a complex name. Though she knew the individual words along with the rest of the language, she still didn't quite understand how they worked together to make a title. At this rate, she would be lucky to finish a simple greeting, much less memorize any of the other points of etiquette her father had marked. It all seemed unnecessarily complex to her. Was keeping the peace over such long life spans really that difficult? Then again, humans couldn't manage it for more than a few years. Maybe all of this formality did have a point.

Just as she decoded the last part of her mentor's title, Arlyn heard a soft knock at the door. She wrote down her last observation and closed the book. Most of the title had been useless information as far as she was concerned. What did she care about where, precisely, the lady's family fell on the Taian branch? It made no difference to her since she had no real grasp of what that placement meant. But she had discovered her new mentor was part of a noble house and was indeed a recognized teacher, both of which called for extra formality. Writing this welcome speech was going to take hours.

Ready for a distraction, she put her book aside and went to answer the door. Arlyn was surprised to find her grandmother on the other side. "Hello."

"Hello," Lynia answered with a smile. "I hope I am not disturbing you."

Arlyn looked back at the stack of books taunting her from the desk, then gave her grandmother a smile. "Not at all. I could use a break."

"Your father mentioned that you didn't bring many clothes appropriate for our clime." Lynia grimaced at Arlyn's long-sleeved shirt. "I see he was right."

Arlyn found herself blushing. "I didn't consider emerging from the Veil in a different season."

"I did not intend to offer insult." With widened eyes, her grandmother gestured to her door. "My friend is a seamstress, and I thought you might enjoy something new. She is waiting in my rooms."

"I…" Arlyn remembered the diamonds Kai had offered for her phone. "I don't think I have anything of value to trade for it."

"Your father will make sure she is compensated."

"That doesn't seem right."

"Arlyn, it is our way." Lynia's brow rose. "Did he not explain? You are young and in training. Any apprentice under Lyr's dominion would have their basic needs met until their learning is complete and they can earn their own coin or make goods to trade. Either the student's family or the leader of our House is responsible, and your father is both."

Arlyn frowned. "What does he get out of it?"

Her grandmother's face went blank with surprise. "Well-trained citizens? The unskilled do not do well, for themselves or anyone else, over millennia." She smiled. "But if this both-ers you, just consider it a gift."

Arlyn had spent so long earning her own way that the idea still bothered her a little. But why? She'd never hesitated to accept gifts from her mother. Mind made up, she nodded to her grandmother and followed the elder woman across the hall. Then halted, mouth agape, in the doorway. She spotted countless bolts of fabrics stacked around the room in a stun-ning blend of color, and in the middle of the cloth chaos, three women and a man stood, their gazes already taking in Arlyn's appearance. It looked for all the world like something an elite Victorian modiste might have done for her wealthiest clients. Did modern fashion designers do stuff like this? Arlyn had no idea.

Lynia glanced back, frowning to see Arlyn still standing by the door. "Come. I will introduce you."

With slow steps, Arlyn made her way over to the group. She forced her hands still by her side as her grandmother gave the formal introductions, the array of titles making a little more sense now that she understood the words. At least she could pick out what parts described their occupation and which their names. Progress.

At the edge of consciousness, she sensed her grandmother and struggled to open a connection. When she heard only words and not a rush of crazed emotion, she sighed in relief. *"Arlyn, please do not treat these people as you would human servants. We do not consider those not of a noble house to be menials. Telia is a good friend."*

"I can't imagine treating anyone like that, but I still appreciate the warning. Maybe after I get this presentation over with you can tell me more about how nobles and non-nobles interact."

"Of course."

A couple of hours later, Arlyn stood on a small platform with swathes of green fabric in various shades draped and pinned around her body. At Telia's command, one of her assistants would lift a portion of the fabric and wait until Telia used a spell to alter it. Without scissors. Arlyn stared down with wide eyes as the cloth seemed to separate under its own power. They had another spell to aid in the sewing, although two of the assistants also stitched with conventional needle and thread.

The male glanced up from where he knelt, holding out a corner of the fabric. A smile crossed his face when he took in Arlyn's expression. "My wife looks much the same when I make something for her."

"I've never seen anything like this." Arlyn waved a hand, then stilled at an irritated hum from the seamstress. "No measuring or cutting."

A lock of blond hair fell into his eyes as he nodded, and he paused to brush it aside. "They are specialized spells that take a fair amount of energy but with much less waste and far more accuracy."

He bent back to his work, leaving Arlyn to her thoughts. She should have spent the time considering her speech, but watching the elves work enthralled her. By the time they lifted the half-finished garment over her head and sent her to change out of the thin shift her grandmother had provided, her head spun with the questions she longed to ask.

When Arlyn returned from the dressing room, the seamstress had just turned to Lynia. "I will finish the embroidery and such by hand tonight and begin work on other outfits based on these measurements. The gown should be lovely, Lyni."

"Excuse me. It is not my intention to be rude, but I have to ask." Arlyn bit her lip and hoped she wasn't about to commit a huge breach of etiquette. "Why are you doing the rest by hand? In fact, why are you doing any of it by hand? Why not just, I don't know, magic a dress?"

Telia smiled gently. "Where would be the art in that? I have spent seven hundred years creating clothing for others, but I doubt I would have lasted one if the only thing I did was copy the same spell over and over. Any magician could do that. The joy is in the process, not the product."

Arlyn's nose scrunched at the memory of the mostly mass produced clothing she had worn in the human world. "That makes sense. I guess I'm just not used to thinking about how magic should or shouldn't be used. Or, really, thinking of it at all."

Curiosity brightened the seamstress's dark eyes. "You are from a place of no magic? And daughter of the Myern?"

"His child with Aimee," Lynia answered for her. "Do you remember me telling you of the mate he found and lost? My fool son rushed off without ever bothering to check her. Arlyn had to come find him."

"You mean she crossed the Veil?" Telia stopped herself, waving a hand. "Never mind, at least until later. I have too much work to do to gossip now, but I will have the story from you eventually."

Then, with surprising efficiency, Telia and her assistants gathered their supplies and rushed off. Arlyn stared after them, more than a little confused by all she'd seen and heard. "Where is she from?"

"Who, Telia?" Lynia's brow pinched. "The village."

"It's just, her skin…" Arlyn tried to come up with a word for the grayish-brown color and failed. "Or maybe she's ill?"

Her grandmother's expression cleared, and she gave a small laugh. "Oh, that. Her grandfather was a Dökkálfar immigrant. One of the Dark Elves, you'd call them. He bonded with a woman in the village, and their family has been here since. The black of Dökkálfar skin grays with the blending."

"It's unusual, at least to my eyes," Arlyn answered. "But beautiful."

"Your father brought me a few books about elves from the human world." Lynia's eyes twinkled with humor. "I imagine you are surprised. We're not so simple as light and dark, as you'll see."

Arlyn recalled the guard at her father's door and nodded. "I've noticed."

And Arlyn wondered, as she returned to her room, what *else* might be more complicated than it seemed.

Arlyn's chin slipped off her palm, and she jerked upright. Rubbing a hand across her heavy eyes, she glared at the rain dripping down the dark window by the desk. With all of the trees and flowers, the sound of the evening shower hitting the leaves soothed her more than any white noise machine could. So much for concentration.

She squinted down at the paper on the desk, barely illuminated by the globe on the wall. She still didn't know how to control the thing, so it stayed at the same level of light the healer had left it on after his last healing session with Kai. The elven text shimmered in her sight, the shadows highlighting its foreignness, though she'd written it herself not long before.

A yawn slipped free, and Arlyn glanced at the bed. The speech she'd written would have to do for now. She'd spent hours on it, even taking dinner in her room. At least her Moranaian had improved after the day's reading. The grammar had settled more easily in her mind, and none had looked her askance when she spoke.

Arlyn moved over to the chair by the bed, but she didn't sit. Her body was leaden with exhaustion, her mind fuzzy. She could *not* sleep an entire night slumped in that damned seat again. Her gaze skimmed Kai, still under Lial's sleeping spell. Kai's color was better after his latest healing, and the healer had told her he might wake him tomorrow. But he shouldn't stir tonight.

Besides, the bed was huge. Probably larger than a king size on Earth. She could slip into the far end and never even notice Kai was there. Arlyn pulled back the covers and glanced once more at Kai's still form before sliding in. A groan escaped her lips as her head met the pillow. *So* much better than a chair.

Kai woke instantly; there was no transition, no pleasant climb to awareness. One moment oblivious darkness, the next murky consciousness. His thoughts tumbled together like leaves in a storm. Where was he? Why was he in pain? Fighting panic, he lifted his head and looked around. A dim spell globe was the only source of light, the blue haze revealing little of the bedroom. A window. A desk. But not his own room. He was almost certain he had never been in this place before.

Pain radiated from his side with an intensity too great to be mere muscle strain. And was that—he glanced down and confirmed that an arm *was* draped over his chest. Small, obviously female. Pain and female companionship did not go together for him. His breath came in shallow pants as Kai followed the arm to the figure sleeping against his side. Long hair streamed around her body, but he couldn't quite make out the color. If only he could remember what had happened.

She turned in her sleep, exposing her face to the hint of light that shaded the room, and Kai gasped. Arlyn! His mind went blank for a moment before the memories, more focused this time, rushed back in. Coming back from his mission, meeting her on the trail and fearing he would never see her again, giving her the necklace, facing Lyr and his father, getting attacked. And over it all, a kind of hazy exhaustion blended with pain that blurred the details. How had he even functioned? In fact, how had he survived? He should have died in those woods, as drained of energy and blood as he'd been. Nothing made sense.

Had he really started the bond? Ignoring the pain moving caused, he shifted a lock of her hair aside. The necklace he'd worn for centuries tangled in the folds of her nightgown. *He had.* Bile surged into his throat, and he moved her arm to her side so he could sit. Kai gasped with the agony of his injury and his realizations. He pulled up his legs, his head dropping to his knees.

He'd started the bonding without even asking her name. His mate. His best friend's daughter. If Kai'd had any food in his stomach, he would have lost it. Unforgiveable. He couldn't fathom why she rested beside him instead of pacing Meyanen's temple until a priest could be found to break the bond.

The memory of her in the clearing trickled through. *If anyone or anything is going to kill you, it'll be me.* Maybe she'd decided to break the bond in another way. Kai pulled at his hair, not even noticing the sting of his scalp over the searing pain of his side. Maybe he would help her.

Kai's head jerked up at the soft click of the door opening. He tensed, ready to defend himself and Arlyn despite his injury, then relaxed when he recognized Lial's face in the soft glow of the mage light floating in behind him. The healer stopped by the bed with a scowl. "Why are you sitting? You shouldn't even be awake."

"You didn't release the spell?"

"No." Lial pushed Kai's shoulder until he lowered himself back onto the bed. "Perhaps your slight healing gift interfered. The wound is finally knit, but I would rather you not move around just yet."

Kai winced. "My body agrees."

"Then why?"

"Just drop it."

Lial glanced at Arlyn, but he said nothing, only pulled power into himself for another healing. Kai let the blue glow sweep through him, easing his physical pain and even the nausea. The healer made no comment on that, either, much to Kai's relief. When Lial finally stepped back, his brows rose in question.

"Will you rest if I allow you to stay conscious?"

Kai rolled his eyes. "I'll do my best."

Some of the hardness Lial wore like armor slipped away, revealing the hint of compassion in his eyes. That, or it was a trick of the light. "All will be well. She has Lyr's strength."

"Hopefully not his temper," Kai muttered.

Lial chuckled. "Ah, but Lyr usually forgives in the end."

"*Usually* being the key."

Lial shook his head, not bothering to argue. After a few more instructions, the healer left, and Kai drifted in the haze the healing had brought. What was he going to do about Arlyn? Nothing he could do or say would justify binding them without her permission. More, he had cheated her. It should have been a beautiful occasion, a memory they would both treasure. A proper mate would have spent much time and effort courting his intended.

With a groan, he closed his eyes. His body grew so heavy with exhaustion that he half expected Lial to be standing over him casting another spell of sleep, but he knew the feeling was normal. Despite the hours of rest he'd already had, his body had suffered serious trauma on top of being perilously low on energy. Even as his mind raced, his exhausted body pulled him back down into sleep.

Lyr signed off on the last paper in the most urgent stack and leaned back in his seat. He glanced at his water clock, then grimaced. He'd worked until the twenty-eighth hour, only two before dawn. At least estate business had kept him from sword work. Without the drain of his combat magic on his personal reserves, he could get by for a few days with little sleep.

As he stood, the mirror beside his desk chimed. Lyr frowned. Who would call at this time of night? He walked around the chair and placed his hand on the mirror's frame. With a resigned sigh, he activated the waiting connection. Might as well get the next crisis handled now. For what else could it be at this point but a crisis?

Lyr winced against the sunlight that filtered through the windows on the other end of the connection and made the black-haired elf seem to glow. The man leaned against the frame of his own mirror, his face pale from the exertion of holding the connection.

"Ralan?"

"Hello, Lyr."

Because he knew it irritated Ralan, Lyr bowed. "Forgive me, Anderteriorn Ralantayan. I was too surprised to greet Your Highness properly."

Ralan laughed. "Stuff it, Lyr. You know I hate that crap."

Stuff it? Clearly he was behind on his slang. "Whatever you wish, Your Highness. I would not think to do aught but what my prince commands."

"Yeah, right." Ralan frowned. "It is night there. I did not think to calculate the time. What are you doing in your father's office so late?"

The quick jolt of pain stole Lyr's breath. He had not spoken to his friend since just before he had met Aimee, in large part because he had never returned to the human world. Ralan rarely called Moranaia. "My father is no longer alive. He was assassinated some twenty-two years ago. Not long after my last visit."

"I am sorry to hear that," Ralan answered, his voice tinged with genuine regret. "I was beginning to wonder why I hadn't seen you. I've never known you to go more than twenty years between missions."

"It was not only because of my father." Lyr took a deep breath, forcing the pain down. "But you did not expend the energy to call me across the Veil to discuss my personal life. I will not drain you by drawing this out, as I can only assume you need something significant."

Ralan's expression tightened. "Yes. I need a guide. You have to send me Kai."

"What could you possibly need with a guide? You vowed never to return."

"I know perfectly well what I vowed. It is irrelevant." Ralan's jaw clenched, his eyes burning with anger. Then some of the tension left his expression. "Sorry. That wasn't directed at you. The energy here is growing toxic. My daughter doesn't have long to live."

"Daughter?"

Ralan swayed on his feet. "I don't have the energy to explain."

"Let me bolster the connection."

"Just send Kai. No more than three days from now." The prince paused, his expression grave. "I have Seen it."

Lyr let out a curse. "Kai was just injured. I might have to send another."

"He'll be ready," Ralan said. "He has to be."

The prince closed the connection before Lyr could argue. His fists clenched, and he cursed again. Of all the things he needed at the moment, a self-exiled seer was low on the list. As soon as the king heard, there'd be trouble. Growling at fate, Lyr stalked from the room. Ralan's timing was terrible. Though perhaps not coincidental. He paused in the middle of the hall as he recalled the prince's words. Toxic energy. Was Earth affected by the same poison as the underhill?

Miaran, he cursed to himself. *Not good.*

With a smile, Arlyn burrowed closer to the warm, firm surface beneath her cheek and let herself drift in a haze of half-sleep. For the first time in longer than she could remember, everything seemed right. Her body was lax with contentment, the tension she'd carried gone. For a moment, she basked in it, unquestioning, and snuggled happily against the apparent source of her serenity. Then that source groaned.

Her eyes snapped open as she tensed. She was tucked up tight against Kai's side, her arm around his waist. His eyes were still closed, his breathing still rhythmic and heavy, but he was grimacing in his sleep. What was wrong? She started to move away from him, and he groaned again. With a gasp, she jerked her arm back. Her hand had shifted to his injured side while she slept.

Arlyn darted up to kneel over him. The neat stitches, already faded to a dark pink, seemed undisturbed. Had she hurt him deep inside, where she couldn't see? She cursed herself for rolling over to him in her sleep. So much for not even noticing she was there. Of their own volition, her fingers trailed across the firm muscles of his side before she pulled them back. So strong.

Arlyn was about to try to call the healer when a hand closed over her wrist. She jumped, biting down hard enough to draw blood on the lip she had been worrying between her teeth, and yelped. Before she could process what had happened, she felt fingers on her lip, then a warm flood of energy similar to Lial's when he had healed her headache. She looked down to find Kai's eyes opened and focused on her face. Realizing what had just occurred, the warmth of her blush traveled all the way to her toes.

The energy faded, and Kai pulled his fingers away to leave her lip unblemished. "I'm sorry I startled you."

"I thought you were asleep." Her face grew hotter. "Are you okay? I didn't mean to hurt you. I was about to call the healer."

Kai smiled at the breathless rush of her words. "I'm fine. The area is just sore to the touch still. It wasn't even bad enough to fully wake me."

She couldn't look away from his beautiful gray eyes, and the peace of waking beside him rushed through her, confusing her even more. Was she angry or happy? For the life of her, she couldn't tell.

With a shake of her head, she broke from his gaze. "You seem awake enough to me."

"After you jumped up, yes."

Silence stretched between them. There were so many things Arlyn needed to ask him. So many things to say. But the feelings he'd stirred in her still pounded through her blood like life. She had to get some distance. She needed a distraction.

"You healed my lip. If you're able to do that kind of magic, why didn't you do something for yourself after you were attacked? It might have made the situation a little less dangerous."

"I couldn't." Kai rubbed some of the sleep from his eyes. "I'm not sure what you know about how magic works for us. We have our own personal reserves, our capacity to handle energy. We can convert natural energy from the world around us, but we have to sacrifice our own to do it. The only way to replenish *that* is sleep. By the time I was returning here from my father's house, my reserves were gone. I couldn't even convert natural energy, much less heal myself. Besides, my healing gift is slight. I could only have kept an injury that bad from worsening."

"So either you have a really low capacity for magic, or you hadn't slept for a while." Arlyn frowned. "Wait, I remember my father saying you were sleep-deprived, but I forgot for how long. Just how long *had* you been awake?"

Kai shrugged. "About a human week."

"A *week?*" She considered shaking him. "Are you crazy?"

"I hadn't believed so, but now, who knows?" He ran a hand through his hair, frustration and pain tightening his face. "I was energy-crazed for certain though I didn't realize it at the time. But it couldn't be avoided. I had good reason for going so long without rest."

"Good reason? What could possibly—"

The sharp knock on the door stopped her words mid-sentence. Frowning, Arlyn glanced at the pale trickle of light beyond the window. It was barely past dawn. Why would someone be at her door so early? Her heart gave a leap as she called for them to enter. When Lyr walked in, a smile on his face, she dropped back to her heels in surprise at the pleasure filling her.

When had she begun to enjoy his presence?

Lyr froze, and the smile dropped from his face. His hands tightened at his sides as he took in the scene. Arlyn reddened when she realized what was upsetting him. She knelt beside Kai on the bed with her nightgown bunched around her knees. And *he* wore no shirt. Mortified, she pulled the blanket over them both.

"I was just checking his side."

"If he has caused you further distress…"

Kai tensed beside her as she shook her head. "No. We were talking."

"You have a right to your anger," Kai said, his voice colder than she'd ever heard it. "But imply that I would cause her physical harm again, and we will come to blows."

Lyr's face went blank with shock. "I meant no such thing. But she looked upset."

Though a hiss of pain left him at the movement, Kai sat up. Arlyn scrambled back, her eyes narrowing on the two men. "Stop it. If anyone is going to defend my honor, it's me."

They stared at her with wide eyes for a moment. Then Lyr let out a cough, and Kai's lips twisted into a smile. Her father rubbed the back of his neck, his expression sheepish. "Indeed. I meant no offense."

Arlyn pushed Kai back. "Rest."

"I'm well enough to sit up."

"I'd rather not add being glared at by the healer to the morning's entertainment." Kai huffed out a laugh, but he sank back to the bed. Then she turned a glare on Lyr. "I'm assuming you didn't come by to beat up Kai?"

"As much merit as the idea holds, no." Some of the tension eased from her father despite his words. "I wanted to let you know that I set your presentation to the household at the ninth hour, right before the midday meal. We will have a celebratory feast directly after."

Arlyn glanced at the window again with a frown. It was still fairly early in the morning, but not that early. "Nine o'clock? That can't be far away."

"A while yet, as we're only at the second hour." At her blank look, he laughed. "I'm sorry, I forgot you count time differently. We start our day at dawn, not in the middle of the night like people in the human world."

"Oh. Logical, I suppose." She shook her head. "That gives me seven hours. What am I going to have to do for this? Do I need to do something special to prepare?"

"Not a great deal. Telia should be by soon with new clothing for you, and she will show you what best to wear. Otherwise, most of the speaking at this event will be done by me. It will be in Moranaian, though. Since Kai is awake, he should be able to help you prepare what words you might need to say. Speaking of which…" A small frown pinched between his eyebrows. "Kai must be introduced as your soulbonded since he is now also part of our house."

"Great, now I will have others pressuring me about it."

"Arlyn," Kai's voice was soft, though his eyes were alive with harsh emotion. "Do not worry about the others. Do what you feel you must. If you end up deciding to go before a priest of Arneen to break our bond, I will not stop you, for what I did is hard to forgive. It doesn't matter what anyone else thinks."

Her hand went to her throat at the guilt and sick grief that trickled to her along their bond. The echo of his emotions weren't what she would expect from a man who had tried to trap her. No smugness or pride. Instead, she got such a strong wash of remorse that she was not sure what to do with it. She couldn't yell at someone who felt like the proverbial kicked puppy.

"I don't even know what *I* think. If we have time after preparing for the presentation, you can explain to me what happened. Maybe that will help me understand it all."

"Don't wear yourself out too much, Kai. You need to be there as well." Lyr opened the door, then turned back. "I'll need you fit to guide in a day or two. Try not to injure him more, Arlyn."

Kai's brow rose. "To guide? Now?"

"A new mission we were given last night." Frowning, her father waved a hand. "I'll tell you more after lunch. We have to get this presentation done before Arlyn's teacher arrives."

14

"So." Kai's eyes settled on Arlyn's mouth as she bit into a berry and chewed. "My speech is done. We have some time. Explain."

He pulled his gaze back to her eyes. "Now?"

"It should have been yesterday," she snapped, tone icy.

Kai dropped the fruit he held, his appetite gone. But she was right. "What do you want to know first?"

"Why hadn't you slept for a week?"

"I was on a difficult mission. Crossing through the Veil takes more energy than it used to, but that was only part of the problem." Kai pushed his plate aside. "What do you know of the Sidhe?"

Arlyn wiped her hands on her napkin and leaned forward. "Father mentioned that the Moranaians are related. The Sidhe live in fairy hills in another dimension connected to Earth, right?"

Kai nodded. "But a dimension more closely joined than this one. Only a breath away, really. I was negotiating with them. Poisoned energy has been sickening the Sidhe, driving them insane, sometimes even killing them. Every time they rest to restore their reserves, they draw in more sickness."

"Oh." Her eyes widened. "That's why you didn't sleep."

"Yes." Kai tensed against the memory of the dark energy that had beaten at the edge of his senses the entire week. "By the time I made it back, I had next to nothing left. The Veil has grown just that turbulent. How did you make it through so easily?"

She shrugged. "I just walked."

His eyes narrowed on her face. "When my energy is fully restored, I should test you for the gift of the guide. If you permit."

"Later." Arlyn waved a hand. Her eyes sparked at him. "Right now I want to know why you decided to *bind my soul* to yours. So you didn't sleep. You were low on energy. Is that supposed to be an excuse?"

Kai gripped the table to still his trembling hands. "No. A factor, but not an excuse. I was energy-crazed. Deprived, you might say. We run on energy, which is partially why we so rarely sicken and why we live so long. Without it, our bodies do strange things. "

"Right."

"It's hard to explain." He shook his head. "Everything was jumbled. I'd found your camp with the steel sword and feared there was an assassin on the loose." Kai gave a laugh at that. "Guess I was right, if accidentally. But when I noticed you on the path, I pulled in energy in case I needed to fend off an attack. The pain of it disoriented me."

Her brow furrowed. "Pain?"

"If you're low enough, converting energy *hurts*." Kai shuddered at the memory. "I thought my head was going to split. I just wasn't thinking. When I realized you were my bonded, I acted on instinct. But I believed you were from a distant branch. I thought you understood when I activated the magic. Even out of my head, I wouldn't have proceeded if I'd known you didn't recognize the bond."

Arlyn's eyes shifted away, and she toyed with a piece of cheese on her plate. "I felt something."

His heart pounded. "Something?"

The fire was back in her eyes when she looked up at him. "But that doesn't mean I'm letting you off easy. I need to think about this. This is major. No matter how you make me feel."

His grip tightened, and his fingers went white around the table's edge. "Would you care to expand on that?"

Another knock sounded on the door, and he cursed. If Lyr had come back to insult him again, there would be a fight. Kai would *lose*, but still. Then the healer entered, and Kai sagged in relief. He would never bridge the anger between himself and Lyr if they kept snapping at one another. Besides, he was in no shape to be trounced.

"Back to bed," Lial said. "I want to do another healing session before the presentation. I believe Lynia wanted to see you, Arlyn."

Kai's jaw clenched, but he nodded. "We'll continue this later."

Arlyn's brow rose. "Maybe."

Arlyn fought the urge to cross her arms over her chest, although the mirror had already told her she was covered. But she might as well be naked. The fabric of the dress, layers and layers of green gauze, was just that light. She ran the thumb of her free hand along the golden leaves embroidered on the top layer of cloth as Kai's warmth burned into her other side.

Their steps were slow as they made their way to her presentation, and she could tell by his tight expression how much he hated leaning on her so heavily. But walk he did. Moranaian healing was potent, though not without cost. Arlyn had passed Lial on the way back from her grandmother's room, and the healer's face had been gray. Not the vital gray of Telia's skin, either. He'd looked as though he was going to sink into himself. But Kai was well enough now to walk.

Finally, they approached the large doors leading to the convening room. She stumbled to a halt at the sight of the man standing before the doors. A long, heavy-looking overcoat draped behind him, the fabric embroidered to look like the shifting mists of the Veil, and his brown hair fell unbound down his back. Was that her father? He looked over his shoulder, and she caught Lyr's face in profile. It was the first time she'd seen him looking, well, *elven*.

He turned. Behind him, she caught a glimpse of the people milling in the room beyond the partly opened doors. But she could only stare at her father. In a gesture that should have been feminine but somehow wasn't, Lyr flipped the length of his coat behind him and approached, a smile on his lips. How could he even move under all that weight? Besides the coat, he wore a jeweled sword strapped over a tunic and pants that gleamed like the silver circlet bound across his brow. Arlyn shivered as the blood rushed from her face. She'd managed to forget he was a noble.

And so was she.

Lyr's smile faded when he took in her expression. "Are you unwell?"

"Just nervous." Arlyn swallowed back the rest of her concerns. How could she explain the fear that shuddered through her at the evidence of his rank? "I'm ready to get this over with."

His eyes twinkled. "It's not an execution. I assure you, those are rare."

That surprised a chuckle out of her. "No. But I still think you have better things to worry about."

"Arlyn," Lyr began, taking her free hand. "There is nothing more important than presenting you as my child. Nothing."

She choked back a sudden sob, her gaze breaking from his long enough to compose herself. Arlyn took a few deep breaths and shoved down as much of the emotion as she could. She'd rather not be blotchy in front of a room full of elves. A few sniffles and a reassuring squeeze on her arm from Kai, and she smiled up at her father. "Thank you."

Her grandmother arrived, and the moment was broken. Lyr stepped back and offered Lynia his arm, then looked back at Kai and Arlyn. "Ready?"

Arlyn forced herself to straighten, her spine so stiff she thought it would crack, and nodded. Lyr gave her one last smile of reassurance, then led them through the huge double doors. *"Take heart,"* he sent her, his mental voice soft.

If Lyr hadn't been moving so quickly, Arlyn would have stopped and stared. The ballroom she had admired her first night was now filled with elves, and the sight stole her breath. They wore a dazzling array of clothes, some simple, others elaborate, in a varied but somehow harmonious blend of colors. Like an extension of the flowers beyond the windows, as though the garden had come alive to mingle beneath the carved trees above them. And the ceiling *had* changed. Now it was a gentle light blue.

The crowd parted for them, revealing a small dais on the far end of the room. Arlyn tried to study all the different people as they passed, but the task was almost impossible. So much variety. More than she had ever imagined. Humans painted elves as all the same—tall, gorgeous, perfect—but the reality somehow surpassed that ideal.

Like Telia, a few had grayish skin tones, and some were as dark as the night. And though many *were* tall and slim, a few elves were short and some almost plump. Arlyn's hand tightened around Kai's arm until he huffed out a breath. *"What is it?"*

"It's so overwhelming. Why didn't anyone warn me?"

His confusion flowed through their bond. *"Of what?"*

"I thought I knew about this world. But this..." She forced her fingers to relax. *"Everything is different than I expected."*

"We will help. Or Lyr, if you wish me gone."

He said it matter-of-factly, but he couldn't hide the pain behind the words. Not with their link. *"It's not that I wish you gone."*

"I know."

They reached the dais before Arlyn could continue, but she didn't know what to say to him anyway. She forced her fingers to relax and her free hand to hang loosely at her side, though she wanted to lift it against the ache in her chest. Her heart pounded, and her lungs burned with the effort to control her breath. The strangers' stares pinned her as surely as the pain she felt from Kai, blending in her heart.

She'd never considered herself as shy before this.

Her father led Lynia to the center of the platform, and she shifted to Lyr's left as Arlyn took her place at his right hand. Then prayed her terror didn't show to the crowd. Kai's weight eased from her, and she gave him a startled glance. Though his expression was neutral—how long would it take to master *that* talent?—she was close enough to make out the fine, white lines that creased near his eyes and mouth. His pride would cost him much in energy.

Lyr held up his hands for a moment, and the hushed whispers of the audience faded to nothing. "I bid good day to the House of Dianore and thank you for the indulgence of your presence. It is my wish that the month of Belen finds you well and much blessed by the high summer sun. With much happiness, I have invited you here this day to meet one too long gone from our domain and to welcome one you might recognize but know no more."

Arlyn's eyes widened at the formality of his words. Here was the elven lord she'd expected to find. Her stomach pitched. She had started to get used to him, to anticipate how he might act. And now she had another side of him to learn. A side so very foreign.

His eyes scanned the crowd. "But with joy often comes sorrow. As such, I mourn that not all in our House could be here this day, and I must ask you to carry the news of this event to those who cannot now hear."

Lyr paused again as murmurs of consent filled the room before dropping away to silence. "Though an occasion such as this deserves much more elegant speech and celebration, I realize many of you were brought unexpectedly from work that cannot be long delayed. Know that my brevity is not a sign of disrespect but is meant as an honor toward those who still have much to do this day. The event for which we are present must not be lessened by the shortness of my words."

Arlyn almost rolled her eyes. How much longer could it take to present her as his daughter? Her nerves were frayed enough by this alone. Then he took her hand and stepped forward, lifting it, and the sound of her pounding heart drowned out her thoughts.

"So I present to you now in the light of the Sacred Sun and by the Nine Gods of Arneen a daughter long lost to the House of Dianore, whose courage brought her to us just two days prior. My daughter, Callian Ayala i Arlyn Dianore se Kaienan nai Braelyn." He pulled a chain from a silver pouch at his waist and raised her hand higher. "As my child, and child of the House of Dianore, I offer her this necklace, hers to give or to hold."

At her father's words, a slice of pain darted from Kai to Arlyn. Worried, she looked over at him, but his expression was blank. *"What is it?"*

"Nothing." His voice was a bare whisper in her mind. *"Run a little of your energy through the pendant to seal it to you."*

Lyr squeezed her hand to get her attention, then draped the necklace around her neck. She wrapped her hand around the silver disk and did as Kai instructed, feeling a slight hum followed by a click. Then she remembered. Hers to give or hold. The second part of the bonding. Kai was probably worried about it. Before she could decide what to say to him, her father turned back to the crowd.

"As she returned to us, so she also found her soul's match in a friend of our House. Now, the first step of their bonding complete, I introduce to you Callian Myal i Kaienan Dianore se Arlyn nai Braelyn. Our House is blessed to have them both."

Everyone in that room had to be wondering about this turn of events, but Arlyn detected no sign of their curiosity. Instead, they tapped fists to chest and bowed, their words in almost perfect unison. "We of the House Dianore welcome you as our own."

Magic thrummed through her as they spoke, a sort of linking like the estate key her father had given her. A belonging. Arlyn gasped with it, but she had little time to process it. Their words were her cue. Her hand convulsed around the pendant as she took a small step forward. They looked at her—really looked *at her*—a hint of curiosity in the eyes of some.

Arlyn swallowed against the lump in her throat. God, she hoped she didn't mess this up. She took a deep, bracing breath as Lynia gave her an encouraging smile. "I thank you for your welcome. It honors me that you would leave home and hearth and tasks undone to receive me into the great House of Dianore. I cannot possibly express the pleasure it has brought me to find true family in this House, far from my former home. I could never have imagined such acceptance on my long journey here. As Heir to my father, Myern Lyrnis, I will do my utmost to serve with fairness, justice, and equality. Know that I wish to bring only honor and glory to us all."

"As do I," Kai spoke from behind her. "And I offer to Myern Lyrnis, my House, and my mate, the Heir, my long and faithful service as *Sonal*. May we all grow and prosper beneath the light of the Sacred Sun and the gods of Arneen."

Detecting Kai's growing weakness, Arlyn stepped back to let him latch onto her arm once more. He was going to collapse if they stood there much longer. She nudged Lyr mentally and was gratified by his quick response. *"Father, we need to end this. Kai needs to sit before he falls on his face."*

After a quick glance at Kai, Lyr gave a slight nod. "The House of Dianore acknowledges and returns your oaths of service with gratitude. And now, I fear that I have kept us too long from our tasks. I give thanks once more to all who shared in this joyous occasion. For those who wish, Merryl has been kind enough to prepare a midday feast for all to enjoy in the garden. We will join you there in a moment, and you may introduce yourselves informally to my daughter."

On a swell of murmurs and curious glances, the crowd dispersed. Arlyn turned to her father, her brow raised. *"After the length of your intro, I can't believe you ended that so quickly."*

"You called me father again."

"So I did." A smile trembled on her lips. *"We can discuss it later if you like, but we need to get Kai sitting. Otherwise, you'll have to help carry him in addition to all those clothes."*

Lyr laughed, drawing looks from those still around them. "To the garden, then."

Ralan had few preparations to complete since Mandy already handled much of the daily operations of his business. Officially, he was taking his daughter out of the country in search of a cure for a rare form of cancer. He had ensured she was diagnosed with something that had several experimental treatments in other countries in case of this exact scenario, so there would be little media speculation over his actions. And if she had to stay in Moranaia, it would be easy to pretend she had not recovered. If that were the case, he would simply disappear from the human world. He would never be able to pretend such a thing.

Ralan only hoped he could avoid his father for as long as possible. He did not want to be put in the position of having to disobey the king, but he refused to allow himself to be used again. The things he had Seen still haunted his dreams. Hopefully, his father had found another seer to guide his hand. Even 312 years after their argument, Ralan still wouldn't use his talent on purpose. He could not stop the random, spontaneous visions, but he refused to intentionally look into the lives of others. Not after Kenaren.

He would not think of Kenaren.

With an angry shove, Ralan closed the lid on the trunk he had just finished packing. There weren't many things he needed to carry across the Veil. For himself, only a few favorite robes and tunics he'd once brought from Moranaia. Despite the centuries he'd been gone, they shouldn't be too out of fashion. He hoped. The other items were for Eri. He'd packed a set of clothes he'd designed for her in the elven style, a picture of her mother, and a few of her toys.

His brow furrowed. How could Eri have so few attachments to the human world? She'd been born and raised here, but his daughter seemed to care as little for life on Earth as he did. She hadn't even asked about her mother. Thank the gods. *That* bitch would never get closer to *his* daughter than a picture in a frame. He had included it in case Eri ever asked what she'd looked like.

"Are you done now, *laial?*"

He spun around, surprised to find Eri standing behind him. She rarely had the energy to walk anymore, but today she looked better than she had in quite some time. Her color was good, and she did not waver on her feet. "What are you doing in here, beloved? You should be resting for the journey."

"I wanted to see you. 'Sides, I'm too excited to sleep. I can't wait to go home."

He frowned. "I never knew you considered Moranaia home."

"I knew we weren't going back yet, and it would have hurt you if I'd said so."

His heart ached at the serious, almost adult expression on her face. "Eri, are you sure you are well?"

"At the moment. I just had to tell you…" She brushed back a lock of her long, black hair and shifted on her feet. "You won't like it."

"Eri," he said, the tone of his voice enough to warn her of his impatience.

"Try not to be too hard on Lord Kai, even when he gets upset. He doesn't know what a good thing this is for him. He's only worried about Lady Arlyn, and he's afraid of causing more tension with Lord Lyr. He'll be a good ally, you know, even if you're going to have to do things you don't want to."

Ralan froze, his breath coming out in a rush. She had never met Kai or Lyr, and he could only guess who Arlyn was. "Where did you hear those names, Eri?"

She twisted her fingers together, a sure sign she was worried, and looked down at her feet. "I dreamed them."

He closed his eyes in defeat. He had prayed she would not inherit his talent as a seer. It had been that hope, he knew, that had kept him from testing her, and it had been easy to put off since it should have been a few more years before she displayed such talents. Ralan had not been able to bring himself to do it, had procrastinated. Gods. If his father found out, he would try to use her, too. She had to be protected at all costs.

"Please don't be angry. Don't hate me," she whispered.

"What?" His pushed aside his own concerns and pulled his daughter into his arms. "How could I ever hate you? I love you more than my life."

"I knew you weren't going to like it, but you look so upset."

He leaned her back so she could gaze into his eyes. "Not at you, Eri. I'm afraid for you. I didn't want you to get this curse from me. Tell me, are you able to look for yourself yet, or do you only see in dreams?"

"I could look, but I don't. Not unless the lady tells me to."

His heart seemed to stop, though his feet still carried him toward Eri's room. "The lady?"

"The goddess, silly." She giggled. "Great Lady Megelien tells me when it's okay to look and when it's bad."

He stopped in the doorway of her room and stared down at her for a moment. "The goddess Megelien has been talking to you? One of the nine of Arneen, though we are on Earth?"

"Yeah, but she isn't strong here. Just whispers, sometimes."

Ralan took a deep breath and tried not to let her see the fear her words caused. Not only had Eri displayed the talent of the seer, but she had been guided *by the Goddess of Time.* If Megelien had taken an interest in Eri at such a young age and across such a distance, it could only mean she was destined to be a Great Seer. He'd believed nothing could ever worry him more than her strange illness. But he had just been proved wrong.

15

Arlyn paused outside the door to the convening room, her gaze taking in the odd celebration. Where was the luncheon? There was no table of food, no real sign of the promised feast. To her left, a table just large enough for the family had been placed, but she had no idea where anyone else would eat. In fact, where had everyone gone? Had they all pleaded exhaustion as Lynia had? A few people milled around the small courtyard but hardly as many as she'd seen during the presentation.

Kai tugged on her arm. "Arlyn?"

"Huh?" She blinked, shaking her head. "Sorry. Where is everyone?"

"Wandering the gardens, most likely." He tugged again. "Come on. They'll bring the food once we are seated."

A chuckle escaped as she walked with him to the table. *Like he's really eager for food.* Kai wasn't fooling her, not with his exhaustion beating at her through their bond. Besides, they'd had a late breakfast. He probably wasn't any hungrier than she was. But she let him keep his pride as they made their slow way to their seats.

Arlyn settled between her father and Kai. She clenched her hands in her lap, hidden from view by the table. The dozen or so people standing in the courtyard rarely even glanced at her, but that didn't make this situation any easier. What was she going to say to these elves as they came to meet her? How in the world was she going to keep from causing unintentional offense?

A few people slipped around the table, leaving plates of meat and cheese in their wake. Arlyn wasn't sure how, but those who milled in the courtyard found plates, too. One moment, they were standing there. The next, eating. Her eyes narrowed on the group. Were they even the same elves?

Lyr leaned forward, looking around Arlyn at Kai. "Will you make it through?"

Though pale, Kai nodded. "As long as I must. Then I'll sleep. I have an assassin to catch."

"You?" Arlyn's eyes darted to the people around them, but none seemed to hear. "Don't you have some kind of police force? People who catch criminals?"

A slow smile lit Kai's eyes. "Worried about me?"

She found her own lips curving up. "I'd rather you not die before I can kill you."

"We do have quite a few *sonal* out looking," Lyr said, his hand closing over Arlyn's. She turned to meet his worried gaze. "Maybe Arlyn's right. With you so newly bonded, the risk is high."

Kai tensed. "This is personal. I'll not be used as a warning."

"Indeed not." Lyr released Arlyn's hand and picked up a piece of bread. "We'll talk before you rest. I want to hear exactly what was said. But not here."

One elf from the crowd finally dared to approach, cutting off any further discussion. A pale, blue dress shone against the woman's midnight skin, and her long, black hair streamed around her. She stopped in front of Arlyn and repeated the chest tap and bow of earlier. Her eyes, when they lifted, gleamed with good humor.

Had she seen this woman before? Arlyn smiled even as her mind scrambled for the memory. "Good day."

"May the light of the gods shine upon you, Ayala. It is good to truly meet you."

"Forgive me. This is blunt and rude, but..." Arlyn huffed out a breath. "Have we met?"

The woman laughed, waving a hand. "No offense is taken. We have not been introduced, but I was the first to see you, other than your father." Her grin grew broader. "I was the guard at his door the day you arrived."

Arlyn's eyes widened as she examined the woman again. This was the same person who'd stood so formally in leather armor? Difficult to believe. But if her hair were pulled back, maybe. Arlyn squinted. Yes, it *was* the guard. "It is a pleasure to meet you."

"I'm Kera." The guard leaned forward, her voice lowering. "I won't burden you with my full name, considering."

Arlyn's brow rose. "You know where I'm from?"

"There are things it is impossible to miss while guarding the Myern's door. But I am bound to keep the information to myself."

A shiver danced up Arlyn's back, and her fingers stilled around the cheese she'd been about to take from the tray. A strange sort of energy trembled through the air, a hum like a television with no signal. Her heart pounding, Arlyn shoved to her feet, searching the courtyard for the source. She saw nothing out of place. Nothing but confused looks as everyone stopped what they were doing to stare at her.

"What is it?" Lyr murmured.

She met his eyes. "Don't you feel it? I think someone's watching."

Kera shifted, her muscles tightening as her hands reached for the weapons she wasn't wearing, and Kai shot to his feet. He placed a hand on Arlyn's shoulder and pushed at her. "Get down."

She shoved his hand away. "Back off. I'm not a damsel in distress."

"You're not a warrior, either."

Her eyes pinned him. "You don't know what I am."

His face grayed as he studied her, but he shook his head. "True enough. But you're unarmed."

"Find me a bow."

For several heartbeats, Kai's world was as red as Arlyn's hair. But he didn't need anger. He needed calm. He ran his fingers down Arlyn's cheek, letting the peace of her presence soak through him. "You can shoot?"

"Obviously." She rolled her eyes even as she trembled at his touch. "Even better, I can find him. Or her."

Kai pulled his hand away as the rage returned, along with the memory of the man who'd smirked over his bleeding body. "Him."

Arlyn sucked her bottom lip in to nibble on it, her eyes narrowing on the western side of the gardens, and lust slammed into Kai to join the fury. The world swayed sickly for a moment as he pulled energy into himself, his instincts overriding sense. Kai would protect her. He would eliminate this threat even if he drained his reserves to the dregs.

"Kai!" Lyr snapped as power surged around them.

"Where?" Kai ground out. "And we'll end this."

"To the west, I think." Her hand slapped his chest as he started to move forward. "Stop. You're in no shape for this."

Lyr rose, his expression placid as he nodded to several of the guards. But Kai knew him. He could see Lyr's fury in the set of his shoulders and the cold look in his eyes. "A threat to our House has been detected. Search the gardens with everyone you can spare."

As Kai shifted Arlyn's hand aside and turned toward the house—and his weapons—pain seared through his side and sparks of light danced across his vision. He peered down, thinking he'd been hit again, but found no injury. Then Arlyn slipped under his arm, a fierce glare in her eyes. The energy he'd gathered began to drain away as his reserves lowered, and he fought not to slump against her.

"God, you're an idiot."

"I..." He clamped his mouth shut, his free hand grabbing for the back of his chair. Then he huffed out a breath. "I guess I am. Leave me here and guide the others."

"I can't."

"I'll be fine."

Her sigh was deep enough to ruffle his hair. "The energy signature faded while I was trying to stop you from killing yourself."

"Iron in the heart," Kai cursed.

The look Lyr turned on him froze him cold. "Next time, control yourself."

Shame trickled through Kai even as his eyes hardened. "All I could see was that smirk. I doubt you'd handle it better."

"Would I have a choice?"

Lyr turned, issuing commands as he strode to the doors of the convening room. Kai leaned on Arlyn as they followed, though his eyes kept straying to the garden. Beside him, Kera did the same. When she looked at him, all hint of her earlier humor was gone. "You've done it, now."

Kai blew out a breath. "Lyr and I have things to settle between us. And soon."

Kai let his head fall back against the chair where he slumped. Arlyn sat at the desk, pretending to read over the speech she'd prepared for her teacher, and Lyr paced the floor with angry steps. Kai knew better than to defend himself now when his friend's anger was at its highest. Not that there was much defense for his foolishness.

When Lyr finally paused, his face was still white with fury. But his hands were no longer clenched, at least. "What was that, Kai? You are better trained than to try to go off by yourself like that."

"I know." Kai rubbed his forehead, unable to meet his friend's eyes. "Through our bond, I kept getting flickers of what Arlyn sensed. It reminded me of the clearing. The pain. The helpless rage while he gloated. All mixed with the need to protect Arlyn."

His bonded looked up to glare at him. "I told you I didn't need protecting."

"It doesn't matter if you did or not." He held her gaze. "Every time I touch you, I just... I don't know if I can even describe it."

"If it makes you so heedless, perhaps I should appoint another *Taysonal*," Lyr muttered.

Kai sucked in a breath against the pain. "Do what you must."

"*Clechtan.*" Lyr's shoulders drooped as the last of his anger faded. "I didn't mean that. Perhaps I'm as reckless as you, for I wanted to chase the fiend myself."

"Do we need to have this out, Lyr?" Kai asked, his voice soft. "I should be well enough tomorrow."

Arlyn pushed back from the desk. "You are *not* going to duel over me."

Kai leaned forward. "I'll not throw away more than five hundred years of friendship. If Lyr needs to trounce me to feel better, I'll let him."

A tense silence settled on the room, Arlyn glaring at them both as they stared at one another. Then Lyr sighed and ran a hand through his hair. "I don't. But you have to take control of your reactions. And don't try to go after the assassin on your own. That's an order."

Kai nodded, and some of the tension eased from his muscles. Maybe, just maybe, their friendship would survive.

16

Her feet sounding out an anxious beat, Arlyn paced the entry hall a full half hour before her new mentor was expected to arrive. Kai had been asleep for a couple of hours. Her father was off consulting with the captain of the guard. And Arlyn was stuck waiting with nothing but her fractured thoughts.

They whirled around her brain like the mists of the Veil, leaving her just as lost. So many things to consider. So many decisions. She'd never experienced such a sense of belonging—of rightness—as she had during her presentation, despite her nerves. Her hands still shook with the joy of it. That and Kai's touch.

Oh, God, Kai's touch. Arlyn's eyes closed.

The memory of his fingers brushing her cheek shuddered through her, deeper than the bone and into her very essence. Beyond pleasure. More than the desire that heated her body at the sight of him. In the moments when Kai touched her, he was her blood and breath. Arlyn's heart jumped at the memory. But with fear? Or excitement? She couldn't tell.

And how could she feel that way when she was still so angry at him? Not *as* angry. Arlyn understood what had happened now. Intellectually, she accepted the accident of events that had led to his mistake. But her heart hadn't caught up. Part of her still wanted to pound against the bond. To rage at him for the trap.

The rest of her wanted to jump him.

Arlyn stopped by the huge tree on the other side of the entry, hoping its calm might steady her nerves. How had the elves formed the house around it without having leaks every time it rained? She looked up, but the floor above her was built closer to the trunk, blocking her view. Maybe it was magic.

"Her name is Eradisel, Sacred Tree of Dorenal, Goddess of the Veils. She is one of the Nine Trees of Arneen, each guarded by one of the first three dukes along each branch. Our family protects her."

Startled, Arlyn took a step back, the hand she'd been lifting dropping to her side. She bit her lip as she turned to meet her father's eyes. "She is beautiful. But I hope I'm not too close."

"Sacred is not the same thing as inaccessible, Arlyn." He smiled. "Unless you have something harmful on your hands—

and if you have good intent—you are more than welcome to touch. She might even speak to you."

"Speak?" Her eyebrow quirked. "Are you serious?"

With a laugh, Lyr walked over. "I'll introduce you. As my heir, you are next in line to guard her." He peered at her until she turned back to the tree. "Place your hand on the trunk as I do, then open your mind to mine."

Though she worried her lip again, Arlyn complied. Her hand hovered for a moment, then she let it settle against the cool bark. She jumped at the shock of magic, strong yet gentle, which pulsed through her like a heartbeat. Then her father placed his hand on the tree, and the energy surged, stealing her breath.

She sensed her father's presence at the edge of her mind, and she opened to it, comforted by the familiarity in the middle of the tumult. *"This is so weird."*

"Let it settle through you. Don't fight it. Here, observe."

With the patience of a true teacher, Lyr showed her how to connect. Arlyn watched with her inner eye, then fumbled to copy the way his energy stretched toward the tree. Sweat began to bead on her brow as she struggled. Almost as though she were battling herself, making her essence move away from her body.

"Not so much of yourself. More like a communication link."

Arlyn jerked back, her palm almost leaving the tree along with her energy. After a few gasping breaths, she closed her eyes and focused on her task. Her father made no comment, merely showing her again how the connection was formed. *Like a communication link.* She bit her lip and tried again.

Then the link snapped into place, and an additional presence joined them. Her hand trembled against the trunk. She would never mistake this mental essence for a person, human or elven. A timeless patience thrummed, a song so low and deep her whole world seemed to throb with it. Calm poured through her, easing her shaking muscles.

Lyr's voice broke through. *"Eradisel, I present to you my daughter and heir, Arlyn. She is next in line to ensure your safety."*

After a pause, Arlyn's mind filled with an odd sort of voice. She heard words, though she was certain there were none. *"You were not born in this place but crossed the Veil from another world."*

"I...yes." It seemed wise to be honest with a tree of the gods.

"You bear the blessing of Dorenal. You may pass through her Veil at will."

Arlyn frowned. *"I wandered for a long time."*

"You are untrained." A pause. A hint of amusement. *"You are a match for your soulbonded in this. He can show you."*

Her breath caught. *"You are saying I should keep him and the bond?"*

"There are many futures and many paths. Only you will know the proper way."

"Thank you," Arlyn answered, though her teeth ground together in frustration. Why had she expected an answer? Nothing was ever that easy.

"Arlyn, Blessed of Dorenal, I accept you as a guardian." There was another pause and a slight shifting sensation, but she still heard

the next words. *"Lyrnis. I like you. Do not leave just because you have someone to take your place. I would miss our talks."*

"As would I, Eradisel." His mental laugh resounded pleasantly along the connection. *"I have no intention of leaving."*

Arlyn felt a wash of amusement and acceptance before the tree's presence faded. Ending both connections, she forced her hand away. "Your talks? You are down here often?"

"No, not here. This place is used mostly by the priests who tend her health and those who come to honor her or the goddess. An altar is located on the other side."

He followed the circle of the wall as it curved around the tree, gesturing for her to follow, until they stood before the altar in question. "Offerings are generally left here, and sometimes I come for that. But to talk? Recall that our rooms are on the floor above. I have a balcony that opens over this chamber, close enough for me to touch her."

Lyr pointed up, and she noticed the walls stretched unbroken to a distant ceiling on the side of the tree where they stood. Well, her father's room explained why her view had been blocked on the other side. Arlyn glanced down at the low, stone altar, bare of everything but a handful of flowers and its own adornment. The whorls carved into the gray rock reminded her so strongly of the Veil that her stomach pitched.

"We'd better go," Lyr said, pulling her attention back to him. "Your teacher should be here any moment. If I'm not mistaken, she might even be a little late."

He frowned at the water clock when they'd made their way back around. Her teacher *was* late. Arlyn hid a smile as they stopped before the large, stone arch. At least she hadn't made the first mistake in etiquette. Her gaze slid back to the tree as water dripped the time behind her. "So do you worship the tree, too? Eradisel?"

Lyr shook his head. "More of a reverence. Or communion. Our worship is for Dorenal and the other eight gods of Arneen. It was because of the Nine that our ancestors settled in this place. According to legend, the first queen of Moranaia heard Their call from within the Veil."

His explanation was cut off by the light that flared from the portal, then settled to reveal an elven woman and a boy standing in a small stone chamber. Arlyn blinked at the plainness of the room; the woman was supposed to be from a noble house, so Arlyn had expected a place as elaborate as Braelyn. But they were dressed in elegant clothing, the elder in a long, delicately embroidered linen gown and the boy in a deep purple tunic and trousers, so maybe such rooms were normal.

Then the pair stepped through and the light flared once more, ending the view and Arlyn's contemplation. The light faded with one last glint against the other woman's honey blond hair, leaving the arch as empty as before. Arlyn twisted her fingers together against their shaking, the calm Eradisel had provided swept away by the cool, rose-gold face of her new teacher.

Lyr took one step forward. "May the great God Ayanel bless you as you enter our home."

Arlyn struggled to focus on their words as they exchanged pleasantries, then titles. She already knew her teacher's name, and the exchange of estate news and discussion of the weather were useless to her. She dug a fingernail into her palm, the twinge drawing her from her daze just in time to hear the last one.

Her teacher gestured to the boy. "And may I present my son, Taian ia'Kelore ai'Flerin ay'mornia Calel i Irenel Baran nai Fiorn."

Calel. What was that title? Arlyn was certain she had not studied that one, nor had she read about greeting children. Her heart dropped. She was supposed to go next. *"Arlyn. Don't worry about his title. In a situation like this, just be polite as you acknowledge him."*

Arlyn relaxed at her father's mental nudge. Forcing her lips into a slight smile, she began. "I welcome you both to our home. It is a great honor for the House of Dianore to host a teacher. If it pleases you—"

"Is this the new student?" the boy interrupted.

"Iren!" The blond elf turned as red as the embroidery on her white robe. "Please, forgive my son. Eleven years old and born to our ways, yet he has not your grace for polite greeting. I suspect we will have difficulty maintaining proper manners around him."

"Well, why should I have to stay so formal if we're going to have classes together? I don't have to talk to Morick like this."

Arlyn shoved down the grin that wanted to break free. "Together?"

"My father did not ask you about this?" If possible, the lady reddened further. "Iren has just begun his magical studies, and I thought I could teach you at the same time, at least until you surpass him. He is young and lacks discipline so that likely will not take long. If this is not acceptable, please say so. You were supposed to be asked before I was sent."

"I spoke to your father, but I do not recall such a question," Lyr replied. "However, the last couple of days have been hectic to say the least. I apologize if I missed that part."

"Oh, I doubt it was your error." Lady Selia winced. "My father has been trying to get me to return to teaching since Iren turned five. If you do not wish my son's presence here, I would prefer to know now. I understand that having a child under foot might cause difficulty."

"I cannot speak for Arlyn concerning your teaching sessions," Lyr began. "But Irenel is most certainly welcome here. It is always an honor to have a child in one's home."

The lady shook her head. "Let us hope you still feel that way in a month. He has his father's rather adventurous spirit."

Arlyn did smile then, for she could see the truth in her teacher's words. Iren fidgeted where he stood, and his gaze darted around the room as though deciding what to explore first. Despite that, his eyes held kindness. He seemed excitable but not mean. And though normally her ego would have objected to taking classes with a child, the arrangement might end up working rather well. With Iren present, she wouldn't have to worry as much about formality. Her introduction had certainly been easier than expected.

"I do not mind combining our lessons for a while." She grinned at the boy. "So long as Iren promises not to make fun of me. I know little about magic, after all."

"Why would I do that?" He rolled his eyes. "It's not like it's your fault you had to grow up with stupid humans. They can't even cast a simple fire spell."

"Iren!" Selia snapped again. "You will not speak to our host, and your elder, in such a way. Nor will you denigrate an entire race for their differences. The lady Arlyn has human blood herself, in case you have forgotten."

"I am sorry for my offense." Though his face sobered, it was belied by the twinkle in his eyes as he bowed before her. "It was not my intention to insult you, Ayala. Please accept my most humble apologies."

Arlyn's brows rose at the shift in his manners. It seemed he did know how to be polite. And as he smiled winsomely at her, his light brown hair falling around his handsome face, she could see he would soon be causing his mother a different kind of trouble. She did not envy her teacher that.

"I am not insulted. You see, I know humans aren't stupid. They may not be able to cast fire spells, but they have created ships to take them into space. People are circling Earth in a space station even as we speak."

"Seriously?" His eyes widened. "We can cross the Veil between worlds, but no one I know can actually live above a planet. Maybe I should visit this Earth someday."

"Yes, well, you may speak with Ayala Arlyn about her birth world at a later date." Despite the underlying frustration in her words, Selia looked at her son with love in her eyes. "Myern, the House of Baran would like to thank the House of Dianore for your hospitality. Please tell me at once if I, or my son, cause offense or become an imposition."

"I am certain you could never do such a thing," Lyr responded in a polite tone. "Now, as we wait for my people to finish gathering your belongings from the portal room, would you like to pay homage to Eradisel?"

"Of course." Lady Selia's eyes lit upon the great tree. "Our branch is not blessed enough to host one of the nine, but I have visited Terial, sacred tree of Petoren. It would be good to honor Dorenal, as we have just passed safely through one of her portals. If you will excuse us, we will return in a moment."

Lyr nodded, watching the two newcomers until they had passed around the broad tree toward the altar. Then he turned to wink at Arlyn. *"You did well. And I think we are lucky. Selia seems much less formal than the other Taians I have met."*

"She is nice," Arlyn answered. *"I like her son, too. Aren't elven children rare?"*

"Not quite rare, but not numerous either." He gazed toward the tree. *"I wonder what happened to his father."*

"Maybe they are no longer together?"

He shook his head. *"Unlikely. Even if they come to dislike each other, elven parents will usually stay together until the child is a few years past sexual maturity. Children are precious, and besides, what is a couple of decades when one lives thousands of years?"*

"I suppose." She shrugged, then grinned over at him. *"So are you interested in my teacher? She is quite lovely."*

"Indeed." The smile didn't reach his shadowed eyes. *"But no. Perhaps in a couple hundred years or so I can contemplate being with another. No other can compare to your mother."*

Though connected lightly during their communication, Arlyn could still perceive his sincerity through the bond, and the true tragedy of *his* loss struck her. Most humans started dating a few years after losing a mate. But *centuries?* That he would not even consider a casual relationship with someone like Selia took Arlyn aback. It was another example of how truly different he was from how she had so long thought of him.

Was the soulbond really that special? Could she consider being with someone other than Kai? If she had their bond severed, she would certainly be free to find another. So far, Arlyn had not seen an unattractive elf; in fact, she had encountered quite a few she'd found downright sexy earlier that day. But thinking back, she had not felt anything but friendly interest for any of them, nor had she ever been particularly concerned with human men. Like most women, she had dated on occasion, but unlike her acquaintances, not seriously. Was it because of this bond?

Had something in her always known?

"Have I upset you, Arlyn?"

"What?" She jerked her gaze back to his and realized she had let their conversation drop. *"Oh. No, your comment just got me to thinking. This soulbond thing is scary."*

"A little, yes. But it is worth it. Despite my pain now, I would undo none of the time I spent with your mother."

Selia and Iren came back into view, ending Arlyn's conversation with her father. Her teacher appeared more relaxed despite Iren's impish grin, and Arlyn wondered if the tree had spoken to them. Or was it simply a result of being near something sacred? The boy didn't look particularly awed, his expression more of happiness than mischief.

"You have returned in good time." Lyr gestured to the staircase on the opposite end of the entry hall. "I received word that your belongings are in your rooms. If you would please follow, we will show you there now."

"That would be lovely. Thank you."

They trailed behind Lyr as he climbed the stairs. Arlyn's knees wobbled a bit with each step, her nerves increasing the farther she went. Would they start right away? Could she even learn to use this magic? By the time Lyr stopped at the room across from hers, Arlyn had to force herself not to run.

Lyr opened the door for Lady Selia. "While I would not normally request you stay in our wing of the house, I have placed you across from my daughter in consideration of the possible instability of her magic. Iren, of course, will have the room between you and my mother. I hope it does not make you uncomfortable to stay so close to those with whom you are unfamiliar."

"I do not wish to intrude on your family's space," Selia answered with uncertain politeness.

"If it would be too much of an imposition, I would be happy to have your things moved to a guest tower."

Selia looked into the room, a line between her brows. Finally, she nodded. "We would be honored to stay here. You are correct about the need for proximity, at least at first."

Lyr inclined his head. "Then we will leave you to prepare for the evening meal. I will return right before sunset to escort you to the dining room."

Arlyn's stomach pitched at that. Another formal meal, and this one with guests? One more thing for her to possibly flub.

As her teacher lead Iren to his room, Arlyn prayed to whatever god here might listen. *Please don't let me fail at this. Or, you know, blow something up.*

After leaving her teacher to get settled, Arlyn slipped inside her room, only to freeze when the door clicked shut behind her. Kai stood in the center of the floor, his body moving in a complicated pattern that reminded her of tai chi. Shirtless. Light from the mage globes played across his muscles as he flowed through the moves. Her fingers twitched to follow the glow. Heat flashed through her as her mouth went dry.

Then her gaze landed on the angry-looking scar on his side. "What the hell are you doing?"

Kai glanced up but didn't pause as his body shifted to a new position. "Working out the stiffness."

She gaped at him. "You were practically dead yesterday. And you think it's a good idea to work out?"

"Lial did another session. I have some residual weakness, but nothing major."

Even she couldn't tell if the sound she made was a choke or a laugh. "Nothing major."

"You know," he began, dropping into a low lunge, "if not for the iron, I would have walked away from that wound. Lial is an excellent healer. Stop worrying."

How could he say that? She'd knelt in a pool of his blood less than two days ago after he'd linked their *souls*. And he told her *not to worry?* Eyes narrowing, Arlyn strode forward. Something in her expression must have finally caught his attention, for he straightened, his hands coming up as though in defense.

"Why are you so angry?"

Wrong. Question. Arlyn poked a finger into his chest and glared. "Over and over I've heard about the dangers of our new bond. That you could drag me with you if you die. And here you are, risking yourself for *fucking exercise.*"

His forehead wrinkled in confusion even as a glint of anger sparked in his eyes. "I'm not risking anything. I'm fine."

"I had to hold you up just a few hours ago. You almost passed out."

"I only needed another healing session." Kai's hand wrapped around her finger. "I'm not ready to go into battle, but I can do this well enough."

Arlyn jerked her hand free and pushed at his side. She tried to ignore the rock-hard muscle beneath her fingers as she watched for his wince, but he only stared steadily into her eyes. No sign of pain or discomfort. Her breath shuddered out. "That doesn't hurt?"

His lips curved up. "I told you it didn't."

The burn of embarrassment started on her face and worked like wildfire across her skin. What the hell was wrong with her? "I'm sorry."

Kai cupped her face with both hands. "What's really the matter?"

"I don't know." Her heart tripped at the tenderness of his touch. "This day. So much pressure. And whatever this is between us."

"It's my fault."

"Yes. And no." Arlyn gripped the pendant he'd given her. Though it tangled with the one she'd received from her father, she didn't have to look to know which she'd grabbed. "Maybe I didn't guess our souls would be bound, but I knew something existed between us even then. And I took the necklace anyway."

"Thank you for telling me." His hands slid down to her shoulders. "You were right earlier. That I don't really know you. But I'd like to."

"You can start by not treating me like a helpless girl."

"Girl?" Kai raised an eyebrow. "You are most definitely a woman."

"What about earlier, when I sensed the assassin?"

"You think that was because of your sex?" His grip tightened. "It's because you were unarmed and untrained, at least as far as I know. Warriors protect, Arlyn. You can't ask me not to do that."

She bit at her bottom lip, and his gaze snapped down to her mouth. His fingers tightened on her shoulders. Arlyn waved a hand in front of his face, drawing his attention back to her eyes. "What?"

"Gods, it makes me crazy when you do that."

Kai's hands glided up her neck and cradled her face once more. Trembling, Arlyn let him. "Kiss me. Just once. I need to know."

He didn't ask what she meant. Her eyes closed as his mouth brushed against hers. Soft, almost tentative. Then Kai pulled her against him, her body molding to his, and the tenderness was gone. Arlyn gripped his hair, straining closer to the heat exploding between them. As their mouths tangled, as the fire built, her soul sang with it.

His hands fisted in her tunic, shifting her even closer. She gasped against his mouth as their hearts pounded in a single, frenzied beat. Her hands slid down Kai's back, and his muscles tensed against her touch. His groan rumbled against her own chest. Just a few touches, and they were both on fire. Her hazy brain tried to remember how far they were from the bed.

Kai ripped his mouth free and rested his forehead against hers. "I should go."

Blinking, she pushed back to meet his eyes. "Huh?"

"If you don't want to end up in bed, I need to go," he answered, his voice rough. "Now."

"Oh."

Arlyn was tempted. *So* tempted. Her body burned with need. And if just touching him, kissing him, affected her like this, what would happen if they went further? A shiver tripped through her. For a moment, her fingers tightened against him.

· **202** ·

Then she forced herself to release him. To step back. She had to think.

"Where will you go?"

He rubbed the back of his neck, not quite meeting her eyes. "One of the guest towers."

"I'm supposed to be watching you."

"Another night of sleep is all I need." His lips twisted up, though the smile held little humor. "After what just happened, I might have to get Lial to put me under if I hope to rest."

Arlyn grimaced. "I shouldn't have asked."

"You can ask me for anything." Kai looked up, his gaze burning. "Anything. You deserve far more than a single kiss."

She almost reached for him as he strode to the door, but the knot of fear in her chest held her back. A soulbond was momentous. *Forever.* Not something to be decided out of lust. Arlyn made herself stand tall until the door closed behind him. Then she sank into the chair behind the desk and dropped her head into her hands.

Arlyn had already lifted her hand three times but still hadn't found the nerve to knock. They'd finished dinner an hour before, and Lady Selia had been nothing but pleasant, telling them stories of her life and training. But, damn, the woman had been a teacher for nearly five hundred years, and that after another half a millennium mastering her skills. Almost a thousand years old—and she was worried enough about Arlyn's power to stay in the room across the hall.

The door opened before she could gather her courage. With a wince, Arlyn dropped her hand, but Selia only gave a gentle smile. "Please, do come in. There is no need to stand there fretting. I will do my best to ensure nothing bad happens to you or your home while you are learning to control your powers."

Arlyn frowned. "How did you know?"

"Your shielding falters when you experience strong emotion. That is one of the first things we will work on."

Arlyn followed her teacher into the room and shut the door. Iren sat in a chair next to the window, his feet kicking restlessly, as Selia led her to the other two chairs surrounding a small table. Arlyn forced herself to sit, though she was as antsy as Iren. "Are you sure you want your son here? If I am dangerous, it might be best for him to be elsewhere."

"May I call you Arlyn?" At her nod, Selia continued. "As you may call me Selia." She leaned forward. "Anyway, Arlyn, I hope I have not frightened you with my quick arrival. Your situation is serious but not so dire that we should fear for our lives."

Arlyn gripped the arm of her chair. "Everyone seems so concerned."

"If you pulled in that much energy, then lost control, you could level much of the estate." Without even looking, Selia tapped a hand on her son's legs until he stilled. "As could Iren, here. It isn't a matter of power. The problem is knowing how to keep it contained."

Arlyn swallowed against the knot in her throat. *Level the estate?* "I don't feel especially powerful."

Selia smiled again. "I doubt you pull in as much as you could. Or maybe you do not even notice anymore. Mages start learning early as a matter of necessity. Perhaps you formed your own methods before you were old enough to understand."

Arlyn thought back to her childhood. The way the world had always seemed to glow with power. "Maybe."

"In any case, it is not sheer power that most concerns me about you. It is the ease with which you have used it. That in your fear for your bonded you could do a type of magic you likely did not even think possible? *Quite* remarkable."

"Not to mention painful."

"Doubtless," Selia agreed. "In the normal course of things, you would have been taught how to use your magic in stages. But what you did blasted everything open at once. The healer must have done a remarkable job, as did your father in shielding you, or there would likely be strange happenings around you."

Arlyn's heart skipped a beat. "I have no idea what they did."

"I suppose the first thing I should do is test you to see what types of magical channels you have, how well they have healed, and how much power you possess." She turned to frown at her son. "Iren, stop squirming. If you want something to do, then observe how I test Arlyn. But do not do anything yourself."

The boy perked up at his mother's suggestion, but Arlyn stiffened. It didn't sound like a pleasant process. "What do I do?"

"Just relax. Your father dropped the shielding he had on you, but I still need to worry about your normal defenses. The calmer you are, the better." Selia studied her a moment. "Though if you have learned to communicate telepathically, then try this—when you sense my presence, allow me in as though we were going to speak."

Arlyn took several deep breaths and let her hands fall lax into her lap. Her stomach still churned, but she closed her eyes. After a moment, her teacher's energies brushed against her own, and Arlyn let Selia through. When Selia's thoughts touched hers briefly in reassurance, no actual connection happened between their minds. Only a strange sort of buzzing in her head, almost like a tickle.

Shivering, Arlyn dug her fingers into her leg to keep from pushing back against the maddening sensation. But before she started squirming in her seat like Iren, the odd humming stopped, and her teacher's presence receded. She opened her eyes to find Selia and Iren staring at her. "What? That bad?"

"Not bad, precisely." Selia shook her head. "Your channels are well healed from the teleportation incident, and you are only a little above average in power. But I noticed several odd things about your energy patterns and the types of talents you possess. Most of them are remarkably similar to mine and Iren's, so much so that I wonder how closely you might be related. But I did not recognize a couple of those talents. And I can identify every type of magic on every branch, even if I can't use it myself."

Arlyn gripped her hands together. "So you can't teach me."

"I did not say that. But until I can figure out what those talents are, we will need to use greater caution." Selia gave her son a frustrated look as he started bouncing in his seat. "What is the matter?"

"Does she have space magic? Can we circle the planet?"

Arlyn laughed at the blank look on her teacher's face. "Humans don't use magic for that, just technology. In fact, most humans think magic is a myth."

"Most?" Selia's eyes narrowed.

"A few religions believe in it still, but it is different than true magic. There is rarely an effect you can see, like fire, or lightning, or teleportation." Arlyn frowned, struggling to put her thoughts into words. "A lot of modern paganism revolves around using your will to make changes in the world around you, but it is subtle. Like putting all of your energy toward a goal until it becomes reality. Sometimes it is as much about altering the flow of what already exists than in creating something new."

"Perhaps that is it," Selia whispered, and a sudden grin split her face. "How interesting. I was not aware such a thing as human magic existed. Do you have any of these pagans in your human ancestry?"

Arlyn laughed. "Much of it is religious, not genetic, though I suppose the talent for the magical part might run in the family."

"Genetic?" Iren asked, brow furrowed.

"Part of your bloodline," Arlyn answered. "Anyway, I'm not sure. My mother was psychic, sort of like a seer, but that's all I've ever heard."

"Well, I suppose we will find out as we work. What you were saying about using your will—that sounds similar to what happened when you teleported. While elves certainly use their will to do magic, we almost always need to know what the result should be. But you wished yourself and the others to safety without knowing how, and your magic found what was needed to make that happen. Accomplishing the goal without knowing the path? Now *that* is fascinating."

Lyr relaxed his fingers where they clenched on the pen and scrawled out his command. By Emora, if Lady Alarele couldn't find a way to make House Nari behave, he was going to have to go down there himself. Holding a summer solstice festival a handbreadth from the border they shared with House Amar after pointedly not inviting them? He dropped the pen to rub a tired hand across his eyes. At least the feud was petty.

Petty but annoying.

When the door opened, Lyr sagged against his chair in relief. He would welcome almost any distraction not involving bloodshed. But the solemn look in his mother's eyes as she approached, a heavy book clasped against her chest, had him questioning that thought almost at once. He shot a glance at the window and the moons riding high. She must have been deep into research to work so late.

"Good, you are still here," she said as she hurried up to his desk. "Well, not *good*. I hope you aren't working too hard."

Lyr smiled up at his mother. "I'm a little behind. But I am rested enough."

Her return smile was strained as she set the book on his desk and opened it to the page she'd marked. "Rest may soon be in short supply. I finally found something."

"Wonderful," he answered, his voice dry.

"I couldn't locate any records of the underhill experiencing this type of energy poisoning before." Lynia ran her finger along a line of text. "But in this report, there is mention of a spell devised by a mage student that caused the same effect. Not on Earth. On Moranaia, about seven thousand years ago."

Lyr turned the book, reading the report for himself. Then his curse broke through the silence. "The source is here. Or *from* here. But why?"

"A good question."

His fingers tapped on the surface of his desk as he considered the problem. "Could you do a bit more research for me?"

Lynia smiled. "Of course."

"Search through the records of those who have traveled to Earth or been exiled there and narrow down those with the ability to do such a spell."

"The exiles should be easy, but mere visitors are much more numerous." She settled a finger over her lips as she considered the problem. "It might take a day or two."

"The Sidhe have waited this long. That is more than soon enough."

With another smile, his mother leaned over to kiss him on the cheek. "Get some rest. I'll not see you as drained as Kai."

"I'm nowhere near that far gone." Lyr grinned. "But a good reminder, nonetheless. One more report, then I'll go to bed. I promise."

"See that you do."

His smile lingered after she was gone, even when faced with another petty dispute. If House Anar planted their crops over the border one more time... Lyr ran a hand through his hair, then lifted his pen. Energy poisoning or no, his work wouldn't wait. His people deserved no less.

Even when they were acting like iron-cursed idiots.

Arlyn flipped onto her stomach, her arm stretched across the mattress. Her body was heavy with exhaustion, but her mind refused to still. How many hours had she tossed and turned since leaving Selia? Did she even want to know? Her sigh warmed the pillow beneath her cheek. One pleasant spot in an otherwise cold bed.

Dammit, it wasn't the same without Kai.

She ran her hand along the empty space where he'd lain. For God's sake, he'd been unconscious when she slipped into bed the night before. It wasn't as if they'd really slept together. But just his presence had been a silent comfort, a balm she hadn't realized she needed. Not even the thought of visiting the sacred tree again filled the hole of his absence.

Arlyn pounded a fist against his pillow, then pushed herself to sitting. With a groan, she dropped her head to her knees. She didn't even know him. Did she? They *had* spent much of the day together as he'd helped her get ready for the presentation and her teacher's arrival. She knew the curve his lips made when he teased her. The gleam in his eyes as he'd offered bad suggestions for her speech to make her laugh.

His mouth moving over hers.

Groaning again, Arlyn flopped back onto the bed. It was going to be a long, long night.

18

Arlyn glared at the cup of tea in her hand and wished it was coffee. Too bad she couldn't transmute it as easily as she'd transported them back to the estate. But *no*. No matter how hard she stared, the herbal tea gleamed back at her, unchanged in the morning light. What use was magic if she couldn't will herself some caffeine?

Her father entered, then drew up short a few paces from his seat. His brow rose. "What are you doing?"

"Trying to make coffee."

She was certain the sound he smothered was a laugh. Her glare turned on him, and he lifted his hands in surrender. "Sorry. According to Lady Selia's report, you don't have the ability to transmute. Good thing. I'd rather not be turned into coffee, myself."

His wry comment had drawn a chuckle before she processed the rest of his words. "She is giving you reports on me?"

"Relax," Lyr answered as he took his seat. "I receive progress reports on all apprentices. Though I admit yours made it to the top of the pile."

She couldn't help squirming. "Did I make an A?"

He paused to look it her, syrup plopping from the fruit he'd just dipped into the bowl. "What?"

"High marks. Good grades." Arlyn huffed at his blank look. "Was it a good report?"

"Ah, I think I see." His eyes cleared of confusion as he lifted the fruit and took a bite. She tried not to squirm again at the wait as he chewed. "Learning requires both success and failure. It isn't a matter of grading. You'll apprentice until you've mastered what you need to know."

"But what did she say?"

Lyr smiled at the fingers she tapped on the table. Arlyn jerked her hands into her lap as he met her gaze. "Lady Selia detailed what she found when she tested you. That is all."

Arlyn glared down at her tea again. "She didn't even tell *me* that."

"I doubt she will until she finishes shielding the workroom I've provided for your practice. The less you know, the less you can accidentally manifest."

"Not fair."

"If you'd believed you could really turn that into coffee, would you have put more energy into it? Even untrained?"

Her breath made ripples in the tea. "As tired as I am? Probably."

"Tired?" Lyr frowned. "Have you not restored your reserves? You shouldn't have used much yesterday. We don't really *need* to sleep otherwise."

"Maybe it's the human in me."

Before he could answer, Kai strode in, looking so rested she had to grip her hands together to keep from smacking him as he leaned over her chair. It seemed *he* hadn't lost any sleep over her absence. Then he placed another cup in front of her before dropping into the seat beside her. She frowned down at it a moment before meeting his amused gaze.

"What's this?"

"Something to perk you up." His lips twisted into a smile. "I could sense how much you needed it."

Arlyn lifted the cup and sniffed. The blend reminded her of black tea and peppermint. She took a long drink and savored the warmth as it slid down her throat. Only after half of it was gone did she look up at him again. "You seem to have passed the night well enough."

"After Lial got angry enough to force me under." The humor dropped from Kai's face. "I'm sorry you didn't sleep well."

With a shrug, Arlyn looked away. "I'll live."

"Do you think you are up for some training?"

Her gaze shot back to Kai. "Training for what?"

"I want to see what you can do." He smirked. "Then maybe you won't have to worry about me treating you like a damsel in distress."

"Maybe?"

He mirrored her shrug, but a teasing gleam had entered his eyes. "I suppose it depends on what you can do."

Lyr cleared his throat, and Arlyn blushed. She'd forgotten he was even there. She pulled her gaze from Kai's to focus on her father. Though he lifted a brow, he didn't comment on the exchange. "That's a good idea," Lyr said. "I can't get away this morning, or I'd come, too. Sword and bow, I'm thinking."

Arlyn finished off the last of her tea, then stood. "Fine. I'll get my things."

Arlyn stopped short at the sight of Iren sitting on the low stone wall separating the practice field from the gardens. He gave a cheerful wave, then returned to watching a couple of her father's soldiers practicing with their swords. The smile she'd given the boy dropped when she followed his gaze. These soldiers moved with a speed, grace, and skill that had nerves dancing through her gut. Human fighters looked like children playing with wooden sticks in comparison.

Swallowing hard, she glanced at Kai. "Maybe I won't practice."

"Why are you so nervous?"

"Let's just say I'm glad I never tried to use my blade. I would've been dead in seconds."

He pulled her toward a small stone building at the edge of the field. "Well, come on. The sooner I test you, the sooner I'll know how much you need to learn."

"Kai, stop." She jerked her arm out of his grasp. "I really hate being laughed at. Maybe we should come back when the field is empty."

"This from the woman who demanded a bow so she could charge after an assassin?" He frowned back at her. "Seriously, Arlyn, I don't think anyone is going to laugh at you. Most elves, especially here, where there are a few of us who have been to Earth recently, wouldn't expect a human to know what to do with a sword at all. They'll be impressed if you can even hold it properly."

"That's a condescending way to try to comfort me," she said with a huff, though she did give up and follow him.

Kai shrugged. "It wasn't intended to be. You must admit sword work is hardly common in the human world these days."

Remembering the scorn she had often gotten for her strange hobbies, she could not disagree. "Fine. I'll show you what I know. But don't say I didn't warn you."

Kai led her into the small building and turned toward the right side. The place was filled with shelves, each stacked full of weapons and armor, a surprising array considering how few soldiers she had seen so far. "Who uses all of this?"

Brows lifting, he glanced at her. "Lyr's warriors, of course. You have the key to this estate and should be able to find out how many there are and where they're located."

She paused, concentrating on her inner map for a moment, and gasped at what she found. They were everywhere—some in the barracks, a few in towers scattered around the estate, others perched in trees along the gardens—and she had not noticed any of them. "Why are there so many?"

"Your father is three down from the king on this branch, Arlyn, and he also guards one of the nine sacred trees. Even when we're at peace, this place is heavily protected." He stopped before a wall stacked with swords and gestured. "Now, pick one you'll be comfortable using. There are several sizes and weights here."

Arlyn sorted through quite a few before finding one similar in size to her own. She held her choice up to the light and examined it carefully, amazed by the workmanship. It was a magnificent blade, well-weighted and beautifully engraved along the hilt with trailing vines. Her brows raised. "This is a practice sword?"

"Yes. If you learn with something poorly made, you'll hardly be prepared to use something finer." He shrugged. "Besides, it isn't perfect. It's rather plain and likely forged with a lower-quality *peresten* ore. Our artisans would never call something like that battle-worthy."

"And people used to call *me* a perfectionist," she muttered. "Well, let's go. Might as well get this over with."

She trudged behind him until he found a spot he liked. "Stand there. I'll sit over here by Iren."

Kai leaned against the wall next to the boy, who turned his attention to them with a grin. This time, Arlyn was too nervous to return the smile as she took her place a few feet away. Though her bow was well secured to her back, she shifted it, then turned the blade around in her hand. After another glimpse at the hilt, she stiffened her spine. No more stalling.

Kai studied her, his arms folded across his chest and his eyes dancing with humor. "First, I want to know what basic forms you know."

"Forms?"

"Sword positions. Offensive first."

Trying to ignore the warriors who had stopped their own practice to stare, Arlyn went through the basic moves she had been taught. As soon as she finished, she sensed what Kai was going to ask next and shifted directly into defensive positions. Her muscles shook with the weight of the onlookers' gazes. She'd often performed at Renaissance festivals, where most of the audience found her strange but amusing, but this was in no way the same. Her palms were sweating so much the hilt grew slick in her hand.

But she managed to get through all the stances. Arlyn lowered her sword and stood, panting, while she waited to hear what Kai would say.

"Your form is not bad. I don't know why you were so worried." He stood and started walking back toward the armory. "Stay there. I'll be right back."

As she had feared, he returned in a moment carrying another sword. "I don't think this is a good idea."

"I'm doing fine today, Arlyn. I'm almost completely recovered." He stopped in front of her and fell into an attack position. "I want to go through the moves with you slowly. If I start to feel strain, I'll stop."

Though she shook her head, Arlyn got ready to counter; she could tell there was no use arguing with him. They moved through the combat positions slowly, and when she made it through once without any major mistakes, she grew more confident. Kai picked up the pace until they were sparring at the same sort of speed she would have used in a tournament on Earth. Then he went beyond what she was used to. She scrambled to keep up, and she began to lose her form. When she failed to bring her sword up in time, forcing Kai to pull the blow, he stopped them.

"That's enough for now. Let's sit."

She scowled over at Kai, wondering why *he* needed a rest. It was difficult for her to comprehend that the same elf who had been mortally wounded a couple of days ago now looked no more strained after their battle than he had before they had begun. And she was ready to drop. She plopped down beside Iren, every muscle in her body aching. It had been entirely too long since she'd trained.

After taking a few moments to regain her breath, Arlyn turned to the boy. "What are you doing out here, Iren? Especially this early?"

"Oh, it's not that early," he answered with glee. "I wanted to come see the warriors practicing. We don't have that many at home."

"You don't have people guarding your estate?"

Iren shrugged. "Some, but it's mostly protected by magic. I thought there would be a lot of people fighting, but before you got here, there were only those two."

She glanced at the soldiers he mentioned and was glad to see they had resumed their own practice. "Why aren't there more people out here?"

"It is just now the breakfast hour," Kai responded. "More will come later."

Unable to avoid the issue any longer, she turned to him. "So how bad was I?"

"Not too bad. You have the basics down, at least." He grinned at her. "I will have to show you more forms, though, and work on your speed. And there are many different ways to fight. Most combat situations won't follow those forms so cleanly, for one. But you'll be easy to teach. Especially if you have any of Lyr's gift."

"Great," she muttered. Arlyn had been considered quite good in the human world. But as she regarded the elven warriors practicing on the other side of the field, she had to concede she'd be lucky to be considered even a beginner. "I'm not sure I'll ever be that good."

"Of course, you will. When you've been training for a few hundred years, like those two." He turned to wink at Iren. "So how would you like to see archery practice? We're about to go there next."

The boy practically vibrated with excitement. "Sure! Will you show me how to shoot?"

"I can try." With a smile, he gestured to the stone building. "Go pick out a bow, a fairly small one, and meet us by the targets. They're on the far side of the field."

Arlyn followed Kai to the other end of the practice grounds and over another low stone wall. The targets were set back against the trees and opposite the field they had just left, undoubtedly to prevent injuries from stray arrows. Though they could still hear the clang of swords behind them, the surrounding trees blocked them from view, making the place fairly private. As she unstrapped the bow from her back and began to string it, Arlyn looked around and relaxed to find no one nearby. At least if she made a fool of herself, only Kai and Iren would see. Well, them and the few guards likely stationed in the surrounding trees.

Arlyn turned to the targets, but before she could draw an arrow, a strange current of energy washed over her. Similar to yesterday. Her gaze darted to the tree line, just in time to see the arrow fly. Straight toward Kai where he stood behind her. Without thought, she threw herself in front of him, pushing him back even as the pain exploded in her arm. Crying out, she fell back against Kai, so stunned by the searing agony she barely heard her bonded's shout.

Dazed, Arlyn could only stare as another arrow arced through the air toward them. She needed to do something. *Had* to do something. But her limbs wouldn't cooperate, tangling woodenly with Kai's as she tried to move. Helpless, she stared as though mesmerized as the arrow neared. Then, almost before her frazzled mind could process the scene, the wooden shaft burst into flames, burning with such quick intensity that the few remaining pieces plummeted awkwardly to the ground.

And was that a fireball flying toward the tree where the archer perched? Her sluggish mind struggled to comprehend what she was seeing. The man in the tree had just lifted his bow, ready for another strike, when the flames reached him. Either unprepared or unshielded, it hit him directly, and his startled scream filled the clearing to mingle with Arlyn's moans. As the flaming body toppled from the tree and several warriors ran from the other field, the pain became too much, and her world faded to black.

For a few precious moments, Kai was as helpless as Arlyn. Pain seared through him so strongly that the second arrow had burst into flame before he even realized the agony might not be his own. He checked his arm and found nothing there. If he was not wounded, then what had happened? His scattered mind focused on Arlyn's weight on top of him.

She tossed against him, her limbs tangling with his as she tried to get up. His breath rushed out as her pain surged along the bond and her body went limp. Kai barely noticed the fireball that shot over them or the shriek filling the air. Steadying his thoughts, he shifted Arlyn to the side and sat up. On the other side of the field, a figure struggled to its feet and raced into the forest without even trying to put out the flames engulfing it.

The two warriors from the practice field burst into the clearing, hardly sparing a glance for Kai as they darted after the assassin. He didn't care what they did with the *drec*. His eyes focused on the blood flowing freely from a deep gash on Arlyn's left upper arm. Her face was gray, her eyes closed. His heart tripped in his chest. Unless the point had been poisoned, she should not have been so easily incapacitated by so minor a wound.

He glanced up at the sound of ripping fabric. A pale Iren jerked a long strip of cloth from the bottom of his own tunic and held it out. Nodding his thanks, Kai tied the cloth around Arlyn's arm to stop the blood. Even unconscious, she cried out as he tightened the bandage, and her body started to convulse. She must have been poisoned; no simple gash from an arrow would cause that kind of reaction.

The pain coursing through the bond shattered his concentration. What was he supposed to do? As he struggled to keep his own muscles from convulsing, he tugged at the knots he had made to bind the cloth. Though they were looser, his trembling fingers and the blood saturating the fabric made the task seem impossible. Why couldn't he untangle a few simple knots?

As he turned to ask Iren for help, Lial burst into the clearing. The healer took in the scene without pausing, moving to crouch beside Kai. "What happened? I felt the pain through the link I've been using to monitor your injury and believed it was you."

"An arrow. Just a gash, but she collapsed almost immediately. I tried to bandage the wound, but that only made it worse."

"Calm down, Kai. Separate *her* pain from *your* body, or you will just send it back to her."

"Is that why she's writhing like that?"

"Doubtful." Lial untangled the cloth from around Arlyn's arm. The wound glowed blue with the healer's energy for only a heartbeat before Lial jerked back. "*Miaran.*"

"What is it?" Kai plopped down beside them, his face pale, and struggled to shield himself from her pain until his disorientation started to fade. "I've never known you to curse over a patient. Is it that bad?"

Lial wrapped the bandage loosely around her arm before turning his focus on Kai. "I meant that literally. Iron."

"But—"

"No time to argue. There is iron in that wound, and I cannot heal it until all traces are physically removed. If you can carry her, do so. If not, I will."

Without hesitation, Kai shot to his feet and lifted her into his arms. "Let's go."

Iren ran beside them as Kai and the healer rushed back toward the estate. "Myal Kaienan, when you send someone out, have them look for more iron. Even though I incinerated the wooden shaft on the other arrow, I don't think I hurt the arrowhead. And I bet he dropped more like them."

"Call me Kai."

"*Laiala* would kill me."

"Irenel, you have saved the life of both myself and my soulbonded. You have certainly earned the right to address me familiarly."

The boy jogged silently beside them, considering the etiquette of the situation. "Even she will have difficulty arguing that, I suppose."

Kai took the first door he came to, entering into the hallway connecting the barracks to the Great Tower. Even though the entrance to the barracks was slightly closer, he carried her to the empty bottom floor of the tower, where war councils and other important meetings were held. In the time it took Iren to push a few of the chairs aside and Kai to stretch her out on the edge of the huge, round table, her convulsions had gotten markedly worse, and her low, keening moan filled the room.

As Kai shifted out of the way, Lial's assistant rushed in behind them, a kit of delicate, *peresten* tools in his hands. The healer grabbed a pair of tweezers from the bag before the other had it fully opened and turned to unwrap the bandage from around Arlyn's arm. Kai's heart lurched to see the pool of blood that had already started forming beneath her. As Lial began to place the small fragments of iron he removed onto the piece of silk his assistant held out, the pool only spread.

Kai forced the connection without hesitation. *"Lyr, come to the council room. Now."*

"What? Why?"

"There has been another attack. Arlyn was injured, and the healer is working on her."

"*Attack? In the council room?*" Confusion was replaced by panic as soon as Lyr processed the rest of Kai's words. "*Arlyn? How bad?*"

"*I don't know. I dare not interrupt the healer to ask. But she took a cut to the arm with an iron-tipped arrow. He's pulling out pieces now.*"

"*Pieces? I'll be right there.*"

The healer was frowning over Arlyn's wound when Kai focused on them once more. His hands shook to see how pale and still she was, her body no longer thrashing. Worse, her soul shuddered with shock and confusion. Though unconscious, part of her was trying to process what had happened, but the amount of blood she had lost made it difficult. Did the healer know she was contemplating retreating from the chaos of her body? Kai leapt up on the table and moved to her other side to hold her right hand. And struggled to keep her soul near while Lial finished his work.

As he took in the scene, Lyr stumbled to a halt, stunned by the blood pooling beneath his daughter and dripping from the edge of the table. Lial's assistant was folding a red-stained piece of silk around several fragments of iron, but Lyr barely noticed the poisonous metal as his stomach lurched. Shoving down the nausea, he rushed past a startled Iren to stand by the edge of the table. When the healer frowned at his position, Lyr jumped up to sit beside Kai.

They stared in silent apprehension as Lial stitched the wound. Throughout the process, Arlyn was still, giving no indication she felt the bite of the needle in her arm. Finally, the healer tied off the thread, passed his tools back to his assistant, and held his hands over the wound. The blue glow of healing energy flowed over her arm, then across the rest of her body. When Lial straightened and the energy faded a few moments later, some color had returned to her face. Beside him, Kai slumped in relief.

Lial stumbled over to one of the chairs and dropped into it, his face lined with exhaustion. "I can do little for the wound itself. Because of the iron, it will mostly have to heal on its own. But I was able to place spells over her body to aid her in recovering from the blood loss. She is quite sensitive to iron, though not as bad as you, Lyr. I can't imagine how she survived in the human world."

"Her powers hadn't fully awakened. The magical effects will be much worse now that they have," Selia announced from the doorway. At their startled looks, she smiled. "Iren called for me."

The boy ran to his mother, his bravery crumpling in her presence. She looked down at him in surprise when he wrapped his arms tightly around her waist. "Iren? What is it?"

"I take it he did not tell you what happened," Kai said.

"He said Arlyn was injured." Selia frowned down at her son. "He has seen injuries before without reacting like this."

Without delay, Kai and Iren pieced together the morning's events. Lyr's muscles tightened with each word until he feared he'd break from it. He looked down at his daughter's pale face and shuddered. Why hadn't she been protected? Where were her guards? The eyes he lifted were so full of fury that Iren jumped. Lyr shoved his temper back with great effort.

"So you see, your son saved us both. That second arrow likely would have killed me."

Lyr unclenched his fists and forced his lips into a smile. "You have the eternal gratitude of House Dianore, Calel Irenel."

The boy's arms tightened around his mother. "But you look upset."

"My anger is not for you, young one." Lyr let out a long breath. "But for the one who dared attack my daughter."

Selia crouched down to meet her son's eyes. "Where in the world did you *learn* such a thing?"

The boy blushed. "I watched some of the older mages practice."

"However you managed it, my House will not forget this deed," Lyr announced. Then he turned back to Kai. "But I must say, several things about this do not make sense."

"What do you mean?"

Lyr frowned down at Arlyn. "How did the attacker get through our wards and past our guards without being noticed? How could anyone make an arrow with a shattering iron head? And he only shot two arrows? He must have been inept to fire so few in that length of time. There is something inordinately strange about this entire situation."

Kai grimaced. "You're right."

"If you don't mind," Arlyn whispered from beside him. "Could we figure it out while I'm lying somewhere more comfortable?"

Lyr paced his office, his stomach churning with impotent fury, and waited for his captain to return with news. He was alone. Kai had carried Arlyn to her room to clean her up and put her to bed, Selia was comforting Iren, and Lial had gone to rest. So Lyr circled his office, unable to sit and work despite being so far behind. If crises like this kept happening, he *would* have to find an assistant. His life had become a maelstrom, chaotic and strange, and he did not like it.

This latest attack was unacceptable. Not only had his magical wards been breached, but none of his guards had seen the assassin. His warriors were supposed to be some of the best-trained in Moranaia. Someone should have been scanning the area around his daughter, and he would know why they had not. Arlyn had been recognized as his heir; she should have had three guards protecting her any time she left the house.

And if someone could slip through to attack Arlyn, then they might be able to reach the sacred tree. Eradisel had to be protected at all costs. He would have to assign more warriors to guard her. As for the wards? He would ask Selia if she could construct something stronger. It was said that many families along the Taian branch guarded their homes almost exclusively with magic.

Lyr had circled his desk again and was pacing back toward the door when Norin entered. His captain stopped in the middle of the room, tapped his chest twice in the customary salute, and waited with head slightly bowed. Part of Lyr wanted to make him wait, but it would have been a rude and pointless gesture born of frustration. He knew it was not the captain's fault though he did bear some responsibility as a leader. No, it was the guard who had failed to protect Arlyn whom Lyr truly wanted to punish.

"Good morn to you, Belore Norin. How do you fare this day?" Lyr asked in the traditional manner.

"I am well, Myern. I trust you and your family are the same."

Lyr almost winced at the equally traditional response. "Arlyn has survived, so I suppose we are better than we could be. Enough of this. Relax and tell me what you have found."

Norin shifted to a more natural pose. "Too little. Lieren picked up all of the iron fragments we could find. As you expected, there was also a quiver on the ground with several of those arrows spilling out. The heads were all shattered, though. They seem to be quite fragile."

"Did you find the assassin? He would have been gravely injured."

"No." Norin scowled. "We tracked his trail for a short distance before it just disappeared."

"Someone had to have seen what happened," Lyr snapped. "Scouts and warriors are positioned in trees all over this estate, that portion included. I want the ones guarding that area to be brought before me at once. I also want to know what happened to the three guards assigned to protect my daughter. A young boy was able to see the attacker. My own warriors should have been able to do the same."

Norin reddened. "I would also like to know why they failed, Myern. While you speak with the Land Guards, I will question the lady Arlyn's bodyguards, then send them to you as well."

"Please do, though I would like them reassigned no matter their reasons." Lyr paused to take a deep breath, struggling to overcome his anger. "I also want extra guards around the sacred tree and at each entrance to the estate. She must be protected at all costs."

"Of course, Myern. If you give me leave, I will go now and carry out your commands."

With a flick of the wrist, Lyr dismissed the captain and resumed his restless pacing. He had to discover who was behind the recent attacks as soon as possible. Not only was his household at risk, but Eradisel and the army Lyr commanded as well. Most of his warriors were not on active duty, but some of them lived in the barracks with the estate and personal guards. Those who did not were hardly difficult to find. They were scattered in villages and on estates throughout his lands. Lyr had to consider they could be at risk.

While not likely, it was possible these assaults had heavier implications than he had first assumed. The first three dukes on the Callian branch were also the three main generals of the king's armed forces; these warriors had not been called to battle for thousands of years, but they were kept trained and ready for the king's command. However improbable, Lyr could not discount the possibility that their true enemy might be working against the king, trying to cause sabotage in his army. And if that wasn't the original intention? Well, the type of skills that allowed an iron-wielding assassin to sneak through wards unnoticed could easily be used in such a way.

Jaw set, Lyr called for Lady Selia.

Allafon nudged the smoking heap with his boot before scowling up at the guard who had brought it. "Where did you find him?"

"He...he crawled to the edge of the estate, milord," the soldier explained, anxiety dripping from his words. "I did not detect a breach in the wards, I swear it. He was suddenly just *there.*"

"So you say." Allafon laughed at the blind fear crossing the fool's face. "Relax. I know who it is. Now leave me."

As the other rushed from the room, Allafon kicked the pathetic form over on its back. The man groaned mindlessly, obviously unconscious. Allafon spelled him to sudden awareness and laughed again at the long, keening moan of agony. He used another spell to cut off the pain, a necessity rather than kindness, and one more to force an answer.

"Tell me, did you accomplish your task? Is Kaienan dead?"

"No," he gasped. "But I hit the woman. Then the fire came. I don't know."

"I should have known not to use a half-breed whelp like you." Allafon pulled the knife free from his belt.

"Milord, but the iron—"

"Being able to use magic on iron is useless if you are too inept to complete such simple tasks. Your failure is intolerable." He considered leaving the pathetic human-spawn in the dungeon to die in slow, relentless agony, but it hardly seemed worth the effort. Without a word, he shoved the blade into the man's heart and twisted, watching in satisfaction until the last spark of life had left his eyes. And basking in the energy that flowed into his soul.

"What a shame." Allafon grinned, filled with euphoria from the death and the influx of energy, then wiped his blade clean and stood. His gaze caught on the cloak still smoldering around the corpse, and displeasure slipped through. He'd paid a fortune to have the thing enchanted to hide the wearer from Lyrnis's wards. "I may have to find another way onto the estate."

Allafon summoned the guard with a nudge of his mind and gestured for him to take the body away. "I have dispatched the traitor. Have you seen my son today?"

"No, milord." The soldier kept his gaze down. "I believe he departed yesterday to attend a friend's wedding."

"I had forgotten," Allafon muttered, dismissing the other's presence almost before he finished speaking. It was unfortunate that Morenial was not at home. Who else could he trust with such a mission? He would have to pick someone soon. Kai needed to die before he had time to reproduce with that Dianore spawn. And Lyrnis? He looked forward to taking care of that one himself. Only then could he begin his vengeance on Earth.

Allafon smiled as the guard removed the body from the room. The Dianore line was foolish. Keeping up relations with other types of fae. Traveling amidst humans. If not for their fixation, his bonded would still be alive. When he took over as Myern, the portal would be sealed. And the useless fae could languish in their own poisoned holes. He would be too busy breaking Lynia to his will.

I ren had known nothing. Bile rose in Lyr's throat at the memory of questioning the trembling boy, but there had been little choice. And it hadn't even helped. Lyr let his head thump against the back of his chair. If Iren were a bit older, more trained, perhaps he could have described the energy he'd sensed in the clearing. *If.*

At least Lady Selia had worked with Lyr on the wards. They had no way to know if the changes would *help* since the source of the invasion remained unknown. But they certainly wouldn't hurt. Lyr could only hope some of the Taian methods would close the hole in his own defenses.

Ten millennia of peace and someone had found a breach.

Unacceptable.

Lyr straightened at the knock on his door. A brief word, and five of the *Tayianeln*, the Land Guards, entered. Though their job seemed simple—to patrol through the forest of the surrounding estate and ensure order was kept—the Tayn were some of the most important warriors under his command. Connected to the spirit of the forest, they were linked with the wards in a bond almost as strong as the family key Lyr had shared with Arlyn. Each undertook at least two centuries of training and, if they were approved by Eradisel herself, another century of apprenticeship. Lyr trusted them implicitly.

They advanced in a line to the exact center of the room as Lyr stood. As one, they tapped fists to chests twice and dropped to their knees, heads bowed, despite the leather armor they all wore. The warrior in the center, a female named Nerinen, spoke without looking up.

"We have come as our Captain has bid us to kneel at the feet of our General, Commander of the Third Branch, Blood of Land and King, Callian Myern i Lyrnis Dianore nai Braelyn. Our failure has fallen as a blight to reach into the hearts of all in our trust. It is hoped most fervently that our words and experience may help those with more wisdom to find the origin of the harm that threatens Braelyn. By witness of the Nine Gods of Arneen, we are ever sworn to uphold the three branches of our king."

"Then stand and be heard, faithful of the *Tayianeln*," Lyr responded. Though he had not expected such formality, he hid his surprise. What had Norin said to them to cause such a reaction? They were only a few steps away from showing their necks for his blade. "In the name of the king and in witness of the Nine, I ask only that you answer my questions with honesty and heart. Do this, and the hand of honor will remain upon you so long as you remain faithful. No dishonor exists in failure when one has put forth true and earnest effort. Rise without shame and be gladdened your words may bring aid."

The five stood with fluid synchronicity, but none of them would meet his eyes. Nerinen, at least, managed to get close. "Ask us what you will. We are grateful to help."

He questioned them for more than half a mark, but they had little to report. Not a single one of the five had sensed a disturbance in the wards; their first indication had been Arlyn's scream. Only Nerinen had been in a position to see the source of the attack, but the assailant had already started tumbling from the tree by the time her first arrow reached him. Nerinen's gaze fell again as she described what she'd done, and her hands trembled.

"It was to my great dishonor that I did not react at once." Nerinen bowed her head in shame. "I was stunned, and for a precious moment, I could not think what to do. My arrow should have been loosed before he could fire his second. There is no excuse for my failure, and I will resign at once if that is your wish."

Lyr repressed a sigh. Nerinen was a fairly new member of the Tayn, having served for a little over a decade, and obviously believed his daughter had been injured because of that inexperience.

"It is *not* my wish. This is a situation that none, save for those who patrol the perimeter of the wards, were prepared for, and that is my own failure. You could not have expected someone to attack without setting off the wards, and although you *should* have acted more quickly, it was an easy error to make. Besides, my daughter was assigned three bodyguards, none of whom acted. They bear the greatest responsibility."

"Three?" Nerinen glanced at the others, who shook their heads. "Myern, no others were present. We saw no body-guards."

"None?" He struggled to pull back the renewed wash of fury. Only centuries of experience allowed him to keep his expression blank. "I am hopeful that, when Norin brings them forth, a reasonable explanation will be forthcoming. Thank you for watching out for my daughter, though it was largely not your task."

"It is our honor to care for all who pass beneath our trees, and it grieves us to have seen one injured beneath our protection. Our vigilance will now be greater than our enemy can comprehend."

"I trust that it is so." Lyr inclined his head to all five. "Carry on your duties with honor, keeping ever in mind the lessons learned this day. Our strength of purpose will see us prevail."

At the formal dismissal, the five Tayn tapped their chests twice in salute, bowed, and left. Lyr waited, his blood pounding a furious beat in his ears, through several drips of the clock. Waited until the Tayn were well-gone. Then slammed his fist onto the desk and let the curses fly.

Arlyn gazed up at the monkey bars, wanting to climb up and swing from the rungs but uncertain if she should. Her mother had warned her to be careful about a lot of strange things, and this might be one of them. The shiny silver bars were obviously steel, which she knew she was supposed to avoid, and there was always a chance her hair would fall down if she wasn't careful.

But her hair was pulled back pretty securely, and anyway, she'd touched steel before without it doing too much to bother her. She was almost halfway through second grade, definitely old enough to play on the monkey bars. Her friends made fun of her for being afraid, never guessing how much she truly wanted to try. And today, she finally decided, she was going to do it. Arlyn scurried up the side before she could change her mind and grasped the first rung.

Her hand was itching with nerves she would not acknowledge, but it was soon forgotten as she swung to the next rung, then the next. She crossed twice before she finally grew daring enough to copy James. Arlyn rocked back and forth until she got one of her legs, then the other, over a bar, then let herself drop to hang by her knees. The world looked glorious and strange upside down.

She felt a sudden tug on her head and gasped to see her long hair drifting in the breeze around her. Arlyn struggled to pull herself up before the mysterious thief got a look at her ears, but it was harder than she had expected. Before she could grab one of the rungs, Mark had already called for their classmates. As her hand connected with the metal, two of the boys pulled her down.

They taunted her mercilessly about her pointed ears and her lack of a father. Some said her father was a fairy or a Keebler elf, but most of them claimed he must have left when he'd seen what a freak she was. She was confused, at first, until they pointed at their own round ears. She'd never paid a lot of attention to ears before, except to make sure her own were covered. Were hers really that unusual?

By the time her mother came to get her from the school playground, she was fighting back tears. Arlyn didn't say a word until they pulled into the driveway. "Did my dad leave because I'm a freak?"

"What?" Aimee slammed on the brakes so hard she and Arlyn jolted against their seat belts. "Where in the world would you get an idea like that?"

"I'm sorry, Mom. I know I was supposed to be careful. But I just had to try the monkey bars. I just had to. And then Mark pulled my hair down, and everyone was laughing at my ears. Am I a Keebler elf, or a fairy, or a freak?"

"I knew this would happen soon," her mother said with a frown. After shutting off the car, she turned to Arlyn. "I've told you all your life how much your father would love you if he'd ever been able to meet you. Why would you ever believe he left because there was something wrong with you?"

"Maybe you just didn't want to say."

"Arlyn Dianore Moore, you know I never lie to you."

She turned a belligerent frown on her mother. "Fine. Then tell me now. Why are my ears funny? And what happened to my father?"

"I suppose you're ready to know, but most of the tale will have to wait until you're older." Aimee gripped her hand and squeezed. "Your father is not from this world, Arlyn. He is what many would call an elf, though not the Keebler or Santa's helper kind. He never knew about you. He had to return to the land of the elves long before you were born."

The sob jerked Arlyn awake as it ripped from her throat. So real. Her mother had appeared so real, so alive. An arm tightened around her waist, and she looked up into Kai's eyes. She was bundled against his side, her tears soaking into his shirt.

His hand played softly with her long hair where it draped around them both.

Arlyn shifted her arm—to push him away or gather him closer?—and let out a cry at the pain the movement brought. "What happened?"

Then memory poured in, answering the question she hadn't asked. The clearing. The arrow. Drifting away on a table in a room she'd never seen before. Kai's spirit anchoring hers. As she stared into his eyes, his worry washed over her, and her heart lurched. "Am I going to be okay?"

"Shh." His other hand lifted to caress her face. "Lial says so. Forgive my worry."

Her eyes grew heavy, but she didn't want to sleep. "Mom was in my dream for a moment. Then nothing. Just lonely darkness."

"You aren't alone now." Kai kissed her brow. "Rest. I'll be here with you."

Arlyn let herself drift in the comfort of his arms. Peace.

And maybe love.

Lyr was about to go visit Eradisel when Norin returned with three young males. Part of the Home Guard, he realized with a frown, by their *peresten* armor. Unlike the Tayn, these were the visible protectors of the estate and those who would remain if the army itself were to ride to battle. But Arlyn's bodyguards should not have come from this group; no, they should have been drawn from Lyr's Elite. Not only that, but these three were quite young. He would be surprised if they were out of their apprenticeships.

They stopped before him with the ritual salute, but he detected little concern in their gazes. It was a sharp contrast to the Tayn, who had seemed near to prostrating themselves. "Who do you bring before me, Belore Norin?"

"Those not worthy of introduction, Myern. Korel, Leral, and Fenere of the Home Guard, former bodyguards of Ayala Arlyn."

"I have been told by the Tayn that you were not seen near my daughter, though you were assigned to guard her life. What words have you to explain your failure?"

The one named Fenere shrugged. "She left with Kaienan. We thought her safe enough with a scout."

Lyr could only stare at them for one stunned moment. "You thought her safe enough? Unless I am somehow mistaken on this point, you were not ordered to sit around letting others guard her. You were *ordered* to protect her any time she left the walls of the estate. This type of incompetence is inexcusable."

"As they are newly bonded, we assumed they were going into the woods to be alone," Korel snapped, face tight with anger. "I did not consider you the type to watch such things uninvited. Especially not your own daughter."

Before the others had even registered the insult, Korel was on the ground, holding a hand to his bloody lip. Lyr stood over him, cold eyes pinning him in place. "You must be a child, to speak so rudely to me."

The other two shuffled back, eyes averted, as Korel sat up. "What respect should I give to one who names a half-human his heir?"

"Indeed?" Lyr gripped the other's tunic and jerked him up-right. "Seems you're in the wrong place." He glanced at the other two. "Do you feel this way, as well?"

Fenere shook his head, and Leral paled. "No, Myern. This was my first time as a bodyguard. Like Fenere, I believed—"

"Your first time as bodyguard." Lyr shoved Korel aside, uncaring that the other stumbled. Body tight with fury, he turned to Norin. "Explain to me why these three, and not vet-erans of my Elite Guard, were chosen to protect my daugh-ter."

"They needed experience, Myern, and Arlyn is but a child."

"She is old enough to be soulbonded, a state the gods do not grant to children. In any case, I was guarded by Elite when I was an infant."

Norin's brow furrowed. "She is part human. It seemed best not to risk offending one of the Elite by assigning them to her."

"You will find three who are willing to protect the heir of our House, or I will order them to do so," Lyr responded im-placably. "As for these three? If Fenere and Leral wish to train as bodyguards, they may apprentice with the Elite for the cus-tomary time. Korel may pack his belongings and return to his family's home."

Korel's hands balled into fists. "That is unjust."

"Is it?" Lyr's brow rose. "We guard the portal to Earth and to many types of fae. I can have no tolerance for a soldier who will not protect one of mixed blood."

"Fae, yes. But human?"

Lyr narrowed his eyes. "Forget your history classes? We evolved from the same line. Perhaps your branching is too distant to know this truth."

Norin stepped forward. "Myern—"

"My decision is final," Lyr snapped. "Go, before I send you all home in disgrace. I will not tolerate insubordination in any of my Guard."

Lyr stood firm as they saluted—even an angry Korel—and left the room, but inside, he burned with rage. This was the first time Norin had shown any sort of prejudice against humans. How many of his warriors shared it? He did not want to replace Norin, yet Lyr might not have a choice. He'd have to pay closer attention. Arlyn was his heir and would one day train to lead the armies he commanded. They could not have a captain who worked against her.

With a worried frown, he started toward his room and the counsel of Eradisel.

rlyn forced her eyelids open as her hazy mind struggled to recall what had happened. She was alone, her left arm propped on a pillow, and sunlight gleamed around the curtains on her window. Then she shifted, and the sudden burst of agony reminded her of the day's events. Her breath came in quick, shallow pants as her chest tightened.

Where was Kai?

He'd said he would stay. Arlyn lifted her right hand to her throat and tried to still her pounding heart. She needed to know everyone else was okay. Iren had been out there. Had she heard him cry out? Shrieks of pain had filled the clearing, but she didn't know whose they'd been.

The door swung open, and Kai strode through, a tray balanced in his hands. He dropped it on the desk with a clatter and rushed to her side. "What's wrong?"

"You said you'd be with me," she gasped out, then squeezed her eyes closed and tried to slow her breathing. "Is the boy okay? Iren?"

"He is well." Kai slipped into the bed and wrapped his arms around her. "Lial said you'd wake soon. I thought you might be hungry."

Though her body protested the movement, Arlyn turned into him, settling her arm gingerly across his chest. After a few deep breaths, she opened her eyes. "Sorry."

A gentle smile slipped across his lips. "No need to apologize. I know firsthand what it's like to wake up this way. Like the world has taken a turn without you."

"Yes." Arlyn burrowed closer, then moved her cheek away in discomfort. Twisting her head, she frowned at the line beneath his shirt. "What's that?"

"What?" Kai followed her gaze. "Oh." He pulled a narrow silver chain from beneath his shirt. "My mother's necklace."

It was beautiful, the hair-thin silver strands woven into such intricate designs that it looked like a solid piece. Had she not been so close, she never would have made out the smaller strands. "It's gorgeous."

"It's one of the few things I have of hers. Moren kept it after she died and made sure I got it when I was old enough."

"I didn't know you had also lost your mother. I'm sorry."

He dropped the chain with a shrug. "Don't be. She died a few days after my birth, so I never knew her. Most of my pain comes from that lack. But I am five hundred and forty-two, Arlyn. I have had plenty of time for the hurt to fade."

"Five hundred and..." She grimaced. "I'm not going to think of that. You are way too old for me."

Kai laughed. "That's the first time I've been considered too old for anything in quite some time. Most still think of me as a youngling. Besides, my parents were a thousand years apart in age. Our difference is nothing."

Arlyn let her head drop against him now since the chain was out of the way. Her body grew heavy with exhaustion, and her arm ached relentlessly. But it had been worth the pain of shifting it. Her defenses down, she let herself relax and just exist with him. If this was the heart of the soulbond, she didn't know how she'd ever give it up.

Not that she had to.

Kai sighed into her hair. "Do you feel well enough to talk to your father?"

"Now?"

"I'm sure he wants to see for himself that you're healing," Kai said. "But he also needs to find out what you remember of the attack."

"Fine," she mumbled. "Help me sit up."

"You should be resting."

She cracked one eye open. "I don't think he'd like finding us like this. Remember last time?"

Kai surprised her by chuckling. "He *was* rather upset, I suppose."

"You didn't find it funny at the time."

"That was then," he answered.

But Kai shifted, helping her move until she was reclined against the headboard and a couple of pillows. Arlyn hissed out a breath as he propped her arm up again. If not for the shock of pain, she might have fallen back to sleep. The simple task of sitting up had her blinking against a jolt of agony.

Kai set the tray of food on her lap as a knock sounded on the door. Frowning down at the loaf of dark bread and the earthenware mug, Arlyn called for her father to enter. She flicked a quick look at Kai. "What is this?"

"Bread and broth."

"Broth?"

"It is good for restoring energy," Lyr answered for Kai as he stopped by the bed. Some of the tension dropped from his shoulders as he met her eyes. "You look better than I expected."

Her brow pinched as she lifted the mug. "Thanks?"

"It was no insult. I didn't expect you to be awake." Lyr stared at the bandage wrapped around her upper arm. "You reacted so poorly to the iron that I assumed it would take you much longer to recover your energy. Especially without training."

"Maybe there's a benefit to my human blood."

Lyr's expression turned thoughtful. "Perhaps so."

Arlyn took a sip of the broth and relaxed as the warmth trickled down her throat. It tasted like a meat broth, probably from some bird similar to chicken, and a blend of herbs. She smiled. "And *this* is better than *I* expected."

Lyr laughed. "I'll pass along your compliments."

Kai took the seat next to the bed—the same one she'd used to watch over him—as Lyr pulled a chair up to her other side. Arlyn took a few more sips of the broth, then a nibble of bread, as her father got settled. "I guess you're ready to hear what happened."

"Are you well enough?" Lyr asked, his brow furled in concern.

"Not really." Arlyn set the mug down with a thunk. "But I want to tell you anyway."

As the communication spell ended, Selia let her hand fall from the edge of the mirror and stared at her own reflection for a long, numb moment. She was unsure how to react to the news she had just received from her father. She almost wished she had not become curious, had not begun to question. But Arlyn's talents were too close to her own for coincidence.

I wondered if you'd figure it out. Even if you had not, it is no matter. Her father's words echoed through her mind once more, still as disturbing as they had been the first time. No matter? Selia had had a brother, dead for decades now. How could her father have hidden such a secret? There had been no real need. He had not been soulbonded to her mother; in fact, her parents had not been together for almost six hundred years. He had not been in any relationship a century ago, when her brother had been conceived, had made no commitments to worry about breaking.

I loved him, Selia, as best I could. But he was half-human. There was no place for him here. She remembered when her father had decided to go to the human world. He had been bored with life, dangerously lonely, and had spent almost a decade exploring there. But she had not known the full story. Apparently, he had grown enamored with a girl in a place called Ireland, and he'd bedded her. At first, there had been a scandal, since the girl was unmarried and with child, but she swore she had been visited by a faerie from the nearby Sidhe hill. When her son, Aidan, was born with pointed ears, the village believed her. Her father had been comfortable leaving him there, knowing the villagers would not mistreat the boy for fear of angering the Sidhe.

As a man, Aidan, scorning the superstitions, had moved to America and married. A few years later, his only child was born. Aimee, Arlyn's mother.

Selia had known Arlyn was descended from someone in the Mornia clan, but she had not expected to discover that Arlyn was her own niece. And her father had urged Selia to come here *perfectly aware* of the relationship. Her hands shook with anger. At 982 years, she was certainly old enough to handle the truth. But had she not figured it out for herself, her father never would have told her. She would have left this place, one more student taught, without ever knowing. Without ever learning of her brother.

Gods of Arneen, she could hardly believe he was dead. He had lived to a mere twenty-nine. A miracle, that, since he had worked in a steel mill. How could her father justify letting his only son, half-human or not, do such a thing? Aidan should have lived for several centuries at least, likely more, had he been taught what things, like iron, to avoid and how to use his own innate magic to regenerate himself. It was inexcusable. She did not know if she could ever forgive her father.

Did her sister know? Niasen was both the eldest and her father's heir, so he might have confided in her. But Selia thought it unlikely, considering how willing he had been to encourage *her* to teach Arlyn without even a word. Despite his claims of love, Loren had not seen his son as worthy of mention. She would have to call her sister to make sure she knew.

But should she tell Arlyn? Selia did not want to continue her own father's deceit, but she did not want to cause her niece pain, either. She might not take this new familial relationship at all well. Arlyn did not seem bothered by being half-elven; perhaps the actual blood connection would make little difference to her. But the neglect Aidan had received would surely cause anger. What was the right choice? Selia rubbed a tired hand across her eyes. Family was everything. To not acknowledge the bond would be the worst kind of insult.

Ah, the problems that would bring. Her father had simply assumed she would remain silent and would be furious if she forged a new bond with House Dianore by revealing the relationship. Letting such a powerful, magical bloodline go untended, eventually to mix with the Callians, would be a scandal. The Taians were as insular as possible, meeting with other branches rarely and mating with them even less, in an attempt to keep their magics to themselves. And now the heir to the third duke in the Callian line held almost all of them. Her father would have much to answer for.

But that did not concern her. She was more worried about the reactions of Arlyn and Lyrnis, each for different reasons.

Arlyn would have to deal with a startling new truth about the supposedly human side of her family, one she might not take well. And Lyr would have to handle the complexities of the new connection between their houses, a social tangle Selia would also have to help unsnarl.

A difficult choice. But she knew, in the end, that there was only one.

Lyr paced his study, his thoughts on his upcoming discussion with Arlyn. It was just past time for the evening meal, but he doubted he would get a chance to eat. Too much to do. Too much to consider. Arlyn had said the energy she'd sensed before the attack had seemed muffled, like a sound heard from a distance, and the estate wards had given no warning.

Muffled. Stifled.

Did their assailant carry or wear something rendering him invisible to the wards? Lyr's stomach lurched, and he was suddenly thankful he hadn't tried to eat. The weight of all those under his protection settled like a boulder in his gut. How could he protect against someone who knew his shields so well? How had they even managed it?

Lyr spun toward the door at the sound of the knock. He was surprised enough to detect Selia's presence that he barely noticed the flash of impatience. With a small sigh, he bid her enter. What was one more distraction? He had another eighteen hours until the morning meal. It might even be enough time to catch up on all he had to do.

Doubtful but possible.

Selia's expression told him this would not be an easy meeting. Had she discovered dire information about the wards? Then she twisted her hands together to still their trembling, and he almost groaned. It had to be another issue to make her so nervous. And these days, surprises were rarely pleasant.

"Good eve to you, Lady Selia. I trust you have been well since last we spoke."

"Of course, Myern Lyrnis. I have everything I need, and your household has been nothing but polite."

Had he heard a hint of nerves in her voice? "I do not see young Irenel. Is he well-settled?"

"He is roaming the gardens even now." Selia averted her gaze. "He was quite shaken up but is rebounding quickly. I believe he will be happy once he becomes accustomed to the estate."

"I hope you will also enjoy your time here," Lyr answered with a smile. Both understood what neither said—that it was Lyr's job to make up for the difficulties his guests had encountered so far.

"I am certain I will." She returned the smile though it did not reach her eyes. "And I hope I am not interrupting your work."

"It is always my pleasure to speak with a guest in my home."

Pleasantries completed, Selia transitioned to her news. "Unfortunately, what I have to say will bring nothing but disruption. I spoke to my father earlier this day and acquired knowledge that I cannot, in good conscience, ignore. Though

Arlyn deserves to know first, I cannot be sure when she will be well enough. It is best to bring this to you now."

"What is wrong, Lady Selia?"

"So great is my shock, I have not the grace of words to express this in any way other than bluntly. Arlyn is my niece. My father is her great-grandfather."

"Come, sit." Lyr gestured for her to take a nearby chair before settling into the one beside her. Lyr paused a moment to gather his thoughts. Her abrupt delivery had been almost as surprising as her words. "We had already learned that Arlyn is of the Taian branch, part of the Mornian clan, but this goes beyond expectation. He mentioned nothing about this before?"

She stiffened. "Of course not. I had believed my father's encouragement to come here was due to his concern for me. He said nothing that would lead me to believe this situation was possible. *Nothing*. My elder sister, his heir, did not even know. We have both agreed this secret must be revealed."

"I am sorry, Lady Selia. I meant no offense." Lyr resisted the urge to rub his forehead in sheer frustration. The last week had sorely strained his ability to remain calm. "I did not expect this news. From what I understand, the Mornian clan is rather large. It seemed most likely that Arlyn was descended from one of the families outside the noble line."

"So I believed as well. Then I tested her." Selia took a deep breath. "Her talents are a close match to my own, closer to Iren's, but for a few differences. More variance is common."

"This news is quite serious. I am certain I do not need to tell you how much. By the gods, Arlyn could be considered fourth in line to your father's title. This alliance will take careful negotiations between our families." Frowning, Lyr clenched his hands. "Beyond that, I must be blunt in turn. It will be difficult for me to negotiate anything with one who would knowingly leave his own child, half-human or not, unacknowledged. I would have given anything to have known about Arlyn, to have been able to claim her even before her birth."

"As I must mourn the loss of my brother, though unmet."

Lyr allowed the anger, and the pain, to wash through him for a moment more before repressing it. "I will have to speak with the duke of your branch, if not the king himself."

"My sister and I both are willing to help in any way. We are shamed by our father's actions." Selia shuddered. "And thank Arneen that Arlyn bonded with Kai so quickly. Had I refused and a male teacher been sent, had she fallen for someone in the House of Baran..."

"Gods," Lyr breathed. There was a reason, beyond family pride, why elves kept such careful track of bloodlines. While inbreeding was bad for humans, they reproduced so quickly that a few isolated incidents would easily become diluted within a few generations. But for elves, who lived so long and had children much less frequently, the results were disastrous. Incest was one of their greatest taboos. In fact, the first three ducal families of each branch, all descended from the nine children of the first queen of Moranaia, still did not intermarry after millennia of the first settling.

Though only three down the Dianore branch, Kai's family, the House of Treinesse, was in no way related. Only the original nine dukes descended from the founding of Moranaia. Other dukes, and all of the sub-branches, had been added over time for various reasons. Lyr's ancestor had created the third earlship for a son of the Treinesse family who had saved his soulbonded and their young child at great cost to himself. The two noble families had never intermarried in the thousands of years since.

"You have an excellent point, Lady Selia." Then he laughed, startling her with the sudden sound. "I am sorry. I just find it amusing that I was so angry at Kai for his haste when it has been at least somewhat beneficial. That is at least one thing in this entire mess I do not have to worry about."

If only the rest of his concerns could be solved so neatly.

"**R**alan just contacted me again."

Arlyn blinked bleary eyes, trying to focus on her father. She'd been awake long enough for Lial to work on her arm and for a few sips of tea, but exhaustion still blurred her thoughts. Lightning flashed outside the window behind Kai and brightened the murky early dawn glow seeping through the curtains. Though her bonded held his own cup of tea, he ignored it as he stared at Lyr.

"And?" Kai asked.

"He reminded me of our deadline." Lyr's jaw clenched. "Today is the last day for you to cross the Veil to bring him and his daughter home."

Kai set his cup on the desk hard enough to slosh a few drops of tea over the rim. "Surely, he isn't still insisting I come?"

Arlyn's brow pinched as she looked between the two. "What's the problem?"

Both men turned incredulous looks her way. Kai shook his head. "You're injured. My soulbonded. How could I leave at a time like this?"

"I'm not dying."

Kai took a few steps toward her. "You almost did."

"I don't think so." Arlyn lifted a hand as he opened his mouth to argue. "I don't think I really would have left my body behind. Not that your comfort wasn't helpful. But the wound wasn't that bad."

"By itself, no," Lyr interrupted. "But your allergy to iron is severe. It's why Lial can't fully heal you. Some flakes were too small for him to extract. If they don't work out on their own, he'll have to find a way to purge them. There is still great risk."

"Yeah, but I'm just sitting here. Kai can travel to Earth."

Kai huffed out a breath. "It's not that simple. Our bond is in the first stage, still tenuous, and you are weak. I'm not sure what the strain of such a distance will cause."

"Maybe nothing," Arlyn said.

"Fuck it all," Kai bit out. "How can I take that chance?" He ran a hand through his hair. "How can I not? It's to save a child."

Arlyn's breath caught at the turmoil he transmitted. "I'll deal with any problems."

Lyr and Kai exchanged glances. Her father frowned down at her. "Perhaps we could have Lial put you into a deep sleep. It would help you heal faster, too."

"You're joking, right?" Arlyn sat forward, jostling the tray on her lap. Thunder cracked outside, a satisfying counterpoint to her anger. "Stop talking around me. If there's pain, or discomfort, or even agony, I'll deal with it. Because I am a *grown woman.*"

Her father looked away. Kai shuffled his feet, then threw up his hands. "You're right. But there are other guides. I don't understand why it has to be me."

Lyr's shoulders slumped. "Ralan has Seen it."

"Seen it?" Arlyn asked.

"He's a seer," Kai answered, frustration laced into his tone. "His vision apparently told him it must be me."

"Then you'll go." Arlyn lifted her brows. "And let me worry about myself. Now get out of here. I want to take a nap."

By the time Kai returned a couple of hours later, Arlyn was almost ready to crawl out of her own skin. How long could a person sit in bed and stay sane? She ran her finger along the flowers embroidered on the coverlet. Again. For the thousandth time. She swung her legs over the side of the bed just as the door opened.

"Arlyn!" Kai rushed forward. "You can't get up."

She shoved against his chest when he urged her to lie back down. "If I stay here much longer, I'm going to scream."

"But your arm—"

"Hurts. The rest of my body doesn't." Arlyn scowled up at him. "Didn't I tell you to stop treating me like a child? As helpless?"

Beneath her hand, his muscles tightened, and heat flared in his eyes. "I assure you I have never considered you such."

"Really?" She pushed at him until she could stand. "You can't blame your protectiveness on me being unarmed the way you did after the presentation."

"That's true. I can't." Kai's hand cupped her cheek. "This is all feeling."

Arlyn shivered. "Oh."

He shifted, pulling her closer. "The thought of you in danger. Hurting. Upset here without me." Kai's hands tightened on her waist. "It rips at my heart."

His mouth found hers, and she was lost in him. Lost in the desire that swirled around and between them. Her hands slid into his hair, and she stifled a wince. Arlyn didn't care about the pain in her arm—she wanted to be closer to him. But Kai sensed the twinge and pulled back to rest his forehead against hers.

"Yet again, my timing is poor," he murmured.

Arlyn couldn't hold back her grin. "Are you forming a habit, or is this normal behavior?"

"I'm not sure." Kai shocked them both by laughing. "You'd have to ask around."

Her breath hissed out as she pulled back, putting strain on her wound. With a huff, she cradled her arm against her chest. Damned inconvenient. "I did want to talk to you."

"Oh?"

The casual tone he tried to put into his voice didn't fool her. His sudden, tense stillness would have given him away even if she couldn't sense his emotions. "About our bond. You say it's tenuous?"

"Arlyn..."

She took his hand. "Maybe we can fix that."

Kai finally understood why people said their blood ran cold. "It's your decision."

"Relax." Arlyn squeezed his hand. "I'm not calling for a priest just yet."

His heart thundered in his chest like the storm that had woken them before dawn. "What do you want to do?"

"I've been thinking about this." Arlyn released him, her hand moving to wrap around the pendant that bore her energy. "There's something about you. About this bond." She smiled. "I could be perfectly complete without you. But I'm not sure I want to be."

Even his breath stilled as she lifted the necklace Lyr had given her over her head and raised it high. *"i'Tayah ay nac-mor kehy ler ehy anan taen."*

Kai looked into her eyes, their green depths filled with amusement and uncertainty, and reached out to enfold her fingers and the chain with his own hand. Light flared, brighter than when he'd given his necklace, and he shivered as the bond tightened. His hand shook as he took the pendant and gathered it, still warm from her body, in his palm.

He caressed the engraving with his thumb as his eyes held hers. Heat sparked between them. And frustration. Kai dropped his gaze to her arm, cradled once more against her chest. Though his body was hard at the thought of completing their bond, he couldn't. When they finally came together, he would have no risk of pain between them.

Gods, he hoped she felt better soon.

"I can't believe you want to do this now," Kai grumbled.

Arlyn smiled and leaned against him as he helped her down the stairs. She was still weak, but her legs only trembled a little as the two of them descended. "If I'm going to give our bond a chance, it means I'm going to stay. My father should know. Besides…"

Kai gave her arm a reassuring squeeze as they stepped into the entryway. "He's not going to tell you to go away."

"Probably not." She lifted worried eyes to meet his amused ones. "But he might want to. I've caused him a great deal of trouble. And I might never fit in here."

He paused beside the hallway that led to Lyr's study. Gentle energy from the sacred tree buffeted Arlyn from behind, and she chuckled at the hint of reprimand within it. Kai lifted an eyebrow. "What?"

"Eradisel did not approve of my words."

Kai glanced toward the tree. "She knows the foolishness behind your fears. If you want to make a place here, then you will. You have centuries to acclimate."

"Easy for you to say." Arlyn rolled her eyes and pulled him forward. "Come on."

She knew he wanted to say more, but he let the subject drop. How could she argue the point, anyway? Only time would tell which one of them was right. So Arlyn walked on in silence, concentrating instead on keeping her steps firm. She couldn't hide her weakness from Kai, but she would prefer her father didn't guess.

Lyr's voice sounded absent as he called for them to enter. Arlyn loosened her grip on Kai as they passed through the tiny hallway linking the estate to the study, then drew up short. Though Kai looked back at her in question, she could only stare. Stacks of papers covered her father's desk, more than she had seen there before. Lyr leaned over one small pile, his forehead resting on his hand as he glared at what he read.

She shuffled her feet, and Lyr looked up. "Forgive me. More reports arrived while you rested. It's always busier as we approach harvest."

Arlyn bit her lip. "We can come back later."

"No." Lyr straightened. Then his eyes narrowed on Kai. "I believe you have news of import?"

Arlyn took a deep breath and stepped closer, letting go of Kai. When she looked back at her bonded to see if he followed, her gaze caught on the pendant gleaming on his chest. No wonder her father seemed to know. She turned back to Lyr, but his expression was closed. Was he upset by what she'd done?

"I guess it's obvious." She locked her trembling legs when she reached the edge of his desk and prayed they would hold. "I decided to give this bond a chance. I hope you aren't angry."

Lyr leaned back, and his posture seemed to ease. Was that a hint of relief in his eyes? "Why would I be?"

Arlyn choked back a laugh. "You almost beat up Kai just a couple of days ago over the issue."

"I'll not deny it's difficult," Lyr said. "Part of me wishes we'd had time together, just the two of us. Time to get to know one another."

Kai took her hand, offering silent support. "I would not interfere with that."

"I know." Her father studied Kai for a long moment. "I know that. I've had time to think, when I take breaks from all this paperwork." His lips twisted up. "If you are happy, then I could be nothing less."

"So you…" Arlyn swallowed against the sudden dryness in her throat. "You don't mind if I stay?"

Lyr stood and joined her on the other side of his desk. "Arlyn. I've come to find that you staying here is my greatest hope. Never think otherwise."

Arlyn sat in a seat by the window, one of her etiquette books open on the table beside her. She'd been hesitant to offer to help, but the weary look in her father's eyes as he'd turned back to his desk had swayed her. Besides, she didn't have anything else to do while Kai gathered supplies for his trip across the Veil.

She could hardly believe her father's easy acceptance of her assistance. Lyr had keyed her to *everything*, including the secured drawer in his desk. No questions asked. Biting her lip, she lifted one of the papers from the pile he'd given her and hoped she wouldn't be useless. He only wanted her to write out a summary. Surely, even she could do that.

After three hours of work and only two reports done, Arlyn had started questioning that assumption. She'd found herself consulting the etiquette book over and over, trying to separate the important information from the layers of politeness. Too bad the spell that gave knowledge of a language could not also give her an instant understanding of the culture.

Another half hour had passed before Arlyn glanced over at her father, a groan of frustration slipping free. "I can't believe this is actually helping you. I bet you would have finished all of these plus ten or twenty more by now."

Smiling, Lyr leaned back in his chair. "That may be so, but the time you have spent on those has allowed me to deal with other issues. The reports I gave you were the least urgent, so there is little rush. Besides, it helps you learn more of our world and of the people and lands you will someday have charge of as my heir."

"Don't remind me." Arlyn rubbed her heavy eyes. At this rate, it would take her decades to pick out a simple greeting. She had to hope he'd live a long time—and *not* give up on life since he didn't have the hope of finding another soulbonded. "If you become suicidal, I'll kill you."

"I'll keep that in mind," Lyr answered with a laugh.

They worked through a light lunch of salad, cheese, and a white, oddly tangy meat. Arlyn found she was getting faster at picking through the reports, but she had still only completed eight in all. Her father had worked his way through countless more, his expression rarely shifting from barely masked boredom. On occasion, he shared with her the more frustrating or amusing cases, like that of a man who petitioned for redress after being temporarily paralyzed by a mage whose wife he had insulted.

Lyr continued to chuckle long after he had finished explaining the situation. "I cannot imagine what he was thinking to insult someone from House Bian. Their tempers are almost as well-known as their magical skills."

"You *did* say it happened in a pub. Glad to know such things aren't limited to humans."

"They are not, indeed, though they tend to happen less frequently here. The repercussions are often more dire." He frowned down at the paper with a shake of his head. "Though I laugh at the situation, it must be handled with care to avoid a feud. Both were in the wrong, but that doesn't always matter."

Arlyn glimpsed out the window at the valley in the distance. "I still find it difficult to believe there is a village down there. I can't see it from here."

"Once we have ended the threat to our House, I will take you. I doubt we would enjoy the trip surrounded by the necessary number of guards. And I'd rather not alert those outside the estate of our troubles."

Shoulder's slumping, Arlyn returned to work on a rather dull report concerning the expected crop yield of a farming estate. Thankfully, her father chose that moment to stop for a while, and she put the paper aside with a great deal of relief. She'd have a difficult time knowing what he would find important in all that information. Was the lord or lady of the estate expected to remember it all? If so, she was doomed as heir. They'd all better hope her father lived a long time.

23

Arlyn walked between Kai and Lyr on the way to the portal, although both had wanted her to rest. But she'd napped again after helping her father—an easy task after the farming reports—and had even gone through another healing session with Lial. So long as they kept the pace slow, she could handle it. Especially since some of the heat had faded with sunset. Not *much* of the heat, but enough.

"So how does one properly greet an elven prince?"

"Greeting a prince and greeting Ralan can be two different things." Lyr laughed. "I would not worry too much about formality with him."

"I disagree, actually," Kai said.

Lyr's brows lifted. "How many times has he gotten angry or irritated at us for being formal?"

"At us, sure. He knows us. But Ralan is a perverse creature." Kai shook his head. "Despite all of his protestations, he is still royal. He spent the first three hundred years of his life being deferred to, and he has hardly led a life of humility in the human world. He might not think he wants formality, but I wager if a stranger greeted him casually on his return, he would be taken aback."

"Do you really think so?"

Kai shrugged. "He has never succeeded as well as he thinks at losing his princely attitudes. Look at how he commanded you to send me through the portal for him. He slips easily into the role at need."

Lyr frowned. "You have a point."

"Which leads us back to my original question," Arlyn said, interrupting their debate.

"If I had time, I would teach you the High Court greeting." Lyr smirked. "He might expect deference, but *that* would really get him."

Arlyn stared at her father. "You seem to take an inordinate amount of pleasure in annoying a prince. Is this some kind of bizarre tradition I should be aware of?"

"No, not at all. I have been good friends with Ralan for centuries. I suppose it is simply a longstanding joke between us."

They reached the portal, the simple stone arch glimmering in the moonlight. Had she not herself emerged from the mists in that very spot, Arlyn would not have believed it marked anything important. It resembled a large doorway missing its building. The stone wasn't even carved, the absence of adornment striking after the beauty of her father's home.

The clearing was equally sparse, with only a few logs that might serve as benches. Arlyn half expected to see crumbling ruins in the background. "It looks quite small for something so important."

"The deception makes it harder to find and easier to guard," Kai answered, hefting the pack he carried.

They stopped a few steps from the stone arch. Though the trees were visible behind it, the energy crackled in Arlyn's bones. The same energy she'd followed from Earth. "How long will this take?"

Kai shrugged. "Depends on the Veil. A few minutes to a couple of hours."

"Great," she muttered, hoping her energy would hold out.

Kai pulled her into a hug, then just as quickly released her. His worried eyes met hers. "I wish you were resting. The pull is going to be uncomfortable."

"Maybe staying close to the portal will help."

"I suppose we'll see." He looked at Lyr. "Try to distract her."

Without another word, Kai turned to the stone arch and walked into the mists. For a heartbeat, he disappeared from her senses just as he had her sight, and she gasped, her hand flying to her chest at the sudden lack. But almost at once, she could detect his presence again. She let out a long, shaky breath. The bond was still there, though her stomach pitched with the twisting and stretching of it.

Lyr gripped her elbow. "Let's sit down."

With a grateful glance, Arlyn plopped down on a nearby log. She tried closing her eyes, but it only made her disorientation worse. Instead, she took a deep breath and focused on her father. "So tell me about the elven prince who has chosen to live with humans for so long."

"Now?"

She nodded. "A distraction, remember?"

"For the whole of the story, you will have to ask Ralan himself. I am sworn to secrecy." Lyr's gaze drew distant, considering. "It is mostly his father's fault. Ralan is the most powerful seer born into the royal family in two generations. After the death of his great aunt not long after his one hundred and twelfth birthday, he provided visions for his father in her stead. Ralan hated it. I can only say that the king went too far in his requests, and Ralan left with a vow never to return. His daughter must be in dire shape for him to break that vow."

"If he is a seer, then why didn't he know he would return?"

"After what his father did, he refused to use his power again. Do not ask him about the future, not unless your life depends on it. He does not react favorably to such requests."

What could cause a prince to do something so drastic? Arlyn shuddered. She wasn't sure she wanted to find out.

Kai stepped from the mists onto the grounds of Ralan's country house, though *house* was a bit too quaint a word for the massive edifice. A mansion built by a wealthy family in the 1840s, the huge place was situated in the middle of five hundred acres completely enclosed by a high stone wall. In large

part because of the natural portal, Ralan had bought and reno-
vated the estate some fifty years before.

The door opened as Kai reached the porch. Ralan himself
stood in the entry; either he no longer employed a housekeep-
er or was too anxious to wait for her. At the sight of his friend,
Kai's fists clenched in anger. The crossing itself had been easy,
but the strain on his bond made him ill. Every muscle in his
body had tensed against the roiling.

"Welcome, Kai." Ralan moved back and gestured for Kai
to enter. "Thank you for granting my request."

"Request? If that is what His Highness wishes to call it,"
Kai snapped, striding into the entry.

Ralan closed the door with a snap. "Lyr would have told
you of my need. This couldn't be helped."

"Another could have come." Kai struggled to fight down
his anger before it bled across to Arlyn. "Do you have any idea
what it's like to cross the Veil with an incomplete bond? Your
selfishness is putting us all in danger."

"No, but I know the pain of watching my daughter die."
Ralan took a step toward Kai. "Do *you* know what it is like to
see your own child waste away? I have to get her back without
my father interfering. Another guide would have gone to him
at once."

"Fuck your father," Kai snarled, heedless of the slur to his
king. "You have spent too long running from him. Your fear
of his power has caused more trouble in a shaky situation, one
you do not even comprehend. Perhaps you would know what
is going on if you weren't too afraid to use your Sight."

Ralan fell back as though shoved. "You are one of the few to know what happened, yet you would still say such a thing to me? Perhaps our friendship is not what I believed. If I did not need your aid in this—"

"*Laial.*"

The small voice cut across Ralan's words more clearly than any shout. Kai glanced over at the source, and his breath caught. He had never seen an elven child in such condition. Her skin was nearly translucent beneath a fall of long, black hair, her body thin and weak. Worse was her energy. Not only did she have little, but Kai could tell she was not pulling in any of the natural energy around them. Why couldn't she connect with the earth to replenish her power?

Kai noticed then how tired Ralan looked; fine lines of exhaustion pinched the prince's pale face. He had likely been replenishing the child's energy himself. Shame burned through Kai's gut, smothering some of the anger. The discomfort of a strained bond was nothing, *nothing* compared to this.

"Forgive me, Ralan. I never imagined."

"Few of our kind could," the prince replied, moving to scoop the girl into his arms. "My daughter, Moranai Aldiaberen i Erinalia Moreln nai Moranaia. She goes by Eri."

"A pleasure to meet you, Eri," Kai said, careful to keep his voice soft so he wouldn't scare her. He glanced around the foyer, noting the trunk waiting over to the side. "Is that all you wish to take?"

Ralan nodded. "There is little I need of my life here."

Kai gasped against the sudden pressure of his bond and the touch of Arlyn's anxiety that slipped through. "We need to go.

I pray to the Nine Gods your vision was true because I'm not sure how easily I can get us all through."

With a glance at Ralan's drawn face, Kai sent forth a trickle of energy designed to levitate the trunk behind him. Normally, he would have left it to Ralan and concentrated on the crossing, but it was not such a large task to do himself. The prince was clearly occupied with giving energy to Eri, and Kai had guided baggage through before. As they made their way to the portal, a rush of energy flowed past, and wards went up around the property. Those spells would hide the estate from prying eyes for perhaps centuries. It seemed his friend did not intend to return for quite some time.

Arlyn exhaled in relief as some of the tension slipped from her body. The bond between her and Kai was growing more solid, more stable. He had to be getting close. "Almost here, I think."

Lyr's lips quirked. "Useful, that you can sense him so well. At least I didn't have to stand there the entire hour."

"How do you do that?" Arlyn asked as they walked back over to the portal. "Know the time so well?"

"Like all measures, it's a matter of experience. After so long, I suppose it is instinct."

Before she could say more, a plain wooden trunk appeared, then Kai, and finally a dark-haired, somehow familiar elf holding a child. Arlyn jerked in surprise as the bond snapped tight, then shoved a fist to her shaky stomach as some of Kai's sick exhaustion leaked through. He leaned back against the stone of the arch, his face almost as pale as after he'd been stabbed.

"What happened?"

"The way was rough. Turbulent. Perhaps Ralan was right to call for me." Kai ran a hand across his face. *"He and his daughter were both too ill for a long crossing."*

Curious, Arlyn glanced toward the prince, then stifled a gasp. His eyes were closed in bliss, and fine lines around his eyes and mouth smoothed as she stared, leaving him looking years younger. But more amazing was the child. The girl had been still and pale as death, but her cheeks were filling with color as she sat upright in her father's arms.

"Welcome to Braelyn, Anderteriorn i Ralantayan." Lyr inclined his head in a slight bow. "We are pleased to host you in our home. Allow me to introduce a stranger to you, Callian Ayala i Arlyn Dianore se Kaienan nai Braelyn."

Though the greeting once would have sounded formal to Arlyn, she could tell now that it was not. Even when introducing the captain of his guard, whom he spoke to daily, Lyr had used the full title. What level of friendship did it reveal to use only a shortened form to address a prince? From the expression on the prince's face, she thought it had surprised him.

Finally, he spoke. "Ayala? When the hell did you have a daughter?" Ralan darted a stunned look at Kai. "And bonded already? It seems our conversation should have been longer despite the strain of distance, Lyr."

Arlyn's careful, planned greeting slipped from her mind at the prince's bluntness. It was obvious even to her that he had been brutally rude by elven standards. But beside her, her father merely laughed. "You have set a fine example for both of our children, my friend."

The prince reddened, but his mouth turned up in a wry smile. "Forgive me, Ayala Arlyn. I have lived too long in the human world. May pleasure, never hardship, reside with you for many years to come."

"Thank you. May you and your daughter prosper in our home." Arlyn grinned. "I'll add that it would be difficult to offend me, Your Highness. I was born and raised in the human world and have been here less than a month."

"Indeed?" He stepped closer. "Then let's dispense with this cursed formality and move to someplace more comfortable. Along the way, you can tell me how you came to be born with humans when your father so clearly is not. And please, call me Ralan."

Kai had been right; though Ralan showed a strong dislike of elven formality, he was unmistakably royal. His birthright was apparent in the way he carried himself, the way he spoke, and how he expected others to answer him without question. Despite that, he listened to her story with obvious interest, and he carried his daughter with gentle care. By the time Arlyn, Lyr, and Kai finished recounting what Ralan had missed, she had begun to hope that she, too, might become a friend to the prince.

"I must apologize." Ralan shook his head. "I never imagined so much could have happened here. Lyr mentioned injuries, that is true, but all of this in a mere week?"

She studied the child, now bouncing in excitement in her father's arms. "You had reason."

They slipped into the door next to the library, and Ralan drew up short, his body tensing. Arlyn followed his gaze to find Lial waiting in the hall. The healer's eyes widened, and she caught a hint of surprise, and maybe hurt, sparking within them before his expression closed. She'd seen him in various states of grumpy but never so reserved.

Lial gave an elaborate bow. "My Prince, it is a pleasure beyond telling to see you returned. Our family will rejoice to see the face of one so long lost."

"Stand the hell up, cousin. You know perfectly well that few of them would notice my absence except when they needed my skill," Ralan snapped.

Scowling, Lial rose. "You would hardly know such a thing considering your hasty departure and lack of contact. Your mother—"

"Cares for no one but herself," Ralan bit out. Then he let out a deep breath. "Forgive me, Lial. I have never had argument with you. There is much you do not know, but it will have to wait. I have need of your skills as a healer."

"You?" Lial's eyes narrowed. "I see nothing that rest will not cure."

"Not for me. For my daughter."

For the first time, Lial seemed to notice the child nestled in Ralan's arms. She met the healer's eyes, no shyness evident in her demeanor, as Lial stared in shock. "You have a daughter?"

"Indeed." Ralan hugged his child a fraction closer. "This is Princess Erinalia. I must insist that my father not be told."

Unbelievably, Lial started to laugh. It took him several moments to compose himself, a process likely hastened by Ralan's anger. "You don't remember, do you? Your great aunt's final prophecy."

The blood drained from Ralan's face. "No," he whispered. "Surely, one of my other siblings has had a child by now. It has been over three hundred years."

"You are the first." Lial's eyes danced with glee. "By declaration of the king at your great aunt's last prophecy, you are the heir." His lips twisted into a smirk. "Have fun with that."

"Well." Arlyn blinked. "That was interesting."

At Lial's words, Ralan had gone white, then stormed out, the healer close behind; Lyr and Kai still stared at the doorway through which they had departed. Should she, a stranger, have seen that argument? Arlyn bit her lip. At least she knew why Lial was so imperious. As Ralan's cousin, he was a member of the freaking royal family.

Kai turned to look at her. "To put it mildly."

"Why have I never heard of such a decree?" Lyr shook his head, still staring at the door. "He called Teyark, his eldest, the heir. We have been introduced. It was in the title. To lie about such a thing is a serious offense."

"Perhaps he did not lie. The decree could have named Teyark heir unless another produced a child first." Kai frowned. "Ralan must know he will have to contact his father now."

Lyr turned away from the door, his brow furrowed. "I don't like this. Poisoned energy, random attacks, and a seer as heir to the throne? The last time such momentous events occurred so close together, there was war."

Ralan tried to slow his pounding heart as Lial led them to the guest tower. What was he going to do? He'd never wanted to be king. Never. Kien had inherited the zeal for that. Ralan fought to keep his hands from clenching around Eri at the memory of his brother's betrayal. Bad enough that Kien had slept with Ralan's beloved—worse that they'd plotted together to kill him.

And his own father hadn't believed what he'd seen.

Of course, the king had wanted Ralan to See that betrayal. He'd known of the relationship between Kien and Kenaren. Known the time they'd planned to meet. And he'd ordered Ralan to look anyway, to search the futures for what his beloved would do that day. The memory of his love in bed with his brother still burned through his blood after a solid three centuries.

"Is Teyark still alive?"

"Yes." Lial looked over his shoulder in surprise. "Is there a reason he shouldn't be?"

"I haven't had a vision, if that's what you're wondering," Ralan answered. "What of Kien?"

"He was banished not long after you left. No one knows why, except for maybe your siblings." Lial opened the door to the guest room. "If your mother knows, she pretends well. She spends much time lamenting the absence of two of her children."

"I have no doubt the rest is spent trying to negotiate another marriage alliance with father," Ralan grumbled. Since the king had never soulbonded, he'd formed marriages to produce and raise his children, but he'd only kept the alliances until the children had been grown. With at least a couple of centuries of freedom between. "That is probably the reason for the lamentations, as well. Too bad for her that father considers four children enough."

Ralan set Eri on the bed and stepped aside for Lial. The healer hunched down beside her with a smile, all tension gone. "Do you mind if I check you with my magic?"

She grinned. "I already know what you'll find."

"Eri," Ralan said, warning her with his tone not to reveal her talents.

"Okay, okay!" She rolled her eyes. "I don't mind."

It took only moments for Lial to move beyond Ralan's limited ability to analyze the health of another. While he waited, Ralan pondered his cousin's words. Why and to where had Kien been exiled? His father had so vehemently denied the possibility of his middle son's betrayal that Ralan could only assume he had been caught in an actual act of treason rather than by another seer. Even when Kenaren had attempted to follow through on the plot Ralan had foreseen her plan with Kien, the king had not believed.

As the blue glow faded from Lial's hands, he turned to Ralan. "Is there supposed to be something wrong with her that a bit of sleep won't cure?"

Ralan frowned. "Did you check for poison?"

"Of course, I checked for poison." Lial shook his head. "I'm beginning to regret working for this House. What, exactly, am I supposed to be looking for? Something unusual or rare, I've no doubt."

"Your sardonic humor is wasted on me, cousin." Ralan examined Eri with his own limited talent and found her to be in almost perfect health. It made no sense. "On Earth, she could not pull in energy for herself. The magic was off somehow. I had to filter it for both of us."

"She shows no sign of any such problem here. Whatever the issue, it was not internal. Perhaps I should check you, as well."

The prince opened himself wordlessly to Lial's magic. The energy swept through, scanning Ralan more thoroughly than he could check himself. His tension eased, his muscles going lax with the peaceful sensation that came with the healer's power. A neat trick for gaining cooperation from their patients. He was almost sorry when Lial finished, so long had it been since he'd been so relaxed.

"Well?"

"You are not poisoned, yet..." Lial hesitated as though searching for the right words. "Your channels are raw. How have you been able to use your talents without intense pain?"

"Easily enough. I have hardly used them at all."

Arlyn lay in bed once more, watching Kai sort through a trunk of his belongings. Someone had come in while they were away, for two trunks were pushed beneath the window and a set of shelves had been installed on the wall by the door. They were wooden, carved in the same delicate designs as the paneling on the bottom half of her walls. Had she not known better, she would have assumed the shelves had always been there. How had such a task been accomplished in a couple of hours? It had to have been, quite literally, magic.

"Did you order the shelves built?"

"I requested it." Kai paused, then straightened. "Does that bother you? I thought after you decided to complete the second step that it would be fine, but if you'd rather wait longer, I can move my things. I do *not* want to pressure you."

"Oh, calm down." Arlyn rolled her eyes. "I was just curious. Unless there's some code that says I have to sleep with you because you put up shelves?"

He let out a startled laugh. "Not that I am aware."

"I don't care where your stuff is. When I decide for sure that I want to complete the bond, I'll let you know."

Heat flared in his eyes, and his hands tightened on the bundle of cloth he held. "I'll do my best to convince you. But after the way we began, the choice is yours."

Arlyn thought he would come close, maybe kiss her again. But his gaze dropped to his hands. Too bad. She could have used some convincing after the craziness of the day. Then he unfurled the cloth, and her breath caught. The item was a tunic, embroidered with an intricate forest scene. Branches seemed to sway in a false breeze as Kai straightened the garment. Dots of color caught her eyes, and she squinted. Were those birds?

Kai draped the gorgeous piece over the desk and turned back to lift a long vest, cut much like the one her father had worn to her presentation, from the trunk. Eager to see more after the tunic, Arlyn sat up and shifted to the end of the bed for a closer look. Unlike the flowing mists of Lyr's vest, this one was embroidered with the exact view of the forested hills she had seen at sunrise through the study window. It could have been a photograph.

"What in the world did you have to pay for something like *that?*" she asked in awe.

"I traded my services as a guide for the work."

Arlyn's brows rose. "You got something like that for just a few minutes in the Veil?"

"Sometimes it takes more effort. In this case, the seam-stress wanted several rare plants used in making several rather expensive dyes." He turned the vest so she could better see the back, where gentle rays of light whispered over the trees. "That shade of gold was one of them, in fact. The place where the plants grow is not easily accessible from this world. I had to make two stops before we reached the place, and it required a great deal of energy. After that, and the fortune I saved her, she was more than happy to make this for me."

"I had no idea that a guide's work was so valuable. You must be quite wealthy."

"I suppose." He shrugged, then set the vest aside with a grin. He pulled another, bulkier bundle from the chest and moved back to the shelves. "Are you bonding with me for my wealth?"

Arlyn gasped, then grinned as his amusement flowed along the bond. "Really, Kai, be serious. You know I'm bonding with you for your body."

His startled laugh shot pleasure through her. "I assure you it is yours whenever you want it."

"Well…" She lost what she had planned to say when he unwrapped the bundle he'd placed on the shelf. It was a breathtaking figure of a fairy rising from the water, so lifelike that for a moment she wondered if it would take flight. "May I see it?"

Kai brought it over, his steps hesitant. He almost seemed to hold his breath as he placed the glass figure in her hands. Her mouth fell open at her first close look. From a distance, it appeared painted, but up close, she realized that the glass itself was painstakingly colored. How long it had taken, how it had even been accomplished, she could only imagine. Done in shades of blue, the figurine was a water fairy come to life in her hands. The wings alone must have taken hours, even days.

Arlyn ran a finger along the delicate tendrils of the fairy's hair. "Where did you have to guide the artisan to earn something this beautiful?"

"I…" Had he reddened? "I made it myself."

Her gaze darted to his in shock. "You *made* this? I had no idea you had such a talent."

"It is only a hobby."

"A hobby?" She stared at him. "A piece like this belongs in a gallery."

He took the figure back from her and placed it on the shelf. "In the human world, perhaps. You should see the work of the artisans on the Rieren branch, as the bulk of their magic lies in craft. I can only aspire to what they create."

"You're not giving yourself enough credit."

Though he shrugged, Kai's eyes held amusement. "One of the greatest artisans built his entire house of glass."

"That sounds inconvenient." Arlyn wrinkled her nose. "Not to mention the lack of privacy."

Kai chuckled. "The inner rooms are shaded. But it's a sight to see, nonetheless."

"Maybe you can take me there sometime." Her gaze shifted back to the figure on the shelf. "So are fairies real? I expected to see more fantastic creatures here."

"Many of them stayed in realms more closely connected to Earth, and the few who decided to come to this world tend to keep to themselves. There's a group of fairies who live at the edge of Braelyn. The largest is the colony of dragons on an island in the eastern ocean."

Her brows rose. "Dragons?"

"Don't expect to see them." His expression hardened. "The history between our races is not peaceful."

Forget etiquette books. She needed to plunder the library for a primer in Moranaian history. Arlyn opened her mouth to ask more questions, but a knock on the door interrupted her. She sighed as Lynia poked her head in to remind them of dinner. She'd much rather hear about dragons than try to navigate a formal meal with a prince.

Even one as friendly as Ralan.

Arlyn sat at Lyr's right hand, Kai beside her. As their highest-ranking guest, Ralan was across from her, with Selia to his left. Then Eri and Iren, with Lynia taking up the other end. So far, this meal was more subdued than any she'd attended before, thanks to the odd blend of family, friends, and new acquaintances.

Out of the corner of her eye, Arlyn thought she caught Lyr fidgeting with his napkin, and she held back a smile. She suspected he'd rather be joking with Kai and Ralan, but his mother's presence kept him at his most formal. Not even elves wanted to tick off their mothers.

Selia had certainly been quick to grip Iren's arm when the prince had been introduced. But although the boy's eyes had twinkled, he'd behaved. When he wasn't staring at Eri. They leaned together even now, talking in quiet tones. Arlyn had the uneasy feeling she didn't want to know what they discussed with such intensity.

A groan from Ralan caught her attention. He'd just taken a bite of bread, and his eyes had slipped closed in appreciation. Arlyn couldn't stop a moment's appreciation herself, though of the prince and not the bread. She was bonded, not dead, and he was one of the most handsome men she'd ever seen. Not that it would go beyond admiration. Even if she'd never met Kai, Ralan wasn't her type. Still, she couldn't help but stare at him. He looked so familiar. But *where* could she have seen him before? A man like him was not easily forgotten.

Kai stiffened beside her even as Ralan caught her gaze. A grin twisted the prince's lips. "Bored with Kai already?"

"Sorry for staring." She frowned. "Have we met? I could swear we have, but I have no idea where."

"He was probably famous," Kai muttered.

"Famous?" Arlyn studied the prince for a moment before it came to her. "Roland Morn, the fashion designer! A couple of my friends were convinced you were gay until—" She cut her words off mid-sentence, suddenly aware that everyone, including the children, had stopped to listen.

Ralan laughed at her blush. "What *is* it with humans and their strict concept of gender roles?"

"I suppose you used that to your advantage." A grin lit her face despite the lingering blush. "You know, I *thought* that eighteenth century court gown you sent down the runway looked quite authentic. I guess it was more so than anyone could have guessed."

He smirked around his teacup. "I saw quite a few of those gowns up close and personal."

"If you don't stop flirting with my bonded," Kai began, leaning forward, "I will flay you. Prince or not."

Selia gasped, and Lynia's eyes narrowed. "Kaienan! You will not threaten a guest at my dinner table." She glanced at Ralan. "Even when said guest has forgotten basic rules of conduct."

Lyr coughed into his hand as Kai murmured an apology. Though Ralan's mouth still curved up, he inclined his head. "Forgive me, Lady Lynia. I have been away too long, I'm afraid. I will cease my teasing if it disturbs you."

Lynia nodded. "If I might suggest another topic, perhaps you could tell us more about the energy on Earth. My research suggests the poison is no accident."

"I would like to hear about that, as well," Kai said. Though he leaned back in his seat, tension radiated from Kai like a living thing. She gave him a concerned glance, but he only shook his head. "So far, the energy problem has seemed restricted to the underrealms. The man who stabbed me warned me away from interfering with the Sidhe. But nothing about Earth."

"Eri couldn't draw in natural energy on her own. I wasn't sure why but assumed it was her human blood." Frowning, Ralan set down his tea cup. "Yet she does so with ease here. Lial said my channels were raw from all of the energy I purified."

"You mean you did not notice?" Selia asked, then pinched her lips closed. "Forgive me, Prince Ralan. That was too personal a question."

He waved a hand. "No, it's fine. It's a valid question. The truth is I rarely used any of my gifts on Earth, especially the last few decades."

Selia's mouth opened, but she snapped it shut. Arlyn watched her teacher struggle not to ask more and took pity on her. "Why not?" Her gaze flicked to Lyr, then back. "I mean, why not use any magic? I'm not sure I could have resisted if I'd known how to use mine."

Ralan's gaze slid to his plate. "It makes discovery more likely. Human technology has made life on Earth more pleasant, anyway."

"Too bad you never tried to track down the source of the poison," Lyr said.

"By the time I realized it wasn't natural, I had my hands full taking care of Eri."

Though she had not appeared to be paying attention, Eri turned from her quiet conversation with Iren. "I know who it is!"

Ralan frowned down the table at his daughter. "Did we not discuss this, Eri?"

"I cannot hide what I am, *laial*," she answered in a serious tone. "Besides, I'm not going to tell you who it is. If you want to know, you'll have to look for yourself."

The manor was quiet as Allafon wandered its halls.
None of his servants—and here, they *were* servants—
would dare to interrupt him in his present mood. He
bunched his hands in his short, white-blond hair and glared
out the nearest window. Where was Morenial? After killing
that nameless, worthless little half-blood failure a few days ago,
Allafon had realized only one of the whelps remained. They
were tough to find and even more difficult to train, a valuable
resource that could not be wasted. Coupling with a human was
repugnant, or he would have created an army himself. Even he
was not willing to go that far for revenge.

He would have to bring his son in on the plot. Morenial
hated the Dianore family as much as he did, so it should not
be a problem. If only he would return from that foolish alliance wedding. Why even bother? The woman would only be-

tray Morenial's friend in the end. Allafon's own mate, his bonded, had done so. Everyone in the Dianore line would die for their part, all but Lynia. Telien's mate would replace his own. Perhaps he would even let Lyrnis live long enough to see it.

His footsteps rang with rage as Allafon returned to the desk in his study and pulled out a piece of parchment. He would not wait for Morenial to return. It was time for him to stop relying on others for his revenge. The letter would require careful wording and much planning, but Allafon might have found a way. Blood would run soon. Much blood.

"What do you mean, you aren't going to tell?" Ralan stared at his daughter with a perplexed frown. "It makes no difference which seer the information comes from. If you know the cause of these problems, then say so."

The girl looked directly at her father, a light in her eyes he knew all too well. "If I tell you now, then everything will be ruined. I see no good future descending from any line where you do not find the truth for yourself. When you Look, you will know."

Ralan's hands gripped the edge of the table. *Megelien.* "The healer told me to avoid using my talents for a day or two while my channels finish healing."

"When you are finally ready, the time will be right," she answered. Then Eri blinked a few times and smiled, and the eerie sense of a Presence was gone.

Why hadn't the goddess spoken in his mind, as she once had?

The table had gone completely silent, all attention focused on the two of them. Honey spread in a puddle from the fruit Lyr had dropped on his plate at Eri's words. Kai gripped his mug of tea with such force his fingers were white. It did not take a seer's ability for Ralan to know that questions would be imminent, but he didn't know how to answer them. Even though Lyr and Kai were friends, two of the people he trusted the most, Ralan had not wanted them to know of Eri's talents. He ground his teeth together at her disobedience. Had he been so reckless with his own abilities as a child?

"She is not yet seven?" Selia whispered from beside him.

Ralan fought the urge to snatch up his daughter and flee. She would not be used. "I was in my eighth year when I began to See. I had hoped she would not inherit this from me, and I beg of you to say nothing."

Before any of them could answer, Eri spoke once more. "We should not hide what we are, *laial*. If anyone should try to force a prophecy from me, I will gladly lead them to a future they do not want. The futures where we live in fear are not good."

His breath left him at her words. *Had* he been living in fear rather than justified anger? It had once seemed logical to abandon his talents after his father's betrayal, for then no one would be able to make him work against his own interests again. But had he allowed himself to be a victim? Though the king had commanded Ralan to Look at Kenaren's activities, he could have refused. Even his father knew it was folly to try to force a seer. So why had he gone along with it? He knew he would have to consider that question carefully.

"Even so, it is not necessarily wise to announce your talent to everyone who will listen. There is much you need to learn of subtlety."

Face pale and expression grave, Lyr met his eyes. "By Arneen, Ralan, teach her."

Kai was too quiet. His shoulders were taut with tension as he carried more glass figures to the shelves, and he avoided meeting her eyes. Worse, Arlyn sensed the upset churning through him, though she was hesitant to intrude upon him by searching deeper along their bond. Was he that bothered by the little girl's words?

That presence had certainly made Arlyn's hands tremble with dread. She'd never been close to a Deity before. Never really felt the pull. After studying so many theories on magic and religion when looking for information on the elves, she'd become decidedly agnostic. How could anyone know which version of the Divine was true? Or if they were all true? Until now, she'd received no direct evidence.

"Did Eri's words bother you?" Arlyn asked.

Kai looked up from the miniature glass forest he'd placed on the shelf. "Not as much as the interference of the goddess. Megelien's interest is concerning."

"Is it that bad?"

"Bad enough," he answered, returning to the open trunk.

She frowned at his back. "Bad enough to put you in this snit?"

"Snit?" Kai spun, and she almost jumped back at the anger in his eyes. "With our bond, you can't tell it's more than that?"

Arlyn's fists clenched, and her eyes narrowed. "I choose not to intrude on your privacy. If you have a problem, talk to me."

The sound of her heart pounding in her ears filled the sudden silence. Hurt and anger surged along the bond even as his face twisted with it. Kai took a few steps forward. "Do you want to break our bond?"

"What?" she asked, brow scrunching in confusion even as pain sliced at her heart.

"Ralan. The way you were with him." His expression hardened. "I could feel your attraction to him. Do you want free of me?"

Her breath whooshed out in a surprised laugh. "Are you kidding?"

Kai closed the distance between them, his gaze capturing hers. "You didn't want this bond in the first place. I would not see you miserable"

"Just like that?" Arlyn's chest squeezed, and she pressed her fist against her breastbone. A futile gesture against the building ache. "You'd let me go, just like that?"

"I don't know."

"You don't *know*? After all of this?" She poked a finger into his chest. "You sound pretty certain to me. I can't believe this."

"*Clechtan,* Arlyn, I…" He yanked her against him, and she caught a hint of the hurt threaded deep through his words. "Fuck it. You will always be mine."

His mouth took hers, and heat flared between them. Kai's hands slid up her side and around her back, catching in her hair, as he consumed her. Emotion pulsed through the bond. His jealousy. Her hurt. Desire. All entwining like their bodies as Arlyn slipped her own arms around him and pulled him closer.

If they didn't join together soon, she was going to explode. And not in the way she'd prefer.

Her heart slammed as he nudged her back, her legs hitting the edge of the bed. Arlyn tugged him, and they both toppled down. She slid her hands under his tunic, along his back. A moan hummed between them at the touch. His sound? Hers? Their fire was one and the same as they started tugging clothing free.

Kai pulled back at her hiss of pain when her dress caught against her arm. Panting, his eyes met hers. "Gods, Arlyn. You're hurt. We shouldn't do this now."

"Not a damsel, remember?"

She tossed the dress aside, the corner of her mouth curving as his focus shifted to her body. Still, he shook his head. "If we do this, the bond..."

"Shut up, Kai."

Arlyn yanked him back down, her mouth cutting off more discussion. Damn, her body burned. Even her soul was on fire as the bond tightened between them. Hadn't she picked him the moment she'd accepted his necklace? Her conscious mind might not have known, but her spirit had. Now the rest of her was on board. Stubborn man. Couldn't he feel it?

She rolled him over. Rose above him. "Are you changing *your* mind?"

"Arlyn." Kai's gaze softened, and he ran a finger along her cheek. "Never."

"Then why?"

He gripped her hips. "I want you to choose me."

"I already did."

Arlyn trembled as she poised above him. Met his eyes. They shivered together as she lowered, joining their bodies. A glow built between them as she began to move, and her breath gasped out as their souls merged. Gripping his hands with hers, she let the passion consume her. Consume them both.

Light filled the room as they exploded together.

She slumped across his chest, energy spent, and snuggled closer as his arms wrapped around her. Peace—rightness— filled her, and her sigh slid against his neck. The tension be- tween them was gone, washed away by their joining. Nothing but happiness remained as his fingers made lazy circles on her back.

Finally, Arlyn tucked herself against Kai's side, settling her injured arm across his waist with a wince. He shifted beneath her, and she could practically feel his frown. "Are you well?"

She cracked one eye open. "You need to ask?"

"Not in *that* way." His chest shook with his chuckle. "I meant your arm."

"No worse than any other scrape I've had over the years," Arlyn answered, shrugging.

"Good." Kai flipped her to her back, his lips curved up in a wicked smile. "Now it's my turn."

After the morning meal, Arlyn convinced Kai to brave the archery field once more. In the days since her injury, no trace of the assassin had been found, and there had been no further disturbances. She still couldn't stop herself from scanning the tree line, her fingers tightening around the bow, even with Selia standing at the ready behind them.

In addition to her teacher, Arlyn could see guards around them even without consulting her inner map. Security had been tightened everywhere, especially after Ralan's arrival. Did elves have an equivalent to the Secret Service? If so, she supposed the king would send them. She tried to amuse herself with a vision of elves dressed in dark suits and wearing sunglasses but found even that could not distract her.

Kai ran a hand down her arm in comfort, and Arlyn shivered. She might not be sure if she'd slipped into love, but she was happy with their bond. Was he? Her fingers shook as she strung her bow. What if she proved inept in archery, her greatest skill? He might not be so pleased to be bonded with her then.

"Do you sense something?" Kai asked, worry in his voice.

"No." Arlyn let out a long breath. "I'm just nervous. I've drawn a bow with worse pain, but I don't want to look foolish."

He gave her arm a squeeze and stepped back. "You'll do fine"

She slipped a glove on her right hand. At four feet long, her Welsh-style bow was the smallest of the three she had brought from Earth, but both her recurve bow and longbow required a greater draw strength and steadiness than she could manage with an injured arm. Had the injury been to her right arm, which she used to pull, Arlyn wouldn't have even tried. Keeping the bow stable enough to get a decent shot would be enough of a challenge.

Arlyn nocked her blunt-tipped practice arrow, drew, and sighted. Smiling, she focused on one of the many targets placed at varying distances and heights. Her insecurities faded, replaced by the peace that archery had always brought her. This was familiar, more home to her than almost anything. Between breaths, the energy flowed through her, and she was so surprised by its unexpected strength that she almost lost focus. But even the burning in her arm ceased to matter as she released the arrow to its target and then replaced it, one after another. No hesitation, no doubt. Wherever she willed each arrow to go, it hit.

She reached back for another arrow and found only air. Lowering her bow, she stood, panting against the pain. Despite the fire raging in her arm, she felt more like herself than she had in days. Grinning, she stepped over to retrieve her arrows, Kai a silent presence behind her. At the first target, she had hit several in the center, a few close enough to touch each other. The second target, placed a few feet higher and farther back, was not as impressive; only two arrows touched in the center, and one was on the outer edge. Still, she was content with her performance.

Leaning back against a tree, Arlyn finally met Kai's gaze and found him smirking. "What?"

"I'm not sure why you were so worried," he answered. "You almost shattered one shaft with another arrow, and you got several so close together that even parchment wouldn't fit between. I guess you could hope for a lucky arrow-splitting shot, but those are pretty rare even for us, at least without using a spell that is generally not worth the energy expended."

Requiring both perfect aim and an arrow shaft with just the right grain of wood, such shots were almost mythical on Earth. She had never met anyone who had actually done it but had assumed the legendary elves could do the trick with ease. "Why do our stories portray elves as such unbelievable archers, then?"

"Mostly because of our speed, accuracy born of centuries of practice, and the superior craftsmanship of our equipment."

She looked down at her bow. "Hey, I made this."

"I imagine you didn't make it at the same time humans and elves mingled enough for them to have such stories of us." Kai laughed. "Your bow is fine. I should introduce you to one of our artisans, though. I have no idea how they are made, but I think you would enjoy comparing techniques."

"Yes, I would." Arlyn unstrung her bow and secured it to her back. "So I really did okay? Better than blade work?"

"I'd have to compare you when you are fully healed, but you might even be better than Lyr," Kai answered as they returned to Selia. "It seems the combat magic you inherited from your father manifests most prominently in this."

"I agree." Selia shook her head. "I studied the energy moving through you, and I don't understand how it flowed properly with the iron in your arm. It must have been painful."

"At first, yes," Arlyn acknowledged, frowning down at the wound. "It still hurts now." She thought back to what had happened. "But the iron seemed to push against my magic. I kept forcing until the iron just gave."

As they turned to go back to the main practice field, Arlyn met her father's eyes.

Eyes full of pride.

The sound of his daughter's laughter filled Ralan with a peace he had never known. Through the window of their tower room, he spotted Eri and Iren playing in the garden below. She was running—actually *running*—around a small, decorative pond while trying to evade Iren in an odd sort of two-person tag. So hard to believe she'd barely had the energy to walk for the last few years. Now the sight of her acting like a normal child filled Ralan with enough joy to make up for his own unhappiness at having to return. He tried to hold onto the feeling as he prepared himself to contact his father. He could delay the inevitable no longer.

Ralan turned back to the communication mirror, full-length and beautifully framed with silver vines of *lari* flowers. Unless his father had changed a routine that spanned a couple of millennia, the king would be taking a break in his study between the meeting with his advisors and the morning court appearance. Since Ralan was not quite healed enough to span the distance with his mind, he would have to use the mirror. At no other time would the king be so readily available to answer. If Ralan waited, he would have to work his way through hapless assistants and countless hours of protocol.

It took less time than Ralan would have liked to activate the spell. There was a brief delay, and then the mirror filled with the image of Moranai Lor i Alianar. Ralan's breath caught when he noted the changes in his father. Before, they could have been mistaken for brothers, but his father's black hair was nearly gray now and his face etched with lines. The effect was even greater when recognition hit and the king's expression filled with surprise, grief, and perhaps even hope. After their angry parting, the greeting was far from expected.

"Ralan?" Alianar breathed, almost as though he was afraid to speak too loudly lest he scare his son away. "After so long, I had given up hope of ever seeing your face again."

For a moment, Ralan was truly at a loss. His father's last words had been a command to leave and never contact him again. Remembering, he stiffened. "How differently you speak to me now. I can only assume you have need of a seer once more."

His father flinched. "I see you are not here because you have forgiven me."

"It is difficult to forgive a father who all but disowns you for telling a truth he manipulated out of you."

Alianar's shoulders slumped. "Come home, Ralan. We have a great deal to discuss. Certainly more than should be said over a mirror connection."

Ralan was almost swayed by the sad, tired look in his father's eyes, but the horror of it all washed over him again. Kien and Kenaren making love before plotting his demise. Alianar's smug smile when Ralan had begun his report on the betrayal followed by anger and cold denial. *You lie because you refuse to accept the future you have seen. What kind of seer are you, then? A son who would betray his brother is no son at all.*

He ground his teeth together. "All you needed to say was said before I left. I will not return to be your puppet once more."

"Why have you contacted me, then, if not to seek redress?" the king asked, his voice cracking in grief.

"I have news," Ralan snapped, surprised by his father's mention of redress. Did he truly believe reconciliation was possible? "I would not have bothered had I not spoken with Lial, but I will not dishonor the rest of my family. I must tell you that I have a daughter."

If the king had seemed surprised before, it was nothing compared to his expression at those words. "A daughter? Just born?"

"She is six in Moranaian years."

Alianar paled. "You have had a child for so long without a word said? Do you realize what you have done?"

"It was unintentional." Ralan grimaced to consider the sheer number of times his brother had been improperly introduced. Thankfully, few outside the family knew of his father's decree, so the results of the dishonor would be lessened. "I thought you would have long ago disowned me. Besides, she is half-human. I assumed that would remove her from succession."

"Did you not know the prophecy, then? Megliana said my heir should be the first to produce a child *with outworld blood*. Why do you think I encouraged a wedding alliance with the Galaren? Teyark was unlikely to have children, Kien was unsuitable, and your sister was just a child herself."

Ralan's hands clenched. "It is good to know that I meant nothing more than the fulfillment of my great aunt's prophecy. Do you not understand? A line of seers should not rule. Gods, the danger… It must not be done."

"A *line* of seers?" Alianar asked, eyebrows raised. "The talent bred true in your daughter as well?"

Miaran, but he had lived too long among humans to let such a thing slip. "Eri is none of your concern. I will not have you hurt her as you did me."

"By Arneen, Ralan, that is low." Alianar shook his head. "I do not understand this. How could you not have Seen all that has happened these three hundred years? You should know how much I have grieved for you."

"I do not know because I will not Look." Ralan tried hard to hide the pain he did not want his father to see. He knew how well the king could lie, and he would not be manipulated. "I will not return. I do not care whom you call your heir."

Alianar looked almost desperate at those words. "At least tell me where you are so I may send the Elite to guard you both."

"You need not." Ralan's smile was grim. "I am at the estate of Callian Myern i Lyrnis Dianore nai Braelyn, and he will see us well-protected. I warn you not to come here or to bother us in any way. Do so and I will take my daughter to a world so far away that whispers of our name will disappear from memory."

Ralan ended the connection so abruptly the gesture couldn't be mistaken for anything other than grave insult. The conversation had hurt more than he could have anticipated. He had believed the only emotion that had remained for his father was anger, but it appeared he'd been wrong. The love and grief ran so deep that it was difficult to bear. Chest aching, he turned away from the mirror, only to meet the tear-stained face of his daughter.

R alan knelt beside his daughter. "What happened, Eri?
Why are you crying?"

"If I ever make a mistake," Eri asked, her watery gaze focused on his. "Will you forgive me?"

He frowned. "Of course."

"And if you were the one to make a mistake?"

"What do you mean?" The pained look in her eyes concerned him as much as the question. "Have you Seen something that bothered you?"

Eri glanced pointedly at the mirror. "Yes, but it was not in the future."

Stunned, Ralan sank back on his heels. It was clear she had heard more than enough of the argument with his father. He pulled her resisting form into his arms and hugged her close.

"I'm sorry, Eri. If you knew all that had happened, you would understand."

"I know better than you do." She jerked away from his hold. "If I try really hard, I can see the past sometimes. You both made mistakes."

He sucked in a ragged breath. "You can see the past, too?"

"When Megelien wills it."

"Then…" Ralan closed his eyes, seeking composure. He couldn't worry about the implications of *that*. Not now. A deep breath and he caught her gaze once more. "Then you know such a thing is not easy to forgive."

Her eyes filled with more tears. "If we ever spoke words in anger, would you want the chance to make it up to me? I'm scared. What if I tell the wrong person I'm a seer and you get mad for good?"

"All you have to do is Look to see—"

"The futures are always uncertain, *laial*, and there are so many paths. You know that. I love you. Don't get mad at me, too."

Ralan could only sit in shock as his daughter ran from the room. Should he go after her? What could he say? He could not deny the truth in her words. He'd made his share of mistakes, growing so embittered over the things his father asked him to See that he had delivered his last report in cruel anger. He could have stayed after Kenaren's attack and tried to convince his father. In truth, he had fled far more than the king's fury; Ralan had been running from himself. If he had been used or manipulated, he had certainly allowed it.

He could never hold a grudge against Eri. Could he? She was his world, and he would love her no matter what she did. How could she believe any anger at her would last? He disliked how easily she revealed her abilities, but he could never stay that upset over it. And if he were the one who made a mistake? His chest tightened with pain at the thought of Eri hating him. Pain, and an undeniable sympathy for his own father.

Arlyn sat next to Selia on the low stone wall around the practice field and waited for Lyr and Kai to return from retrieving their swords. She'd intended to practice her blade work, but the pain in her arm had needed more time to fade. So her father and her bonded would train first. She was supposed to analyze how her father used his magic in combat. If she could figure out how.

"It is good that we have a few moments alone," Selia said, drawing Arlyn's attention.

Arlyn's stomach pitched. "It is?"

"I have things I need to say to you." Selia took in Arlyn's expression and smiled. "Do not panic. You have not done anything wrong."

She took a deep breath. "That's good, at least."

"I hope you will forgive the informality and bluntness of this speech." Selia paused, a hint of unease entering her eyes. "I have discovered the source of your mother's elven blood. This is the first true chance I have had to tell you about it."

"Oh." Arlyn twisted her fingers together in her lap. "Is it bad?"

"No, but it is a dishonor for my House." Selia's gaze slipped away. "Your grandfather was my brother."

Arlyn gasped, the punch of her teacher's words hitting her. "I'm sorry to shame you."

Selia gripped Arlyn's hand when she started to rise. "Oh, no, Arlyn, I did not mean such. The dishonor was my father's in neglecting his son. I would be honored beyond telling to call you family."

"Even with my human blood?"

"My brother was half-human." Selia straightened, her head taking on a regal tilt. "His grandchild should be no less treasured."

"I need to think about this," Arlyn said.

Selia nodded. "I understand. My father's actions…" Her nostrils flared. "I can only apologize. But I hope we might someday become friends."

Arlyn ran her sweaty palms along her pants. She hadn't expected such an offer from her kind but formal teacher, and she wasn't sure how to respond. Accept? Deny? Was there some protocol around friendship? Giving up, she just nodded. "That would be lovely."

It must have been the right thing to say because Selia relaxed. "Thank you."

Arlyn wanted to ask more about her grandfather, but Lyr and Kai returned before she could. As they took their places, Arlyn leaned over to Selia. "Does my father know?" she whispered.

Selia nodded. "I told him while you were injured. I wanted to speak with you first, but it was news that could not wait."

Arlyn opened her mouth to answer, but Lyr caught her gaze from his place on the field. "Remember to study my technique."

"I'll do my best," Arlyn answered, giving Selia a quick smile in apology.

When Kai and Lyr began, the only adjective she could think of was beautiful. Like a dance of death. Both of them flowed like water around stones, their swings moving flawlessly from offense to defense and back again. They stooped and turned, blades clashing over and over yet somehow never meeting flesh. She could not believe how they managed to pull their blows at this speed.

Arlyn gasped as Kai's sword swooped a hairsbreadth from Lyr's stomach. Her father shifted back in one fluid motion, then went on the attack while Kai recovered from the momentum of the swing. He barely glided away from Lyr's blow in time, coming frighteningly close to a wound on his other side. But Kai only turned, spinning in a quick arc. They fought back and forth across the field at a frenzied, amazing pace, their steps so in tune she could almost hear music as if they truly danced.

Though Arlyn tried to focus on how to duplicate such expertise, she wanted to close her eyes against the sight. One stumble could cause one or both of them serious injury. Why hadn't they worn armor if they were going to use live blades? It seemed foolhardy for them not to have done so, and yet their skill was undeniable. She had enough experience to know her father was holding back, taking it easy on her bonded, but Kai was still an amazing swordsman.

None of that knowledge settled the twisting in her stomach.

Before her discomfort could become distress, they stopped. Kai let his sword drop to his side and wiped the sweat from his face with his other hand. Unlike when he had fought her, he was panting for breath. "Enough."

Her father didn't even look tired. "Come on, Kai. We've almost made it the full hour. Can't you go a few minutes longer?"

Arlyn blinked, surprised to realize so much time had passed. "Don't stop on my account."

Kai met her gaze. "I could tell it bothered you."

"Sorry," she muttered as her face reddened. "You're not wearing armor. What if one of you slips?"

"The blades are enchanted to minimize such risks, but the occasional cut does happen." Lyr shrugged. "We've all given Lial our fair share of grief."

With a laugh, Arlyn shook her head. "No wonder he's so surly."

"Indeed." Her father smiled, and for once, she was in on the joke. "If Kai's too tired, how about you? Have you recovered enough for a lesson?"

Arlyn's grin slipped. "I guess so. Just promise not to laugh."

Arlyn shifted the hilt of her practice blade in her hand, then forced herself to stand firm. With a quick nod, she met Lyr's eyes. "Let's get this over with."

His eyebrow rose. "This is a lesson, Arlyn, not an execution. I won't hurt you."

"Of course not." She lifted her blade in resignation. "But you'll probably be embarrassed."

"I highly doubt it."

Lyr tested her, then, going through defensive and offensive sword positions to see what she knew. Her face flamed the entire time, and the gazes of their audience seemed like a living thing on her back. She struggled to ignore the world around her, to forget her awkwardness, but it was impossible. Her father's face never changed from an expression of polite concentration, providing further frustration. She had no way to gauge his opinion of her skills.

Finally, he stopped. "Why don't you pull in energy when you do sword work?"

"What?"

"It flows through you with ease when you practice with your bow." He lifted his sword. "Try again. Feel it."

Arlyn almost groaned to realize he was right. When she held a bow, it was part of her soul. But that never happened with a sword. Maybe because Earth blades were made of steel instead of the *peresten* ore of this world? Her eyes slipped closed as she sought the energy that poured through her during archery. After a few breaths, it filled her, extending down through the blade. Her body hummed with it.

At once, her sword became lighter and her knowledge of the world more pronounced. She worked through the first few positions, hesitantly at first, then with more confidence. Soon, her father joined her, and she started to understand the dance.

The combat magic did not make her an expert; she still fought at less than half the speed of the others. But she recognized the energy as it flowed, how each move her father made rippled in the world around her. She began to trust the music she knew but had never heard.

By the time they stopped, Arlyn held a glimmer of hope for her future. Panting, she stumbled over to the stone wall and plopped down, too tired to even care about the ache in her arm. It hadn't given her the same trouble as it had during archery. Had her exercise worked the iron flakes from her flesh? She'd have to ask Lial.

Lyr—not even sweating, damn him—stopped in front of her. His eyes crinkled up with his smile. "Excellent work. Another fifty years and you will likely beat Kai."

"Fifty years?" Arlyn laughed. "Somehow that isn't as reassuring as I think you intended."

Kai pushed back a strand of hair, still damp from his after-practice swim, and tried not to shuffle his feet. Lyr would finish reading the report as soon as possible, and impatience would help nothing. But restlessness picked at Kai's nerves. Arlyn had loved his glasswork so much that his fingers practically itched to make her something. He just needed a place to work.

"How long do you think it'll take them to finish the building?" Kai asked as soon as Lyr dropped the paper.

Lyr frowned down at the report on the desk before meeting Kai's eyes. "A couple of houses are in line first. Perhaps two weeks if the weather holds."

"I'll start seeing what I can trade for tools, then." Kai shifted, ready to go find his bonded. "I'd get them from my old workshop at Oria, but I don't want to deal with my father. I'd rather guide a caravan of haughty Sidhe traders than that."

"Some of those glasswork components are expensive."

"Very." Kai smirked. "That's fine, though. I hear the head of my new House is wealthy enough."

Lyr let out a snort. "You probably earn more as a guide than I do as Myern."

After a quick knock, Kera slipped in the side door, a folded piece of parchment in her hand. Kai's brows rose as Lyr gestured her forward. Most communicated through spell mirror, saving paper missives for more serious affairs. What could it be?

Lowering the paper, Lyr looked up at Kera. "Did you know the messenger?"

"No, Myern," she answered. "But the guards of Oria are a reserved lot. They tend to avoid us."

"Thank you for bringing this at once, Kera."

She nodded, then gave a salute before returning to her post. Lyr lifted the paper, scanning the words again as Kai stepped closer. "Did she say Oria? That's from my father?"

"He has requested a formal visit from our family as soon as possible so he might meet your new bonded," Lyr answered. "How odd. This is rather short notice for a formal meeting, and he has no love for this family."

Kai drummed his fingers on his knee. "He must want something, but I can't imagine what. He does nothing unless it is to his own benefit."

Lyr pulled out another slip of paper. "Would you like me to refuse?"

"Though it might give me some satisfaction, I think I'd rather get the visit over with. Tradition demands it be done eventually."

"Are you certain?"

Kai tensed against the uneasiness that rose like bile in the back of his throat. The request was an odd gesture from his father. Almost suspicious. A hazy memory surfaced of his brother's warning. It had been a hallucination or a dream, hadn't it, a product of the iron poisoning? Lial had told him Kai's family had not been contacted, and his brother could not have gotten so close without alerting the guards.

But what purpose would his father or brother have in harming him? Though not close, he and Moren had always been friends of a sort. His father had expressed regret at his distance from Kai at their last meeting. Surely, he was making much of nothing, a dream and no more. Perhaps Allafon truly was eager to meet Arlyn and to make amends with his son.

Either way, they needed to know.

"Yes," Kai finally answered. "But let him wait. Tomorrow will be more than soon enough."

The soft reflection of the quarter moon glimmered on the garden stream. Arlyn was not sure how long she had sat in this spot, but the other moon had already shifted behind the trees. Two moons. Did they have names? She knew as soon as she wondered that the one she could still see was called Meridar and the one now set was Torinar. It seemed her father's gift of language had included such things. Useful, if a bit uncanny.

Though she was exhausted, Arlyn couldn't sleep. Worry twisted her insides, so much so that she'd refused even Kai's comfort, blocking him out as much as possible. He could do nothing but stress himself on her behalf, and his concern would only increase her own. The day had just been too much. As he had discussed the intricacies of tomorrow's formal visit, sick, hopeless dread had filled her until she'd left to try to calm herself. Pain at her withdrawal had pierced her across their bond, but Kai hadn't protested. He knew how much she needed this moment to herself.

Despite the difficulties she had faced so far, Arlyn loved Moranaia, and she had given up trying to deny it. But could she ever truly belong? She was a grown woman, sure of herself even when she lived on the fringes of the human world, rarely more than an observer. Here? Here she was a child, unskilled at everything. Iren, and somehow even Eri, had more social skills than Arlyn. She needed a guidebook for the most basic interactions of Moranaian culture. And her father called her his heir. With a bitter laugh, she imagined how appalled his people would be if she were left in charge. She'd probably *lead* them in the rebellion.

Seriously, how many layers of formality did one culture need? Tomorrow would be a delicate balance, and Arlyn was totally unprepared. There were rules for those higher in rank visiting a subordinate. Rules for House alliances formed by the soulbond. Hell, there were probably rules for how she wore her undergarments. She was going to flub something.

Except maybe the undergarments. Maybe.

Moranaia called to her soul, but her mind struggled. If she could not get past her own ego and allow herself time to flounder, to learn as a child learned, then she would never fit in here. Arlyn had no idea what she would do in that case. Earth held no appeal; she had no surviving relatives and no close friends. Perhaps Kai could guide her to a place more suited to her knowledge and skills. Of course, now that she was bound to Kai, he would suffer for her failure, too. The pressure was almost paralyzing.

A soft sound drew her attention, and she glanced up to see Selia a few paces away. A hesitant smile crossed her teacher's face. "Forgive my interruption. I did not think to encounter anyone in the gardens this late."

"It's fine." Arlyn shrugged. "I wanted solitude earlier, but it doesn't seem to be helping much."

"May I sit?"

At Arlyn's assent, Selia settled herself on a nearby stone. She took a long moment to smooth her dress before finally meeting Arlyn's eyes. "I meant what I said earlier about becoming friends. If you need someone to talk to, you may speak with me, so long as you are comfortable."

"Thank you." Arlyn looked at her mentor with new respect. Though Selia's fingers twisted together with nerves, she struggled past her discomfort. "I admit I'm having difficulty adjusting. There's so much in this place I don't understand."

"You must stop thinking like a human. No one here will be." Selia looked into the stream for a moment before glancing back up at Arlyn. "Please understand. I do not mean human thoughts are bad. You should certainly honor that part of yourself. It is just that when you measure your life in such a short span, everything has immediacy. A human who does not adapt quickly is often in peril. You are not living on those terms here. Even if a new skill takes you a century or more to learn fully, well, that is nothing. We are not usually considered full members of society until our two hundred and fiftieth year."

Arlyn considered her teacher's words. "But how can I be an adult and a child at the same time? How can I be bonded so soon?"

"Sexual maturity and the ability to bond have little to do with this. Are all ages of humans regarded equally once they are of an age to wed?"

"It depends on the culture, but not where I am from." Arlyn twirled a strand of grass around her finger. This variety was softer than grass on Earth; her skin slid easily along the blade. "In America, the age of eighteen is the standard for adulthood, but most are not taken seriously until their mid-twenties. A person must be at least thirty-five to be president, a sort of elected king."

Selia nodded. "Exactly so. One can earn respect sooner but is not punished as harshly for transgressions, either. Pretend you are eighteen."

At that, Arlyn couldn't help but laugh, confusing her teacher in the process. "I'm sorry. Your advice was sound. It's just that eighteen is often the age when humans in my country go to college, a place of learning. Many of them spend as much time partying as studying. Imagine my father's face if I started spending my nights drinking alcohol and having loud parties."

Selia grinned. "This college must be a fascinating place."

"Oh, there are plenty of serious students despite the stories. But you are right, it is a fascinating place."

Arlyn smiled back. Some of the knots of worry had unwound themselves during their discussion. Her mentor's words had certainly helped more than all the brooding. Maybe, just maybe, it would all be okay.

A rlyn sat at the table in her dressing room and watched in the mirror as her grandmother braided her hair. Lynia had volunteered for the task when she brought Arlyn's newest dress, a gown composed of at least ten layers of sheer fabric in shades of gray. She was fully covered by the embroidered designs, but she still felt naked. She traced a finger along the shifting whorls of gray thread. Like wearing the mists she'd gone through to get here.

She met Lynia's gaze in the glass. "How is your research going?"

"Not as well as I would like." Lynia winced. "I haven't found a single exile capable of casting the spell behind the energy poisoning."

Arlyn jerked in surprise, then murmured an apology when the motion pulled a strand of hair from her grandmother's hand. "You mean you send your criminals to Earth? You just *leave* them there?"

"No," Lynia answered. "Part of Lyr's job is to monitor them. He used to travel there himself for that reason. Besides, no one dangerous is exiled there. It is mostly the shiftless. Those who refuse to contribute to the greater good."

"Harsh."

Her grandmother shrugged. "Perhaps. But thousands of years is a long lifetime to support. Quite a few have returned after a decade in the magicless human world."

It made a certain sick sense, especially since every citizen was provided with basic food and housing. But damn. Arlyn started to ask what happened to those who *were* dangerous but changed her mind. The churning in her gut suggested she already knew. That and the absence of jails on her inner map.

Lynia's gaze connected with hers again. "You cannot let someone who could and would level a city go free," she said, her voice soft.

Arlyn couldn't stop a shiver. A murderer—a psychopath—with magic? She'd never considered the dark side of life here. Not to this level. And her father was in charge of deciding it all. How could she ever hope to replace him someday? Heaviness settled in her stomach, and she began to regret eating lunch.

"Forgive me, Arlyn." A line formed between Lynia's brows. "I did not intend to distress you. Such people are rare.

It has been at least a decade since we have had a serious offense."

Arlyn took a deep breath, forcing herself to relax. What good would it do her to worry about all this now? After a moment, she managed to smile. "Thank you for helping me with my hair."

"I am pleased to do so. I hope you will forgive me for being so distant this week. Between learning the truth of Telien's death and helping your father, I have been more distracted than usual."

"I understand."

Lynia picked up another section of hair and started to braid. "I just hope I can find some answers. A connection with Telien's murderer. What I would not give to know who is responsible!"

"If I might ask," Arlyn began, then paused. Her fingers picked at the hem of her dress as she met Lynia's eyes in the mirror. "I've wondered how you didn't know what happened to him. With being bonded..."

"I was asleep. His death was so instant that I knew nothing but the severing of the bond. I woke to pain and to an emptiness I hope you never experience."

Lynia's hands shook so hard she dropped half the plait.

"I'm sorry." Heedless of her hair, Arlyn reached back to squeeze her grandmother's hand.

"It was a fair question." Lynia let out a sigh and picked up the wayward strands of Arlyn's braid. "But enough of this dismal talk. I would not have you upset before your meeting with Allafon."

"Do you know him?"

"Not well. He's a strange one."

"How so?"

Her grandmother frowned. "Nothing specific, but I found his relationship with Kai's mother to be odd. She was a guide, too, you know, and Allafon always hated that. He seemed almost jealous, which is unusual between soulbonded if they have been together long. His bitterness has only grown since her death."

"Sounds like this is going to be a wonderful visit," Arlyn said, doubt and sarcasm battling in her voice.

"And now I have made you more nervous." Lynia let out a hoarse chuckled. "Perhaps we should have found another to fix your hair. I'll have you morose and anxious."

"Of course not," Arlyn insisted. "It was information I needed to know."

When her grandmother was finished, she handed Arlyn a hand mirror. Breath still, Arlyn stared at the gorgeous tangle of braids crowning her head. Though coiled tightly, it did not seem to pinch or to weigh her down as she'd expected.

On impulse, she turned and gave Lynia a hug, then jerked back with a blush. "That was probably against some rule of formality."

Her grandmother smiled, true pleasure lighting her eyes. "Not with family."

In less time than she'd have liked, Arlyn was standing in front of the portal through which Selia had arrived. An anxious Kai paced near Eradisel, though Arlyn noted that her bonded stayed a careful and respectful distance from the sacred tree. She had no idea how he managed to walk so swiftly in the heavy overcoat, this one embroidered to look like falling leaves, that flowed at least two feet behind him.

Just as Arlyn was about to mentally contact her father, Lyr arrived. He was dressed like Kai, though his overcoat was even more elaborate. She inched closer to examine what could only be called art; the scene depicted a dark-haired elf kneeling before a queen as a circlet was placed on his head, the same circlet her father wore now over his brow. The embroidery was so fine the image was almost as realistic as a photograph.

"The picture is copied from a painting of the establishment of our House. That is Delvian, the queen's seventh son, who was set as the first Myern of the Callian branch."

"So that is how we are related to the king. A *distant* relation, I'm guessing."

"Yes, though not as far as you might think. The line born of Delvian has not been as prolific as some of the others, but we tend to be long-lived. I am only the fifth Myern since Delvian was given this House over thirty-seven thousand years ago."

"Thirty-seven…" Arlyn's eyes widened. "I *really* need a history book."

Kai grinned. "I'll find you one as soon as we get this foolish errand over with."

Tensing, she turned with them to the portal. Kai strode forward to activate the spell, then frowned at the sight of the plain stone room that appeared. "Odd. The main portal is closed."

Though his eyes narrowed, Lyr shrugged. "He has always skirted insult. Father found it more amusing than I ever have."

Dread tightened Arlyn's chest as she examined the room on the other side of the portal. Was the rest of the house so austere? Her shoulders practically itched for the bow she couldn't carry for this type of visit. At least the men wore ceremonial daggers. She wouldn't be able to do the same until she'd finished formal training.

With a last deep breath, Arlyn gripped Kai's hand and stepped through.

Ralan stared out the window of his tower once more, but this time, the garden was empty. Eri would barely speak to him, and he had no idea what to do. He'd always believed he would be pleased to never return to Moranaia. But had he ever been happy during his time on Earth? He winced. Until the birth of his daughter, no. And now past bitterness was affecting his relationship with her. His very heart.

Perhaps Eri was right. Perhaps it was time to reclaim his place as seer. So much had happened both here and on Earth that he could no longer allow his fear to rule him, and the only way he could understand why his daughter was upset was to Look for himself. He could only hope the talent had not faded too much with disuse. He would need much practice to make up for all of the lost years. With a groan, he turned from the window and settled into his seat, ready to unlock a part of himself he had never intended to use again.

"So you seek me out once more."

Ralan's gaze darted around the room, but he did not find the source of the voice. The voice that sounded like—

"HAVE YOU FORGOTTEN ME?"

He blanched at the raw anger in Her tone. *"My goddess Megelien, of course I have not forgotten you. It has been so long since I was blessed by Your presence it took me but a moment to recognize your voice."*

"Your departure hurt me deeply, even knowing for many years that it would likely be so. Do not make me regret rejoicing at your return."

Despite attempts to do otherwise, Ralan had missed Her as well. Although not clergy in the traditional sense, seers had a deep relationship with the Goddess of Time. Those born with great ability were chosen by Megelien before birth, their innate psychic talents augmented by the goddess. Only She knew why some were elevated, and such secrets were kept even from the seers themselves.

"Please forgive me, my lady. I did not think that You could contact me on Earth." He paused, then shook his head. *"That is not entirely correct. I was afraid—of my abilities and of Your anger when I chose not to use them."*

"All was as it had to be. You have returned to your home and your destiny. Open your mind and See."

His breath whooshed out as images of the futures filled his mind. So many possibilities, so many strands of probability. He was lost in a universe of *what ifs*. What would happen if he sighed, turned his head the other direction? What if the cook in the kitchen took an extra step to the left? Ralan gripped his hands in his hair, squeezing his head as the differing paths overwhelmed him. Too long unused to their raging flow.

Just as he started to falter, to doubt, the steady influence of Megelien filled his mind. Reminded him how to manage the strands. He narrowed his focus and discarded the least probable and the most inconsequential. Then he turned his attention to the strands of those closest to him.

In less than two heartbeats, they passed through the portal. After spending so long crossing between Earth and Moranaia, Arlyn had tensed with fear as she'd stepped through, but this experience had been no worse than stepping over a threshold. She glanced back to see the image of Lyr's home before the portal closed, then blinked in surprise at the two guards who had flanked the entrance. Did her father expect trouble? She'd detected no visible threat in the room they had just entered. It was, in fact, rather small and drab, just gray stone walls and a plain wooden door with no decoration.

The door opened, and a diminutive male elf dressed in a simple tunic and pants quietly bade them to follow. Her father did so without a word, though Arlyn knew from her connection with Kai that something was off. She had prepared to be greeted by Kai's father just as she and Lyr had met Selia. The situation was certainly different than what she had expected, but Arlyn was uncertain if it would be considered rude by Moranaian standards.

"Is this normal?" she asked her bonded.

"I don't like it. Why bother to invite us just to offer this kind of slight?"

Arlyn shivered at the chill of the hall they passed through. *"Maybe we should go home."*

"Lyr will not back down against one under his command. If there's a problem, it's his job to solve it. Just be on your guard."

The elf led them down two short halls, then took a turn to the left. Nothing but eerie silence. Though she'd grown accustomed to the quiet nature of the Moranaians, this went beyond what she had come to consider normal. As if even the cold stone was afraid to settle in its foundation. The walls were bare, no painting or decoration, and the sconces were the simplest she had seen. The whole effect was creepy, if she were honest with herself. Arlyn could hardly imagine Kai growing up in such a place.

"Why is this estate so different?"

"My family came to Moranaia much later than yours. My grandfather chose a style that suited his life from before."

Arlyn didn't want to know where they'd come from if *this* was the result.

The elf trudged toward a large door, this one ornately carved. It was so incongruous that Arlyn skipped a step. Their guide, intent on opening the door as quietly as possible, didn't seem to notice. His gaze darted around the hall before he gestured for them to enter, then rushed away without a word.

Arlyn's fingers tangled in the fabric of her dress as Kai led her forward. With a worried glance, he squeezed her other hand. This wasn't right. Really, *really* wasn't right. Couldn't they feel it? But though she could sense unease from Kai, both he and her father appeared relaxed, their expressions impassive. Maybe this wasn't *that* outside of normal here. How would *she* know?

Without hesitation, her father walked through the door, leaving them to follow. It took all of her willpower not to stop once more in the threshold. The room reminded her of a Great Hall straight out of a medieval castle, from the throne at the end to the tapestries and guards lining the walls. Guards who all carried swords.

An elf with short blond hair sat in a carved stone seat in the middle of a huge dais. His face showed no expression, but something about his eyes, as blank as his face, made Arlyn want to shudder. Shouldn't he show some pleasure at the sight of his son? Though strangers were present, she would have expected that. With his tunic, pants, and overcoat in various shades of red, he could have been another decoration in the ostentatious room. Her mouth went dry.

As they came to a stop at the foot of the dais, Allafon frowned. "Where is Lady Lynia?"

Both males tensed at the abrupt question, and Lyr took another step forward. "My mother is resting at home. Since the loss of her bonded, she rarely leaves Braelyn."

"I am surprised you would let her isolate herself. It is not good for her health."

"Her health is none of your concern," Lyr answered, his tone frigid.

"It will be." Allafon stood, sneering. "Your House owes me."

"Our House has always met its obligations to you." Lyr's shoulders tightened, and Arlyn caught a glimpse of his hand clenching. "What is the meaning of this, Allafon? It is clear your invitation misrepresented the occasion, and your lack of proper greeting goes beyond the bounds of mere insult."

Allafon stepped down from the dais, his red overcoat flowing around him like blood. "Didn't you know, boy? We are at war. We have been since your father sent my bonded on her last mission, the one that led to her death. This meeting has been long in coming."

"What are you talking about?" Kai moved forward, bringing Arlyn with him. "Mother fell down the stairs."

The smile that lighted Allafon's eyes could in no way be called pleasant. "I pushed the cheating whore down those stairs. She came back from that mission carrying you, by whom I could not say. Probably some human wretch. I would have killed her then, but I knew the suspicion that would cause. I had hoped that raising you as my own would provide some benefit, but I should have known better. It is Telien Dianore's fault she was tempted. She should have stayed in this house where she belonged."

The echo of his words faded into silence. Through their bond, Arlyn experienced the sudden nausea that tightened Kai's gut even as he let out a startled breath. As she struggled to push back her own doubt and confusion, Arlyn looked over to see her father's face, blank with shock. Allafon's hostility made no sense. The *story* made no sense. She had not been with Kai for long, but she already knew that cheating on one's bonded would be agonizing. He had to be insane.

Kai's hand went to his dagger. "You lie."

"I assure you, it is the truth." Allafon's smile widened. "And I would not recommend pulling that. I have three archers with iron arrowheads pointed at your hearts."

At a gesture, the three in question shifted on the balcony, their arrows suddenly evident. The guards along the wall stepped forward, three carrying heavy-looking iron shackles. Arlyn's stomach sank as she tried not to panic. If they were bound with those, her father would take the worst of it. She opened her mouth to ask a question, to cause a distraction, but Allafon pulled an iron blade from the belt at his waist. In a move too fast to track, he put it to her neck.

"You will allow yourselves to be chained, or she dies now. Choose wisely."

28

Ralan checked the strands once more, but there was no mistake. And little he could do. With a cry, he pulled himself from the trance and cursed at the seconds it took to regain his bearings. Though he knew what would happen, he sent a thought toward Lyr, only to encounter the expected shield surrounding Allafon's estate. He could take the time to break through, but it would cost him. It would cost them all.

The futures were surprisingly diverse, and so many actions could cause disaster if the right paths were not taken by all involved. Ralan jumped up and ran for the tower door. He had the slimmest chance to help, the slightest possibility. Taking the stairs two at a time, he sent out his consciousness, searching for Lial. When he found his cousin, he broke through his shields with ruthless disregard.

"Meet me in the library."

Anger surged along the link. *"You abuse your gift."*

"I've had a vision." Ralan skidded along the landing, then headed for the proper hall. *"Get your ass to the library.* Now. *By order of your prince."*

Ralan closed off his mind to Lial, not caring to hear his cousin's grumbling. He sent his mind along the strands and hoped something had changed. But no. He picked up speed. And prayed to the Nine Gods he'd get there in time.

The top level of the library was Lynia's favorite place to read. She could see much of the estate through the broad windows, and few bothered to climb so many stairs to break her solitude. After centuries spent here with Telien, this place soothed her loneliness like no other. Sometimes, she could almost hear him whisper, sharing his opinions as he had so long ago.

And when her research grew frustrating, this chair was where she always settled.

Like today.

Lynia tapped her finger on the open page of the book she held. Nothing. She had checked again, and not a single exile to Earth could cast an energy-poisoning spell. In fact, the only capable person exiled anywhere in the last four millennia had been Kien, Ralan's brother, but he had been secluded on a distant world. Could he have found a way to pass the spell through the Veil? She would have to find Selia and ask if the mage knew if it was possible.

She heard the door open below and looked over the railing to see Norin, staring up at her with a smile. He was one of the few who knew of her preference for the library, but he almost never bothered her here. Actually, he had rarely spoken to her at all since her bonded's death. He had been with the Dianore family for almost a thousand years, captain of the guard for nearly six hundred, and had grown quite close to Telien. Out of mutual grief and respect, they spent little time in each other's company.

With a disappointed huff, she watched him climb the stairs that spiraled up the tower. Though she did not dislike him, Lynia would have preferred he turn around and leave. She was no fit company at the moment, and the required pleasantries seemed like too much work. Bad enough that she would have to struggle through polite exchanges with Selia. Though the mage seemed kind, even that formality was exhausting to consider.

Lynia would much rather settle in by the window and read.

Despite her silent hope to the contrary, Norin reached her in short order. "Good day to you, Lady Lynia."

"And to you, Belore Norin," she answered, barely managing to stifle a sigh.

"Please excuse the brevity of my greeting. I have been sent by Myern Lyrnis to request your presence at Oria. Kaienan's father seemed quite distraught by your absence."

He had climbed all the way up the tower to deliver such a message when he could have contacted her telepathically? His expression was pleasant, quite as though he had encountered her on a stroll around the garden, but her hands tightened on the book anyway. Lyr would not have asked her to come no matter how upset Allafon became. Though he had lost his own mate before the bond had been completed, her son came closer than anyone to understanding her pain and seclusion. On this issue, he might have even fought the king.

"What is this really about, Norin? Though Oria is a good distance from here, I've no doubt that Lyr could have contacted me himself with such a request."

Norin's smile hardened. "You will come with me. The Myern was quite insistent."

Lynia snapped the book closed and stood. "I do not believe you."

"Lord Allafon will clear up everything. He will reward us both when his current troubles have been resolved."

"Troubles?"

Norin tried to grab her arm, but she slipped to the side. "We must not mingle with humans, Lynia. Telien considered it. Did you know he was thinking of returning us to their world?

"He considered resuming contact with them, yes." Lynia tightened her grip on the book and hoped she wouldn't have to use it as a weapon. Blood was difficult to get out of paper, even with a spell. "What does that have to do with anything?"

"Did you know Allafon's own bonded betrayed him on a scouting mission?"

She tried not to tremble at the odd, crazed glint in Norin's eyes. "You are not making sense."

"With a *human*, Lynia." Norin's fists clenched. "Allafon thinks she slept with a human. And now Lyr has let more of this foul blood into our House. But Allafon will clear it."

Gods. He was insane. Lynia crept backward toward the stairs, her only hope of escape. Her shields could hold against a magical attack, but Norin was a warrior. And she had not practiced her defensive moves in decades. Her vision narrowed down to only him as her fingers gripped the leather tome she held. Would it even help?

"Elerie never would have betrayed her bonded." She took another slow step back. "And Telien's discussions about the humans were little more than idle thoughts."

"Idle thoughts?" he hissed out, ignoring her other claim. "His plans were solid enough to bring his death."

Her throat tightened around a gasp. "*You*," she choked out. "You killed him. All this time and I never knew."

Norin shrugged. "I tried to change his mind. When I could not, my superiors ordered it."

"This is madness."

"Madness is bringing a half-blood here and calling her heir." Norin drew his blade. "You will come with me now. Perhaps you can talk your son into seeing reason."

"I doubt my ability to reason has anything to do with why Allafon desires my presence. I will not go with you. I will not be used against my son."

Lynia reached the first step as he grabbed her arm. Before she could pull away, the crash of the door and a rush of feet distracted them both. Her eyes widened at the panic on Ralan's face, and for a moment, she froze. Then Norin's hand tightened, and she tugged at her arm with renewed vigor. The book slipped from her sweat-slicked hands to thud on the floor at her feet.

She started to slip just before the bite of Norin's blade seared her side. She screamed with it, the sound echoing through the tower, and a smirk settled over Norin's face. Had Telien seen that same look? With her last bit of strength, she grasped his wrist. A smile of satisfaction curved her mouth as she pulled her bonded's murderer over the side. If she died, she would take him with her.

"No!" Ralan rushed forward. "No, Lynia!"

He knelt beside her still form, partly slumped over Norin's body. She'd managed to turn the captain so he took the brunt of the fall, but her lower half had hit the stone. Ralan lifted his hands. Pulled them back. He couldn't move her with a broken spine. Only Lial could help her now, provided he followed the path that brought him here quickly.

If the healer stopped to talk to his assistant, Lynia was doomed.

She let out a groan as she tried to shift, and Ralan risked a light touch on her head to calm her. "Stay still. You're badly injured."

He felt the gentle brush of her mind, so faint one of lesser talent might not have noticed, and opened his mind to her without hesitation. *"Take care of Lyr. Give him my love."*

"You will *not* die," he answered aloud, hoping to center her in this world. "Hold on."

Her breath shuddered out, and the pain that passed through their mental link made him wince. *"Promise."*

"You know I will protect Lyr. You don't have to die for that."

Her presence grew faint, her breathing shallow. Ralan dropped to his knees and gathered her hand in his, barely glancing at Norin's open, empty eyes. The bastard deserved far worse than such a quick death. If only Lynia had pushed him away instead of trying to tug free. In that future, Norin would have tripped on the book and fallen to his death alone.

Ralan heard Lial's strangled gasp from the open door, then the shuffle of shoes along stone. The healer dropped to Lynia's other side, his hands already glowing blue as he hovered them along her body. Ralan's throat closed in on itself. So many futures. So many possibilities.

If he'd started using his talents sooner, he could have stopped all of this.

"Even the gods can only know the possibilities," Megelien whispered in his mind. *"Free will makes a fool of prophecy more often than you know."*

Lial's hand closed on Ralan's wrist, drawing him back. He met his cousin's worried gaze. "Well?"

"Help me lift her to one of the tables." Hands shaking, Lial stood. "I have cast a spell to keep her spine from further injury while we do. But I can't heal her like this."

Ralan wondered at his cousin's reaction even as he rushed to help. Were Lial and Lynia friends? He could think of no other reason why a healer as experienced as his cousin was so visibly shaken. Lial had once carried on a conversation about lunch options while healing a man who'd impaled himself in a fall. He never faltered.

"Do I need to call for your assistant?" Ralan asked as they settled Lynia on a nearby table, one she and Norin had narrowly missed in the fall.

"I already have." A glint of resolve entered Lial's eyes. "Now move. I need space if I'm to save her."

Ralan took a few paces back and shielded his eyes as the blue glow flared, brighter than before. When it didn't fade after several moments, he moved back farther, turning his face to the door. There Eri waited, her hands twisted together and her face wet with tears. Heart lurching, he went to her.

"I'm sorry. I couldn't warn you."

He sank to his knees. "Come here, Eri."

She shuffled her feet for a moment before moving closer. "I couldn't Look at what you would say. Please don't hate me for not telling."

"Hush." Ralan pulled his daughter into his arms and buried his face in her sweet-smelling hair. "I'm the one who's sorry. We will work out the future together. Always."

Lyr struggled to keep his eyes open as his energy drained steadily away. Kai and Arlyn, chained with their hands above their heads to two of the other three walls, stared at him as he let out a groan. His heavy overcoat pulled at him, adding strain to his shoulders, and his wrists burned from the constant contact with cold iron. How could he be in this ridiculous situation? He was a warrior feared on the battlefield, yet here he was, shackled to a damn wall with his magic draining away with each breath.

His mind grew sluggish, and he struggled to form any kind of plan. Surely, there was a way to get free. They were not in a dungeon; Allafon had only placed them here while he completed some unnamed task. Of course, he hardly had to do more considering the effect iron had on all of them. They couldn't break even these simple shackles with magic.

"I know you said your father didn't like you," Arlyn muttered to Kai. "But damn."

Kai's expression hardened. "If he is my father. Maybe I'm a half-blood, too."

"No." Lyr shook his head, then paused to let the world settle again. "In all the times Lial's healed you, I think he would have noticed. That kind of weakness would have been obvious."

"Hey!" Arlyn cried out.

Lyr winced. "Nothing against humans. But they do not heal the same way we do. It would take Lial more energy to accomplish, at the least."

Though her mouth thinned into a line, she tried to shrug, rattling the chains. "He didn't complain about me. I'd think he would have."

"With your mother a quarter elven, it might—"

Pain tore through him, cutting off his words. Lyr convulsed against the wall, and the iron drew blood as his arms jerked against the restraint. *Laiala.* A mortal wound. A moan slipped from his lips, but he hardly registered the sound.

"It cannot be," he whispered. Surely, it was a trick, some terrible attack.

But the emptiness that trickled in as her soul started to slip away told him otherwise.

29

He would not fail. Could not.

Lial pulled in more power from the world around him and channeled it all to his gift. To the blue fire that swept him up until he could see nothing but the one he healed. Though his own chest was tight with fear, he let his training take over. He'd loved Lynia for too long to let her slip away because he couldn't gain control of himself.

The damage to her spine was grave, but he first had to close the wound on her side. His breath slipped out in a sigh of relief to find that Norin's blade had been stopped by Lynia's rib. A wound meant to slow her, not kill her. Lial sent his power into the cut, knitting muscle and flesh. Still, her breathing stuttered. She started to slip away.

He scanned her abdomen and…there. Internal bleeding. Deftly, he healed that, too, then sent more of his power into her body to bolster her. "Stay with me, Lynia."

Lial let his inner eye follow the length of her spine, and he shuddered. Shattered in at least two places, badly broken in more. He needed more energy, for his reserves would never last through such taxing work. *Clechtan*, but he knew better than to let himself get so worn down. He glanced up, hoping his assistant had arrived, but only Ralan and Eri were there.

"Ralan," Lial called. "Come give me energy. You're close enough in blood that it should take less for me to convert it."

His cousin nodded, then slipped away from the little girl after giving her shoulders a quick squeeze. Lial returned to work. When Ralan connected, he soaked up all the power he could and let it dive into the fire of his magic. Blue light flared, and he shut his eyes. He didn't need to see.

He needed to feel.

Arlyn gasped as her father began to writhe, his unfocused eyes filled with pain. Was it the iron? She pulled at her arms, panic sucking the air from her lungs, but couldn't work herself free. "What is it? What's wrong?"

Lyr's body went lax, his sudden stillness almost more alarming. "It cannot be," he whispered, his voice raw and broken.

Her concern grew. "What?"

"*Laiala*." He looked up then with a face more desolate than she had ever seen. "She was wounded. I can barely sense her now."

Arlyn frowned over at Kai. *"How could he know such a thing?*
He must be wrong."

"We are connected to our mothers in a bond nearly as strong as a
soulbond. We spend the first nine months of our lives held within her soul,
her energy. The more magical the being, the stronger the connection."

"But you can still sense her, right?" Arlyn pushed back the
fear rising up her throat. "Maybe someone there can help her."

"Almost gone," Lyr murmured.

Arlyn shivered at his words. They had to get out of here.
Even without her grandmother injured, Lyr was not doing
well. *At all.* His skin was so pale now it was almost gray, and
even she could tell he was losing energy fast. So was she—and
Kai, to a lesser extent. If they didn't escape soon, they were all
dead.

Another tug against her chains did nothing but bite the
iron harder into her flesh. Arlyn glanced at Kai. "Any ideas?"

"Against iron?" Kai thunked his head against the wall behind him, his eyes slipping closed. "No. None of us can work
magic around it."

She ground her teeth together. "That's stupid. There's iron
in our blood."

"It's something in the energy. We can consume iron from
something that has once been living, plant or animal, because
that iron has already been converted to natural use. But cold
iron, mined from the ground? Magic won't flow through. At
least not if you have the allergy."

With a grimace, Arlyn looked up at the chains. So some
elves could convert iron within their own bodies, but others
couldn't? She glared up at the metal. Could it have to do with

magnetism? The innate polarity of iron? She recalled the burn of her injury during archery practice. The flakes in her arm had almost resisted her power, but she'd been too caught up to worry about it.

Yes, they'd resisted. Until they hadn't.

Arlyn straightened, her eyes slipping closed. She ignored the low moan from her father and the rattle of chains as Kai shifted. But how to proceed? Shrugging, Arlyn thought back to all the times she'd used her magic. She let it sweep through her, filling her body until it reached her wrists and the iron that bound them.

Like two magnets with positive ends shoved together, her magic and the metal pushed against each other. She shoved even harder, willing her power through. Willing herself free. From a distance, she heard Kai let out a curse, but she ignored him. Ignored everything but the battle burning around her wrists.

Then, with a nearly audible click, the iron gave.

Arlyn almost slumped against the wall. But she still wasn't free. She opened her eyes to find Kai staring at her. "What?"

"That trick." He shook his head. "How did you do it?"

"I kept pushing until I won."

A slow grin crossed his face. "I'm not sure if that's insane or brilliant."

"Yet here we still are," Arlyn answered, rattling the chains.

Lyr groaned again, and her breath caught as his head lolled and his eyes slipped closed. Kai exchanged a worried glance with her, then said, "Let me try it."

Lial plopped down onto the table, digging his fingers into the edge to hold himself upright. Too much longer, and he'd fall flat on his face. His gaze fell on Lynia, and he let out a long breath at the color returning to her face. The bones of her spine weren't completely mended, but he'd fixed the worst of her wounds.

It would take him hours of painstaking work to knit shattered bone.

His assistant, Elan, worked with Ralan to levitate Lynia onto a narrow board. Though Elan's power was too minimal to be a full healer in charge of an entire estate, he was invaluable for the small things that had to be done. Like getting patients ready to move to Lial's workroom so Lial could conserve his energy for healing. Or tending to minor injuries during a crisis. Crucial.

Lial pushed to his feet, biting back a curse as he swayed. *Miaran.* He needed a vacation. But then, he'd probably end up healing people there, too. Smirking at the thought, he turned to follow Ralan and Elan as they carried Lynia toward the door. And jumped when a small hand closed around his wrist.

He met his youngest cousin's eyes. "Yes, Erinalia?"

"Just Eri." Her lips curved. "I'm close enough in blood to give you energy, too."

He could only blink at her. "I will be well enough. I could never take from a child, especially one so recently ill."

"You will if you want to save her."

"Eri." His voice cut off as he registered the odd glint in her eyes. One Ralan had so often worn. But a child of that age?

"Your father can help if needed. You are too young to attempt such a thing."

Power flared through her, gleaming from her golden gaze. "I've seen more than you have despite your many years. Take my offering or let her die."

Lial shuddered, even as he fought to stay on his feet. By the Gods, she was right. "Fine. If your father says—"

Energy rushed in, stunning away his words. He straightened as his body converted it with little difficulty and his weakness faded. Tricky child. She'd known perfectly well that Lial was about to tell her to seek permission from her father. He gave her a look of censure, but she merely grinned. Then danced away after Ralan as though nothing had happened.

Lial's mouth curved up into an answering smile. He didn't envy Ralan the raising of that one.

Kai let out a long curse. *So close that time.* So close, but his power never made it past the iron. "I'm not sure I can do this."

Arlyn bit her lip. "Maybe you're giving up too soon."

"Maybe it takes having human blood."

"I'll try something else, then." She huffed out a breath, blowing a strand of hair from her eyes. "Maybe I can force the iron open. I transported us without knowing how."

"No!" Kai jerked forward with a rattle of chains. "That is too risky."

"We need to try *something.*"

Kai forced himself to relax. As well as he *could* relax while chained to a fucking wall. "I'll try again. What's that human saying? Three is a charm?"

"The third time's a charm," she muttered.

Kai's eyes slipped closed, and he took several deep breaths. Once his mind had cleared of worry, he pulled energy from the ground beneath him. His first home—the place of his birth, a connection not even Allafon could sever. His energy wavered, and he had to force his mind away from *that* distracting thought as he gathered more into himself.

He could worry about his father later.

As Kai had seen Arlyn do, he shoved the power up, toward the chains. Like before, it fought him, pushing his energy away. Kai gritted his teeth. He was *not* going to let Arlyn hurt herself trying to find a way free. Gathering himself, pulling in more, he gave one last shove.

And felt something in the iron give.

Panting, Kai fell back against the wall. Sweat dripped into his eyes, and he twisted to rub his face on his sleeve. Arlyn grinned at him. "Guess my threat worked."

His brows rose. "You were bluffing?"

"Only partially," she answered, shrugging. "If you hadn't succeeded, I'd have tried something else."

A groan from Lyr caught his attention. "I need to get us out of here. It should only take a moment to break through these simple locks."

Kai looked up at his shackles, focusing his power on the mechanism. Simple indeed. His fath—Allafon must have relied on the iron itself as a deterrent. Kai had learned the counter to these types of locks playing soldier as a child. A few heartbeats and a breath of magic, and the metal slid free.

Rubbing his wrists, Kai took a few steps forward, then paused to look between Arlyn and Lyr. His bonded met his gaze. "Save my father. He's the worst off."

His leaden feet refused to move, and he glanced between them again. Then Lyr's head shot up, and he pinned Kai with his gaze. "Arlyn first. As Myern, I command it."

"Lyr—"

"Now."

Though Kai's chest ached, he wasted no more time. He rushed to Arlyn, gripping her shackles despite the instinctual shudder that raced through him. But the iron didn't burn his skin, and his magic worked on the lock. The metal let out a soft click, then released her. With a cry, she slumped against him for a few breaths before pushing away.

As his bonded steadied herself against the wall, her pain beat at him. Her injured arm burned as her blood rushed through, making his own breath catch. Kai struggled to separate her feelings from his own as he turned to release Lyr. If he could even convert more iron so soon. Arlyn had been so much better at the trick, but it would be difficult for her to concentrate while dealing with so much pain.

Kai was halfway to Lyr when the door snapped open, Allafon's voice preceding him. "I hope I have given you enough time to appreciate—" His voice cut off at the sight of Kai, and he gave a quick gesture to the two men behind him. "Well, well. Seems you have learned some interesting tricks. Norin said you were allergic to iron."

Lyr's head snapped up, the sorrow in his eyes replaced by fury. *"Norin?"*

"Too bad the fool is dead. I could kill him myself." Allafon strode forward, his iron blade at the ready, then stopped to dance the knife almost playfully across Lyr's chest. "I suggest you two stay where you are unless you want me to kill him immediately. Not that it matters, since he'll die anyway."

Kai froze, even as one of the guards jerked him back. If only his ceremonial blade had not been taken. Decorative though it was, any weapon was better than nothing. Cool metal dug into his neck, just short of breaking the skin. *Peresten*, at least. He heard Arlyn's muttered curse behind him, and he tensed.

"Stay still," he warned.

Exasperation passed along their bond. *"I'm not an idiot."*

"Why are you really doing this?" Lyr asked. "Even if your bonded did betray you, it is not our fault. My father had no control over her actions."

"Oh, but I am certain he did. Your entire line is foolish, forever associating with those beneath us. Had he not sent her to meet with those glamour-wielding…" Allafon's voice choked off as he struggled to control his anger. "Worst of all, you mingle with humans. Our family lived almost like gods until the first Moranaians abandoned Earth. For centuries, we struggled to retain our power until we were finally overrun. There were not enough of us left to face the fast-breeding animals. And now I am expected to serve as some minor lordling for an elf who ruts with humans? I think not. I will rule them, or I will kill them all. Once I have your portal."

Lyr straightened, his head taking on a regal tilt. "I doubt a human would deign to sleep with you. You are more animal than any I have ever met."

With a cry of rage, Allafon struck.

30

The blow seemed to take forever, though it fell so quickly Arlyn barely had time to cry out. She jerked against the guard who held her, his knife breaking through skin before he forced her still. With a curse, the guard lowered the blade but tightened his grip. Blood dripped down her neck, but the pain didn't register. All of her focus was on her father as Allafon stepped back, revealing the gash sliced across Lyr's chest.

Metal glinted, and her eyes widened to see the pendant revealed by the rip in his tunic. The necklace her mother had asked him to wear. Allafon cursed as Lyr glanced down, gaze softening on the pendant that had deflected most of the blow. "Thank you, Aimee."

"You still have the necklace." Allafon scowled down at the wound. "I see you lied about being bonded to the human. Too bad your deceit will not save you again."

Arlyn's body burned. With anger. With pain from where the guard gripped across her wound and from the cut on her neck. She would *be damned* if this asshole killed her father so soon after she'd finally found him. Or Kai, the love she'd never expected to find. Whatever it took.

"Any ideas?" she sent Kai.

"Love? You can't just think that and—"

"Later. After we're all out of here alive?"

His sigh caught Allafon's attention. "Does this bore you?"

"I'm waiting for you to tell us all your plans," Kai drawled. Though she couldn't see it, Arlyn knew he was grinning. "Or is that later?"

"Be quiet." Allafon waved a hand at the guards. "If either of them speak again, slice their throats."

"When my father turns, pretend to faint. It will not see you free, but it will provide distraction."

"You're joking."

"Elven women rarely faint, but they'll expect a human to be weak." He sent amusement along their bond. *"Be the damsel for a moment. Then prove them wrong."*

Arlyn rolled her eyes. Who would fall for such a simple, cli-chéd trick? But then, she wasn't on Earth, and she didn't have enough experience in elven combat to stand a reasonable chance of getting herself free. Might as well try. So she waited until Allafon turned back to her father before letting her body go limp. The guard stumbled against the wall in surprise, not prepared to hold her entire weight. He turned her in his arms and gave her face a slap. She barely managed not to flinch.

At the sound of a sword being drawn, followed by a grunt of pain, sweat broke out on her brow. But Arlyn didn't open her eyes. If Kai were hurt—well, she would sense it, wouldn't she? Then the guard dropped her, and she had no more time to worry. Allowing herself to fall, Arlyn barely managed to keep her head from cracking on the floor. She lay still as he stepped over her, waiting until her captor was about to put his back foot down before grabbing his leg.

Opening her eyes, Arlyn pulled hard, toppling the guard off-balance. He stumbled into a blow that had been meant for Kai and went down with a gash to the stomach. But he wasn't dead. She scrambled for the knife he'd dropped before his searching hand could grip it. Time seemed to slow as her eyes met his until even the sounds of Kai fighting and Allafon's laughter blurred to nothing.

Her stomach heaved against what she had to do. She'd never hurt anyone, not really. Maybe this man was innocent. A pawn. Then his eyes filled with hatred, and his mouth turned up in a snarl as he struggled to rise. Taking in a shaky breath, Arlyn summoned her combat magic, followed her instincts to the best point of attack, and plunged the knife deep.

The squish of her blade slicing through his throat, the crack as it severed his spine—Arlyn lost it, throwing up on the floor where she knelt. Allafon's cackle cut through the sudden silence. "I didn't think you'd actually do it."

Trembling, she looked up, taking in the scene. Lyr had slumped against his chains, frighteningly still. Kai stood panting over the body of the other guard as he pulled a sword free. Where the hell had he gotten *that?* Shaking her head to clear it, she met Allafon's crazed eyes. He still held the iron knife, and if he was worried at their success, he didn't show it.

"Well, come on." Allafon turned back to Lyr. "See if you can get to me before I kill him."

The madman lifted his arm for another strike. Arlyn struggled to her feet, still shaking, as Kai started forward, but neither of them was close enough to make it. As Allafon started to swing, her heart seemed to stop. But he never connected. He let out a shout of pain as the knife dropped from his fingers, the shaft of an arrow sticking from his wrist.

She followed the path it must have taken to find a blond version of her bonded standing in the frame of the door with his bow nocked. Arlyn drew to a halt, uncertain now where the true threat lay. Was the newcomer pointing his next arrow at Allafon or Lyr? She glanced at Kai, and the blank shock on his face didn't offer reassurance.

"Moren?" Kai whispered.

Allafon took one stumbling step toward the newcomer. "What are you doing?"

"Stopping you. Your madness has gone too far."

"My son. My only son." Allafon stood there for a moment looking bewildered before fury consumed him once more. "Even *you* have betrayed me!"

A sudden, mad gleam in his eyes, Allafon pulled the arrow free from his wrist without a single flinch. He stared at the blood pouring forth for a moment before lifting his arm to let it drip over his head. Arlyn heard Moren's swift intake of breath and felt an influx of panic from her link with Kai. The scene, beyond creepy, filled her with a deep sense of dread. Then she heard their enemy begin to chant under his breath. Energy built in the room, an ominous force that twisted into muscle and bone. She shuddered at the dark pulse flowing around her.

Moren pulled back on his bowstring, but Kai shook his head. Allafon lowered his arm to let the blood fall on the smooth stone beneath his feet. The madman closed his eyes for a moment as the tone of the chant shifted to a pitch that made Arlyn want to scream. When his eyes started to open again, Kai sprung. The sword bit through his father's neck in a single blow, and Allafon's head rolled to a stop near Moren's feet as his body slowly crumpled. The malevolent energy cut off as quickly and cleanly as the blow had fallen.

Her stomach heaving again, Arlyn bent over, hands on her knees. She allowed time for several long, deep breaths before forcing herself to straighten. Blood pooled on the floor and splattered the walls. In the middle of it all, Allafon lay, the red of his overcoat blending in until he looked like an odd, gruesome flower. Moren stood frozen, bow now lowered, and stared down at his father's head. Kai's eyes were closed, his sword dragging the ground as he pulled in gasping breaths. His agony and confusion brought tears to her own eyes.

Then Lyr groaned, and they all rushed into action once more. Arlyn tried not to step in the blood as she hurried to her father's side. Barely conscious, Lyr slumped against his shackles. His wound was bleeding profusely with no sign of the clotting that should have already started. She turned at the sound of ripping, and her eyes widened to see Moren holding out a piece of his own tunic. Before she could accept it, Kai reached out to take the cloth and press it to Lyr's wound.

"Convert the iron, *mialn*, so we can take him down." As Arlyn complied, Kai looked over at his brother. "Is Alerielle still healer here?"

"I have summoned her."

Once Arlyn finished, Kai wasted no time unlocking the shackles. He and Moren worked together to lift Lyr, carrying him from the room to a bench in the Great Hall. Several warriors ringed the room, shifting uncertainly as they noted the blood tracked across the stone floors. At a gesture from Moren, they relaxed. Three bodies slumped in the corner, but she didn't bother to ask how or why. Her attention was drawn to her father. He had grown so pale his skin almost looked translucent.

An older woman strode through the doors and approached them without hesitation. Even as she unfastened the leather kit she carried, she nudged aside one of the gawking soldiers. Her gray eyes were gentle but determined, her expression soft but intense. With hair completely white and deep wrinkles molded into her skin, she was the most ancient elf Arlyn had seen. She could only imagine how many millennia the woman had lived, how many wounds she had treated.

"What has been wrought here, Ayal Morenial?" she asked as she knelt beside Lyr and pulled out a needle and a spool of thread.

"I am the Dorn, now, Alerielle," Moren answered with a bow. "My father is no more."

"About time," the healer muttered. She began to stitch the gash on Lyr's chest with a skill born of long practice. "Foolish of you to allow this to go on as long as it has. He should have been disposed of after poor Elerie returned, sooner even."

"Honored Elder," Kai started, his expression hesitant. "Father...Allafon said that I am not his son. Do you know more?"

She gave him a brief but direct look, barely pausing in her work. "You are not. I presided over your birth myself. In her agony, your mother confided in me. Allafon was not her bonded. Your true father was."

In the midst of the greater crisis, Kai found himself struggling with his emotions and his desire to know the truth. There were so many things that were more important—his friend's health, finding others loyal to Allafon, the state of Braelyn—but he couldn't focus on any of them. He wanted to question the healer, to learn if her claims were fact. He had been so concerned when Lyr hadn't known his new name after he had bonded with Arlyn, but his old name was the greatest lie. Her words would remake him. Her words would set him free.

More than five hundred years of guilt and pain, of not understanding why his father hated him, and now Kai finally knew the answer. So simple and yet so complicated. Nothing he could have done would have pleased Allafon. Nothing. No action, no accolade could have overcome his blood. That bit of relief did not stop the pain. His mother was still gone and his true father still unknown. He had no idea who he was anymore.

"Did she give my true father's name?"

The healer shook her head, her eyes full of sorrow. "She feared for his safety if Allafon discovered that she'd told. But I do know he was of the Sidhe."

Lyr's groan reverberated through the hall. Though Alerielle had already closed the wound, Kai was still surprised she had allowed her patient to awaken. The pain had to be excruciating, yet the healer helped Lyr sit up and lean against the wall. His head fell back against the stone, and his breath came in gasps. But still he met Kai's eyes.

"We must return to Braelyn. Did Allafon's shields come down upon his death? Can we use the main portal?"

Kai checked through his key to the estate, a key that had apparently been limited. He hadn't known about the room where they had been held. "Yes, but you should stay here with Moren. You're badly injured."

"Braelyn is my responsibility, as is the protection of Eradisel. More than that, my mother could be at further risk."

Kai turned to his brother. "Do you need help finding others who might have worked with our fa—with Allafon?"

Moren shook his head. "I know every traitor on this estate. Most of them are already dead."

"We have much to discuss," Lyr said, giving Moren a pointed look. "It seems you know a great deal about this plot. Had I the leisure, you can be certain I would be questioning you immediately. For now, I must demand you give your oath of loyalty as was done in old."

"You have always had my loyalty," the other answered in a calm voice.

"You'll excuse me for not taking your word for it." Lyr struggled to his feet and leaned heavily against the wall. Though he swayed, he stayed upright. "Morenial Treinesse, do you swear your oath to me as Dorn of the lands of Oria, third branch beneath the authority of the Myern of Braelyn?"

Moren pulled his knife from his belt and sliced it across his palm without flinching. He turned his hand down to let the blood drip onto the floor in front of Lyr. "*i'Bey'i'dahn ay mor kehy ler ehy tai'i narano key merdial Beyar Braelyn.*"

With some difficulty, Lyr bent down to touch the blood, rubbing it symbolically into his skin as he rose. "*i'Tehyn te narno.* You are now to be known as Callian ay'iyn Dorn i Morenial Treinesse nai Oria. Report to me when Oria is secure."

Even as the energy sang through the air, Kai shifted to brace Lyr as he stumbled toward the portal. Kai had never seen a formal oath-bonding before; it was an old tradition rarely used after millennia of peace. *Bound by my blood, my being is sworn unto the House of Braelyn.* Moren's essence was now bound in service to Lyr and his heirs, and if he tried to act against that oath, he would experience pain like no other, pain of blood and soul. At a raised brow from Arlyn, Kai sent her a mental explanation as she ducked under Lyr's other arm, giving more support.

Kai triggered the spell that would return them to Braelyn. The archway flared with light, then settled to show the main room of the estate. Instead of the two they had left, five guards blocked the way forward with others standing at attention around Eradisel. Their faces betrayed no emotion, but they must have been surprised by the sight that greeted them.

Not only was Lyr clearly injured, but they were all splattered with blood, their clothing torn. Still, the guards hesitated for only a moment before stepping back to allow them through.

31

As Lyr stepped back onto his own land, a blessed surge of energy, much of it a gift from Eradisel, filled him. It was not enough to heal him or to remove the bulk of his weakness, but he found himself able to stand on his own once again. He sent silent thanks to the sacred tree as he walked to his second in command, standing next to a somber Ralan. None of the guards looked injured; in fact, he doubted they had even seen battle. Not so much as a scuff marred their armor.

"Koranel, report," he snapped, his energy and patience too thin for politeness.

Though his eyes widened slightly in surprise, the guard merely saluted. "Prince Ralan ordered us to protect the gate after your mother..."

"Was gravely wounded. I felt it," Lyr said, sparing Koranel from having to deliver the news. "What happened?"

Shoulders slumped, Ralan moved forward. "It was Norin. Your mother was reading in the library tower when he went to get her. To take her to Allafon. In the struggle, she fell and pulled Norin down with her."

Lyr frowned. "Who was the witness?"

"I was." Ralan averted his eyes. "I found the future strand moments before it happened, too late to change the bulk of it. Had I not forsaken my talents, had I looked sooner, I could have stopped this. I'm sorry. Lial believes she will live, but her good health is not certain."

"Seeing the future does not make you responsible for the actions of others. Some things are meant to be. Some must be. You, above all, should know that."

"Knowing and feeling are often estranged."

Lyr nodded. "Too often. Where is she?"

"Lial's workroom." Ralan took a step back, his gaze narrowing on Lyr's chest. "Gods. Looks like you need to go there yourself."

"I'll probably live." Lyr shrugged. And tried to ignore how dizzy the movement made him. "I trust there have been no other threats?"

Koranel shook his head. "No, Myern. All has been quiet, save Norin's betrayal. If any others have been working for him, they have not been foolish enough to make themselves known."

"Keep extra guard around Eradisel. The others may return to their normal duties, but tell them to remain vigilant." Lyr headed for the front door, the fastest way to the healing tower, then paused to look back over his shoulder. "If Morenial comes through the portal before I return, have him wait in my study."

Arlyn met his gaze. "May I come? I'd like to see her."

He opened the door wider. "Of course."

Lyr gritted his teeth, forcing himself to take another step. Then another. Lial's workroom wasn't too far from the bulk of the estate, but it could have been a day's journey for the effort it required. After being so perilously drained by the iron, Lyr should have rested. But his mother had always been there for him, and he would do no less for her.

When a seer said her good health was uncertain—

His throat tightened as he cut off *that* speculation. It would do no good to wonder, and there was no way to know if Ralan had Seen something dire. He might even have been repeating Lial's words. Lyr would have to find out for himself. *If* he didn't pass out in the middle of a walk he would normally take in a couple of minutes.

Lyr heard Arlyn and Kai shift closer. His daughter's apprehension slipped through his shields, and he winced. He wasn't fooling anyone. "I can make it."

He didn't miss her soft huff. "If you'd let us support you, the walk would be easier. Better yet, go rest."

"Not without seeing *Laiala*." Though he stumbled with the movement, Lyr spared her a quick glance. "And I cannot afford to show too much weakness. Especially if Norin had allies yet to be revealed."

Arlyn snorted. "You aren't fooling anyone."

Lyr's lips curved as she echoed his own thoughts. They were more alike than he could have imagined. "So you'd stay abed like you were told if I were injured? I doubt it."

Kai's soft chuckle filled the sudden silence.

Another wave of dizziness spun Lyr's head, and it took him a moment to realize that his body had shifted as well. Rough bark bit into his back. Gasping against a surge of pain, he leaned his head against the tree and closed his eyes. *Miaran.* He was never going to make it to his mother like this.

"Fine," Lyr muttered. "I concede."

He expected some teasing, especially from Kai, but they said nothing, only moved forward to help. Arlyn ducked beneath his left shoulder and Kai his right. Lyr grimaced but let them support some of his weight, and they started toward the tower at a much faster pace. His muscles trembled with every step. Actually trembled. He couldn't recall ever being so weak.

Finally, they drew near Lial's workroom. The square building was small compared to some, but it had come to be called "the tower" over the years. Lyr had always wondered if people referred more to Lial's temper than the height of the building. Gods knew it was as bad as *capturing* a tower to seek healing after doing something foolish.

Kera stood in front of the door, her hand resting on the hilt of her sword. Her sharp eyes scanned the area, and though her expression didn't change, Lyr had no doubt she'd already assessed his condition. He would trust few more than Kera to guard his mother during a crisis. No one would make it through so long as she lived.

"Myern," Kera said, saluting.

Lyr inclined his head. "Thank you for watching out for Lady Lynia."

"It is my honor." Her expression darkened. "Too bad I wasn't guarding her in the library."

"You can't be everywhere, Kera," he said. "After your shift is over, please come find me. Provided I'm not unconscious."

"Have I done something wrong, Lord Lyrnis?"

Lyr smiled. "No. But you might want to consider whether you'd be willing to take Koranel's place when he moves up to Captain. It will be a bit of a shift for you, but I need someone I can trust."

"Myern," she choked out, her eyes wide.

"Please consider the position."

"Of course."

A soft chuckle slipped out at her stunned expression, but levity fled as soon as Elan opened the door. With a raised brow, he stopped them, gesturing to the broad stone washing stand beside the entrance. Lyr looked down at himself and grimaced. "I can stand well enough to wash my hands."

He scrubbed the blood from his hands and face, then stepped back for Kai and Arlyn to do the same. Gods, they were all a mess. He should have at least changed clothes, but he feared he'd collapse at the sight of his bed. *Laiala* came first. Forcing aside the lightness in his head, Lyr walked through the door on his own. The sharp tang of herbs swirled through the air as he made his way to the bed along the right-hand wall. Lynia rested there, so still and pale he drew up short, his throat squeezing tight in fear.

When Lyr saw her chest rise and fall, he could breathe again.

Rubbing his temples with his fingers, Lial slumped in a chair beside her, his pallor almost as striking. He glanced up at Lyr, and a scowl twisted his face as he noticed the gash on Lyr's chest. "*Miaran.* Can I not leave you alone for any length of time?"

"Don't start," Lyr said, dropping into the other chair and taking Lynia's hand. "Norin was working for Allafon. If I'd realized sooner, none of this would have happened. We all paid for my failure, didn't we?"

For once, Lial didn't give a sharp retort. "I'm sorry. Lynia's healing was difficult, and I am not certain I have the energy to do much for you." He sighed. "Alerielle sewed you up? Iron must have been involved."

"Yes and yes." Lyr's eyes slipped closed, his grip tightening on his mother's hand. But not enough to hurt her. Never that. "How bad is it?"

"Parts of her spine were completely shattered, and there was a great deal of internal damage." Lial's hand shook as he brushed a lock of hair from her face. "I've stopped the bleeding, healed her organs, and begun work on her spine. But that is the most delicate of all things to repair. The damage to her spinal column alone was extensive."

Lyr's breath caught. "What are you saying?"

"I think I can ensure that she walks again, but it will be a long journey, even for one of our kind. It will not be easy."

"You *think?* But elves—" Arlyn began, then cut herself off. Startled, Lyr glanced up to find that she and Kai had stepped up beside him. Her face pinched as she struggled to find the words. "Elves can heal from just about anything. Can't they? It's what I've always heard."

"Our innate magic fixes many things," Lial answered softly. "But we are not gods. No matter what some humans believe."

An odd note in Lial's tone caught Lyr's attention. A hint of grief he hadn't expected. The healer tended to avoid Lynia and had for as long as Lyr could remember. But the look in Lial's eyes as he stared at her. The way his hands shook. Could he be in love with Lynia? Lyr's eyes widened. Surely not.

"Lial?"

The healer looked up, his gaze sharpening at the question in Lyr's voice. "It is not for you to know."

Lyr nodded, accepting both the acknowledgement and the rebuke, and shifted uncomfortably in his seat. Lial and *his mother?* He *really* did not want to consider that. "But she will live?"

"Yes. And if *you* care to live?" Lial's eyebrow rose. "Go rest."

Back in their room, Arlyn wrapped her arms around Kai's waist, pulling him close. Her heart, still heavy from seeing her grandmother, ached with the pain radiating from her bonded. "Are you okay?"

"Yes." His breath ruffled her hair. "No."

Her hair. Her hand went to her braids, now in disarray, as she jerked away. "Gods, we're covered in blood. Father's. The guards'." She shuddered. "Allafon's. I can't even think about this. Come on, let's clean off and find some new clothes. Anything but these."

Later—much later—they lay together in bed, Arlyn's head on Kai's chest. "Do you want to talk about it?"

"I don't know."

She offered him the only things she could. Comfort…and her love. Kai jerked in surprise as she passed both along their bond, and her lips curved against his chest. "Whenever you are ready."

"How?" His hand sank into her unbound hair where it twisted around her waist. "I don't understand how I've come to deserve your love."

Arlyn chuckled. "Maybe you haven't. But you have it anyway."

A spark of humor flickered to life in the middle of his grief. "Fair enough."

"And?" Her heart pounded, and she bit her lip. "Maybe it hasn't been long enough for you to feel the same."

"Arlyn, you have to know I love you, too," Kai rushed out, voice cracking. "But I don't even know who I am anymore. How can you? My true father could be anyone among the Sidhe."

Frowning, she lifted herself up to meet his eyes. "Are you kidding? By all of your gods, I don't see how you could do worse than Allafon. But even if your real father *is* worse, what does it matter? I *do* know you. I'm part of you. None could know you better."

"If we have children…"

Arlyn rested her arms against his chest as her lips turned up again. "Then they'll be a wonderful blend of our mixed blood."

Relaxing, Kai hugged her close. "Yes. Perfect."

The only sound heard in Lyr's study was the dripping of the water clock. He slumped in his chair behind the desk, waiting for Moren, and wished he dared take another nap where he sat. But he had to focus on his duty to the estate and the protection of all. No matter if his muscles shook with fatigue or his chest burned with unrelenting fire.

At least Moren had sent word that cleaning up Allafon's mess—both literal and figurative—was taking longer than expected. Two hours of rest allowed Lyr to sit upright without the threat of passing out. Barely. Even with Eradisel's help, his energy regeneration was sluggish. Cursed iron. If not for his relationship with the sacred tree, he probably wouldn't be awake.

Maybe he deserved the pain. The weakness. How could he not have seen Allafon's treachery? Norin's? Lyr had trusted Norin to investigate his father's and Kai's attacks, had believed in his captain's lack of success. Had Norin himself murdered Telien? Lyr would have to ask his mother what the traitor had told her, if anything, once she woke. The thought of it pushed bile up the back of his throat.

And Allafon? He had always been dark, openly resentful of the Dianore family. Still, there were many such resentments among Moranaian houses. Lyr had not expected it to turn to treachery. He had not known how far Allafon had gone, turning to long-forbidden blood magic spells. Kai had stopped their foe the only way he could have without knowing a counter-spell. Instant death. Had Allafon seen the attack coming, he would have released his power at once, killing them all. Lyr could hardly fathom a hate so intense it had led Allafon to such extremes.

How could he have missed such a thing?

As he sensed the portal flare to life, Lyr leaned back in his seat, closed his eyes, and tried to conserve as much energy as possible. He'd asked Kai and Arlyn to meet Moren there at the time he'd given, saving Lyr from that. Standing for long was *not* advised. Not if he hoped to make it through this meeting.

At the knock on his door, Lyr straightened, forcing his expression blank and calling for them to enter. Kai, Arlyn, and Moren stopped in the middle of the room, Moren bowing without hesitation. He had changed from his blood-splattered clothes into a tunic and vest fit for the formal occasion, and his long, blond hair was held back with a gold chain. Lyr studied him for a long moment and was pleased to find no evidence of tension in the other's demeanor. His newest lord was either adept at hiding his nerves or was confident in what he had to report.

Bracing himself against his desk, Lyr stood as Arlyn and Kai shifted to flank him. At least high formality would not be expected under the circumstances. "Callian ay'iyn Dorn i Morenial Treinesse nai Oria, I greet your presence here."

Moren gave a quick salute. "I thank you for allowing me to come before you, Myern. My House has much for which we must atone."

"Indeed. You may not long remain the Dorn of Oria if you cannot explain your actions to my satisfaction." Lyr held the other's gaze. "Morenial Treinesse, did you work with your father to bring harm to the people under your care?"

"Though my father believed otherwise, none of my people were harmed by my word or deed."

"You seem to know a great deal about Allafon's crimes, yet you have reported nothing to me or, to my knowledge, my father before me. I will hear your explanation."

Moren straightened almost imperceptibly, his expression resolute. "I cannot say with certainty when my father's madness began, though it must have been some time before my birth. I know he was obsessed with my mother, made her claim to be his bonded or risk death. Still, I did not suspect the depth of his evil until Kai's birth. Mother's death was suspicious, but I could never prove he ordered her murdered. I started to scrutinize his actions then. It was difficult, as he had no trust for me, but after two or three hundred years, I convinced him of my loyalty. During that time, he did nothing overt. He often spoke of his hatred for your father and your House, but I did not see any indication of further action."

"Did you warn my father of this?"

"I did not. Many speak words of anger or dislike in the privacy of their homes. I found no proof of any kind of plot. I wondered when your father died, but by all accounts, it was an accident."

Lyr reached into a drawer and pulled out the knife that had been used on Kai. He held the pommel up as he gestured the other forward. "Do you recognize this seal?"

Lyr's brows lifted at the string of curses Moren let loose. "Oh, indeed. I have been trying to trace its origin for some time. Where did you get it?"

"Your brother pulled it from his body after someone tried to kill him. The same seal was on the sword used to murder my father. You know of the seal but not of these events?"

"I learned of the attempt on Kai's life after the fact. I tried later to warn him to leave, but that clearly did not work." Moren gave Kai an irritated frown before turning back to Lyr. "Myern, trying to spy on my father was no easy task. His hatred of you was so great that I dared not come to you. Instead, I did my best to discover what he planned. Most recently, he'd started working with a few half-bloods he'd found, though I could not say from where, who were able to do magic around iron. He also commissioned two cloaks that could slip through wards, one of which I have. I think he has been working with another, but I am uncertain."

Moren let out a deep, frustrated groan. "Though I've caught sight of that seal on missives, I have yet to discover who sent them. I was close. I had gone to follow a lead not long after warning Kai, only to return, unsuccessful once more, to be forced to stop my father in his attack on you. Now I have nothing."

Lyr shook his head. "How did it come to this, Moren? Why did *no one* come to me as they should? Five hundred years is a long time for such madness to go unchecked."

"Fear. He killed those who opposed him, or he held their loved ones captive. He told them it was under your command. After a while, they believed him." Moren's composure slipped, and his face pinched with sadness. "I helped those whom I could when I could, but my father was perverse beyond imagining. Those I failed will always haunt my dreams."

"You have failed no one." Lyr set the knife on his desk and leaned forward. "It is the responsibility of this House to ensure all on this branch are cared for. It seems that over time we have become complacent. I shudder to think how many others could have hidden such madness. Perhaps the old form of oath-bonding should be used once more."

"Maybe so." Moren's gaze slid back to his brother. "Forgive me, Kai. In my attempt to earn father's trust, I was a poor brother to you. I do not know your true father's name, for mother refused to tell me any but the smallest of details. She would only say that the key is the silver chain she left for you. Find its original owner, and you find your father."

As Kai pulled the chain in question free from his tunic, Lyr stared down at the small knife. So many questions unanswered despite all they had learned. "Do you know about the poisoned energy affecting Earth and the underrealms?"

"My father was involved, but he told me little. I will search his papers for any information I can find."

Lyr stifled a groan. He had nothing but Moren's suspicions that another had been involved. He wanted to believe Allafon had acted alone. But he couldn't. "Get me everything."

Moren nodded. "As soon as possible."

"Thank you. It seems we all have a great deal of work ahead."

As the other elf departed, Lyr plopped down on his seat. Maybe it couldn't be avoided. Maybe the elves would have to return to Earth after all.

Epilogue

As the sun rose over the horizon, Arlyn looked down at the village nestled in the gilded valley. It was empty and still, the inhabitants gathered on the hill that sloped down from the large dais where she stood with her father and Kai. Before them, a line of Moranaian nobles stretched, prepared to give their blood-oaths.

The preceding week had been a harried one as her father sent messages to all under his command. No small number. But Arlyn needed no special talent to read the anger that seethed under Lyr's calm exterior. It flared into his eyes every time Lial carried Lynia in to dinner. Every time Kai's brother sent another useless report on all he hadn't found.

If another elf was behind Allafon's actions, their identity had died with him. Would the poisoned energy remain? She'd had precious little time to ask as they'd all scrambled to pre-pare for the influx of nobles. *Later,* Lyr had said, *once Braelyn is secure. We'll plan later.* But she knew he lingered in his study un-til all hours of the night, brooding over the issue.

Kai might have to go to Earth himself to investigate, and if he did, she would be at his side. But Arlyn would return to Moranaia. Even with all the strangeness, despite the struggle of learning their ways, she would always come back. For the first time in her life, she fit.

And wasn't that what she'd always wanted?

ABOUT THE AUTHOR

Ever since finding a copy of *The Hero and the Crown* in her elementary school library, Bethany has loved fantasy. After subjecting her friends to stories scrawled in notebooks during study breaks all through high school, she decided to pursue an English degree at Middle Tennessee State University. When not writing or wrangling her two small children, Bethany enjoys reading, photography, and video games.

For more information, please visit
www.bethanyadamsbooks.com

Made in the USA
Coppell, TX
27 December 2020

47183027R00225